AMERICA
FANTASTICA

AMERICA
FANTASTICA

A NOVEL

TIM O'BRIEN

MARINER BOOKS
New York   Boston

AMERICA FANTASTICA. Copyright © 2023 by Tim O'Brien. All rights
reserved. Printed in the United States of America. No part of this
book may be used or reproduced in any manner whatsoever without
written permission except in the case of brief quotations embodied in
critical articles and reviews. For information, address HarperCollins
Publishers, 195 Broadway, New York, NY 10007.

HarperCollins books may be purchased for educational, business,
or sales promotional use. For information, please email the
Special Markets Department at SPsales@harpercollins.com.

FIRST EDITION

Designed by Jen Overstreet
Title page image © Chutima Chaochaiya/Shutterstock

Library of Congress Cataloging-in-Publication Data
has been applied for.

ISBN 978-0-06-331850-2

23 24 25 26 27 LBC 5 4 3 2 1

For Meredith, Timmy, and Tad

WE HAD FED THE HEART ON FANTASIES,
THE HEART'S GROWN BRUTAL FROM THE FARE . . .

—WILLIAM BUTLER YEATS

WE ARE NOT A NATION OF TRUTH LOVERS.

—HUNTER S. THOMPSON

AMERICA
FANTASTICA

PART I

CARS, GUNS, CRIME,
CASINOS, MONEY, MOVIES, SKIN CARE, GOD,
MONOPOLY, RVS, TALK RADIO, BASEBALL,
AND LIARS IN PUBLIC PLACES

1

THE CONTAGION WAS AS OLD AS AFRICA, OLDER
than Babylon, wafting from century to century upon sunlight
and moonbeams and the vibrations of wagging tongues. During
the second decade of the twenty-first century, the contagion
alighted in Fulda, California, riding aboard the bytes of a Mac-
Book Air. Dink O'Neill, warlord of the Fulda Holy Rollers, infected his brother Chub, Fulda's mayor, who infected Chamber
of Commerce President Earl Fenstermacher, who that evening
headlined his weekly blog with the bulletin that a South Beach
ingenue had been imprisoned in the U.S. Senate cloakroom
for disclosing that Form 1040 caused infidelity, infertility,
and testicular cancers. The news spread swiftly. From Mont-
pelier to Brownsville, from Eastport to Barstow, dull reality
was replaced by fanciful delusion. Reinvigorated by repeated
utterance, fertilized by outrage, mythomania claimed its ear-
liest victims among chat room patrons—the disappointed, the
defeated, the disrespected, and the genetically suspicious. In
Fulda, immunocompromised Kiwanis club members transmitted the infection to Shriners and American Legionnaires, who
transmitted it to their children, who carried it off to Sunday
school. Masks were worthless. The disease spread northward
into Oregon, eastward into Idaho, arriving on Pennsylvania Avenue in January of 2017. Soon afterward, the whistle-blowing
South Beach ingenue, a seventeen-year-old rollerblader, was

secretly transferred to a federal prison in upstate Wisconsin. Reptiles manned the IRS phone banks. Locusts ate the truth. Walls went up along the Rio Grande. Alt-Right fellow travelers, women included, had long ago forgiven POTUS's locker-room lies. Time passed. By the summer of 2019, as glaciers melted and as chunks of civility calved from the Body Politic, mytho-maniacs had taken refuge in a world of their own construction. In St. Joseph, Missouri, a forty-seven-year-old patriarch named Willard Swift announced to his wife and seven children that he had been crowned king of America in the frozen-foods aisle of a thriving Walmart. That evening King Swift deposited the remains of his family in eight fifty-gallon Rubbermaid recy-cling bins topped off with kitty litter. Almost simultaneously, a thousand miles away, in a suburb outside Baltimore, a racist, politically engaged orthopedist reported that the bones of disinterred slaves indicated "healthy, pleasant, and privileged lifestyles"; the Thirteenth Amendment, he said, was a "waste of words." In New Mexico, highway speed limits were challenged as infringements on core liberties. In Washington, D.C., well-heeled lobbyists declared that handguns were "living human creatures." And on talk radio, in the late hours of the night, it was revealed that Alka-Seltzer had become the Chinese "weapon of choice," that a daily dab of Brylcreem remedied the common cold, and that Lee Harvey Oswald *war nicht so schlecht.*

2

ON AN AFTERNOON IN LATE AUGUST OF THE YEAR 2019, after locking up the JCPenney store on South Spruce Street, Boyd Halverson strode out to his car, started the engine, sat without moving for several minutes, then blinked and wiped his eyes and resolved to make changes in his life. He had grown sick and tired of synthetics, rayon in particular.

That evening he packed a suitcase. As an afterthought, he tossed in two passports, a copy of the *Iliad*, his expired *Trib* ID card, and a pair of swimming trunks. He ate supper and went to bed with a biography of Winston Churchill.

Late the next morning—a Saturday morning—Boyd attended his bimonthly Kiwanis brunch. Midway through the proceedings, he excused himself and made his way across the street to Community National Bank. It was 11:34 a.m. The bank closed at noon on Saturdays, and only a single employee was on duty, a diminutive redhead named Angie Bing. Boyd filled out a withdrawal slip, signed his name, and approached the teller.

Angie chuckled.

"That's a boatload of money," she said. "If you're headed for Vegas, Boyd, take me along."

Then she laughed again. She had been flirting with Boyd over the better part of two years.

She tore up the withdrawal slip.

"Three hundred grand we don't have. What else can I do for you?"

"How much is on hand, would you say?"

"On hand?"

"I'll want it all."

"You're robbing me?"

"Not you," said Boyd.

He took out his gun and showed it to her. It was not a toy. It was a Temptation .38 Special.

Angie Bing managed to scrape up just under eighty-one thousand dollars, a significant sum for a small bank in the small town of Fulda, California.

Boyd stuffed the cash into a paper grocery bag.

"I'm sorry about this," he said, "but I'll have to ask you to take a ride with me."

As they drove south out of town, Angie Bing predicted he wouldn't make it fifty miles. But on Sunday morning they were in a motel near Bakersfield. By Monday afternoon they were in Mexico. The two passports had been a wise bit of last-minute whimsy even if Angie only dimly resembled one of the photos. After an unnerving and venal discussion with Customs, Boyd counted himself lucky to drive away with almost all of his eighty-one thousand.

He ditched the car—a traceable 1993 Buick LeSabre he'd owned for nine years—and then afterward, over an early dinner, he asked Angie if she'd consider giving him a head start before contacting the police. They were in a beachfront restaurant in the town of San Felipe. Angie was having grilled tuna; Boyd was working on a plate of chicken wings. Outside, framed by a latticed picture window, the Gulf of California presented itself in bewitching shades of twilight.

"How big of a head start?" Angie asked. "I don't want to get in trouble."

"Three days. Four days."

"What'll I do with myself?"

"You can swim, tune up your Spanish. Treat it like a holiday. I'll leave you some cash."

"How much?" Angie said.

"I don't know. A thousand?"

"You're kidding, I hope. Out of eighty-one?"

"Make it two thousand."

"Make it forty-two."

Boyd shrugged. "Greed is a carcinogen, Angie. You'd better sleep on it."

"I'd better."

In the morning she said, "I'm not a criminal. No deal."

They caught a bus south, grinding in fits and starts through a day without flaw. Had he not long ago robbed a bank, Boyd Halverson would have perhaps envisioned nine pleasant holes of golf, succeeded by two very dry martinis on the stone terrace of the Fulda Country Club. There was, he reflected, something dazzling about the robust and undeniable reality of the Mexican vistas, and of this beat-up old Greyhound jolting along beneath him. There were the mixed smells of oranges and body waste. Across the aisle, a weathered old gentleman in a black Stetson and a red bow tie sat stoically with a large unhappy rooster flapping in his lap. All this, Boyd reasoned, would have seemed extraordinary only a few days ago. A slideshow for the Kiwanis boys—Here's one of me robbing a bank!—Here's Mexico!—Here's a rooster!

Halfway to Santa Rosalía, Angie asked for his honest opinion: How far did he think eighty-one thousand dollars would take him?

Boyd shrugged and said nothing.

"I hope you've thought this out," she said. "Because you're in one tremendous pickle. You stuck up a bank, Boyd. You kidnapped me."

"I was in a pickle anyway," said Boyd.

"Maybe we should say a prayer. You and me."

"There's an idea."

"Seriously, you go first," she told him. "Just start with 'Dear precious God,' then if you get stuck, I'll hop right in. Whenever I'm in a jam—like if I steal something or get squirmy for somebody's husband—I don't wait around to put things right with Jesus. It's the only way, Boyd." She closed her eyes briefly and then raised a finger to her nose. "See this little hole here? When I'm not at work, I wear a cross there, a little silver nose stud. People at the bank, they don't go for it; they think it's like—you know—too freaky, too metro. But I'm Pentecostal, the real deal, just so you've got the picture."

"Stout of you," said Boyd.

"Right, stout's the word, and we don't do holdups. It's a strict religion." Angie laced her fingers together and fell silent for a few thoughtful moments. "The thing is, just because the Lord Jesus saved me, that doesn't make me a fanatic or a virgin or anything. He's coming back, that's all. Probably a lot sooner than you think."

"Coming back?"

"Your Redeemer."

"Ah, then," said Boyd, eyes closed, feeling vaguely threatened. "Let's hope he's taking the overnight express."

Angie looked at him with a disapproving frown. "You think Christ the Lamb finds that funny?"

"I wouldn't know."

"He doesn't."

"All right then. Give the flock my apologies."

"That's not funny either. You better get prepared, Boyd. Especially now. After robbing a bank and all." Angie glanced across the aisle at the rooster, which had quieted some, then she chuckled to herself. "Let me ask a question. How much would you say you've got tucked away in your Community National account?"

"I'm not sure, something like—"

"Seventy-two thousand and change. I should know, right?"

"You should," said Boyd.

"Right. And you robbed us for eighty-one. So unless you plan to go back for another stickup—which, by the way, isn't the greatest idea in the world—that looks to me like a net take of barely nine even." She paused. "You didn't do it for the money, did you?"

"No."

"Why then?"

Boyd gave it some thought. The question, much like the bus and the rooster, seemed alarmingly surreal.

"Well," he said, "I did it for entertainment."

"Oh, right. Instead of square dancing, you mean?"

"Just the novelty, Angie."

"Sure. Okay."

"Okay?"

Angie pushed up her chin in annoyance. "I'm being polite, Boyd. Okay means you're mentally ill."

The bus passed through a dusty village and began climbing a purplish-red plateau that rimmed the Gulf of California. The terrain had more or less emptied itself of plant and animal life, and for a few sober miles Boyd marveled at the emptying turn his own life had taken.

How barren, he mused. One would've anticipated anxiety. How very otherwise.

Several miles later Angie sighed. "Well, if you ask me, entertainment isn't a good answer. What if I did something like that? Like right now, what if I strangled that rooster for the pure fun of it?"

"Be my guest," said Boyd. "Anything to occupy the soul."

"Yeah, the soul, at least you know the word. Which is a start, I guess, except I hope you have a plan."

"I wouldn't call it a plan. Maybe an idea."

Angie appraised him sternly. "A delusion, you mean, except we both know it can't pan out."

"Probably not."

"It can't," she said. She waited a moment, watching the Gulf go by. The countryside was parched and desolate. "Listen, Boyd, I was afraid of you at first but not anymore. Not even a tiny bit. Right this instant, if I wanted to, I could jump up and start screaming bloody murder. What then? Take out your gun and shoot me?"

"I doubt it."

"You're not sure?"

"I'm pretty sure."

"How sure?"

"Eighty percent."

"Eighty?"

"About that."

"I thought you liked me."

"I do. You're fine, Angie. But you talk a lot."

In Santa Rosalía they got off the bus and walked four blocks to a modest seaside hotel. They had supper in the dining room downstairs in the company of an elderly, bickering couple from Toronto. Later they took a short stroll along the beach before retiring for the night. As had been their practice since Saturday, Angie had first dibs on the toilet and shower, then she slipped into bed fully dressed.

Afterward, Boyd took his turn.

When they'd settled in, Angie said, "I'll need fresh clothes tomorrow. Underwear and jeans and shirts and socks. And an electric toothbrush. And a new nose stud and probably a camera. And a good wristwatch."

Boyd grunted and closed his eyes. Angie Bing exhausted him.

"I'll need shoes, too," she said. "Casual ones, maybe sandals, and a couple pairs of decent heels—I like those spikey ones—and if we'll be eating out all the time—you know, like in restaurants—I'll need dresses and skirts and stuff, and a shawl for when it gets chilly at night, and a manicure set. And spending money."

An unpleasant taste rose in Boyd's throat. "What about going home?"

"How so?"

"Home," he said. "Don't you want that?"

"Of course I do. But until then—whenever 'then' is—I'll need things. I'll need an ankle bracelet."

"Angie—"

"You've got eighty-one thousand under the bed, Boyd. I didn't ask to get kidnapped—that was your idea—so don't go all stingy."

"I'm not stingy, Angie."

"You *sounded* stingy. Like a miser."

"All right, I'm a miser," said Boyd. "What about heading home? Promise me a head start, you're free to go."

"That easy?"

"All I need is the promise."

Angie turned sideways in the overstuffed bed, looking down at him with a concoction of pity and amusement.

"That's naïve, Boyd. What's to stop me from promising and then running straight to the cops? You'd better start using some common sense." She waved a hand at the dark. "Anyhow, here we are—in Mexico, for Pete's sake. In the same bed."

"You'd back out of a promise?"

"I didn't say that. I said quote what's to stop me unquote. What I meant was you're a criminal now, so you shouldn't be naïve. Robbers don't go around trusting everybody."

"Make it a one-day head start. Twenty-four hours."

"I can't honestly promise, Boyd. I'd be fibbing."

"This one time?"

"No, I'm sorry. I can't." She paused to think, then shook her head. "I told you before, I'm the Lord's servant and, by the way, that doesn't mean I'm some goodie-goodie who never got naked. Christians fool around, too."

"So I've heard," said Boyd.

For a while they lay silent, then Angie sighed and kicked back the sheets and wiggled out of her skirt. The room's ancient air conditioner made grinding noises in the dark.

"Boyd, how old are you? Be honest."

"Forty-nine."

"Yeah? I'll be thirty soon."

"Too bad," Boyd said.

"What is?"

"That you won't promise me a head start."

"We weren't *talking* about that. We were talking about *life*. If you can't be friendly—"

"Angie, I'm trying to let you go. That's friendly."

"It's not."

"I'd say it is."

"I'd say it's not."

Boyd got up and made a bed for himself on the tile floor.

"Friendly," Angie said from the musty dark, "is when you talk about personal things."

In the morning they bought a blue Samsonite suitcase, which Angie Bing filled with clothing and jewelry and toiletries and corn-husk memorabilia of the Baja.

Then it was dead time. They spent eight days at the hotel in Santa Rosalía, mostly spending Community National's money, sometimes sitting at a wrought iron table on the veranda to watch the sun go down. In the late evenings they listened to an English-language radio broadcast out of San Diego—no bank stickup news, not a word, but plenty of turmoil north of the border: POTUS on the road to impeachment, Russians campaigning on Facebook, spree shootings in Philadelphia, Tucson, West Texas, and Biloxi. "Gunfire," declared an enthusiastic Senate staffer, "is the dance music of American liberty."

There were no other guests in the hotel except for the combative old couple from Toronto. The nights were long, black, ancient, and arid. The days were fever-hot. Angie talked a great deal; Boyd tried not to listen. She had been a gymnast back in high school. She did not care for the color yellow. Her mother had once whacked her in the eye with a stapler when she'd taken the Almighty's name in vain. She had a steady boyfriend, an electrician named Randy something. "If you'd pay attention," she said one afternoon, "you might learn something about the modern world, the modern woman. Like, you know, why turnips make a good, nutritious casserole, and why the word *chick* is offensive, and how it's not such a great idea to pretend you're asleep right now."

Around noon on September 12, they boarded an express bus to Los Angeles.

As far as Boyd had a plan at all, he hoped to scatter a trail into Mexico and then double back on a cash basis, buying himself time to take care of a few personal matters. He had no illusions. This would end badly, he knew that, but for the present he found it hard to care. After nearly a decade managing a JCPenney store, Boyd had reached the end of an awfully long rope. He'd grown weary not only of his job, which was dull enough, but also of his own tedious companionship—polite, frugal, unremarkable of dress and manner, all but invisible even to himself. He hated his fourteen handicap. He hated Kiwanis and women's hosiery. He hated going to bed with the likes of Winston Churchill.

With no real future, and with a past he cared not to dwell on, Boyd had nothing much to lose. Or, more precisely, nothing left to be. He was done hiding from the world. Dishonor was one thing—a terrible thing—but he'd paid for it with a divorce and a scuttled career and the loss of all appetite for the future. That seemed penalty enough.

The truth, give or take a detail, was that he had robbed a bank because he could think of nothing better to do. And maybe, if things worked out, he might settle a score or two with Jim Dooney.

These and associated reflections kept him busy until Angie Bing gave him a nudge. "Hey, robber," she said. "You're talking to yourself."

"Sorry," said Boyd.

"You all right?"

"I think so."

She studied him for a time, then said, "I guess talking's healthy even if it's to yourself. It's like a pressure valve, sort of— blow out all the unhealthy vapors—or like when you get down on your knees and pray to win the lottery. It's how people figure things out." Angie contemplated the wisdom of this, her face a banquet of self-congratulation. "So, who's Dooney?"

"It doesn't matter."

"No kidding."

"It doesn't."

Angie shrugged.

Five or ten minutes passed.

There were pigs and chickens along the road. There was a man on a bicycle, succeeded by a great many miles of nothing.

Then Angie said, "Look, I'm not the pushy type—I hate that—but sooner or later you'll have to explain what all this is about. The Boyd Halverson I used to know; he wasn't a bank robber. He didn't run around kidnapping people."

"That part was impromptu," said Boyd.

"Impromptu?"

"Pretty much. I didn't want you hitting the alarm."

"That's why you kidnapped me?"

"I could've shot you instead."

"Ha-ha."

"It isn't funny, Angie."

"I *know* it isn't funny. That's why I said 'ha-ha.'"

She glanced down at Boyd's coat pocket, where the pistol was, and then rearranged her hands in her lap.

"Scary you," she muttered.

This young woman, Boyd decided, was a problem. Not a hair over four feet ten, barely a hundred pounds, but even so, she looked formidable in her new silver nose stud and turquoise ankle bracelet. Her acutely retroussé nose gave her the look of one of the Emerald Isle's darker, somewhat roguish little people.

After a few minutes, she said, "One other thing, Boyd. This isn't easy to say, but I thought—you know—I thought you had a crush on me. The way you flirted all the time."

"No."

"Why did I think that?"

"I'm not sure."

"Me either. Maybe I'm not nice enough."

"You're plenty nice, Angie."

"Smart, too. I've got a brain in my head."

"You sure do."

"So?"

"Nothing," Boyd said. "It was a holdup."

"That's all?"

"I'm positive."

She put her mind to it for a moment, her thin lips poised for invective, but then she shrugged and said, "Probably I scare you. Most older guys, they get threatened by cute, spiritual women."

"Yeah," he said. "I bet that's it."

The miles went by and Angie Bing dozed off. Outside San Felipe, as the sky passed from blue to desert lavender, Boyd slid down inside himself. The first squeakings of disaster were upon him—metal fatigue, a wreck in progress. He was struck by the enormity of what he'd done. The novelty of robbing banks had worn thin.

He took out snapshots of Evelyn and Teddy, looked at them briefly, then put them away. He thought about Jim Dooney for a while.

At dusk the bus pulled into a gas station that sold pre-wrapped sandwiches and chips and candy bars. Boyd and Angie sat on a curb outside the station and ate their sandwiches. At what seemed a promising moment, Boyd asked where she stood on the issue of a head start.

Angie blew out a breath. "I haven't decided yet. Everything's different now."

"What's different?"

"Everything."

"You want to give me an example?"

"Well, for one thing," she said, "I was sure you had a crush on me, and you don't, and that changes the whole deal."

"I don't see how."

"It just does."

Boyd nodded. "Let's pretend I have a crush. Then what?"

"You just said you don't."

"Hypothetically. Would I get a head start?"

She looked at him as if he were the dimmest man on earth.

"If you had a crush, Boyd, you wouldn't *want* a head start. You wouldn't be spending all this time trying to dump me." She unwrapped a Mars bar, took a bite, and chewed thoroughly. "I told you I'm smart. And while we're at it, here's another thing you haven't thought about. I bet the police think I helped you. They'll look at the camera clips and figure I'm an accomplice."

"They might."

"Not might. That's exactly what they'll think. For all I know, you probably planned it that way."

"Of course I didn't, Angie. Why would I?"

"Who the heck *knows* why? That's for you to answer. The point is, how can I go home? The rest of my life, every single day, people will look at me and think, Hey, there goes a bank robber. How do I prove I'm not?"

"I could write a letter."

"A letter?"

"Sure."

Angie Bing stood up.

She stared at him for what seemed a long while, then shook her head and turned and walked to the bus.

They crossed back into the States around two in the morning. At daybreak they were in Los Angeles.

They took a cab to a small stucco house in Santa Monica.

Angie said, "What's this?"

3

THERE ARE TWO SANTA MONICAS. ONE IS A FAIRY tale of spangled gowns and improbable breasts and faces from the tabloids, of big money and fixed noses and strung-out voice teachers and heiresses on skateboards and even bigger big money; of movie stars you thought were dead and look dead; of terraced apartment buildings cascading down perilous yellow bluffs toward the sea; of Olympic swimmers and hip-hop hit men and impresarios of salvation and twenty-six-year-old agents backing out of deals in the lounge bar at Shutters; of yoga masters and street magicians; of porn kings and fast cars and microdosing prophets and shuck-and-jive evangelists and tattooed tycoons and considerably bigger big money; of Sudanese busboys with capped teeth and eight-by-ten glossies in their back pockets; of Ivy League panhandlers, teenage has-beens, home-run kings in diamonds and fur coats, daughters of sultans, sons of felons, widows of the silver screen, and the kind of meaningless big money that has forgotten what money is.

There is that.

But start at the pier and head southeast until you reach a neighborhood of tidy, more or less identical stucco houses separated by fourteen feet of scorched grass. In a number of these homes, you will find families, or the descendants of families, who have lived here since the mid-to-late forties. For them, upscale was a Chevy in the driveway. Mom mixed up Kool-Aid at ten cents a gallon, Pop pushed used cars at a dealership off Wilshire Boulevard, Junior had a paper route, Sis did some weekend babysitting. Nowadays, the house Pop bought for $37,000 will fetch just under two million in a sluggish market, but as Pop loved to say, secretly proud, "What kind of house do you buy with the profit? A pup tent? A toolshed in Laguna?"

Sis drowned in 1995. Pop's heart ticked erratically until fifteen minutes into the twenty-first century—or so Junior would later claim. Mom kept chugging away, fat but indestructible, fortified by milkshakes and late-night Cyd Charisse movies and a well-mannered suitor whose aspect compared favorably with an aging Cesar Romero.

As for Junior—whose name was not yet Boyd Halverson but soon would be—he did well for himself. An ambitious window-shopper of a child, a Peeping Tom just outside the magic kingdom, Junior dreamed a boy's glamorous dreams, reading hungrily, faking what he had to fake. He shilled his way through three semesters at USC, dropped out, vanished for two years, showed up again in Santa Monica with a Purple Heart and a Silver Star, slept for a month, and then awakened to find himself on the metro desk of a newspaper for which he had once been a twelve-year-old delivery boy. Still a window-shopper, yes, but in journalism, Junior—now Boyd—discovered a calling. After all, since boyhood he'd had practice ogling other people's lives. And thus over time this led to that: Pasadena, Sacramento, a botched marriage, Mexico City, Manila, almost a Pulitzer, Evelyn, wedding bells again, a year in Hong Kong, nearly two years in Jakarta, Teddy's arrival, then eventually back to L.A., where at last he collided with the sudden, brutal, and well-earned catastrophe he'd been patiently anticipating for decades. In a single afternoon, Junior's fortunes spun upside down. "You're a liar, man, and a rotten human being," said a ponytailed copyboy, for which there was no reply but to shrug and step aboard a downward-bound elevator. Liar? For sure. Rotten? Pretty obviously. Outside, standing unemployed on a blindingly white California sidewalk, Junior was struck by the apprehension that he had dropped something—a small watermelon, say, or his life, which lay pulpy and putrefying at his feet—after which came excessive booze, lethargy, and a glorious romance on the rocks. One humid evening, gazing into the wary eyes of a barmaid he'd twice bedded, Junior found himself startled by the discovery that he had slipped into the sour melancholy of his thirty-ninth year. "You kind of depress me," said the barmaid, who nonetheless continued filling his glass for another month or so.

Drifting north, Junior washed up in small-town Fulda, twelve miles off the Oregon border.

He signed on with JCPenney.

He expected nothing and the world delivered. A whiskey at breakfast, a whiskey at lunch, a double at day's end.

To recognize one's own life as a breathtaking failure was an experience Junior would recommend to all. Relieved of illusion, he was relieved of disappointment. There was, in fact, a harsh cleansing effect that accompanied the knowledge that he could do no worse than he had already done. Dry goods demanded little of him, and for close to a decade Junior was content to erase himself amid the bustle of returned sweaters and a four o'clock golf league. The years did not speed by. But they did pass. He wasn't happy and he wasn't sad. Having grown up on the slow side of some extremely fast tracks, he now surrendered to the becalmed world of mediocre-anywhere—a triumph for a man who had once played fetch with Robert Stack's dog outside an ice cream parlor on Ocean Avenue. He boiled his eggs for three and a half minutes. He smiled at people and dressed neatly. On occasion he wrote poetry. Some of the poems were about dropping things; some were about make-believe sappers and concertina wire; some were about Evelyn; and a good many were about the .38 caliber Temptation Special he kept in a Kleenex box on the top shelf of his bedroom closet.

There were few inquiries about his past. There were none he couldn't graciously dodge.

He mowed his grass, paid his bills, prepared his meals, dressed up as a clown for Krazy Days sales, and casually wondered if he would ever find the desire to dive back into the disaster of his own reckless creation. And then in July of his ninth year in Fulda, Junior began having trouble sleeping at night. He roamed the house and talked to himself. He contemplated suicide. A great deal. Constantly. He imagined holding up Community National Bank. His mother had finally died, which was part of it, but he'd also come to recognize that even the manager of a JCPenney store might have felony in his heart.

He didn't plan much—just the basics.

Boyd would rob the bank on a Saturday, leave a false trail into Mexico, then head home to attend to things he should have attended to long ago.

4

"WHAT'S THIS?" ANGIE SAID, AND BOYD FORCED A rusted key into the front door. He gave it a wiggle, kicked with his knee, and said, "A pigsty, but it's mine."

There were no cop cars in front of the house, which Boyd took as a gift, but already he was feeling the pressure of the clock. He was exhausted and jumpy. Soon enough he'd be hearing sirens, or whatever a man hears when he's on the run with eighty-one thousand dollars of somebody else's money. The jaunt down to Mexico may have bought him a few extra days, maybe a week, but a quick bit of fact-checking would connect him to this modest but now pricey bungalow off Ocean Park Boulevard.

The house had been vacant since his mother's death nearly two months ago. In the front yard stood a forlorn For Sale sign, almost lost amid a stand of weeds that obscured the Realtor's name and phone number. The electricity and water had been left on for prospective buyers, but it was the land, not the shabby old house, that might someday produce riches. By that point, Boyd knew, capital gains would be irrelevant.

He opened windows, switched on a ceiling fan, and stood surveying the unfashionable environs of his youth. There were cooking smells from thirty years ago, a scattering of upside-down water bugs on the kitchen floor. It was from this, Boyd thought, that ambitious Junior had made his youthful escape—an ascent, if one wished to be generous—a ruthless, dissembling scramble away from laminate furniture and plastic tablecloths. Poor Mom and Pop, he thought. Poor go-getter Junior.

"Well," Angie said.

"I know," said Boyd. "Not much to look at."

Angie put down her suitcase and sprawled wearily in a dusty upholstered chair—the very chair in which Junior's father had once studied self-improvement books late into the night.

"Open up more windows," Angie said. "My God, this place smells like . . . like I don't know what. Like burned sausages or Wesson oil or something." She kicked off her new sandals. "On the other hand, try a trailer park for sixteen years, you won't complain. A good airing out, some elbow grease, we'll be fine."

Boyd shrugged. "We won't be here that long. A day or two. It depends."

"Depends on?"

"I need to find a few people."

"And then?"

"I don't know," Boyd admitted.

"Oh, right, I forgot how you love planning ahead." Angie made a fed-up sound and closed her eyes. She was wearing a black tank top with HE RETURNS stenciled in gaudy silver across the chest. Her hair was in pigtails. "Anyway, whatever's going on, I figure it's bad."

"It is," he said.

"And you don't want to explain?"

Briefly, a menu of clarifications appeared before him, supplemented by the lurid image of Jim Dooney's smirking blue eyes. Clarification, he decided, would confuse things.

"You're right," he said. "We should clean the place up."

"You okay, Boyd?"

"Sure."

"Well, I'll tell you this much, you don't look okay. You look like somebody getting ready to eat brussels sprouts."

He turned away from her, his gaze skidding down a hallway toward the tiny bedroom he'd shared with his sister for fourteen years. Such waste, he thought.

His nerves were shot—eighteen hours on a Greyhound.

"For a royal fuckup," he said, "I'm tip-top."

"You should take a nap."

"I should."

"You should. Before you start dismembering people." She took his arm and steered him down to a bedroom. "And don't swear, Boyd. I hate swearing."

He managed to sleep awhile—a jittery, someone's-knocking-on-the-door sleep—then he got up, opened his cell phone, and dialed Evelyn's number in Bel Air. There was no answer, so he left a short message: *robbed a bank, visited Mexico, need to talk, where's Dooney?*

He showered, shaved, and began mopping and dusting.

Angie slept a little longer.

Later, plainly refreshed, she stood with a bottle of mineral water and watched him work, idly chattering about the miscellany of her life, whatever odds and ends popped into her bumblebee mind. She had been chattering, it seemed, for two breathless weeks.

As Boyd extracted a wad of his mother's hair from the bathroom sink, Angie told him about growing up Pentecostal in east

Sacramento, church four nights a week, but how, to be fair, it had made her the decent and moral person she was. She talked about her fourth kiss. She talked about being extra petite, how hard it was to find clothes and how you had to do backflips to get respect from people. She talked about her sister, Ruth, who sold beauty products door to door, and who, before that, had been an assistant blacksmith in a rodeo, which was how Angie had met Randy, her current boyfriend. An electrician, she said, but the guy did some rodeoing himself, at least when he wasn't busy breaking into houses or stealing cars.

"Maybe I attract that type, the criminal element," Angie said, her voice both resigned and whimsical, as if proud of herself. "But at least he's six three and not fat or boring or old or anything. How tall are you?"

"Five eleven," said Boyd. "And I'm not fat."

"No," she said. "And I'm not Angie Bing, kidnap victim. In any case, who says I'm talking about you? The subject was I, I believe."

"It certainly was," said Boyd.

He turned away, opened his suitcases, and put on a clean shirt and necktie.

Angie seemed not to notice.

She rattled on about how she'd waitressed her way through two years of college, how vaccinations were Satan's handiwork, how her boss at the bank had trouble with long division, and how Randy had gotten a little upset one afternoon and picked up a guy's HP Jet Pro printer and hauled it outside and tossed it into a swimming pool. Same with the guy's freezer.

The girl's voice box, Boyd reasoned, was constructed of space-age titanium.

Angie shot him a look, and said, "Titanium?"

"Thinking aloud," said Boyd. "That electrician of yours, he sounds classy."

Angie frowned. "What's that got to do with titanium?"

"No idea," said Boyd.

"Well, listen, if it was criticism, I don't care, because Randy has a crush on me, a huge one. We're engaged. And he's thirty-one. How old are you again?"

"Forty-nine."

"So, what makes you think I'd trade him in?"

"I don't think that."

"So you say."

"I do say."

"You *say* you say."

Boyd's head hurt. He went to the kitchen, dug out a bottle of his mother's vodka, looked for a clean glass, gave up, and took a slug from the bottle. He straightened his tie and glanced at his wristwatch.

"On top of everything else," Angie was saying, "I should probably tell you that Randy's got a temper like you wouldn't believe. In this bar one time, I saw him stick a cigar in a guy, a lighted one, boom, just like that, right in the ear, and the guy wasn't even flirting with me. Hardly at all." She flicked her eyebrows gaily. "Anyhow, I'll bet eighty-one thousand bucks Randy's pretty steamed about this kidnapping business. Running off to Mexico and buying me jewelry and sleeping in the same bed and who knows what the heck else."

"Angie, there wasn't anything else."

"Oh, sure. Tell that to Randy."

"How would he ever find out?"

"Well, I don't know. He can read, can't he?"

Boyd looked at her. "Read what?"

"Anything. Catalogs, comic books. He's not a dummy, Boyd. Remember those picture postcards in the hotel down in Santa Rosalía, those ones in the lobby?"

"You sent him a postcard?"

"He's my fiancé, isn't he?"

Boyd took another hit on the vodka. Later he confiscated her cell phone and tied her to a kitchen chair.

"I guess you'll gag me, too?" said Angie.

"I guess I'd better," said Boyd.

He changed buses twice, ate a burger, then hiked the last quarter mile to Evelyn's white palace in the supercharged regions of Bel Air. His ex-wife had remarried wisely. And of course that was fine. Boyd couldn't begrudge her a Bentley in the driveway.

It was a disappointment when no one answered the doorbell. For close to forty minutes, he sat on Evelyn's white marble steps, unsure what else to do. Plainly, he should've thought things out in advance—if this, then that—except any such foresight would've led to another decade as a JCPenney man. He'd already done enough thinking to fill a lifetime: night after pathetic night, wired to his own flamboyant misdeeds. Even now, squinting into the sunlight bouncing off Evelyn's expensive marble, he found himself amazed at the inexcusable things he had done, the disgrace he had brought upon his wife and upon himself. The lies alone should have been enough to send Evelyn scampering away, and yet they hadn't, not immediately, because she'd stuck it out through weeks of boozy apologies that weren't entirely apologetic. To blame only himself had seemed excessive, especially when those same things could just as easily be blamed on circumstance or a nationwide lying infection or his fellow man. He blamed Jim Dooney. He blamed a small stucco house in Santa Monica. Above all—for it was undeniably true—he blamed the twelve-year-old kid who had wanted so desperately to be anything but what he was, a crummy paper-boy pedaling a borrowed Schwinn. He had explained all this to Evelyn, and for a few weeks it seemed he might be forgiven. But things had gotten worse before they got better, because things had never gotten better.

Eventually, to shut down history, Boyd stood up and followed a winding walkway to Evelyn's expertly groomed backyard.

Here, the grass was greener.

The place had the look of a well-kept Mediterranean estate, with lemon trees, date palms, and a huge Olympic-plus-size pool guarded by statues of menacing Greeks. A pair of fountains bubbled in the sunshine, each of them backed by beds of bougainvillea that made Evelyn's immaculate green lawn all the more ferociously green.

Such wealth, Boyd reflected, could certainly file off the grit of a tough day on Rodeo Drive. He tried to recall what her new husband did for a living. Something related to travel. Yachts, life rafts? Not life rafts, no, but of that general stripe—seat belts, perhaps. Or parachutes.

Boyd returned to the front steps, gave the doorbell a last poke, then turned and trudged fifteen long blocks until encountering a decent-looking bar on Sepulveda. Over the next two hours he unloaded ninety-four dollars, chatted with an aspiring screenwriter from South Dakota, and eventually departed with the wobbly, out-of-body bafflement of a man seriously on the ropes. During the slow bus ride back to Santa Monica, Boyd found himself close to tears. It had become evident how pitiable he was, and how absurdly out of control.

At one point he took out his pistol and showed it to a young, smartly dressed Pakistani gentleman seated next to him. "If you want this, it's yours," he said. "I'm almost positive it works."

The man shook his head and looked out the window.

"Your call," said Boyd. "But it's a good honest gun."

Something lurched in his stomach. He cocked the pistol and shot a hole in the bus's plastic-lined ceiling. "Perfectly decent gun," he said.

5

THE PICTURE POSTCARD FEATURED A HOTEL VE-
randa overlooking a sunny white beach in Santa Rosalía, Mexico. On the veranda was a wrought iron table, and on the table
were two fluted glasses, a bowl of oranges, a bud vase, and a
sweating bottle of champagne. A red carnation peeked up from
the vase. Seated at the table, lounging in white wicker—and this
truly hurt, it really did—was a pair of lovebirds gazing out to
sea with a head-over-heels look in their eyes, all kissy-kissy goo-
goo, as if they'd swallowed a barrel of oysters. Honeymooners,
maybe. Or who cared what. It was all the same to Randy Zapf,
who sat now at the very wrought iron table and stared bitterly
at the very sea.

In recent days Randy had slept only a wink or two. Though
a working man—an electrician with burglary experience—he
was worn to the bone by twelve hundred miles of fast driving.

Before him was a warm Coca-Cola. Before him, too, on the
wrought iron table, was Angie's inflammatory postcard.

Randy had arrived in Santa Rosalía only hours ago. Already
he'd interviewed the hotel manager, a smart-aleck maid, and an
elderly couple from Toronto with firm opinions and a lifetime's
bitter harvest. The Toronto couple, in particular, had recalled
Angie with indignant clarity. "The yapping dwarf," one had
said, the female of the pair. "Nonstop," said her husband—"A

Chihuahua on speed." Asked about Angie's companion, the couple had squabbled over details, agreeing only that the man was of middling age and middling construction and could not be faulted for his manners. "How he tolerated her, I don't know," said the more infirm of the two, the frail and stoop-shouldered husband, whose milky eyes then swiveled uneasily in their sockets toward his wife. "Earplugs, I guess."

With the sun on its downtick, Randy Zapf had been dallying on the veranda for a considerable length of time, occasionally permitting himself whimsies about what he would do to Boyd Halverson.

A screwdriver. Up a nostril might be interesting.

Yes, sir, Randy thought, and Angie, too. Robbing a bank, that was one thing—it was institutional—but this postcard was provocation. He'd been dating Angie for something like six years, not all that long, but plenty long enough to figure out her code. On the postcard, where she'd written, "We robbed a bank—Boyd bought me a camera!" the deciphered meaning, Randy understood, was that he'd better bust ass south.

Needle-nose pliers. Maybe a box of thumbtacks and a roll of electrical tape.

Randy knew tricks.

One time in Fresno he'd seen a rodeo buddy stick a crowbar through the eye of a three-quarter-ton bucking bull; he'd seen a pig electrocute itself pig-diving. He'd seen some good, cool stuff. What he would do to Boyd Halverson was up in the air, but in the morning, he'd track down that express bus somebody had mentioned, and after that, he wasn't quite sure how, but after that, Katy bar the door.

Randy kicked off his boots.

Man oh man, he mused, what kind of woman robs a bank,

shacks up with a Kiwanis stiff, sends you a picture postcard? Man, he thought.

He polished off his Coke and ordered another, no ice, this was Mexico.

In the dull, southernmost stupor of Southeast Texas, Jim Dooney was in his hot tub when the phone rang. He should've answered, but instead he said to his partner, Calvin, "Ignore it, we're busy," and it wasn't until later in the evening that Dooney retrieved his daughter's message and called Evelyn back.

"A bank?" he said.

He listened for a time, then said, "No, I don't believe it either, not a chance. But either way he doesn't know where to find me, right?"

Then he said, "You *should* hate me."

And later, just before he hung up, he said, "Well, I'm sorry. It's what I am, honey."

Dooney checked his doors and windows, and went to bed.

"What's all this about?" said Calvin, and Dooney said, "I think tomorrow we'll hop up to my place in Minnesota."

"There's a problem?"

"There may be."

Dooney switched off his bedside lamp, lay thinking for a while, then said, "If I haven't mentioned this lately, I adore you, Cal."

"Do you?"

"Yes, sir. You're a beautiful man."

"Well, that's sweet to hear," said Calvin. "I love the fantasy, of course, but—you know—I'm seventy-three. Beautiful might be stretching it." He hesitated for a moment. "Would you mind, Jimmy, if I asked a serious question?"

"Not a bit," said Dooney.

"Are we safe?"

"Is anybody?"

Calvin went silent briefly and then sighed. "Details, please. I'm all ears."

"Not *all* ears," said Dooney.

Evelyn had been lucky to spot Boyd coming up the sidewalk, and for almost an hour she'd been sitting quietly in her upstairs dressing room, waiting for him to get off the steps and go away. There was nothing to be said between them. Boyd was an interesting man in one or two ways, and Evelyn had once loved him, but history was too much for her. Granted, it was cowardly to hide like this. Ridiculous, too. Even so, she had struggled hard to make a new life with Junius—a good life if not a wholly and perfectly wonderful life—and right now the best thing for everyone, Boyd included, was to avoid scenes.

What Evelyn now needed was the icy calm of this house in the hills. No laments, no weepy excuses. After ten more minutes passed, when she went to the window again, Boyd was gone. A little prickle of guilt went through her.

Evelyn sighed, slipped on a pair of Lanvin trousers and a white silk blouse, looked in a mirror, then added a set of earrings that Junius or one of his assistants had picked out in remembrance of her forty-fifth birthday. In two hours she would be playing dutiful host to a dozen or so of Junius's friends. She would drink moderately. She would avoid the word *lament*. She would smile her most genuine smile and be sure to circulate, which was important at these gatherings, for not to circulate was to risk intimacy and of course intimacy was of interest to no one. She would not mention Boyd Halverson.

She would not mention Dooney. This was to be a modest get-together, drinks and finger food, nothing pretentious, but it was nonetheless understood that neither she nor her guests desired cocktail confessions. Wire fraud would not be a topic of conversation this evening, nor would steroids or Botox or unfavorable movie reviews. People would laugh and circulate and pretend to be informed about current events, and then they would jump in their fancy cars and go home—early, she hoped.

Briskly, giving her thigh a little slap, Evelyn moved to her vanity and applied a thin coat of lipstick.

The thing to do, she reasoned, was to put Boyd back where he belonged, down at the bottom of her thoughts. Try to enjoy herself.

Maybe a Xanax beforehand. Maybe one and a half.

It wasn't as if Boyd had a claim on her.

Again, she examined herself in the mirror. "So there," she murmured, then she went downstairs to see about opening up the bar.

Seven hundred miles up-country, in small-town Fulda, California, Community National President Douglas Cutterby was explaining a complicated situation to his wife, Lois Cutterby, who doubled as the bank's executive officer. "At this point," Douglas was saying, "we don't actually know much, so let's neither of us jump to conclusions. Stay calm, lovebug. Calm's the secret word."

Douglas's tone was jolly, a trifle condescending. He was a tall, silver-haired, bluff-faced man who looked sleekly imposing in his black banker's suit, but who looked far less sleek in the bathtub. Now, as he appraised his wife, even his smile was sleek.

Lois had seen him in the bathtub.

"Don't we know that eighty-one thousand dollars are gone?"

"Not gone, darling. Unaccounted for."

"The tills are empty. The vault is empty."

"So it appears."

"Then I'm blind, is that it?"

"Well, no," Douglas said gently. "But maybe a touch myopic. Bear in mind, bad often goes to worse."

"Is that your experience?"

"It certainly is."

They regarded each other in silence for several moments, then Lois thumped the rosewood desk behind which her husband sat with bland, infuriating complacency.

"Our goddamn bank was robbed," she said sharply. "And you're telling me you're too stupid to call the cops?"

Douglas beamed at her. "Not at all. Stupid would be summoning law enforcement. Stupid would be triggering, so to speak, a top to bottom audit of our profitable little enterprise— bank examiners, forensic accountants, FDIC snoops. Do we want that?" He raised his eyebrows. "We do not. You especially do not."

"But we can't ignore—"

"Of course we can," said Douglas. "Business as usual. No foul, no harm. For a short time, a month or two at most, we'll have to economize a bit, maybe delay the down payment on that South African diamond mine you've been eyeing."

"It's a hairpin. Two stones."

"And the matching cigarette case?"

"The cigarette case," Lois said, "looks spectacular against a blackjack table."

"And your island retreat?"

Lois scowled at him. "For Chrissake, Douglas. The place was dirt cheap, barely seven hundred an acre. Plus a whole house."

"And should I therefore assume you'll want to keep it?"

"Sure, let's assume that. So what do we do?"

"We wait, of course," Douglas said. "In due time we'll take measures to retrieve the missing funds."

Lois looked at her husband with the sour expression of a woman dealing with digestive issues.

"The funds are not *missing*, Dougie. Those camera videos—we watched Halverson waltz out of here with eighty-one thousand in cash. My money, your money."

"Ah, yes. But technically, I suppose, it's the institution's money."

"Technically? We've been robbing our own bank for years."

"Borrowing," said Douglas.

"Whatever."

Douglas rose behind his desk, buttoned his suit jacket, and again smiled broadly at his wife. "In any case, my dove, I've put the immediate precautions in place. Videos erased. Cameras on the fritz. Cash on credit order." He circled from behind the desk and diplomatically embraced her. "Oh, and for the moment I've transferred a hundred thousand from your checking account over to Community National. To tide us over, you understand—liquidity and all that. You see the point, I'm sure."

Lois nodded stiffly. "Yeah, I do see, even poor myopic me. We sacrifice the eighty-one to stop some thieving FBI bean counter from stealing the four million we've already worked hard to steal."

"Four point eight," Douglas said affably. "But it's our bank, isn't it?"

"Lock, stock, and barrel," said Lois. "Do I keep my island?"

"And the hairpin," said Douglas. "Except no cops, no courtesy calls from the Federal Reserve. As far as we're concerned, no bank heist period."

"Fair enough," said Lois.

Arm in arm, as they left the bank and crossed the street for lunch, Lois said, "I think I'll pop down to the Bellagio next week."

"Perhaps I'll join you," said Douglas.

Despite a brocaded quilt and flannel sheets, Calvin was feeling a chill. He'd listened to Dooney without interruption for a good ten minutes, long enough to understand that a trip to Minnesota might be prudent. "You're very, very lucky," Calvin said, "that he's not coming after you with a chain saw."

"A faux pas," said Dooney. "And it wasn't my fault."

"Except he thinks it was?"

"Apparently."

"Well, the man sounds"—Calvin shivered, partly feigning—"he sounds berserk."

"It'll blow over," said Dooney.

"I don't know. A bank robber?"

"Look, for all we know, it's a pile of shit," Dooney said. "Worst-case scenario, bank or no bank, Boyd's still your basic bumbler. Give it a few days; he'll shoot off his own dick." Dooney turned and looked at Calvin. "You didn't cringe."

Calvin shook his head. "The man wants to kill you."

"He wanted that ten years ago."

"But a baby."

"A toddler, Cal. And I told you, it wasn't my fault."

"Let's hope not."

"Well, it wasn't," said Dooney. He gave Calvin's arm a reassuring squeeze. "Take my word; we're dealing with second-rate. I actually said to Evelyn once, I said, 'Honey, this gentleman is second-rate.'"

"What'd she say?"

"All kinds of crap. Said he'd almost won a Pulitzer. So naturally I said, 'There you *are*, my dear. Almost.'"

"Are the doors locked?"

"Of course they're locked."

Randy liked to drive with one thumb on the wheel, nothing else, all that horsepower under light rein, exactly like hopping aboard a nasty-ass bronc, how you don't try to manhandle the critter, you don't even *think* about that, you're just along for an eight-second ride that feels like eight bumpy years, and so you keep your toes pointed out when you dig in with the spurs— pointed toes gets you points, proves you're not a pussy—and you don't muscle the critter, you don't clamp on with your legs, you're pure balance, you're pure horse, and the bronc could no more shake you off than he could shake off his own smelly hide.

That's how Randy drove—like a rodeo pro.

At the moment, he was doing a safe seventy-eight mph in his '87 Cutlass, a pretty fair set of wheels except when you needed spare parts. He'd crossed back into the States forty-five minutes ago.

Now, with San Diego behind him, it was a straight shot into L.A., and Randy's deliberations had turned to the upcoming pleasures of tracking down Angie Bing and Boyd Halverson. One thing about steering with your thumbs, you saved energy for stuff like revenge.

As he approached the outskirts of Newport Beach, Randy was paging through a personal catalog of possibilities. Like, for instance, that time in Sacramento, way back whenever, the time he'd bet a guy he could nail a goat to a sheet of plywood, all four hooves, bang-bang, like one of those bolted-down statues in front of a courthouse. Unhappy goat, no question about it, but a nice fat payday, that one.

Hammer and nails, it was one option.

For a few seconds Randy indulged in goat nostalgia, which got him to chuckling, and which then led to the contemplation of more innovative methods.

Something slow might be interesting.

Amazing what you could do with a softball and Saran Wrap. Or one of those old-fashioned potato mashers. Or—what the heck—maybe acupuncture, nice and slow, except the needles go in moist new places.

He smiled at the thought. Randy had studied these things. He pitied people who squeezed through life without useful knowledge.

He zigzagged his Cutlass around Newport Beach, punched up the speed, and took aim at a silver Vette six lengths in front of him, juicing the accelerator just so, smooth and steady, until the Vette shriveled to a pitiful, panting speck in his rearview mirror.

Randy made L.A. three hours after dark.

He checked into a Super 8, hit the showers, and then called a cop buddy up in Fulda. There was no answer, just his luck, so after a couple of frosty Dr Peppers, he slid back into his Cutlass and headed over to the Greyhound station on East Seventh. Last he'd heard, Halverson and Angie had caught the L.A. express from Santa Rosalía. It was a long shot, but long shots carried the big-kahuna payouts.

Trick was, you had to think positive.

Randy checked with the baggage guys and a ticket agent and three or four dusted-out Greyhound drivers blinking away the NoDoz. Nobody remembered a saucy little redhead, four foot ten, or a middle-aged, middle-height, middle-of-the-road nobody without a future.

Don't bet on the greyhounds. Somebody told him that once.

No sweat, though, because Randy had ideas. By coincidence, he happened to know a certain somebody who could find anybody, and it just so happened that this supersleuth somebody who could find anybody was himself.

Outside, he lit up a cigarette, thinking, and then he crossed the street to a passable-looking diner. He sat at the counter, ordered the liver and onions, switched to the rib eye, switched back to the liver.

There were a few ways you could play this.

The hard way, you find a public library, start digging, see what you can come up with on Mr. Bullshit Bank Robber.

Another way, you chill and wait to hear from your cop buddy in Fulda.

Easiest way of all, you enjoy your liver, wash it down with iced tea, and then you get up and walk over to that big old phone book hanging from a chain on the wall. You lick your finger and flip pages till you get to the *H*s. Next thing, you cross the licking finger over some other finger and think to yourself, Lucky me, and hope for a hit or two, and if you get the hits, like in Halverson, well, then you take out your Bic and start writing down addresses.

Randy should've been a cop. Cops hogged all the fun. Got to carry tasers and fuck with people.

As it turned out, the phone book was ancient—1994—and the greasy old pay phone had been out of service for at least as long. A tough piece of luck. Still, Randy found listings for fourteen Halversons, plus four Halversens with an *e* and one Hallverson with double *l*'s. Any way you cut it, he decided, that amounted to a sizable bunch of Swedes to hunt down. He borrowed a pen from the gal behind the counter, copied the addresses, then sat down again and ordered a slice of the coconut cream pie.

Next life, he'd be a cop. He had the instincts.

Evelyn had remarried for a number of excellent reasons, almost every excellent reason except love. Although, of course, she liked Junius absolutely fine. She liked his resolve and stability. She liked his marble house in the hills, his hands-off policy as a husband, and she felt nothing but gratitude for how the man never complained, never cried over spilt milk, just lumbered on like the cutthroat money machine he was. Granted, Junius tended toward the skeletal and emaciated, with the face of an undernourished bulldog, but all the same he had proven to be an altogether reliable, unemotional, and stinking rich variety of bulldog.

Only a moment ago, for instance, when Junius said, "What's wrong?" he hadn't tacked on any life-or-death spin. He hadn't even looked at her. Instead, as he was still doing, he'd gazed out over the pool at a pretty young woman who last week had been acquitted on two counts of wire fraud. The party was in the young woman's honor.

"Nothing's wrong," Evelyn said. "I'm fine."

"You seem distracted," said Junius.

"No."

He shrugged and murmured, "All righty then," and wandered away.

Briefly, Evelyn considered retreating to her upstairs bedroom, chaining the door, and hiding out for the duration. The last couple of hours had been difficult for her, at times unbearable. Not that it wasn't a perfectly civilized little party. Torches burned. Fountains sparkled. Counterfeit white statuary looked on as people sat chatting in deck chairs around the pool. Among them were two actors, a retired linebacker, a rugged-looking CFO, a landscape architect, and the second wife of California's freshly defeated lieutenant governor. Beautiful evening, beautiful grounds, and the backyard had the Technicolored shimmer of an Esther Williams movie. One of the actors, in fact, had commented as much. "Esther was nothing," he'd remarked conspiratorially, "if not baroque," to which Junius's CFO had nodded and replied, "I have no idea what that even *means.*"

Evelyn had circulated. She had drunk moderately. Xanax had helped.

The time was now closing in on 11:00 p.m., and she embarked on a next-to-last round of hospitality. She passed out mineral water, charmed a man she didn't know, took a dip with the CFO, pulled on a robe, sat smiling at poolside, and then, after ten excruciating minutes, whispered something to her husband and glided off into the shadows beyond the torches. Barefoot, still in her robe, she lay on Junius's furiously green lawn, inspecting a night sky clear of smog, listening idly to the party chatter, telling herself to forget Boyd Halverson, duty done, out of her hands, and besides, it wasn't as if she didn't have troubles of her own.

How, for example, do you deal with a CFO whose hands had just swept expertly across your butt beneath the surface of an Esther Williams pool?

You deal baroquely, she decided. Perhaps with gratitude.

And how, for another example, do you deal with not being a mother anymore?

You don't because it's undealable.

What you do instead, you hire a guy with a truck, and when the truck comes, you fill it with playpens and cribs and changing tables and battery-powered mobiles that play twinkle-twinkle until you want to butcher somebody. You keep piling on the toys and monitors and strollers, then you tote it all out to the truck and dump it in, and later, when the truck guy asks if you want the stuff taken to Goodwill, you tell him no; you tell him you want the goddamn shit off the planet, you want it rocketed to Jupiter, and then you weep on the guy's shoulder because Boyd is indisposed and there's nobody else to weep with.

Evelyn rose to her feet, swayed for a second, found her balance, and rejoined the now all but dead party.

"I'm fine," she told her husband, a little crossly. "So stop asking."

Junius suspected his wife was not fine. He suspected, too, that Boyd Halverson was involved.

As the pool party broke up, Junius took his CFO aside and asked him to look into the matter. "I want this handled," Junius said, "by somebody unpleasant."

"I know the guy," said the CFO, whose name was Henry Speck.

"I know you know," said Junius.

6

MY NAME IS BOYD HALVERSON, BOYD THOUGHT MER-
rily, and I am a lying, bank-robbing, somewhat erratic alcoholic.
I am the source of untold misery. I am a contagion. I am an
infection sweeping through wheat fields and river valleys and
forests and sleepy villages and internet chat rooms, a liar's liar,
mendacity incarnate, the stale, stalwart breath of birthers and
Ruby Ridgers, the wind beneath the wings of fake unfake news,
the last false hope of the disregarded and disappointed and
plain old dissed.

It was two in the morning, a tick or two after, and Boyd
sprawled comfortably in a chair at his mother's kitchen table.
Before him, a large bottle of potato spirits seemed to have swallowed itself.

Angie Bing sat across from him.

"Stop drinking," she was saying, though oddly enough her
voice emerged from the mouth of the mostly empty bottle. "I'm
asking politely, Boyd. Right now. Dump it out."

He examined the remaining half inch of liquid potatoes in
his chipped coffee cup.

"I shot a bus," he said. "A big blue one."

"Right, you explained all that," said Angie. "Probably ten
kabillion times. You were lucky you didn't get arrested. You're
even luckier that I'm still talking to you."

"Yeah, I was wondering about that."

"About what?"

"You know. How you make your voice come out of a bottle, how you never come up for air. Just talk and talk."

Angie glowered at him. She was still securely tied to a kitchen chair. "Well, one thing for sure," she said, "I'm definitely seeing the real Boyd Halverson now." She waited a few moments. "Do you plan to untie me?"

"I doubt it. No offense. I already ungagged you, didn't I?"

"Untie me, Boyd."

"That bus I shot, it actually had a name—Big Blue Bus. Pretty strange, don't you think? I guess now they call it Big Blue Bus with a Hole."

"Boyd, I'm starting to get upset, so if you don't—"

"Would you care to know why I shot a bus?"

"No," she said, then frowned. "Why?"

"Well," said Boyd, but no satisfactory answer presented itself. His stomach wobbled.

He set down his coffee cup, smiled dizzily, then stood and moved with exacting strides toward what he hoped would be a bathroom.

He emptied his bladder, then his stomach. He wiped up the mess.

After an indefinite period of time—more likely minutes than seconds—Boyd found himself inspecting a mirror above the sink, where a sad, puffy-fleshed creature loomed before him, the eyes bloodshot, the posture defeated, an unattractive black and gray stubble coating the beast's cheeks and jaw. Could this, he wondered, be I? Instantly, he congratulated himself on the impeccable grammar. Still the journalist. Still civilized, too, because what was grammar if not civilization, or the delegate of civilization, or its last decaying bulwark? It is indeed I in this mirror, Boyd surmised, and as he splashed cold water on his face, he noted something dark and flaky on what was pretty obviously his own upper lip. The substance, he reasoned, was no doubt a foodstuff, yet he had no recollection of consuming so much as a bite over the past twenty or thirty hours. He did, however, recall Evelyn's white marble steps. He remembered a screenwriter from South Dakota and several overpriced glasses of extremely hard liquor. Most vividly, he recalled boarding the Big Blue Bus, and the shockingly loud retort of the Temptation .38, and a Pakistani gentleman's yelp of dismay.

"I shot a bus," Boyd said to the mirror, which flashed him a weary grin. "I do not lie. A bus."

Boyd grinned right back at himself, plucked the suspicious substance from his lip, emptied his bladder once more, stood motionless at the mirror, and came to the conclusion that he was now a wanted man in need of one last nightcap. Wanted man—Boyd liked that. It had been a while since anyone had properly wanted him.

Refreshed, he found his way back to the kitchen, where Angie said, "How was the bathroom vacation?"

"Not bad," he said, and rummaged through a cupboard. He discovered two mini bottles of his mother's bourbon and carefully deposited their contents in his coffee cup. "Would you care for a slug?"

"No. Untie me."

"Can you think of a good reason?"

"Because I'm sane," said Angie, "and you're not. Because, as far as I can tell, I'm your only friend on earth. And because I could've run away a million times and I didn't." She studied him for signs of weakness. "If you'd just trust me—if you'd try to explain things to me—maybe I could help somehow."

"Help how?"

"Do you trust me?"

"Not a smidgen," said Boyd.

Angie feigned a humorless little laugh. "Look, just because I sent Randy that totally innocent postcard . . . Grow up, Boyd. You can't hold grudges for eternity."

"Grudges," he said, "are my strong suit." He held out his cup. "Here, take a sip."

"I want you to untie me."

"Yes, I understand that. It's a legitimate request."

"It's not a request, for God's sake. Do it."

Boyd polished off the bourbon.

"By the way," he said, "did you know that Rosemary Clooney once lived barely a block from here? She was no longer young then, I'll admit. Getting plump."

"Who?"

"You're asking *who*? Rosemary Clooney?"

"Come on, Boyd, please untie me."

"No kidding, I delivered Rosemary's morning paper—nice lady, an angel really."

"I said please," Angie snapped.

"Please what?"

"Pretty please."

"Maybe so, maybe not," said Boyd. "If you promise to go home, that's the maybe so. If you don't promise, that's the maybe not."

"Why would I go home?" she asked.

"I'm sick, Angie."

"You're intoxicated. You're a disgusting old man."

"Yes, but I'm truly sick. I'm headed . . . I'm headed somewhere bad, I think. *Sick* isn't the word. *Dark* is the word."

Angie nodded. "Well, that's exactly what Our Lord and Host is there for. Day and night. He's there for the darkness."

"Indeed! Does the Host make house calls?"

"Sure," she said. "If you untie people."

Again, a seesawing sensation swept over him, beginning in his stomach, sliding downward, then rocketing to the roof of his mouth. "Boy oh boy," he said. "I've been drinking, Angie."

"Yeah," she said.

"I should untie you, shouldn't I?"

"Any day now."

He untied her, fumbling a little, and said, "I'm hungry. Do we have food?"

"No," she said. "Let's get you to bed."

"Did I mention I was married once or twice?"

"You overlooked that. The twice part."

"I had a little boy."

"Did you?"

"I did. Yes, I did. I dropped him."

She shook blood into her hands, and then, more gently than he would've expected, led him by the arm into his mother's bedroom. She pulled back the quilt, took off his shoes, and settled him in.

A while later she got into bed beside him.

"I think I'm in trouble," he said.

"You are, Boyd."

"I'm sorry I gagged you. You talk too much."

"I do sometimes."

"You do. You talk a lot."

"Go to sleep."

"I'm hungry. I miss my little boy."

7

THE COCONUT CREAM WAS FIRST-RATE. RANDY ORdered a second slice and ate it slowly, thinking contented thoughts about diners and pie and that perky waitress behind the counter, perky but could stand to drop a dozen pounds, maybe lay off the coconuts and the cream. Diners were pretty special, Randy decided. Especially diners across from bus stations where you get the kind of customer who could appreciate a piece of liver topped off with coconut cream pie that tasted like coconuts and not stewed pigeon guts, like in certain fancy truck stops he could name. In diners you met interesting people, too—for example the big Black guy sitting three stools down. Randy would've bet the max that this individual had some history behind him, the ink work alone, not to mention the biceps, not to mention the fact that the fella was telling a scrawny white guy next to him about spotting Charlie Manson in the flesh one time, which where else would you spot Charlie Manson except in Corcoran State Prison? It was a medium-fair conversation, Randy figured, and he nudged his plate down the counter and asked if it was true that Charlie Manson liked to read the Bible backward. "I heard that," Randy said, "but not at Corcoran."

The big tatted guy looked at his companion and said, "Never noticed any Bible; you ever notice a Bible?" and the scrawny guy just shook his head.

"Eats popsicles, too," said Randy, getting into it. "Charlie eats popsicles, reads the Bible backward, that's how he does his time."

"Yeah?" the big guy said.

"Yeah," Randy said.

"I guess you'd know, right?"

"I would and I do."

"How's that coconut cream?"

"Good," Randy said. "It's good."

"You ever eat shit?"

Randy didn't blink; he knew the program. "Couple times I did. Not down at Corcoran, though." Then he put his hand out, and said, "Randy Zapf," and the two guys waited a second, then shook his hand, and the inked Black guy said, "Zapf, there's a name for you."

"German," Randy said.

"How you spell it?"

"Like it sounds, except there's a *p*."

"Zaff?"

"Almost like that."

"There's a name."

"It's a name, all right," Randy said, then they talked for a good while about the Black guy's tattoos, what they meant, where he got them, and afterward they paid up and ambled over to a place on East Ninth where they watched tennis on TV and some overdressed dancing gals in rubber thongs. It turned out that the inked dude hadn't been in Corcoran at all, which didn't bother Randy a bit, because Randy hadn't been there either. On the other hand, all three of them had done brick time in the Glendale lockup—quite a nifty coincidence, actually—and the inked guy's scrawny friend claimed he'd heard Johnny Cash in person, which probably meant Folsom '68, which meant the guy had to be one very ancient criminal.

Randy didn't see any reason to brag. He could've mentioned Snake River Correctional up in Oregon. He could've told rodeo stories. Instead, he said, "Them rubber thongs, where you figure I could pick one up? Not too expensive?"

"You wear thongs?" said the old white guy.

"Yeah, I wear thongs." Randy gave the dude a look, just so, a polite warning. "Now let's say I asked one of them young ladies, like that sassy bleached-up one over there, you think she'd sell me her thong?"

"Can always try," the inked guy said.

"Yes, sir," Randy said. "I'll do that."

He got up and went over and talked to the girl and came back with a yellow thong.

"Twenty bucks," he said, proud. "And she looks better now."

"Bunch," said the big inked guy. "Who's the thong for?"

So Randy unloaded on them about Angie and the bank and the postcard and the trip down to Mexico and how he was eager to get a line on Boyd Halverson. He asked if they had ideas.

The two men looked at him.

"Robbed a bank?" the big one said.

"Community National up in Fulda—right off the state line. Not much of a bank, but I figure their money spends."

"Prob'bly does if it's real money."

"No lie," said Randy. "And you see why I need to track her down. Takes off with this amateur crook, sends me a postcard."

"I do see that," the big guy said.

About then it crossed Randy's mind that he should probably give his sayonaras and scoot back to the Super 8, rest up for tomorrow, get ready to ring doorbells, but on the other hand, these two boys were taking an interest. "All I know for sure," Randy said, "is what I read in the postcard. You know, like when a bank gets robbed, sometimes they show robbing tapes on TV, those black-and-white ones, look like the silent movies? Well, all I got was the postcard, says she robbed a bank, but it's like this video in my head, it keeps going round and round."

"Carl and me—I'm Cyrus—we starred in one of those," said the big tatted guy.

"Oh, yeah?"

"Sure. Carl and me and that sassy stripper."

It was a joke probably, and Randy laughed. "Anyhow, it's like Angie—Angie, she's my gal—it's like she's thumbing her nose at me, you know? Ticks me off. And the bank robber guy, he bought her a goddamn camera, you believe it?"

"Ticks me off, too," said the elderly white guy, Carl.

The big Black one said, "So what's the plan? Strangle her with a thong?"

"Well, no, I don't figure she was in on the heist. Not Angie."

"You don't, don't you?"

"No way." Randy hesitated. "Angie sort of—I don't know— she's a cooperative gal, easy to manipulate, got herself sucked into something."

"How much they get?"

"Money?" Randy said.

"No, Cyrus means honey-sweet nookie," said the scrawny old white guy. "Don't you mean nookie, Cyrus?"

"Uh-uh," said Cyrus. "Randy's on to me. I mean how much money."

Uneasily, Randy put the yellow thong in his pocket.

He started to get up, but Cyrus said, "Sit on down, Randy Zipper. We might got business to do."

It wasn't as though Randy hadn't given thought to all that tax-free income floating around out there, because he had, and because lifting the cash off a girlfriend-thief would've been half the fun, like a citizen's arrest except he wouldn't be arresting anybody and he wouldn't be giving any money back.

Randy didn't need business partners.

He was pretty sure he should've kept his mouth shut about the bank money. And not shown his list of Halverson addresses to a couple of prison bozos. Or mentioned the Super 8.

So here it was, middle of the night, and he's on the freakin' floor, not even a blanket, Carl and Cyrus bunked out in the king-size bed Randy had paid out-of-pocket for. One thing Randy hated, it was roommates, especially the kind with tats and testicles and prison time. The truth was, if he had it to do over again, he never would've crossed the street for liver and onions.

His back was killing him.

The smart thing to do, he thought, was wait until about four in the morning and then sneak out to the Cutlass and make fast tracks.

Randy grinned in the dark, thinking, Yes sir, that's what you'll do.

Swipe some wallets for fun.

When he opened his eyes, it was broad daylight and the scrawny old white guy, Carl, stood a couple of feet away, toweling off after a shower. Randy shut his eyes, then opened them again, but the picture didn't improve.

Cyrus sat filing his fingernails at an imitation-walnut desk.

Without glancing up, almost like he had eyes in his shoulder blades, he said, "How's that floor, Zipper?"

"Pretty fine," said Randy. "How's the bed?"

"You bein' smart?"

"Well, no. Since I paid and everything."

Cyrus thought about it. "I'd rank the bed," he said, "about Super 8."

The elderly white guy laughed. It was a bouncy laugh, full of energy, balls swinging like in a Senior Olympics hammer throw. Randy watched the action and reminded himself to ditch these jerks ASAP.

Breakfast came with the room. Afterward, the three of them piled into the Cutlass, and Randy pointed it where Cyrus told him to, west toward Culver City. The list of addresses lay on Cyrus's lap. Scrawny Carl sat in back, not liking it much.

"Your girlfriend," Cyrus was saying, "she won't be a problem? Don't want problems, do we?"

Randy shook his head. "The only problem," he said, more chipper than he was feeling, "is Angie finding the right gunk at Walgreens to cover up the thong bruises."

"And the robber dude?"

"He's a nothing."

"A nothing with the nuts to rob a bank."

"Sure, but I'll put it this way," said Randy, and then he stopped to figure out a way to put it. He'd read somewhere that pauses make people respect you. "The deal is, this slimeball isn't Jesse James. He's JCPenney."

"You know the fella, then?"

"Personally, you mean?"

"Whichever way you might know him, Zipper."

Randy kept his eyes on the road, looking for the Culver City exit. It was a Monday morning, mid-September, and traffic was enough to make you invest in solar. "Can't say I know him, Cyrus. Spotted him around a few times, I guess, but you don't really notice department store managers. They're like the lady sells you a movie ticket, the one in the ticket booth. You don't pay attention."

"I married that lady," said Carl from the backseat.

"Your sweetheart," Cyrus said.

"Yeah, my sweetheart," Carl said.

They laughed awhile, then Cyrus said, "So, Randy, here's what we're wondering about. If you ran across this Boyd fella, you think you'd know him? If he happens to come to the door when we knock?"

"Oh, right," Randy said. "I see what you mean."

"He sees what you mean," Carl said.

Randy pulled on a pair of sunglasses. The disrespect thing was getting on his nerves. What these hotshots needed to appreciate was they weren't dealing with a civilian. He wished one of them would bring up the subject of, say, grape burglary, so then Randy could chime in with his story about a certain grape farmer down in Napa, a lady grape farmer—in fact, a real sharp-looking lady grape farmer if you go for eighty-year-olds with skin you can see through—how she hired Randy to rewire her great big mother of a grape barn, which was full of way more grapes than anybody needed, and how the old bat showed up just when Randy was busy loading a fourth barrel of grapes into a pickup he'd borrowed, and how she came at him with a broadfork until he muscled her into the barn and pretty much turned her into grape juice, nice and slushy, a good story, but before Randy could even get started, Cyrus said, "Hey, Zipper, there's your exit."

It took a couple of U-turns, but they found the house, first one on Randy's list, a fixer-upper if there ever was one. A kid was playing in the front yard, nine or ten years old.

"That your bank robber?" scrawny Carl asked.

"Better check," said Cyrus.

"Go check, Randy," said Carl.

Randy shrugged. He tipped up his shades, got out of the car, strolled past the kid, rang the front doorbell, waited a minute, then leaned on it hard. Part of him was wondering how he looked with the shades up on his forehead. Like in the movies, he thought. Some of the best stuff Randy knew, he knew from the movies.

He gave the doorbell another poke, no dice, so he moved over to a window along the porch and leaned up close, cupping his hands against the glare. There wasn't much to see except his own nose. The sunglasses, he figured, looked fairly fine tipped up like that.

He turned to the kid in the yard, and said, "Any Halversons around? Mom and Pop?"

The kid didn't look up from the scooter he was playing with.

"Hey," Randy said. He stepped off the porch and walked over to the boy and gave his arm a pinch. "I'm talking to you, Buster Brown."

The kid backed away.

"Pipe up," Randy said.

Even then the boy didn't say anything, which got Randy's goat. He didn't have patience for brats who wouldn't look at you and wouldn't hardly give you the time of day.

"Man, are you *deaf*?" he said, then realized that was probably the problem.

The little shithead was crying now.

Randy kicked the kid's scooter and walked back to the Cutlass and hopped in. Why the kid had to be hearing crippled, Randy didn't know. It was like somebody planned it that way.

"You're the nasty one," Cyrus said.

"I can be," said Randy.

They tried three more Halverson addresses before noon, another four after lunch, but nothing popped up except zeros. Cyrus and Carl stayed in the car while Randy did the doorbell chores, which struck him as unfair. Their last stop was in Anaheim, an old man watering his roses, but by that point, Randy was thinking he should try his cop buddy again.

The ride back to the Super 8 was stone quiet.

In the parking lot, Cyrus said, "So, Zipper, where'd you come up with these bullshit addresses?"

"The phone book," Randy said.

"Phone book? There ain't no more phone books. Phone books went out with culottes."

"Yeah, well, I found myself one—'94, I think. What's the big deal?"

Cyrus shot a look at Carl. "Chasin' names in a twenty-year-old phone book? Not to mention, this bank robber of yours, he ain't even from L.A., so what makes you think he'd be in a brand-*new* phone book?"

"I don't know . . . Family maybe. He came here for a reason, I figure."

Cyrus closed his eyes, blew out a breath, looked at Carl again.

Carl said, "Donkey dumb."

Randy waited for a good zinger to jump into his head, but nothing did, so he said, "What'd you say?"

"Donkey dumb," said Carl, "and that's stretching it."

For a while the three of them went silent, then Cyrus sighed and laid a hand on Randy's shoulder.

"What Carl's pointing out," he said, almost gently, "he's sayin' what if our stickup man came here for some *other* reason? Phone book's useless in that case. Even a phone book that ain't from the Dark Ages."

"Yeah," Randy said.

"You follow?"

"Sure I do. But what if he came here for family?"

Cyrus wagged his head. "Zipper, you're not grasping this. What if he came for some *other* reason?"

"Like what?"

"Well, it don't matter. To take a leak in the Hollywood Bowl."

"Huh?"

"I'll explain later. Let's eat."

"Brain food," said Carl.

They crossed the parking lot to an Applebee's. Randy was willing to drop the whole subject, but over a plate of almost perfect-looking onion rings, which they didn't share, Cyrus and Carl went into way too much detail about all the various reasons Boyd Halverson could've come to L.A. He could've come because it was a big city and he wanted to get lost with his heist money. He could've come because he had buddies here. He could've come to see a prize fight, or rob another bank, or jump a cruise ship for Hawaii. "In other words," Cyrus said, and plopped the list of addresses in front of Randy, "this phone book shitola is a pure shot in the dark, am I right?"

"Okay," Randy said.

"See the problem?"

"I guess, sure." Randy stared at the onion rings. "How you like being Black, Cyrus?"

"Say again?"

"You like it all right?"

Cyrus looked at Carl, then at Randy. "What the fuck's Black got to do with anything? I'm asking if you see a problem with a twenty-year-old phone book."

"Course I do. I said okay, didn't I?"

"But do you *see*?"

"Yeah, I see," Randy said. "Except if Halverson has family in L.A., they'll be in the phone book."

"Oh, man," said Carl.

Randy shrugged and looked down at the address list. The next stop was out in Santa Monica, just off Ocean Park Boulevard.

He stuffed the list in his pocket, and said, "Forget the phone book. I've got other ideas—this cop buddy of mine in Fulda. Might be he can help out. Not a buddy exactly. But he arrested me one time."

Carl lifted his eyebrows. "Holy cow, you're a criminal, are you?"

"You want to say that, say that," said Randy. "Can I try them onion rings?"

8

MYTHOMANIA, THE LYING DISEASE, CAME WITH AN odor: a mix of sulfides and rotting crawfish. By the late summer of 2019, in the nation's capital, White House limousines and Senate hearing rooms had become unpleasant places. To smell a rat or to smell something fishy were now literal responses to an avalanche of oratorical whoppers issued by occupants of high, medium, and low office. According to NIH epidemiologists, the onslaught of shameless, matter-of-fact mendacity was creating its own epidemic of olfactory nerve damage, endangering not only constitutional democracy but human life. Two presidential advance men perished in Butte, Montana, after failing to detect leaking natural gas. A six-man, one-woman presidential Advisory Committee on Locker Room Talk was hospitalized after ingesting a banquet of spoiled chicken tarragon, again undetected.

Nose disease took its toll. Toilets went unflushed; milk soured; children ate stewed kale.

More alarming, the causal connection between epidemic lying and epidemic nasal malfunction represented only one of the many consequences of mythomania. Bullyism skyrocketed. Marriages collapsed. Prayer groups turned violent. By the last day in July of that year, perjury had become a feather in the cap, E no longer equaled MC squared, and the interchangeability of truth and falsehood filled psychiatric waiting rooms. Editorial fact-checkers complained of dizziness, confusion, rage, hopelessness, and isolation—easy pickings for the nation's seventy-six Truth Teller Seeds.

From Cape Cod to Pearl Harbor, creative Truth Tellers flooded cyberspace with the manna of make-believe. Burbank's popular Truth Teller Seed relayed the news that television screens were flashing "subconscious LGBTQ propaganda targeting six-year-olds." *SpongeBob*, the Seed claimed, had been conceived by whale-hugging, clean-water Democrats; Japanese anime was aimed at "reversing the outcome of World War Two"; *American Dad!* was an "atheistic assault on the Fifth Commandment." Similarly, in Black Hawk, Colorado, a Truth Teller Seed had posted a fake unfake video of a former vice presidential candidate pinning a merit badge to the shirt of a thirteen-year-old Boy Scout, Edgar Pitts, who had developed the world's first fully portable nuclear weapon.

About a third of the nation's adult citizenry—sixty-nine million Americans—believed one or more of these ridiculous falsehoods.

Thus, in small-town Fulda, California, the country's leading Source Seed (as opposed to Relay Seeds) found itself under pressure to deliver fresh untrue truth content.

Earl Fenstermacher had been struggling.

"How do you top Boy Scout nukes?" Earl complained to his confederates. "I'm creative director, sure, but I'm not . . . I'm not a magician. I'm not Boyd Halverson. The cupboard's bare. Anti-vax, anti-diapers—all the good stuff's used up. Where do you go after Boyd proved the FDA won't come clean about guns preventing tonsillitis? What's left?"

"Hillary?" Dink O'Neill said.

"Done to death."

"Civil war?" suggested Chub O'Neill. "Stock up on ammo—us against the EPA?"

"Ancient history." Earl wagged his head wearily. "Look, I'll level with you. We need something so new it hasn't happened yet, and never *could* happen, except with libtards running the show. We need sexy. We need preposterous. Like—I don't know—like how the feds are sticking spy cameras inside hummingbirds, that kind of thing."

"Halverson already tweeted that one, I believe," said Doug Cutterby. "The lad had a gift."

Earl nodded. "Yes, sir, and there's our problem. Say what you want, but Halverson—bless his twisted tongue—he was right up there with POTUS himself." He paused. "God bless America, of course."

"Amen," said Dink.

"Double amen," said his brother Chub.

The four men fell silent. They were seated at a back table in the Twilight Club, Fulda's answer to upscale L.A. drinking establishments. Dink picked idly at one of his Klan tattoos, Doug Cutterby daydreamed about Taylor Swift, whom he'd spotted at the Bellagio, and Chub sat stirring his vodka tonic until he cleared his throat and said to Earl, "Face it. Dink's right. Hillary it is."

"What's the spin?"

"Who cares? She wrote *The Story of Little Black Sambo*?"

"Dated," said Earl. "Nobody under forty will get it."

"Yeah, I guess," said Chub. "How about this? We headline it: Hillary Expecting Quintuplets, Obama Denies Parentage."

"Or she already *had* the quintuplets!" said Dink. "And ate them!"

Earl puckered his lips in distaste. "Forget it, too stale, old news. Think crazy. Think *impossible*."

Again, the Source Seed went silent. Several minutes passed before Earl smiled and grunted and jerked up straight in his chair.

"What?" said Dink.

"Remember that last Kiwanis brunch, the one where Boyd walked out on us, said he had to get to the bank before it closed? Right before he walked out, Boyd was riffing—trying out new ideas—mostly that one about how twelve American presidents never actually *existed*. Remember that? Rutherford B. Hayes—a nobody. Literally. Never drew a breath. John Tyler—pure fiction. Millard Fillmore, James Polk, Jack Kennedy, William Henry Harrison—not one of them was even half as real as Santa Claus. I forget the details, but do you remember who was behind it all?" Earl looked at Dink, then Chub, then Doug Cutterby. "The Electoral College, that's who! If they don't like who wins an election, the bastards *invent* a president. They *invent* a whole biography. They hire washed-up actors to show up at inaugurations. They drum up videos of fake presidents saluting on fake airplane steps. Election fraud! That's how Boyd pitched it. Hell, the Electoral College staged the Kennedy assassination because there *wasn't* a Kennedy, never *was* a Kennedy, just like there was never a McKinley or a Lincoln."

"No Lincoln?" Dink said.

"Not if you listened to Boyd."

"So no Emancipation Proclamation? They're still slaves?"

"Draw your own conclusions," Earl said happily. He drained his whiskey sour, glanced at his watch, and said, "Unless somebody's got a better idea, I vote we float it on Instagram. Pronto. Right now. There's an election coming up, a biggie, and it can't hurt to start tilling the soil. I swear to God, it's like Boyd gave us this last fantastic goodbye gift."

Dink frowned. "I don't know. No Lincoln? Who'd buy it?"

"You'd be surprised," Earl said. "A third of the country, I'm betting."

9

THEY WERE PICKING UP GROCERIES IN RALPHS, NOT
yet eight in the morning, and the cart was piled high with items
Boyd had not realized were edible. "Somebody your age," Angie
Bing was saying, "somebody with a drinking problem, you'd
better start watching your heart. Fish oil helps with that. Fish
oil and Tremella and spinach and lots of fruit; maybe you won't
keel over tomorrow. Not that I give a teeny-weeny hoot."

She was there under a gag order. Not one peep, Boyd had
warned her, but that had been a half hour ago.

"I'm forty-three," Boyd said wearily. "Or maybe forty-nine,
and last night was an exception, and you promised you wouldn't
say a word."

"We're *grocery* shopping."

"So?"

"Well, so that's different."

"It's not different."

"Boyd," she said, and swiveled toward him. "Am I making
a scene? Look at me. Am I yelling?"

"No."

"You want me to yell?"

"No."

"If you want, I can yell. I'm a good yeller."

"Don't, Angie."

"All right, so lay off. All I'm doing, I'm trying to keep you alive. Don't ask me why."

Angie seized the cart handle, which for her was a reach, then shot a warning glance at him. At the pharmacy she loaded up on ginger extract and St. John's wort and mushroom powder and stool softener; in the knickknack section she picked up a garlic press and a measuring tape. There was no point, Boyd decided, in asking questions. He wanted out of the store, out of the eye of three-dozen watchful cameras scanning the aisles. This excursion was supposed to have been a quickie, in and out, and Angie had sworn she would stay silent.

His own gullibility irritated him.

After a time, he took her arm. "That's it," he said.

"Boyd, that hurts a little."

"It's supposed to hurt. Let's go."

"I can still yell, mister."

"Fine, then. Yell up a storm."

"Sure, and get arrested?" She pried his hand away. "Let's go pick up some cow meat. It'll be fun watching your veins explode."

She spent five minutes squeezing steaks and pot roasts.

Boyd finally sighed and said, "Please? I mean, really, aren't you ready to get back to your boyfriend and job and all?"

Angie tossed three pork chops into the cart. "No," she said. "Because life's for living. If *you* get to have a big glamorous adventure, why can't I? And my job sucks. You think I get a kick out of counting other people's money? You think that's fun?"

"Jail won't be fun either."

She pushed the cart over to a bin of persimmons and said,

"You're the crook, Boyd. Not me. Which, by the way, you haven't explained yet. Last night you swore you'd explain."

"Not in a Ralphs," he said.

"Excuses," said Angie.

"All right. If you do me a favor, I'll explain."

Angie turned and studied him like a poker player deciding whether to fold or go all in.

"What's the favor?" she asked.

"A couple of phone calls."

"That's it? Then you start talking?"

"Tonight for sure. It'll take a while."

Angie stood motionless for a moment, just watching him.

"Okay, deal," she finally said. "But don't forget, I'm a pro when it comes to yelling."

After checking out, and after Boyd had dropped another three hundred dollars, Angie pulled out her cell phone, placed two calls, then handed him a scrap of paper on which she'd scribbled the word *YOU!*

"Good luck," she said. "How long will this take?"

"Two, three hours," said Boyd.

"You want to say thank you?"

"Thank you, Angie."

"You're welcome. And remember that promise of yours—no drinking. It's Satan's conscience killer."

"If only," said Boyd.

"Three hours max," Angie said. "Don't shoot anybody."

Off Beverly Boulevard, near where it cuts across North La Cienega, stood a black-granite office building that, by the posh face of it, catered to those with excessive amounts of time and capital on their hands. Curiously, like the Big Blue Bus, this streamlined structure had been christened with its own name—YOU!—but that excited pronoun very plainly did not embrace the scuff-shoed, thin-walleted clodhopper just off the bus from Fulda. YOU! did not mean *you*. The *you* of YOU! meant celebrity, or those attending celebrity: perhaps the agent or the spouse or the weary bankroller. And if you—just any you—were to wander into the building's lobby bedecked in the apparel, say, of JCPenney, your welcome would be less than enthusiastic—a security guard's cheerless stare, a receptionist's unfailing eye for mediocrity.

Near the building's revolving front door, behind an imposing, nearly opaque smoked-glass window, several discreetly engraved plaques announced the enterprises housed within, among which were a health spa, a cosmetician, and a surgical service specializing in the human eyelid. Apparently, too, a few ludicrously upscale retail shops committed larceny on the premises: a perfumery, an antique store, a jeweler, a Cuban tobacconist, and a suite of law offices. Displayed upon white satin in the lower portion of the window lay a number of items that may or may not have been for sale, most prominently a chess set, a clinquant tiara, a gold spoon embedded with shards of emerald or convincing glass, a weathered Noh mask, a pair of safety pins, and an urn that appeared to be made of concrete but almost certainly was not. No prices were advertised.

The top six floors of this handsome, buffed-black building were occupied by the U.S. headquarters of Pacific Ships and Shipping. A discreet bronze plaque listed Junius Kirakossian as CEO, James R. Dooney as chairman emeritus. Their likenesses had been imprinted upon the plaque like the faces of Octavian and Caesar.

Boyd Halverson had been loitering at the smoked-glass

windows for some while. At the moment, on this brilliant mid-September morning, he found himself reflecting on the relativity of wealth and privilege. Not long ago he had robbed a bank, lifting every nickel from the till, yet here he stood, all but impoverished by the standards of YOU!, with barely the wherewithal to purchase a simple safety pin.

Forever the window-shopper.

As a diversion, Boyd mused, it would be interesting to shoot the smoked-glass window—inviting target, hard to miss—and it was a disappointment when he recalled that Angie had removed the bullets from the handgun now weighting his coat pocket. "You can have them back," she'd said, "after you talk to your ex. I'm not getting involved in murder."

Not an hour ago, he'd left Angie in his mother's kitchen, where Boyd had renewed his pledge to swear off alcohol. He had acknowledged lapses of judgment and common sense. Shooting buses, he had sworn, was off-limits.

"Or shooting anything else," Angie had said. "Nothing illegal."

"Correct."

"And tonight you'll tell me what all this is about. Everything. That's our deal, right?"

"Only fair."

Angie had gazed at him over the rim of her coffee cup. "Right here, right now, Boyd. This is what trust is. Now give me the bullets."

Angie's earlier phone calls had yielded two results, the first of which led to the discovery that Evelyn was having her face resurfaced that morning; the second of which located a suite of high-end cosmetology offices on the third floor of YOU! A few minutes after ten o'clock, with the unloaded pistol in his pocket, they had parted ways on his mother's doorstep. "Don't think you've snowed me," Angie said. "Because you haven't. Total honesty from now on." She'd gone up on her toes and deftly kissed his chin. "I'm not your enemy."

Now, appraising himself in the smoked-glass window, Boyd regretted his reckless pledge of sobriety.

He needed a drink.

He needed three.

After a moment, he gave a feeble rap on the smoked-glass window, passed through the revolving door, and boarded an elevator to the third floor. At the end of a corridor lighted in calming ocean blues, he found an establishment called The Inner You, an earnest but illogical designation for a concern that serviced the outer hides of well-ticketed women. As he stepped inside, a melodic chime played Chopin or Bach or somebody with piano experience. Wind and surf sounds surrounded him. Ocean smells percolated from the carpets and tapestries.

Grandiosity was Boyd's weakness—it always had been—and his stomach churned with a familiar wrong-side-of-the-tracks anxiety. There was wealth at work here. Someone had taste.

Directly in front of him, a well-tanned and impossibly lovely young receptionist seemed to levitate behind an antique walnut desk—one hundred and very few pounds of Los Angeles starlet.

Boyd's stomach muscles tightened. He squared up his posture.

"One sec," whispered the starlet.

She appeared to be doing absolutely nothing. Her gaze was fixed on the oxygen between them.

Boyd smiled. His dislike for the girl was instantaneous and intense.

"No sweat," he whispered back.

The young woman neither spoke nor shifted her foreground focus. Seconds ticked by. Her glassy, greenish-blue eyes seemed to have frozen in their sockets. He wondered if she was breathing.

More time elapsed.

"Anybody home?" he said mildly.

The girl wiggled some fingers—just barely—and Boyd's dislike morphed into loathing. At the same time, shamefully, he had risen to his full height. With women like this—Evelyn herself, not so long ago—he was a sucker for what could not, in any ripe sense, be had. Invisible me, he thought. It occurred to him that he might find a way to announce himself as an emissary of George Clooney, or better yet, get her attention with his pistol.

"Hey, you," he said, "is this a puppet show?"

The girl blinked up at him with a quick, startled smile.

"Sorry?" she said.

"In case you were worried," said Boyd, "I'm not a nobody. I run with the pack."

The young woman smiled again, her teeth afire with dentistry. "You're a joker," she said, "aren't you?"

"I'm a joker. There's a gun in my pocket."

The girl nodded without affect.

Magically, she seemed to levitate a trifle higher as she opened a desk drawer and extracted a leather-bound log.

"You have an appointment then," she murmured, not quite a question, not quite much of anything. "And you would be . . ."

"Mr. Cranston," said Boyd. "Bryan."

Her eyes found focus.

"Just kidding," Boyd said. "Yu. Mr. Yu. Here to pick up my wife."

"That would be Mrs. Yu?"

"No, that would be Mrs. Evelyn Kirakossian."

"Ah," she whispered. "How do you pronounce it again?"

"Evelyn."

"No, the last name."

"Kirakossian."

"That's a mouthful."

"You're telling me," said Boyd. "But listen, I need to ask something. Did you hear that chime just now?"

"The what?"

"The *chime*. The one that says, 'Hey, somebody walked in, I'd better look up and be polite.'"

"Have a seat," she said.

"Seriously. Did you hear it?"

"Mr. Yu," she said. "Please."

Boyd shrugged and sat down directly across from her. Astonishing, he thought, what will fly off a man's tongue once he has robbed a bank. It occurred to him, too, that after a decade of penitent silence, he was beginning to find his mojo again. Vaguely, he wondered who Mr. Yu might be—a well-groomed flunky, no doubt—but in any event this was playing out better than expected.

The girl spoke into a telephone, hung up, and, without looking at him, said, "Five minutes, she'll be out."

"Fine," said Boyd.

Some oceanic time went by.

Then Boyd said, "May I ask how you do that?"

"Do what?"

"Levitate like that."

The receptionist smiled abstractly. She had heard it all.

"Honest to God," he said, "it looks exactly like you're floating there. Is it an air cushion or something?"

"Mr. Yu, I wish—"

"I'm actually not Mr. Yu," Boyd said. "But I buy and sell things. Real estate mostly. This building for instance."

"You own it?"

"I certainly do. Chimes, tapestries, elevators—I own YOU!"

The young woman looked up at him sharply. "If that's your idea of a come-on," she said, "you're out of luck. Nobody owns me."

"Not you. YOU! I own the place."

"You own YOU!?"

"I do," said Boyd. "And I shot a bus yesterday."

This was liberating, Boyd decided. There was a taste to a good lie, like smoked sausage, something fatty and unhealthful, but delicious. He would've continued in the same vein had not Evelyn then stepped out into the reception area. She was dressed, it seemed, for afternoon tea.

"Look, I'm sorry," the girl said to her. "I thought he was Mr. Yu, but he's—"

"I know who he is," Evelyn said.

"He owns YOU!"

Evelyn's gaze swept sideways.

She began backing away, but Boyd stood up and took her arm and told her he wouldn't need but ten minutes, that he should've called first, very sorry, but would she be willing to let the past be past and head out for a drink and maybe reminisce for a while and then hop in her Bentley and take a quick spin to paradise or nirvana or wherever?

"You're something," Evelyn said.

"That's true, but not long ago I was nothing. Then I stuck up a bank."

He showed her his gun.

"All right," she said. "Ten minutes."

"That's kind of you, Evelyn," said Boyd. "Your skin, I must say, looks good as new."

"Put the gun away," she said.

10

THEY FOUND A PLACE TWO BLOCKS DOWN LA
Cienega, a sidewalk café where they sat beneath a cheerful yellow awning. Evelyn took a defensive posture, arms folded, her
upper body on a rigid forward cant, regarding him with equal
parts apprehension and fatigue. Little had changed over nine
years. She was still slim and self-possessed, still scrupulously
put together, still many light-years out of his league. Boyd felt
for her what he had always felt, which was mostly awe.

Some elastic moments went by before Evelyn said, "The gun
wasn't funny, Junior. Following me around isn't funny either.
Next time wait for an invitation before you ring my doorbell."
She glared. "So what do you want?"

"Well," he said, "a gin and tonic."

"Junior."

"A celebration, isn't it? Old times, just the two of us." He
hesitated. "I did rob a bank, you know. Broad daylight."

"Sure you did."

"It was a mistake, I'm beginning to think."

"And the gun?"

"For show," he said, then thought about it for a second. "Or
maybe not. I'll say this, it gets people's attention. The whole
experience—robbing banks—it's been a personality shaper. The
important stuff just slams you in the face."

"Such as?"

"Such as here I am. About to share a drink with my ex-beloved."

Evelyn closed her eyes briefly, then sighed and leaned back in her chair. "You don't quit, do you? Such bullshit."

"You don't believe I robbed a bank?"

"Of course I don't."

"Ten, twelve, sixteen days ago. I'm losing track."

"What do you want?"

"Dooney," Boyd said.

"Dooney. For what?"

Boyd grinned self-consciously. "For what? You know what." He felt the grin slipping away. "Where would I find him these days?"

"Not a clue."

"Oh," he said, "I'll bet you *do* have a clue. Just an itsy-bitsy-spider clue?"

Stone-faced, with only the slightest show of unease, she said, "I actually don't. Dooney uncloseted himself, resigned as CEO, installed my husband, then hit the road with Calvin. Where I have no idea. We don't speak."

Evelyn put on a pair of sunglasses then immediately pulled them off. "Do you plan to shoot him with that great big gun of yours?"

"Not necessarily, but I do expect a bloodbath," said Boyd, looking around for a waiter. "Incidentally, do you want to know why I robbed a bank?"

"You didn't rob a bank. You're a liar, remember?"

"Oh, yeah."

"You never, never tell the truth."

"I wouldn't say never, never."

"Almost never."

Boyd shrugged to show he was a good sport. "Well, listen—this is fascinating—you'll be happy to learn I've cleaned up my act. A rayon specialist. Fourteen handicap, not bad with the putter. A Kiwanis stalwart these past nine years. Maybe you didn't know that."

"I didn't."

"Absolutely. Kiwanis every other Saturday. Our motto is Service, Pride, Charity."

"That's you," Evelyn said.

"Is it?"

"No."

Boyd nodded, and said, "Alas, right you are, so why not rob a bank? Where's Dooney?"

"He's my fucking father, Junior."

"He certainly is all of that . . . Hang on a second."

Boyd reached out, stopped a passing waiter, and ordered four gin and tonics.

"Four?" said the waiter.

"Well, six," said Boyd. "And two big glasses to pour them in. And if possible, make the ETA sometime soon, just so I believe you actually work here."

Evelyn said, "Be polite or I'm leaving."

"As you wish," Boyd said.

For a while they sat in silence, then Evelyn said, "How'd you find me this morning?"

"A friend's assistance. Phone call. Not all that difficult."

"You have a friend, do you?"

"Well, not per se," Boyd said. "I kidnapped her."

"And your friend—?"

"Ting-a-ling. Seems you've hired an indiscreet manservant

or whoever does the heavy lifting with your telephone. My friend—her name's Angie, a bank teller—she's a talker, doesn't quit, tongue hooked to the L.A. power grid, so I wouldn't be too harsh with the reprimands."

Evelyn nodded. She was making a mental note, Boyd knew, to have a word with the help.

"So then," she said. "You're back."

"I am," said Boyd. "With what we might call a vengeance."

"To spin more tall tales?"

He chuckled at that.

"In all fairness," he said, "my tales were pretty stubby. Compared to Dooney's, I'm saying." He paused. "Help me out here. Where is he?"

"We've been through that. I don't—"

"I think you do."

Boyd pulled the snapshot of Teddy from his wallet and slid it across the table toward her. Her expression didn't change.

"Just give me a hint," Boyd said. "Houston? Jakarta?"

"I told you, Junior, I don't have the foggiest. Call information."

"I've tried that."

"Well then," she said, "you're out of luck, aren't you?"

It was admirable, Boyd thought, how Evelyn did not so much as glance at the snapshot nor move it out of harm's way when the waiter arrived with six gin and tonics. The man had forgotten the lime slices and big glasses.

"Cheers," Boyd said. "So Dooney resigned?"

Evelyn nodded impatiently. "Retired actually. Junius runs the show now. Dooney and Calvin—it's love, I guess—they're a couple of globetrotters, just hop from house to house. Last I heard, Dooney owns nine of them." She watched Boyd finish a drink and reach for the next. "We all had to start over, didn't we? Dooney, too."

"Almost all of us," said Boyd.

"What do you want me to say? It was your own fault."

"Pretty much, I'll admit. Not entirely. There was some blackmail if you'll remember."

"All he did was hand you the rope, Junior. You opened the trapdoor. Blame Dooney all you want, but let's not rewrite history."

"Sure," he said, and smiled. "So then. Is it nice being rich?"

Evelyn made an abrupt tossing motion with her head. This gesture, Boyd recalled, meant I'm not in the mood. It also meant don't think I won't bite. She stiffened her jaw, still avoiding the little boy between them. The tendons along her neck stood out like jail bars.

"Rich is fine," she said. "I've always been rich. And nobody's lying to me."

"Just curious."

"Tough luck. You forfeited curiosity rights."

"Perhaps I did. But listen, I'm a little nervous, all I want is Dooney's—"

Her cell phone buzzed and Evelyn lasered him with a shut-your-mouth scowl. She snagged the phone from her purse, stood up, and moved out of earshot a few feet down the sidewalk.

Again, Boyd couldn't help marveling at how little had changed.

A tuck here, a tuck there, but the basics were squarely in place. She'd always had a stern, almost eerie command of her emotions, as if a thermostat had been built into her brain stem. He'd never figured it out. Even during their early years in Jakarta, Evelyn had struck him as a woman living inside a giant Ziploc baggie. Nothing much got in; nothing much got out.

After a bit, she disconnected and stepped back to the table. She took a punitive amount of time sitting down.

"Five more minutes," she said. "I'm putting a timer on it."

"The chauffeur's on the way?"

"Correct."

"Starched uniform, I'm guessing. Gray cap with one of those shiny black visors? Calls you ma'am a lot?"

"Five minutes."

Boyd motioned at the snapshot. "That's your son on the table."

"It is. Do you want me to cry?"

"If you'd like."

"I won't."

"All right then," Boyd said. "Give me a hint on Dooney. We'll see if *he* cries. I'll bet I can make him cry."

Evelyn put on her sunglasses again and this time did not take them off. She turned slightly in her chair.

"All this does," she said quietly, "is make me tired."

"He's a monster," said Boyd.

"Yes, obviously. Who isn't?"

Boyd waited a moment, then reached out and retrieved the snapshot.

"Boy, aren't you the strong one, Evelyn."

"I sure am."

"Cute kid, though."

They looked at each other. It occurred to Boyd that life in the baggie made things endurable for her.

He finished off the second gin and tonic, dented the third,

and said, "So here's the situation. Tell me where Dooney is, we'll kiss goodbye, you won't have to put up with me ever again."

"Ever?" she asked.

"Never ever-ever. Might seem like a long time, I guess, but not after you rob a bank."

For an instant, something like repugnance passed through her eyes. "If you think I believe that shit," she said, "you forget who you're talking to. Funny I haven't read about it in the papers, seen it on TV."

"You're skeptical?"

"Not skeptical. Sad, I guess. You really can't stop lying, can you? It's a disease, Junior."

"The name isn't Junior," he told her. "Plain old Boyd."

"Is that so? Boyd what? Boyd Halverson or Boyd Birdsong or Boyd something brand-new? Part of the new disguise?"

Boyd shrugged and said, "Turning a new leaf."

A silver Bentley pulled to the curb forty feet from their table. Evelyn rose and gathered up her purse and cell phone.

"Just so you know," she said, "I gave Dooney a heads-up after you left that garbled message yesterday. I doubt he'll be eager to sit down for one of your in-depth interviews. Leave him alone."

"So, in fact, you *do* know where to find him?"

"I know his mobile number. He travels."

"Right, the globetrotter, you said."

"Not the whole globe, maybe, but he certainly trots. Dooney and Calvin, they're a couple of harmless old men, no fangs, no pitchfork tails. You'll be disappointed, I'm afraid."

"We'll see," Boyd said. "I still think I can make him cry."

Evelyn took a step toward the parked car, then turned back toward him. For a breathtaking instant, Boyd wondered if she might sprint into his arms.

"Goodbye," she said.

"Yeah, bye," said Boyd. "May I ask one last question?"

"Please don't."

"Did you rat me out?"

"Rat you out?"

"Betray confidences."

"Junior, I hope you're kidding."

"I'm not," he said.

Evelyn laughed a false laugh. "You're asking did I tell anyone you lied to me for three and a half years? Automatic lying. Compulsive lying. That kind?"

"Right," Boyd said.

"Lying to the *Trib*? Lying to five million readers every time they opened a newspaper? Exeter, for God's sake? Princeton? Rosemary Clooney—your *godmother*? You lied to me about your name. You lied about your birthday. You lied about your shaving habits and bowel movements . . . I'm not *finished* here . . . You lied about expense accounts. You lied about smoking, all those push-ups you couldn't do. You lied about your mother . . . she called the money shots at one of the big studios, wasn't it? Fox? Paramount? And dear old dad the fighter pilot, dead from a heart attack—isn't that what you told me? Except one day he shows up at the door, wants to say hello, not so completely dead after all. Amnesia victim. Poor man forgot he got cremated, forgot he flew fighter jets. You lied about dental work. You lied about oysters. You lied about teaching trapeze, the Boston Marathon, that dinner with Alfred Hitchcock. You lied about your pile of war medals—buck fifty for the whole lot. You lied about that so-called bullet wound on your arm. You lied about polo and your poor drowned sister and your pension plan and those hotels you never stayed in and the brain tumor you didn't have and all those bills you stuffed in a back drawer and never paid . . . Did I betray *those* confidences?"

"Right again," said Boyd.

Evelyn started to laugh, but then said, "Wow," and strode briskly toward the waiting Bentley.

11

A HALF MILE AWAY, JUNIUS'S CFO SAID, "I'VE found a guy for the job, sir. Very well qualified, I think."

"Does he get nasty?"

"That he does."

"Am I looking at him?"

"You are."

"Excellent," said Junius.

"Anything else?" asked the CFO.

"Yeah, maybe, let me think."

Junius swiveled in his Wegner swivel chair, a chair that had set him back thirteen thousand and change—ludicrous, he thought every time he swiveled. The price tag made him wonder if he should get out of ships and get into the chair business.

Behind him, CFO Henry Speck waited with a counterfeit, somewhat greasy forbearance.

"When I say get nasty," Junius explained slowly, "I'm not talking metaphors. I see this Halverson slimeball again, I want to see a hospital bed."

"Goes without saying."

"Fine, but I said it."

Junius stared out toward Catalina, a view that had also cost him a bundle, then he swiveled again and inspected his youthful, rugged-looking CFO. "Henry, you realize you're not an actual CFO, right? That's just our private little nickname for being my chief fuck off, getting paid for doing almost nothing. You understand that, I hope?"

"Sir, I wouldn't say almost nothing. Anything you ask, I'm on top of it."

"Okay," Junius said. "But not finance, correct?"

"Not strictly speaking."

"Well, strictly speaking, Henry, I don't pay you for brains. You're my muscle, *comprendes*? I pay you for those impressive pecs you keep flexing. I mean, you work out a good bit, am I right?"

"Not every day, but—"

"Every other day, minimum," said Junius. "You're in tip-top shape; I noticed that in my pool last night. So did Evelyn."

"I like to think I'm fit, sir."

"I can tell you like to think so."

"Sir?"

Junius swiveled back toward Catalina.

"Here's another question, Henry. Right now, how many vessels do we have under construction down in Long Beach? Two, is it?"

"Three, I believe. Four on order."

"And Jakarta?"

"Five, sir. Fifteen to eighty-five mil apiece, depending. Our ship business, if you'll excuse the pun, is pretty shipshape. Better than exceptional."

"Yeah, good," Junius grunted, looking down pensively at his fingernails. "So, in other words, we've got lots of happy employees in the yards? Ironworkers, carpenters, riggers?"

"I'd definitely agree, sir."

"Okay then. Write this down. Just in case you're not quite as athletically shipshape as you think, I want you to pick out one or two helpers. Beefy types. The hospital bed, I'm talking about."

"If you say so. Is that all?"

"Sure, almost." Junius fell silent for a moment. "You know what drives me nuts, Henry?"

"No, sir."

"Prices these days. Ironworkers, carpenters, Cheerios, wives, a pack of Winstons. Can't find cheap air anymore—buck a tire at the Texaco over on Alameda." Junius half swiveled. "Like, for example, how much do I pay you?"

"Salary, you mean?"

"Yeah, salary."

"Enough. I could check my stubs, Junius. Let you know."

"Forget it." Junius made a sorrowful sucking sound. "Just hurt the guy, but do it on the cheap. The whole shebang, it ought to take three, four days. Track him down, deliver the message. Real simple. No frills."

"Yes, sir. Is that all?"

"Not quite," said Junius. "That party I threw last night, you know what that cost me? Take a guess."

"A ton," said the CFO.

"Some lousy finger food, four hundred Franklins, nobody touches it, everybody's on a carrot diet."

"Good party, though."

Junius shrugged. "You have fun?"

"I did, thank you."

"You know what else, Henry?"

"What?"

"Keep your claws off my wife's ass."

"Well, sir, I didn't—"

Junius swiveled away and said, "Hell, you didn't. And you

know what I wish? I wish I was back in the candy business. Way back when, that's how I got my start. Not ships. Candy. Boil your sugar, boil your corn syrup, stir in some flavor at twelve cents a gallon. Turn product into cash. Cut-and-dried, right? Nobody guzzling your champagne. No bodybuilders flexing in the pool with your wife."

The CFO said nothing.

"After you hurt this moron," said Junius, "maybe you better show me some pay stubs."

12

IN THE NINETEENTH YEAR OF THE TWENTY-FIRST century, mythomania careened down interstate highways, into truck stops, across bridges and viaducts and ideologies, hurtling off exit ramps, breeding in motels and restaurants and RV parks from Rhode Island to Alaska, borne on idle chatter, validated by repetition, revved up on cable news, hot-wired to America by the shortwaves of citizens band radio.

By mid-September of 2019, the Truth Teller Seed in Fulda, California, had become the fourth most prolific in America, fourth only to those in Monteagle, Tennessee; Storm Lake, Iowa; and Creedmoor, Texas. In all, seventy-six Seeds in forty-nine states reigned as the wellsprings of fake unfake news. The Fulda chapter had rocketed up this list on the heels of Dink O'Neill's series of tweets celebrating the news that Timothy McVeigh had survived execution and was alive and well in Omaha, where he worked under an alias for a distributor of guaranteed inorganic fruits and vegetables. McVeigh's "comeback," as Dink called it, had positioned him for secretary of agriculture under POTUS's upcoming second term. Ridiculous, except for a hundred and forty thousand enthusiastic retweeters.

Mythomania—or plain old lying—infiltrated churches, schools, hair salons, corporate boardrooms, courtrooms, and nightclubs. Smith & Wesson received seven hundred write-in votes in Topeka's mayoral race. The Library of Congress was under pressure to ban its copy of the Gutenberg Bible for flaunting the word *fornicate* and the first two syllables of the word *sodomy*. Speechwriters jumped aboard. Nannies and city councilmen in Prescott, Arizona, denounced the devil's codex implanted in the due process clause of the U.S. Constitution; NASA was burning down forests in Idaho; the Census Bureau was refusing to count people with blue eyes; Grover Cleveland's skull was buried under the Watergate complex; vigilantes roamed the nighttime streets of Fargo in search of Democrats and Kenyans; Columbine was a CIA operation; Pearl Harbor never happened; corporations were people; Amazon was a distinguished citizen. In Fulda, where the Truth Tellers were led by Dink O'Neill, his brother Chub, and Chamber of Commerce President Earl Fenstermacher, the burdens of seeding fake unfake news kept them hopping through the hot days of September 2019. Boyd Halverson's contributions were sorely missed. "Boyd had a knack for it," Chub told Earl after their bimonthly Kiwanis brunch. "I don't know how we'll replace him."

"I *did* replace him," said Earl, a little miffed. "I'm creative director, right? Who came up with that killer post about presidents who never existed? Yours truly. And it went viral, I believe."

"Boyd's idea. You said so yourself."

"Okay, but I added two more fake presidents, changed twelve to fourteen, plus I tacked on that cool wrinkle about how John Quincy Adams was Napoleon's bastard daughter. Give credit where credit's due."

Chub shrugged. "All right, just do me a favor with those tweets of yours—watch your spelling. It's President P-O-L-K, not P-O-K-E. And I don't think Andrew Johnson was LBJ's love partner."

"Who cares? Andrew never existed, remember?"

"True. But he didn't exist in a different *century*."

"Hairsplitting," Earl muttered. "We're getting quoted on Fox. Lay off!"

13

IT TOOK A DOZEN TRIES, BUT RANDY FINALLY reached his cop buddy up in Fulda, Toby Van Der Kellen, who in the strictest sense wasn't a buddy, more the exact opposite, except they shared hobbies like cars and crime and so on. Carl and Cyrus were leaning way too close to Randy's cell phone, listening in while the Fulda cop kept saying, "What bank heist?"

Randy could hardly pay attention.

Cyrus's breath was medium bad, but Carl's . . . Was there a word for it? Sort of like the fertilizer you use for blowing up courthouses. The Super 8 room wasn't any florist shop either.

"Community National, how many freakin' banks you got up there?" Randy was saying to his cop buddy. "Joint got hit for eighty thou plus. Couple weeks ago, I figure."

"A stickup, you're telling me?"

"Bet your handcuffs a stickup. What kinda cop are you, don't even know your own banks are getting robbed?"

There was some silence on the line, too much, too long.

"You there?" said Randy.

"He hung up," said Cyrus.

"He hung up," Carl said. "And I'm thinking there ain't no eighty-one thousand up for grabs."

Randy stood staring at his cell phone, thinking maybe it malfunctioned, maybe it was scrambling the words coming out of it.

"Zipper, you dealin' in fiction?" said Cyrus.

"Maybe crime fiction?" said Carl, and playfully slapped Randy's ear.

Randy kept punching buttons until his pal in Fulda picked up again a half hour later. Things went back and forth for a while, names getting batted around, Angie Bing, Boyd Halverson, but finally the Fulda cop said, "Don't know how many times I have to say this—maybe as many times as I arrested you—but there hasn't been any bank stickup. I checked just now. Horse's mouth."

"Which horse?" Randy asked.

"Doug Cutterby. Bank president. Heard the name?"

"Yeah, I think so. From Angie."

"Want to know what Doug says?"

"Sure I do."

"Nothing."

"Sorry?"

"Nothing. Laughs at me. *Then* he says something."

"What's he say?"

"Doug says—I think I've got this exact—he says, 'What's the jail time for false police reports?' I tell him I'll look into it. He says, 'Good idea.'"

Randy thought as fast as he could think, but fast thinking wasn't all that fast when you had Carl's breath rolling over you like a death cloud.

"He's lying," Randy told Toby.

"Who's lying?" said Toby.

"The bank dude, what's his name—?"

"Doug's lying?"

"Sure."

Toby the cop buddy went quiet for a second. "You're telling

me a man's bank gets hit for eighty-one grand and he says, 'No way, we're hunky fuckin' dory'?"

"Well, yeah."

There was a sound coming from Fulda that was hard to identify.

"Here's what I wish," the cop said. "I wish you'd smarten up. Replace your brains with cookie dough. Then you'd be smarter."

Randy had a comeback for that, one he'd practiced quite a bit, except there wasn't anybody on the line to come back to.

Cyrus said, "Lunchtime, Zipper. Your treat."

On the walk over to Applebee's, Randy decided it was time to deep-six these two amateurs, get over to that address in Santa Monica and throw a Q-&-A party for Angie Bing, starting with how the heck you rob a bank and nobody knows you robbed a bank.

Randy was grinning as he slid into the booth at Applebee's.

Say what you want, he thought, but the perfect crime had to be the crime that never happened.

"What you having, Zipper?" Cyrus said.

Randy gave the dude a nice level stare and said, "Blackened chicken, that sound good?"

Lois was at table three, Douglas sat across the pit at table sixteen, and at the moment Lois stared in disbelief at still another fifteen. Nine and six this time—probably her trillionth fifteen since she'd sat down yesterday morning. The dealer showed the usual ten. Okay, she was supposed to take a card—that was basic strategy—except she hadn't filled a fifteen in her lifetime, not with two thousand riding, so she waved it off and watched the dealer turn over his own fifteen, then hammer it with the six of clubs.

"So sorry," the dealer murmured.

"Yeah, yeah," said Lois.

She glanced across the pit at Douglas, who wasn't doing much better. It was getting on toward noon, a solid twenty-four hours with only pee breaks, and she figured it wouldn't hurt to stretch her legs, probably pee again, then force down that comped lunch that so far had cost her thirty-two thousand and change. Maybe closer to thirty-three.

She tucked away two chocolate chips, wiggled off her stool with a little vacuum-sealed pop, and circled the pit to where Douglas was busy busting on his own fifteen.

"That takes skill, Dougie," she said bitterly. "Let's get lunch."

"One last hand," Douglas said.

Amiably, like the bank president he was, Douglas grinned at the dealer and made a joke about how he'd arrived at the Bellagio in a ninety-two-thousand-dollar Mercedes and would be leaving in a half-million-dollar Greyhound.

The dealer, a pretty Asian woman, chuckled politely. She peeled off a six and a ten for Douglas, a red queen for herself.

"Jesus," Lois said to the dealer. "How the fuck you do that?"

The dealer made a sound that meant nothing.

"Okay, here goes," said Douglas.

He slapped the table and drew a four. Miraculously, the pretty dealer turned her ten into a twenty-six.

"Lunch!" Douglas crowed.

Lunch, they decided, would be olives, and they convened over double-shot Bloody Marys just off the gaming floor. Lois was down the thirty-three, Douglas was down twenty-six, and already they were itching to get back to blackjack business.

"Up our bet to five hundred a hand, we'll be back to even-steven in no time," Douglas said. "Make good the losses and tack on a tidy profit."

"And if we lose," Lois said, "we still own a bank."

"Exactly. No problem a cooked book can't solve." He beamed at her. "And, of course, I married the master chef."

"That you damn well did," said Lois.

For a few moments Douglas chewed dutifully on an olive.

"One tiny item I should mention," he said. "An hour ago, hour and a half, I had a call from Fulda. Toby Van Der Kellen."

"Who?"

"Toby the cop."

"You mean . . . ?"

"That's the one. Hubcap Toby."

Lois searched Douglas's face for a giveaway. Off and on for four months she'd been testing mattresses with Hubcap Toby.

"What's he want?" she asked carefully.

Douglas explained.

When he'd finished, Lois relaxed and said, "No problem then."

"Exactly what I'm hoping," said Douglas. "Far as Toby's concerned, no harm, no foul."

"And no bank robbery," said Lois.

"Well said, no bank robbery," said Douglas. "Still, I'll urge caution. Toby seemed maybe a little too interested. Also, let's bear in mind that this particular law enforcement officer happens to be banging my wife."

"Banging?"

"Banging."

"I didn't think you knew," said Lois.

"Well, I didn't. Wild guess."

Lois worked on her Bloody Mary with a straw.

"Good guess," she finally muttered.

"Thank you, pet."

"How about you do that at the tables? Guess which card's on the way."

Douglas laughed heartily. "I'll do my banker's best. Right now, though, let's see if you can stay away from Toby for a few weeks. You know, until we retrieve our money, get the ledgers squared away."

"I can manage that," Lois said.

"Excellent," said Douglas. "Back to the tables?"

"Back to the tables."

Calvin wasn't doing cartwheels over Bemidji, Minnesota. He didn't care one bit for the blackflies, or for the three-mile drive down to the nearest mini-mart for a quart of milk and some frozen potpies, or for how the house smelled like a minnow tank, or for the dense, humid fog that rolled in every evening just after dusk, or for how the sheets on his bed felt damp and creepy even after giving them a good going-over with his hair dryer. Calvin didn't care for the mosquitoes either. Already he'd lost enough blood to keep the Red Cross in business.

Door to door, it had been a thirteen-hour trip from Port Aransas. Departure at dawn, hardly time to pack, then ten miserable hours of regional jets and layovers and delays.

All that, Calvin thought, to end up here.

He was not in the least dazzled by the big blue lake out the window. Nor by the dock or the boathouse or the bowling alley in the mansion's east wing or the thick stands of conifers and birches along the shoreline. The eleven-bedroom vacation castle, which Dooney had conned off a now-deceased client, was tightly built and well screened, but each night a forest full of mosquitoes put on their bibs and sat down for a Calvin banquet.

"Your fault, not mine," he was whining to Jim Dooney, "and it's not asking the world to get my back scratched."

"Scratching only makes it worse," said Dooney.

"That's in the long run," Calvin said, digging at his rib cage. "It itches in the short run."

"Okay, hold your horses."

"I *can't* hold my horses. Scratch. Don't be a tease."

Dooney slipped a pair of potpies into the oven, put a salad on the table, and used Calvin's swim trunks to wipe his hands. "No scratching—that's verboten—but we can rub on some calamine." He wagged his head. "Such a baby, Cal. A few dinky mosquito bites."

"Few? I'm a *polka* dot."

"Stay put."

Dooney found the lotion, had Cal lean over the table, and greased him up.

"Scratch!" Calvin said.

"Can't do that. Start scratching, I'll be at it all night."

"One quick scratch."

"No can do."

"Jimmy!"

Calvin fidgeted through dinner, complaining about flies, mosquitoes, and getting chased into the wilderness by a department store manager with a pistol and a vendetta. "I thought we were a team," Calvin said. "You and me. I thought we'd told all our secrets."

"I overlooked this one," Dooney said.

"You overlooked a guy wants to kill you?"

"Not kill. He's too subtle for that. Something else."

"Whatever, you should've told me. I'm hurt."

"And I'm sorry, Cal. I apologize."

"This potpie is awful."

"Agreed. Should we go out for a pizza?"

Cal stood and went to the kitchen wall and scraped his back against it.

"Can the guy find us here?"

Dooney shrugged. "I doubt it. Come on now, let's go round up a pizza. I'll scratch your back afterward, show how sorry I am."

"Do you have other secrets?"

"One or two," said Dooney.

"Give me a hint," Cal said feebly, almost mewling. "Why are we . . . I mean, it's a nice place and everything, mansion made out of logs, very unusual, but why are we here? What happened exactly?"

For a few moments, Dooney seemed to be considering options: what to say, what not to say. "It's complicated, Cal— economics, grades of steel, naval architecture. Can you handle all that?"

"Simplify it. I'm a hair therapist."

"You're *my* hair therapist," Dooney said. "And my partner for life. Pull that shirt off, I'll scratch your back." Dooney took a breath, regathered his thoughts. "Okay, start with this. I'm chairman emeritus of PS&S, ex-CEO, you understand all that, right?"

"Pretty much. Scratch lower."

"And what does PS&S stand for? It stands for Pacific Ships and Shipping. So that's our core business."

"Boats?" Calvin said.

"Ships, not boats. There's a difference. Big ships. Oceangoers. Monsters. Hundreds of tons, mostly cargo ships, and we—"

"Harder! I'm going crazy here."

"Cal, for Chrissake, stand still. I'm trying to simplify. Ships. We own them, we sail them, we transport stuff. That's half the core business. But we also manufacture them. Ships, I mean. Great, big, expensive mothers, we design them, build them from scratch, mostly over in Jakarta—tax reasons, labor costs, a lot less red tape, nobody looking over your shoulder every three seconds. And so . . ."

"That's good, Jimmy, but try boiling it down for me. All I want . . . Scratch harder! . . . All I want is to know why we're here."

Dooney sighed and said, "I'll boil it down to three sentences. Those ships we manufactured? Two of them sank. Seven months apart, different oceans."

"Your ships sank?"

"Two of them. Another one capsized, didn't sink. Well, I take that back, eventually it did sink, sort of bobbed in the North Pacific for about a month. Then it sank."

Calvin turned, looked at Dooney, and put his shirt on.

"That's why we're mosquito food? Your ships sank?"

"Partly why. Mostly why. Bad steel. Cheap steel—wrong grade. No steel at all in a couple of unfortunate places. Un-welded joints. No inspections. Few innocent bribes here and there. Bunch of sissy sailors who couldn't swim."

"Oh-oh."

"Evelyn tattled. Told Halverson. He was a reporter."

"So you're a criminal?"

"I'm a businessman," said Dooney. "I put a lid on it, played some hardball. Now let's go get that pizza."

In the Super 8, Randy was explaining to Carl and Cyrus his technique for riding a really nasty bronc, or at least a medium-nasty one. "The mount," Randy was saying, "can't just trot around like somebody's poodle, it has to—in case you didn't know, we call them mounts—the mount has to be a mean mother, has to feel like you're aboard a pissed-off attack dog, otherwise the judges start scribbling down bad shit and docking points left and right, even if you're digging in with the spurs, even if you're giving your mount a kidney transplant. Now, on the other hand, you don't want what you'd call a killer bronc, you don't want that either, because sometimes you'll end up—"

Cyrus raised his hand.

"Yeah?" Randy said.

"The hell you talkin' broncs for?"

Randy knew why, and he knew Cyrus knew why, but right now wasn't the time to discuss eighty-one grand that may or may not have been robbed. The subject was sensitive.

"Just saying," Randy said. "You don't want a pansy mount."

"Is that so?" said Cyrus.

"Well, yeah," said Randy. "That's what I was just saying, wasn't it?"

Carl, who lay in his undershorts on the Super 8's king-size bed, sat up and stripped off the undershorts and waddled to the john. Over his shoulder, he said, "Ride me, Zipper. I'm pretty medium mean."

Cyrus laughed.

The shower kicked on.

"What Carl's too polite to say," Cyrus explained, almost cooing, "is he gets the feeling you're changing the subject. Wants to know why you been misleading us, you know? Maybe stringing us along, getting yourself some free bodyguards."

"Who asked for bodyguards?"

"Not in so many words," said Cyrus.

"Not in *any* words," Randy said, knowing instantly he should have stayed away from absolutes. Now he had to follow through or look like his own brand of pansy. "In that diner, remember? The word *money*, you guys jumped all over it."

"Money?" said Cyrus. "You think Carl and me care about eighty-one thousand green?"

Randy thought quickly.

"Nah," he said.

"Nah is right," said Cyrus. "Because there *ain't* any eighty-one thousand. Didn't we establish that today?"

"Sort of. I trust Angie, though. She's . . . she's religious. Angie wouldn't say she robbed a bank if she didn't rob a bank."

Cyrus sighed and hoisted himself out of the room's only easy chair. He was a large and impressive man.

"How much is that Cutlass of yours worth, Zipper?"

"My Cutlass?"

"You know. Cash money. The stuff Carl and me don't care about."

There was singing coming from the john's shower.

"Not worth a whole lot, I guess," Randy said. "Unless you got good taste in cars."

"Well, maybe tomorrow we unload it. Split the take three ways. Seems fair, don't it? Carl and me, we can't rightly accept the whole kit 'n' caboodle, know what I'm saying?" He chuckled. "The three of us, Zipper, we're thick as thieves."

"Jeez, Cyrus," Randy said, "I kinda love that Cutlass."

"Tell you what, I want you to think about it," said Cyrus. "See what you can find in that big heart of yours."

He pulled off his T-shirt, then his briefs, and maneuvered his way into the Super 8's miniature john.

Randy stood still—he'd been standing the whole time.

The Cutlass? he thought.

Swiftly, humming along to a pretty fair shower duet, Randy swept up jeans, T-shirts, underpants, shoes, socks, one wristwatch, and two wallets. A minute later he was in the car, cruising down East Seventh past his favorite diner, heading for a Days Inn he'd scoped out that very morning.

His lips hurt from smiling.

Why, he wondered, does everybody underestimate me except me?

14

AFTER EVELYN'S BENTLEY DEPARTED, BOYD LIN-
gered twenty minutes at the sidewalk café on La Cienega, reviewing things, watching mostly nothing. Five decades on the
planet, all that time, but only two or three seconds mattered.

Sixty seconds to a minute, sixty minutes to the hour, 3,600
seconds in each hour. Multiply by all the hours you've lived.

Amazing, he mused.

Subtract three seconds, you're a different human being.
You're not a bank robber. You're not packing a pistol. You're
not sitting by yourself on La Cienega, your ex-wife halfway to
Bel Air in her swanky vehicle. He couldn't get over it. The time
it takes to suck in a breath and, whoops, you drop your little
boy, splash, and that's that and always will be that.

More than a few minutes elapsed before Boyd sighed and
sat up straight. He tucked the snapshot back in his wallet, finished off the drinks on the table, guiltily beckoned the young
waiter, and ordered a spine stiffener for the road.

He thought: Boyd, your beloved is one true-blue sufferer in
silence. As ex-wives go, Evelyn was far and away the cream of
the crop, an awesome and very classy bearer of life's carnage.
She knew how to tough it out. And, of course, the material trea-
sures of a new marriage remedied some of the hurt, a mansion
jammed with balm for the soul, a silver Bentley to chase away
the late-night shivers.

Sure enough.

A while later he thought: Not to deny, of course, that you've got your own perverse take on the pain.

For indeed you do.

A fresh drink in hand, Boyd sat observing the Beverly Hills crowd hustle by, most of them clad for the kill, not one of them less than eye-catching. He noted any number of serviceable breasts and Superman biceps. Even the children looked hip and stylish. What did these people consume, he wondered, to cut such wholesome figures? Where were the saddlebag thighs and bulging tummies? Where were the goddamn liver spots? Alas, he thought, no one is forty-nine anymore. No one lunches on fried pork bellies and quarts of beer.

Down the hatch.

His spine had stiffened. Now, perhaps, one more for the road. He was alert to a shifting world.

On a park bench opposite La Cienega, within hailing distance, the surly young receptionist from YOU! sat eating what appeared to be a small peach; a bottle of Topo Chico rested at her side. For what reason Boyd wasn't sure, but he briefly considered beckoning the girl to his table. She might appreciate, he thought, a splash of gin at the noon hour; perhaps, too, if he played his cards right, she might share with him the mechanical principles behind that floating-girl trick of hers.

Forlorn was his mood, and forlorn was the fact of the matter, thus why dwell on it? Moreover, the sunlit morning had now gone noticeably threatening at its western fringe.

Weather, he thought, was on the way.

Après moi, indeed—a fantasist's deluge!—and he imagined that soon all of Los Angeles would be lying through its teeth— the receptionist, she'd be counting ballots on her fingers and children would be reading *Cinderella* in civics classes and Hollywooders would be footnoting tweets with citations from *I Love Lucy*—it was in the clouds, it was in the cards, a communicable disease rolling across America like Noah's killer flood. When you dwell in the rabbit hole, as Boyd did, the rabbit hole is home sweet home, ergo: Off with their heads! Climatologists? Chemists? Off with their tongues! Who needs reality when you have *Venom*? Who needs history when you can manufacture your own? Evelyn's catalog of his lies had been impressive, to be sure, but far from exhaustive. Little did she know. Boyd was a man of his times—a trailblazer; he was the hanging judge at Salem and the bug in Joe McCarthy's ear and the author of magnificent whoppers still rattling around on Facebook— *Hiroshima was a clever hoax; the Holocaust was science fiction; Jackie Robinson was a white man in blackface; reptiles manned the IRS phone banks . . .*

Upsy-daisy, and Boyd pushed to his feet, reached back, and tapped a dead son through his wallet.

Cautiously then, he found his sea legs and began working his way across the street. The tides soon cast him within two feet of the young receptionist, who stared vacantly ahead, savoring the last of her peach, not a flicker of cognition in her starlit eyes. Maybe this explained, Boyd reasoned, why the cops had not yet tossed him behind bars. Like arresting a ghost.

He swayed in a gust of wind, resecured balance, and made his way to a bus stop. Do not, he thought, shoot this bus.

The stop-and-start ride to Santa Monica amounted to a replay of Evelyn's inventory of sins. The oysters bothered him. He hadn't lied about the oysters. Six dozen of them. With a guy who mowed Hitchcock's lawn.

He disembarked three blocks from his mother's house.

Oh, my, he thought. Why would the sky be dumping gin on the sidewalks?

There were no police cars along the street, no SWAT teams, which Boyd took as a gift.

Inside, Angie sat in the living room painting her toenails. She glowered at him, but Boyd said nothing and hurried to the kitchen. He filled a coffeepot with water, leaned over the sink, and dumped the pot's contents over his head. Better, he concluded, but not much. A few minutes later, after preparing an actual pot of coffee, he filled two cups and carried them out to the living room.

As he'd guessed, Angie was displeased with him.

"What gets me," she said petulantly, "is you swore to God Himself, to your Creator and Knower of All Things. No more booze, you said, or you hoped to roast in hell."

"I got thirsty," Boyd said.

"As if *that* pulls you off the hook."

"Angie, go to the window—God's raining gin on us. I'm exhausted; I need a nap. Should I go find a gag?"

"You promised your Savior on High, my friend. Not to mention me."

"Okay, I misspoke," he said. "I'm sorry."

She made a face. "Boyd, there wouldn't be anybody in hell if God took sorry for an answer. What good is sorry? This coffee's way too strong."

"I need strong."

"And what about me? Cooling my wheels here, wondering if you'll even—"

"I'm getting a gag," said Boyd.

"Good luck. You can't gag Jehovah."

Briefly, Boyd slept a deep sleep on his feet, then snapped awake and went to the kitchen and returned with a yellow sponge and a roll of tape.

Angie looked up at him.

"Did you disinfect that thing?"

"No. If you shut up, I'll explain."

She eyed the sponge for a few seconds. "Okay, I'll listen, but it better make sense."

At first Boyd was tongue-tied, not sure where to start, but more swiftly than he would've imagined, he summarized the last decade of his life, skipping the embarrassing details.

When he'd finished, Angie said, "So you're a compulsive liar. About everything."

"Yes."

"And your name's not Halverson? It's Birdsong?"

"Correct. Halverson was my mother's name. Maiden name. She didn't care for Birdsong. Changed it back when my dad died. So did I."

"I see. And what's wrong with Birdsong?"

"Everything," said Boyd. "What's right with it?"

"Well, it's lyrical."

"And ridiculous. I wanted a name you can't laugh at. Birdsong, chirp-chirp . . . All the shit I took as a kid."

Angie replaced the cap on her bottle of nail polish and gazed at the floor for a long, awkward time. Twice she began to speak; twice she stopped.

"All right," she finally said. "You're an addictive, nonstop, godless liar. Big things, little things. Lie, lie, lie. Your whole life. Then this Dooney guy finds out—he's the ex-wife's father, right?—and he uses the lies to bust up your marital paradise.

Scandal. Ruined life. Uxorial issues. You end up in Fulda selling brassieres. Does that cover it?"

"Uxorial?" said Boyd.

"Look it up."

"I know what it means; I'm surprised you do."

"Why? I'm ignorant?" She stared at him until he looked away. "Anyway, uxorial issues. And so later, lo and behold, your ex ends up with Julius What's His Face, who used to be Dooney's gofer, except now he's a stinking rich CEO. Is that it in a nutshell?"

"Junius, not Julius."

"Yeah, Junius," said Angie. "The point is, this Dooney nuked you. Turned Birdsong into dust."

"Right," Boyd admitted. "I glow in the dark."

"And now you're the pistol-packing wrath of God."

Boyd looked into his coffee cup, calculating what he could and could not get away with.

"Good synopsis," he said. "Should we have a drink?"

"I told you before, I'm not trailer trash." Angie waited a second and then wiggled into a pair of sandals. "I've got some thinking to do."

She went to the front door.

"I'm going for a walk, Boyd—probably a long one. Put the sponge away. Get on your knees and pray to Saint Despicable that I come back."

"Okay," he said.

For an hour or so, the coffee kept Boyd awake, but eventually he dozed off on his mother's lumpy, gaudily upholstered sofa. When he awakened, it was with the sudden, startled recognition of how pitiable he had become, how desolate, and how even in the act of confession he had been unable to utter the whole and exact truth. For him, it seemed, lying was not only automatic, it was biological. He lied the way other people have orgasms.

Angie wasn't back yet.

He washed and dried the coffeepot, pulled Winston Churchill from his suitcase, sat in his father's easy chair, read half a sentence, then got up and went outside and sat on the front steps. A hot day had become a hotter night. There was the smell of gin in the air.

A while later Angie came briskly up the sidewalk.

She plopped down on the steps beside him. It took her thirty seconds to let out an exasperated sigh.

"Aren't you going to ask what I'm thinking?"

"What?" Boyd said.

"A few things," said Angie. She squinted into the silky, polluted night. "No particular order, but start with this. Anybody messes with a marriage, that's a sin in God's book, so I see why you've got a score to settle. Revenge, it's as old as the Bible, except even in the Bible it never ends very well unless it's God getting the revenge. I'm on your side, Boyd, but you need to start showing some common sense."

"Such as?"

"Well, for example," she said. "Haven't you noticed how *easy* everything has been? Somebody robs a bank, you'd expect trouble, but not a cop in sight. And like when you used your ex's passport to get me into Mexico. I'm a redhead, she's a bottle brunette, and I'm ten years younger, minimum, but even so, we sail through customs. And another thing. How hard would it be to find you here—your own mother's house? Six seconds on the internet. You'd expect trouble."

"It'll come," he said.

She shook her head. "I'm not so sure. That's partly what I've been thinking about. Remember when I told you about my boss, how she can barely do long division?"

"No," Boyd said.

"You should start *listening* to me."

"Angie, that's all I've done for—"

"You're *still* not listening. My boss, her name's Lois, she's Community National's second top dog, she basically runs things. Five or six times—more than that—I've gone to her with my till printouts and showed her how nothing's adding up right, deposits versus withdrawals. All Lois does, she says she'll check it out, gives me this smile like I'm the stupidest hayseed who ever opened a cash register, like I can't even change a fifty."

"And?"

"And what? You see where this is going, right?"

"Sort of. Not really."

"Well, a bunch of stuff," Angie said. "Like that set of books she keeps in her personal safe-deposit box. Or how I'll go to the vault sometimes, and there's this hole where the hundreds used to be. I'll ask Lois what's up and she creams me with that poor-dumb-you smile of hers, says she's on top of it, tells me not to worry my hollow head. And like with all the Mexicans up in Fulda, must be four, five hundred of them, a good half are illegal, probably more. But only one bank in town, Community National. You following this? So all these Mexicans, they wire money home to grandma in Tijuana, right? Except Lois tacks on a seven percent transaction fee, then tacks on a four percent currency exchange fee, then forgets to even send the wire transfer. You're illegal, you're Mexican, what can you do?"

"You're saying she's crooked?"

"No," said Angie. "I'm saying the whole *bank's* crooked. Okay, I'm a lowly teller, but even so . . . What about the big money I never even see? Mortgage payments, car loans, foreclosures, private investing? Maybe Lois doesn't want the feds looking too hard at all that."

Boyd thought about it, more carefully now.

"Far-fetched," he finally said.

"Maybe. But if you're robbing your own bank, you don't start yelling, 'Hey, we've been robbed!'"

"What about cameras?"

"Push a button," she said. "No more camera clips."

They sat in silence for a good while, watching a neighbor walk her dog, then Boyd laughed.

"What's funny?" Angie said.

"Nothing. Except when I rob a bank, it's not even a robbery. Not all that funny, I guess."

"It isn't," she said. "Sooner or later, somebody'll be coming after that cash in your suitcase. Not the law, maybe, but Lois likes her diamonds and blackjack. Douglas is even worse."

"Douglas?"

"Your Kiwanis buddy. Her Beelzebub hubby. All angel till the fangs come out."

"I need a drink, Angie."

"No, you don't. You need somebody with a brain in her head."

Upstairs, as they got ready for bed, Angie said, "Here's what I think—I think it's time you made love to me. You've come clean about what a lying swine you are, that's a start. We've got some basic trust established. The kind you need to actually be fruitful and multiply and maybe give me a shiver or two."

"No, thanks," Boyd said.

He spread a blanket on the floor, snapped off the lights, and lay down.

For a time, Angie sat on the edge of his mother's bed, peering at him, then she took a breath, and said, "I'll tell you a secret, maybe then you'll trust me. Remember how back in high school I was a gymnast?"

"Yes, vaguely," said Boyd, though he didn't.

"Right, and I was good at it. My senior year, we're up at the state finals in Redding and I'm like in, you know, second place in the overall standings. There's one last event still to go, but it's the horse, my weak spot, and the girl in first place, she's Miss All-American Horse, it's her specialty. So, I'm in deep doo-doo. I get through my routine okay, nothing spectacular, but then all I can do is sit there and watch the competition, and naturally Miss Horse is out-of-her-mind perfect. Mount, dismount, everything in between, not a single mistake. So there goes my trophy. Out the window. But do I cry? No way. I trot over and do the kissy-kissy Russian thing."

"Well," Boyd said. "I don't quite see—"

"I'm not done yet."

"Oh."

"So afterward, everybody's in the locker room. I spot the trophy over on this bench. I mean, the thing's just sitting there all by its lonesome, and I think, Well, go on, girl. Take it. So I do. I dump the trophy in my gym bag and zip it shut and walk out to the bus. And that's that."

"Okay," Boyd said. "Now I trust you."

Angie wagged her head irritably. "Boyd, for crying out loud, can't you ever just listen?"

"You returned it?"

"Boyd, let somebody *else* talk."

In the dark he could feel her glaring at him. She stood, went to a window, opened it, and leaned out.

"If you want," she said, "I can scream rape."

"Okay. What happened next?"

She climbed back into bed.

"So two years go by. I'm in college up in Chico, business administration, and I've still got that trophy in my room. Except now I'm starting to feel guilty. Like I've matured, you know? I've grown up. Not physically, I guess, but I've got a conscience now, I've got ethics, and so I think to myself, Angie, if you ever run across Miss Horse—even if it takes a billion years—you're gonna give back that stupid trophy. And guess what?"

She sat in the dark until Boyd said, "I don't know, but I'll bet—"

"Hey, come on, do I interrupt *you*?"

"I thought you asked—"

"Please, please, shut up. So maybe a month later, maybe three weeks, I'm interviewing with banks for my first job, and I drive up to Fulda for an interview. I walk into Community National. And guess who's standing there at the teller cage?"

Boyd said nothing.

"Go on," Angie said. "Guess."

"Nope," Boyd said.

"Come on, guess."

"Okay. Miss Horse."

Angie stared at him. "You *are* naïve, aren't you? That's way too coincidental. Guess again."

"Angie, I haven't got a clue."

"*You* were."

"I was what?"

"You were standing there. In the bank. Cashing a check."

"What's that got to do with gymnastics?"

"Not a thing. It's how I first saw you."

Boyd nodded. It occurred to him, not for the first time, that Angie Bing approached the world in a roundabout way.

"All right," he said. "Finish the story."

"That *is* the finish. I just told you a huge secret."

"Which secret?"

"How I first saw you, Boyd. How I remember exactly where it was when we first met, the whole deal."

"What about the trophy?"

Angie shrugged. "It's mine now. But I hope you at least believe in me a little."

Boyd waited for what he hoped was an appropriate length of time.

"Angie," he said, almost gently. "I can't be fruitful tonight."

"Your loss," she said.

15

TOBY VAN DER KELLEN ROUSTED MEXICANS FOR sport first, profit second, but he didn't mind pocketing ten bucks here, twenty bucks there, especially if Pedro wanted to slip cash through the vent window after a traffic stop. For Toby, they were all Pedros, even the women. And what was ten bucks, twenty bucks, if you're illegal in the first place, if you can't fix a taillight, and if your name doesn't show up on the *Mayflower*'s manifest? It was like duck hunting, Toby figured. The ducks didn't stop at passport control, just flew right on over, so when you've got a duck hunting license, which Toby definitely had because he was a cop, what's the problem with a bunch of feathers on the road? A duck is a duck.

Pluck 'em, he thought.

Then he said it aloud, "Pluck 'em." Flat and firm, which was how he'd tweet it tonight. Pluck 'em: like a headline or something.

At the moment, cruising past the JCPenney store on South Spruce Street, Toby had spotted a pickup with four Pedros in the bed, no seat belts. He hit his brake for a second, but then figured he was feeling international right now, pretty Pan-American, not to mention he had banking to do.

He parked in front of the Kiwanis–Ace Hardware building, ignored the meter, and crossed South Spruce on foot, checking for tire pressure violations as he made his way toward Community National.

A tough job, he thought, being the only full-time cop in a town pushing up on 3,400 potential criminals, a good fifth of them Pedros. There was Elmo, sure, but Elmo was part-time, filling in now and then, and there was Wanda Jane, who sat manicuring her nipples at the dispatch desk. Not that he didn't totally respect Wanda Jane. Respected her nipples, too, mounted like they were on a pair of, what, thirty-nine, forty inchers.

On the sidewalk, one door down from Community National, Toby stopped and lit up a Kool and waited for Lois to make her morning donut run. The thing about Community National—the thing about almost anyplace else in this ex-free country—was you couldn't enjoy a Kool anymore; you had to go outside and stand in a snowdrift and catch pneumonia. Democrats were the problem. Without Democrats, Toby mused, we'd have a country where you could still catch cancer if you wanted to, still hustle a senorita just by flashing your badge.

He stood there for fifteen minutes, smoking, respecting Wanda Jane some more.

When Lois finally popped out the bank's front door, Toby snatched her elbow and said, "Forget the donuts. That fat-head husband of yours lied to me. You got held up, didn't you?"

Lois shook free and gave him a hands-off-right-now look.

"Shut up," she whispered, "and pretend you're a police officer."

She led him down the street, past the donut shop, past the Mobil station, then along a pathway cutting diagonally through Sunrise Park. The park was the Kiwanis Club's nod to community beautification, a half-acre lot featuring a disabled teeter-totter, a bed of scorched asters, and a wildly overgrown hedge that had been configured as a maze. They sat on a rusty iron love seat at the center of the maze. Lois was snapping at him before he could even get started. "What did you expect?" she was saying. "We were in Vegas, people everywhere, what's Doug supposed to say? 'Oh, yeah, our bank got robbed'? Over the *phone*?"

"Well," muttered Toby. He tried to think of something else to say, but couldn't, so he said "Well" again except with a growl to show he wasn't buying it. After a second, he thought to add, "So I guess you did get stuck up?"

"I didn't say that, did I?"

"Not in so many words, but it sure seemed—"

"Toby, take a time-out," said Lois. "I'm not a Mexican, this isn't a traffic stop."

"Well, did you?"

"Did I what?"

"The bank, for Chrissake. Did you get stuck up?"

"You mean robbed?"

"The hell you think I mean?"

"Yes and no," said Lois.

"You're telling me yes and no you got robbed?"

"There you go, you're catching on."

Toby reached for his Kools, shook one out, then remembered Lois liked to smoke only her own smoke. He slipped the cigarette behind an ear, one of his favorite moves.

"Officially," Lois said, "it's a no. Unofficially it's a yes. I shouldn't tell you even that much."

"Halverson?"

"For sure. How'd you guess?"

Toby shrugged and said, "I've got my sources. Guy called

Randy Zapf, thinks he's Al Capone, except he couldn't burgle his way out of bed." Toby smiled, hoping Lois might smile herself, maybe open up some possibilities for later on, but she didn't seem all that smiley. He waited a beat and said, "What about that pip-squeak teller gal, what's her face? Was she in on it?"

"Angie," said Lois. "She's on leave right now."

"Yeah? Is that official or unofficial?"

"Official."

"Well," Toby said, "I hope it's not maternity leave. The baby'll be bigger than she is."

Another pretty good line, he thought, but Lois wasn't biting. What she tended to bite on, by and large, was his dick, money, and ripping off bank customers, a quarter of them Pedros, which gave them something fun to talk about when they had to talk.

"Unofficially," said Lois, hesitating, not sure how much to give away. "Unofficially, it's hard to tell if Angie was in on it. Maybe yes, maybe no. For now, we're sticking with the on-leave story. Obviously, Douglas zapped the bank's camera clips, which was smart, but first he had a good look at what happened. Angie didn't put up much of a struggle. Acted sort of surprised but then went along with scooping up my cash. Didn't even lock the bank." Lois paused and stared at him. "Officially, none of that's official. Didn't happen. Got that?"

"Got it," said Toby.

"You know why, right?"

"Pretty fair notion," he said, and grinned.

They sat quietly for a minute or two before Lois sighed and put her head on his shoulder, a set of greedy fingertips in his lap. Toby liked that. He settled back in the love seat.

"On the other hand," Lois said, "we do want the eighty-one thousand back."

"I'll bet you do," said Toby.

"And this Randy. Sounds like he's got a line on where they might be?"

"Seems that way," Toby said. "You can't never tell. The guy's a piece of stupid wrapped up in cowboy clothes. I wouldn't put money on him."

"I won't," said Lois, "but maybe I'd put money on you."

"You would, would you?"

"Let me talk to Douglas, see what we can arrange. Where's this Randy right now?"

"L.A.," Toby said. He waited a second. "Take it out, babe."

"All of it?" said Lois.

"As much as you can handle."

"I think we might have a job for you."

"I've got one for you, too," Toby said.

True enough, her marriage to Boyd had been cranked tight from day one. The fun times were fun, sometimes gloriously fun, but the miserable times were awful. Manila and Jakarta had been fine, mostly fine, or at least the appearance of fine, the fantasy, the promise of something that had not quite arrived but waited for her just around the corner.

They were in love, of course. Evelyn had never doubted that even when everything else had become falsehood.

Early on, especially in Jakarta, Boyd's variances from absolute truth had seemed frivolous and cute, like those of a boy who substitutes the word *bicycle* for *popsicle*, later the word *Princeton* for *USC*. Partly, she had written it off as simple awkwardness: growing up in the slow lane, now running with the gazelles. In a way, too, she blamed herself—not herself, exactly, but her circumstances, daughter of a tycoon and therefore pretty tycoonish in her own right. There had to have been pressures on Boyd to close an awfully wide gap in their net worth, financial and otherwise.

Pathetic, in a way.

Junior was always junior, always scrambling, but what exactly he yearned for Evelyn had never figured out. Some version of Hollywood happiness, circa 1953; those old movies he'd watched on late-night TV with his mom and pop and undead dead sister—Grace Kelly, Robert Stack—it was as if he'd missed his own era, as if he'd borrowed the fantasies of another generation, cocktail party dreams, Riviera dreams, glamour and money and 3D high society.

They loved each other. They did. But Evelyn sometimes wondered if it had been CinemaScope love. "You're my princess," Boyd murmured to her that night in Jakarta, the night he proposed, and maybe what he meant was you're my Ava Gardner, my Ida Lupino. Or maybe not. Maybe he was whispering to a filthy rich tycooness. Or maybe not that either. Maybe just love.

The irony, Evelyn often thought, was that Boyd had already made his own way; he had no need of princesses. A few hundred thousand eyes gazed at his byline over their bacon and eggs every morning; he dined with ambassadors; he was the *Trib*'s rising superstar, its golden boy, an East Asian correspondent at age thirty. He appeared on CNN, twice on *Meet the Press*. Not that any of this was enough for him. He wanted a Pulitzer. He wanted a dozen Pulitzers. He wanted the next big scoop, the next glass of champagne, the next scrap of gossip he could shape into an exposé of graft or human rights abuse or whatever else the prize committees found worthy of reward. Jakarta became a job.

Now, looking back, she realized it was easy to be unfair to Boyd. The Pacific Basin beat would have been grueling for anyone—typhoons in Bali, power grabs in the Philippines, it never ended.

Briefly, after Boyd was reassigned stateside to the paper's L.A. office, things had improved. Evelyn could finally unpack her suitcase and make friends and stop worrying about tropical diseases and chase-your-tail ambition. The baby had helped, too—Boyd settled down a little. He'd go to work each morning, come home, eat dinner, and get down on the floor to play with Teddy. For once he'd seemed satisfied with what he had. Over those twenty-one months and two weeks and four days, Boyd had turned into the doting daddy, at ease with himself, as though he'd finally cornered whatever elusive fantasy he'd been chasing all his life.

But, of course, all that ended up on the pavement.

Nine years had passed, almost ten, and she was okay now. She coped very nicely with chauffeurs and dinner parties and a bulldog husband like Junius Kirakossian. He paid the bills. He didn't trouble her with passion. What bothered her was that Junius could get ruthless. She shouldn't have called attention to Boyd's reappearance yesterday. She shouldn't have let herself go teary. Statues didn't do that sort of thing.

On a concrete bench outside the law offices of Taylor, Sweet, and Dooney, Boyd and Angie reviewed a number of convergences. After retiring as president and CEO of Pacific Ships and Shipping, Ltd, and after passing the baton to his own son-in-law, Jim Dooney had returned to the former legal practice that still bore his name. Cozily enough, Dooney remained chairman emeritus of PS&S, and even more cozily, his law firm and PS&S were domiciled in the same modern black building, YOU!, which also housed a jeweler, a Cuban tobacconist, and a health spa called The Inner You.

All this Angie had learned in five minutes on her phone.

"You were here yesterday," she was scolding Boyd, "and I don't see how you missed the humongous plaque in the lobby. Taylor, Sweet, and Dooney, it says."

"Hypnotized by a safety pin," said Boyd.

"And by that receptionist you mentioned," said Angie. "The one who levitates."

"Her, too," Boyd admitted. "What's the plan?"

Angie checked her cell phone, stood up, and said, "You stay here, I'm late for a facial. I'll need four hundred bucks."

"For a facial?"

"And a massage. Seven hundred and don't complain."

Reluctantly, Boyd pulled out the cash.

"One piece of advice," she said sharply. "Don't budge. I'm sick of breathing saloon fumes."

With a classy adjustment of her shoulders, Angie swung around and strolled through the revolving glass doors of YOU!

It was another L.A. morning, gas-mask weather, sunny above the smog, and with any luck Angie would emerge with intelligence about Jim Dooney's whereabouts. The thing about facials and massages, she had explained during the cab ride from Santa Monica, is that people get confidential when they've got their hands all over you.

It had seemed a long shot. It still did. On the other hand, Angie Bing was nothing if not dogged.

Boyd folded his arms, crossed his legs, and realized he was still blurry from yesterday's indulgences. Although he smoked only occasionally, he decided now was one of those occasions, and after a moment, he rose from his bench and approached a squad of pariah puffers lined up along the sidewalk outside YOU! He secured a four-dollar Marlboro Light, bent forward to accept a match, and returned to the bench. Seconds later one of the nicotine outcasts sat beside him, and said, "I know you, sir."

"Sorry?" Boyd said.

"I know you maybe."

Boyd looked up. It took him a moment to recognize the Pakistani gentleman whose yelp had accompanied gunfire aboard the Big Blue Bus.

"Well, yes," Boyd said. "And I owe you a drink."

More politely than there was reason to expect, the man chuckled, and said, "No, no, no—it is I who owe the drink." He hesitated. "Of course, I am not permitted, never, never, but perhaps I might learn chemistry of . . . *the* chemistry, sorry, definite article . . . *the* chemistry of booze." He gave his lips a light slap. "I do smoke but God forgives. I sometimes forget perfect English."

"No problem," Boyd said, a little confused. "You owe *me*?"

"Oh, sure. Your pistol—bang!—I jump out of my shoes. Yikes! But the shoot-the-bus story I can now tell to my wife, my friends." The man smiled a bright smile. "Wild West, Jesse James."

"Glad to entertain," said Boyd. "Sure you don't want that drink?"

Again, the man hesitated, longer this time. "I am on break only fifteen minutes but perhaps . . ."

"You work here? At YOU!?"

"I do indeed, sir."

Together they crossed the street to a convenient but expensive-looking bar. Boyd ordered a pair of vodka tonics; the

Pakistani gentleman ordered tomato juice, and they settled into a cozy, dimly lighted booth at the rear of the establishment.

The man's name was Huzaifa. He was thirty-one. He supervised IT for Pacific Ships and Shipping, smiled infectiously, and turned out to be excellent company on a hazy September morning. The man had grown up in Islamabad but had lived in L.A. for three profitable years.

"Islamabad?" Boyd said. An amusing lie alighted on his tongue. He swallowed. There was always a wobbly half second between conception and utterance. "Islamabad, I know the place."

"You know Islamabad?"

"Not well, I admit, but years ago, my job—my former job—took me there. Charming city. Snake pit, too."

What was funny about that, Boyd had no idea, but Huzaifa laughed.

"Maybe, sir, you learned to shoot the bus in Islamabad?"

"Didn't hurt," Boyd said with a shrug. "The Wild East."

"Oh, indeed."

Their fifteen minutes passed jovially, then stretched to a half hour, then stretched again. At one point Boyd inquired about Pacific Ships and Shipping—was Huzaifa acquainted with Junius Kirakossian?

"Oh, yes, yes," said Huzaifa. "You know Mr. Junius?"

"My wife knows him. My ex-wife. Knows him well."

"Ah," said Huzaifa.

"What does 'ah' mean? Good or bad or just something to say?"

"What it means," Huzaifa said, leaning forward, his voice slipping to a lower, almost conspiratorial register, "it means with God's forgiveness I sometimes wish to shoot Mr. Junius the way you shoot the blue bus. Penny-pincher, you know? Big conglomerate, not just ships. Baseball, candy, Stingers. But Mr. Junius mangles the penny. Pinches too hard."

"Stingers?" said Boyd. "The missile, you mean?"

"To be sure. I have friends who . . . You say you know Islamabad?"

"I certainly do," Boyd said. "Another tomato juice?"

Over refills, they traversed a good deal of terrain, comparing notes on topics ranging from lamb stew to Pakistan's nuclear arsenal to Osama bin Laden. They took turns tallying up bin Laden's wives, losing count, which led to a discussion about who was the taller man, Lincoln or Osama, which led to polite give and take about religious body counts over the centuries. Eventually, Huzaifa said, "So in absolute true truth, you never really see Islamabad, correct?"

"Right," Boyd said. "But close. Karachi, '99."

"A spook then?"

It was too tempting. Boyd reached for his drink and flashed a smile. "Hmm," he said, which sounded about right.

"Spooky spook!" said Huzaifa. "Shooting a bus, Stinger missiles, all this adds up."

"Not the missile," Boyd said. "That was my dad."

"What is 'dad'?" Huzaifa said.

"My father. He headed up the development team. Stingers, I mean. Fighter pilot, MIT, Raytheon. That's my pop."

Huzaifa thought about it for a moment. "Excellent father for a spook, yes, sir. In Pakistan we say *waalid*, which is formal, but sometimes we say *abbu*, maybe *abba*." He gave another slap to his lips. "My English, it is broken, yes? Like the USA—broken? Like when you shoot the bus and jump me from my shoes. Guns, guns! Lies, lies! Maybe someday Pakistan can make USA jump from the big-shot shoes. Bang! Maybe the stupid camel jockey will shove a nuke up your too fat ass?"

Boyd nodded with weary wisdom.

"Interesting," he said.

"Great carpets, better bombs." Huzaifa stared at him. His English had improved. "You were never in Karachi, correct?"

"An overnighter. Riyadh, mostly. Damascus. Istanbul now and then."

"But no Pakistan?"

"Never had the pleasure," said Boyd.

The man's eyebrows squeezed into a single eyebrow. He glanced at his wristwatch.

"Perplexing," he said. "Big-shot spy. Pack of lies, of course."

"It's an affliction," said Boyd.

Again, Huzaifa looked at his watch.

The man slid out of the booth, stumbling in his haste, and after a moment Boyd reluctantly followed him to the door. He had forgotten how thrilling it was, how a tall tale tickles the teeth.

Outside, a polluted L.A. morning had become a polluted L.A. afternoon. Angie sat waiting on their concrete bench in front of YOU! It was no surprise that she seemed cranky when Boyd introduced his new old friend.

"Your spooky man, he shot my bus," Huzaifa told her solemnly. "But he is all the way forgiven. Good strange spook."

"Yeah," Angie said. "My hero."

Huzaifa bowed and made his way through the revolving doors of YOU!

"Thanks for not budging," Angie muttered.

Little was spoken until their Uber ride pulled up at the bungalow off Ocean Park Boulevard. Even then, actual words were not spoken until three in the morning when she elbowed him awake and told him to get down on his knees and beg for his Creator's mercy.

It was not until breakfast that she handed him a slip of paper.

"How'd you do it?" said Boyd.

She stared sullenly at a cup of tea. "One thing I didn't do, I didn't get plastered with terrorists."

"Hey, come on, he wasn't a terrorist. Terrific guy, great sense of humor. And I've apologized for the plastered part."

"Not on your knees, you didn't."

"I've been on my knees, Angie. It doesn't help."

"Folding your hands helps. Begging for mercy helps."

"How'd you do it?"

"How the heck do you *think* how?" she said. "My therapist, Peter, who, in case you're interested, is a Baptist and wouldn't mind multiplying a few times."

"What would Peter know?"

"Everything. It's on that piece of paper you're holding." She pushed her cup of tea toward him. "Drink that. It grows back brain cells."

"How would a therapist—?"

"Boyd, for Pete's sake. Haven't you ever had a professional massage? People chitchat! Peter's purring away—can't keep his hands off me, even if that's his job—so this leads to that."

"And?"

"And now," Angie said, "you've got Dooney's address."

"From a masseuse?"

"No, Peter didn't have a clue. Finally, I took the elevator up to Dooney's law office, asked this other guy, Eddie. Took all of ten seconds."

"So what was my seven hundred bucks for?"

"For my therapy, obviously, and it's not *your* seven hundred bucks, it's *our* seven hundred bucks. Either way, you got what you wanted."

She gestured at the slip of paper.

"Where's Port Aransas?" said Boyd.

By 8:00 a.m. the next morning, Boyd had locked up the house, pulled the tarp off his mother's old Eldorado, taken it for a test spin, filled the gas tank, dumped in a quart of oil, inflated the tires, and pointed the vehicle southeastward.

They spent the night outside Phoenix, a much shorter night in El Paso, then they burned up the I-10 before calling it quits in a place called Kerrville, Texas.

They slept for thirteen hours, queen-size bed. In the morning, over pancakes, Angie said, "I guess you really *don't* have a crush on me."

"No offense," said Boyd. "This isn't a crush situation."

"Same bed. That's a crush situation."

"Pass the syrup," said Boyd.

Later Angie said, "So what next?"

"We finish breakfast. We split up. You go your way, I go mine." Boyd inspected his fork; he couldn't look at her. "Things get ugly now. I'm trying to protect you, okay?"

"Just like that? Split up?"

"Yes."

She fell quiet for a while. "I want the truth. What's wrong with me? All I've ever done, I've tried to be nice to you, never once pried, never once asked point-blank why you robbed a bank or why there's that ridiculous gun in your pocket or why . . . I mean, why *did* you rob a bank?"

"I told you why. A sea change."

"The truth! Just try it for once, it won't give you a toothache."

"But I can't—"

She reached across the table, snatched away his fork.

"Look at me, Boyd. In the eyes. If you wanted money, you have that whole house to sell. Santa Monica of all places—worth a couple katrillion easy. The money doesn't matter, does it?"

"No."

"Okay, then. *Why*?"

"I don't know exactly. Burn bridges, I guess. Make myself move."

"Which involves this Dooney guy?"

"Yeah."

"And the gun?"

"That, too. And I need my bullets back."

Gently, almost, Angie Bing made a motion with her head, a kind of invitation. "So what did he do to you? Whatever it was, it had to be bad."

"I've already told you all this. Scandal. Ruined me."

"But that's not everything, is it? There's something else. Something you won't say."

For a dizzy second Boyd felt a kind of slippage, a trapdoor sensation, which he covered by holding out his hand and saying, "Bullets, please."

"They're upstairs, in my purse."

Boyd paid the check, took Angie's arm, and escorted her to their room. She handed over six dull-looking bullets.

"There's a secret you're keeping," she said, her voice flat with certainty, "but I'll tell you this much, you're stuck with me." She drew a breath. "And that reminds me, I've changed my mind about sleeping with you. I'll need new pajamas tomorrow."

"Fine," said Boyd.

"Pink ones," said Angie. "The kind with a lock."

He waited until she was in the shower. Then he hustled out to the Eldorado, tossed in his suitcase, backed out of the motel's parking lot, and swung the vehicle south toward the Gulf. Twenty miles down the road, he nearly turned back—he liked her—but instead he accelerated. It was for the best. Because he liked her.

16

THREE COP CARS WERE PARKED IN FRONT OF THE bungalow in Santa Monica. No yellow tape, Randy noticed, but one of the cars had the word FORENSICS stenciled across its trunk, very classy. A gang of kids stood out front, eyes like Frisbees, as if they'd never seen a cop before. Randy wasn't impressed. Cops, he'd run across a time or two. Strip the uniform off a cop, what you get is a buck-naked deadbeat, couldn't ride a bronc if you stuck him aboard with Velcro. Cops were mucho overrated. Like these particular ones here, that dipstick with a notebook in his hand, sort of squinting at his fingers, probably trying to spell "nobody home," and those two other morons Q-&-Aing a sunburned old lady in curlers who looks like she just finished electrocuting herself.

Didn't take a cop, Randy thought, to figure out this was a bad bust. Flown the coop, sorry about that, more wasted tax dollars. Of course, Randy didn't pay taxes, not a chance, but even so he felt like writing a letter to the editor. He chuckled. Dear Editor: There's this tweeb Boyd Halverson, he robs a bank, hijacks a fiancée, and, guess what, it takes your yo-yo PD a thousand years to run down his hideout in east Santa Monica. Took yours truly a day and a half. All on my own, too, ancient phone book and some gasoline.

Randy settled back in his car, a half block from the house,

and put his mind to rigging a way for this situation to work some magic for him.

Good news, he was on the right track.

Bad news, he was a little late himself.

What he'd have to do, probably, is backpedal. Angie was always good for a clue, like that sick postcard she'd sent him, the one from Mexico. She might just as well've drawn a map, put a big X on it, and said, "Here I am, come get me." Cute gal but totally nutso. Inferiority complex, he figured. Four foot ten, who could blame her, except the four foot ten was like no other four foot ten you'll likely find, very streamlined, all the gadgets in the right places, only miniaturized.

For now, the drill was to sit tight here in the Cutlass, let the kids ooh and aah his wheels, wait till the cops skedaddle, then amble over for a peek at the leftovers.

Randy waited almost an hour. Finally, though, he got fed up, jumped out of the Cutlass, walked over to what looked like the lead cop, and asked point-blank what was what here. The cop wore a plastic ID clipped to his tie, like a dentist at a dentist convention. Unsnazzy, Randy thought. The ID explained that this was Deputy Sheriff Bork, which didn't strike Randy as much of a snazzy name either.

Bork wasn't any motormouth. Chewed gum, stared, acted tall, did all the stuff cops do until you take out your two feet of rebar and go to work.

Anyway, terrific posture for a tall cop.

He asked Randy why he was interested, as if maybe this wasn't any of Randy's particular business, and Randy said, "No reason."

The cop said, "No reason?"

"No reason," said Randy.

What he should've said, Randy realized, was "Bunch of cop cars, who's *not* interested?" Except, naturally, he didn't say that. He kicked his shoe against the curb, looked up at the bungalow, and explained that he was a neighbor, one block down, one block west.

"That so?" Bork said.

"It's so."

"How come your plates say different?"

"Huh?" said Randy.

Right away he regretted it. "Huh" was something a hick might come up with, a straw head just off the bus from Little Rock.

"Your plates," the cop said again. "On that piece of crap '87 Cutlass parked over there. The plates say Siskiyou County. Seven hundred miles, I wouldn't call that a neighbor, neighbor."

"I'm what you call a new neighbor, neighbor," said Randy.

"Are you now? How about you mosey along."

Pretty quickly then, Randy put it together. "So I suppose you're not gonna fill me in?"

"I'm not," Bork said.

"Maybe I could help you out somehow. Pass along leads maybe."

"You can do that?"

"Nope," Randy said. "But if I could?"

"Beat it, pal."

Randy grinned. He was back in form. "Okay, pardon the heck out of me, I didn't mean to bust into any bank-robbing stuff, interrupt all the cop nose picking."

"What bank-robbing stuff?" said Bork, softer than a second ago.

"Huh?" Randy said.

"Buddy, you just said bank robbing, and I'm asking you *what* bank robbing. We're here about a guy shot a bus."

"Shot a what?" Randy said.

"Bus," said the cop. "Shot a goddamn bus."

"Oh, right," said Randy. "That's what I was saying, wasn't it?"

Bork studied him for a second and seemed to decide something. "When I say beat it, what that means is get lost before I arrest you for dumbness in public."

Randy shrugged.

The bus angle confused him, but he smiled and took a few lazy steps back toward his Cutlass. Then after a second, he thought: Why not go for it?

He turned back to the cop.

"You know what?" he said. "I used to hang with a guy, he wanted to be deputy sheriff, just like you. Him and me rodeoed together."

"Another time," the cop said.

"No, this is good," said Randy. "You'll be interested, I'm positive. This was, like, I don't know, probably six years ago. My buddy's a rodeo clown—dangerous work—and he's one tough, kick-ass hombre. Trust him with your life. Problem is, even in the rodeo, clowns gotta be halfway funny. And my buddy, he ain't funny one little bit."

"A rodeo clown, you're saying?"

"That's it."

"So?"

"So it's a bad situation. Put yourself in the guy's shoes. He's a clown, for Chrissake—red wigs and stuff—can't make nobody laugh. So he pokes around for some other line of work, figures he's deputy sheriff qualified. Tough as nails, loves haircuts, stares at shit. And he's real, real, real unfunny. Figures sheriffing's up his alley and so he takes this test. You probably took the same test, right?"

Bork squinted at him.

"The *test*," Randy said, and started backing off. "Somebody tells a joke, you sit there like a dufus, rub your crew cut, finally say, 'I don't get it.' The *unfunny* test, man. The one proves for sure you haven't got no sense of humor."

The cop stared for a while.

Then he said, "You know what I think?"

"Probably not much," said Randy. "But I know what Bork rhymes with."

A block down the street, parked under a pair of browning palms, Junius Kirakossian's CFO sat in his way-too-conspicuous Z3, having just explained to Junius how he'd tracked Halverson to a modest bungalow in east Santa Monica. The cell connection was terrible, in and out, but he'd caught the last half sentence of Junius's standard complaint about how much this was costing him.

Henry Speck had learned to stay silent. In person he would have nodded, but now he was making yeah-yeah faces at the windshield.

"All right, so you traced him," Junius was saying. "How come right now he's not getting fitted for a leg cast? You think I'm paying by the hour?"

Speck rolled his eyes.

"Sir," he said, "bear in mind I'm looking at three police vehicles. Six uniforms with badges. It's not great leg-breaking scenery."

"Christ, a simple thing like this."

"Well, it may not be so simple," Speck said. "I spoke with one of the officers and he—"

"That cost me extra? Talking to cops?"

"Not a dime, sir. I'm on salary."

There was a huffing sound on the line, then Junius said, "You and everybody else—cops, unions, my incompetent baseball team. You know what I pay those bozos?"

"I do, sir. A lot."

"You bet your ass a lot," said Junius. "Seven figures apiece—that's *apiece*—couldn't pull off a hit-and-run in central Watts. What did the cop say?"

Henry Speck presented a blah-blah-up-yours gesture to his windshield.

"Well, first, nobody's here. Place is empty."

"You telling me no balls to squeeze? Guy's screwing with my wife."

"Not literally," Speck said, then said: "I hope."

"You hope, huh?" said Junius.

"Yes, sir."

In the background was a squeaking sound, then quiet, then another squeaking sound. The gold-plated swivel chair, Speck thought.

"That's not all, sir. Halverson, he shot a bus. Guess that's why I'm looking at three cop cars right now."

"Why'd he shoot a bus?"

"For fun, I hear. That's what he told the Pak."

"What Pak?"

"It's complicated, but I think—"

"Uncomplicate it," Junius said, getting testy. "Uncomplicating is what I pay you way too much for."

Speck swung open his door and slammed it shut.

"What the hell was that?" Junius said.

"Not sure, sir." Speck smiled at the recollection of Junius's wife in a pool, fine piece of goods, fine everything. "Anyhow, the story is, some Pakistani woman called in the tip, seems her husband's friendly with your problem boy. Pretty good ID on Halverson."

There was that squeaking sound again.

"Sir?"

"I'm here," Junius said.

"Well, I have an idea if you're interested. About how to find Halverson."

"What's that gonna cost me?"

A shitload, thought Henry Speck. Maybe a wife.

It was a toss-up, Randy thought. Either head back to the Days Inn or wait it out at McDonald's until he could slip inside the bungalow.

Randy flipped a coin in his head, which came up wait, and he spent the next several hours in a red plastic chair watching the citizens fatten up.

At closing time, he drove back to the bungalow.

By then it was a little after midnight, no cop cars. He pulled out his tool kit and strolled up pretty as you please to the front door. He was ready to say open sesame when his cell phone piped up. Randy ignored the phone, stepped inside, flicked on his Crime Stoppers flashlight, and tossed the house in about ten minutes flat.

In the bathroom he found a wastebasket filled with tubes and bottles bearing the last drops of freckle erasers, nasal-hair removers, vitamin A and E skin replenishers, and three fruity-smelling varieties of a well-known feminine hygiene product. This was Angie to an expensive T, he thought, and the thought ticked him off. Running off with an old-fart criminal, that was pretty insulting, but perfuming her privates, that was rude.

Randy swept the kitchen and bedroom, which yielded a turquoise ankle bracelet, a half-empty jar of bone-broth collagen, and an unmade bed.

Man oh man, he was thinking when his cell wailed again.

Randy punched the green button and said, "Get lost, I'm busy."

Angie said, "Not too busy, I hope."

"Huh?" Randy said.

He started to say, "Well, what a coincidence, I was just sniffing this pussy perfume, wondered how you were doing," but the thought hadn't half formed before she was off and running.

She was stranded in Kerrville, Texas. She needed a lift.

"A lift?" he said.

"Like right now, okay?"

"Where the heck's Kerrville, Texas?"

"How would I know?" Angie said. "Get a map, for Pete's sake. You a boyfriend or aren't you?"

"Hard to tell. Aren't you gonna ask how I am or anything?"

"Not right this very instant," she said. "I'm the one who's stranded, right? Why don't you ask *me* how *I* am?"

"Okay, how are you?"

"I'm terrible! I need a lift."

Randy grinned into his cell phone.

"Well, first off," he said, "a lift is where I pick you up at the doctor and dump you at the Walmart, like eight blocks away. That's what they call a lift. A lift ain't Kerrville, Texas. A lift ain't, hey you, gimme a ride over to Moscow, over to Honolulu. That's not what *lift* means. Second off, I'm sittin' here on this unmade bed in Santa Monica. Third thing, I got this almost brand-new yellow thong waitin' on you. A rubber one. And I bet you know what it's for."

"What?" Angie said.

"It's for when I ask what you been up to the last couple of weeks. Like how many banks you robbed, who you robbed them with. Feminine hygiene questions."

"Are you finished?" said Angie.

"Not even started. Why?"

"All I need is to get down to Port Aransas."

"Is that right? And what's Port Aransas?"

"It's a *place*," she said, "where eighty-one thousand dollars will be."

Randy lay back on the unmade bed.

"Yeah?" he said.

"Yeah," said Angie.

He flicked his flashlight on and off, making burglar fireworks on the ceiling. It was his trademark: lying on other people's beds, making fireworks.

"You know what?" he said after a while. "I heard somebody around here shot a bus."

"I heard that, too. Are you on the way yet?"

"On the way where?"

"You know where," Angie said. "Bye."

Randy poked around the house for a few more minutes, nothing much to steal, so he headed out to the street, mounted his Cutlass, checked a map, and rolled east toward the 10. Night driving, it was sex without the bother.

He was two and a half hours down the road, now four in the morning, when his phone played Springsteen.

Angie again—a text this time, which read: *Cancel the lift. Boyd just pulled up. Changed his mind. Now you're the stranded one, cowboy.*

17

MAKING MONEY WAS A CINCH, DOONEY THOUGHT, nothing to it, like when you played vertical poker or ran an international conglomerate. You didn't call your customers pigeons; you called your pigeons customers. You didn't stack the deck, didn't slip too many suited straights up your sleeve. All you did, basically, was play a solid, conservative, vertically organized game, because you were the house and you were the dealer and you were the guy at third base, with employees at first and second and fourth; and, of course, you were the guy who ran the game, so if you went all in and lost, well, the odds were pretty good that one of your vertically organized employees would haul in the chips. In a nutshell, you won even when you lost, which tended to improve your odds. Plus, naturally, you paid yourself the basic seven percent rake just like everybody else at the table, including your customer, whose main job was to cuss and take out markers and write the big fat checks and then come back to do more business after the cussing was over. Customer first, that was Dooney's motto.

The hard part, he kept telling himself, was spending the money you worked like a dog to win.

Like, for example, this million-dollar boat of his. Basically, it was your fifty-two-foot ocean-approved fishing yacht, all the gismos, floating on a not-so-huge Minnesota lake. Two refrigerators, fish freezer, spaceship console, four 560-horsepower

Seven Marine outboards pumping out forty miles per hour at the top end, custom-painted hull, carbon-fiber trim, air-conditioned sleeping berths, sound system blasting decibels that could blow away Bemidji if you cranked it high enough the way Calvin liked it. Problem was, the boat was manufactured by Pacific Ships and Shipping, Dooney's own company, or ex-company, in which, as chairman emeritus, he still held controlling stock, so the million bucks he paid for a boat he didn't want and didn't need and didn't like one little bit, the whole million went from himself right back to himself. Try spending money, you end up making even more money. More headaches, too. Maintenance, refitting, fuel, insurance, on and on. Christ, just getting the tarp off the boat, folding fifty-two feet of stiff canvas, that was manual labor. Tarps get heavy when you're an old man. Tarps get boring. Water gets boring. Fishing gets boring. Then add on flies big enough to eat your ears, mosquitoes lining up for blood transfusions.

Work hard all your life, try to spend the coin you've socked away, and what happens? You end up making your life either boring or miserable or, in this case, both at the same time.

Dooney missed the action. He missed being a son of a bitch.

Five days in Bemidji, he was ready to run down children with all 560 thundering horses in those engines of his. Calvin wasn't any happier. At the moment, bobbing out of gas, waiting for a tow back to shore, they were fantasizing about getting out of Minnesota, maybe spending a chunk of Dooney's money on a smallish, quaintish hotel in the Alps, northern Italy, maybe France, anywhere without flies, and how they'd boot out all the customers and turn up the air-conditioning and sit down for a civilized dinner that wasn't fried walleye and lukewarm baked beans.

"What I want to know," Calvin was saying, "is how a smart guy like you got us into this mess in the first place. Maybe I'm missing something."

"You are," said Dooney. "You're missing verticality."

Calvin shaded his eyes, looked out across the land of sky-blue waters in search of the promised towboat. They'd been bobbing for forty-five minutes.

"Words like *verticality*. I cut hair, give shaves. I get lost, Jim."

"Okay, you know what taconite is?"

"No," Calvin said.

"Taconite is waste rock with some iron ore in it. Used to be, taconite got thrown away, but these days you extract the iron, make the iron into steel, make the steel into cars and ships and skyscrapers and pipelines and paper clips. In other words, you make taconite into money, follow me?"

"Sort of, sure."

"So if you want to make lots and lots of money, a ton of money, then you go vertical. You own the ground where the taconite is. You own the machines that dig up the taconite. You own the companies that make the digging machines. You own the trucks and barges that haul the ore to steel mills. You own the steel mills. You own the car companies that buy the steel. You own the rubber trees that make tires for the cars. You own the ships that carry the rubber. You own paper clip companies, pipeline companies. You own the banks that capitalize skyscrapers. You own the damned skyscrapers."

Calvin wiped his face. "May I ask a question?"

"Ask away," Dooney said.

"I'm hot. When's that tow coming?"

"Soon, I hope," said Dooney. "But I thought you wanted to know this stuff."

"Well, I do," Calvin said. "I guess what I don't understand is . . . I don't see why taconite makes somebody want to shoot you in the face."

"Verticality," Dooney said.

"Yeah?"

"Pyramids are vertical. Iran-Contra was vertical."

"Illegal vertical?"

"Adrenaline vertical. The kind of vertical where you can buy a million-dollar boat you don't want, a boat that runs out of gas twenty yards from the fueling yard."

"But illegal, right?"

"That's for the lawyers, Cal. You a lawyer?"

Dooney reached into the fish freezer and pulled out a hyper chilled 2007 Oenothèque. He popped it open, took a hundred-dollar swig, and handed it to Calvin, who looked great in his Speedo, great for a guy whose seventy-fourth birthday was tomorrow. "Cal, you know who JFK was, correct? His old man, Joe, he was a businessman just like me, ran some rum in his day, played a little loose with rules and regulations, and so when JFK ended up POTUS, old Joe used to tell him, 'Jack, there's one thing you gotta know. All businessmen are sons of bitches.'"

"That's sweet!" Calvin said.

"I thought so, too," said Dooney.

Calvin rubbed his jaw, pondered things, then said, "So this Halverson creature, Lloyd or whatever, he wants to shoot you because you're a son of a bitch?"

"Boyd, not Lloyd," said Dooney. "And he wants to shoot me because I destroyed his pitiful life. Here comes our tow."

Seven miles outside Port Aransas, Angie Bing had completed an exhaustive and highly articulate diagnosis of Boyd's psychological difficulties. In summary, she was saying, he suffered from three or four personality disorders, one of which was a pathological inferiority complex manifesting itself in pseudologia fantastica, sometimes called mythomania, other times called lying through your teeth.

"You're not forty-nine, are you?" she said.

"Fifty-three," Boyd said.

"And you're not five eleven."

"Well, last time I checked—"

"Stop fibbing," she snapped. "I measured you."

"You measured me?"

"I certainly did." Angie's eyes glittered with satisfaction. "That measuring tape I bought in the Ralphs? You were asleep."

"You measured me in my sleep?"

"I sure did, Shorty. You're two gray hairs shy of five ten."

Boyd kept his eyes on the road, which had flattened into the bland, depressing coastal islands of southeastern Texas. Sand and water stretched out to the horizon on both sides of State Highway 361. Straight ahead was a parade of RVs.

"Part of your problem," Angie went on, her voice puckish and indefatigable and irritatingly penetrative, much as it had been for the last two hundred and forty miles, "is you even lie to yourself, Boyd, like that nonsense about not having a crush on me. Why else turn around and come back to get me? Crush, that's all it is."

"Or else I figured I could use you," said Boyd.

"Crush!" Angie yelped. "Aren't you even listening?"

Forty-five minutes later, they flopped into a booth in the Nightcap Café just off Port Aransas Beach Road. Angie ordered crab cakes; Boyd ordered two Buds and the shrimp basket. Apparently, the place specialized in elderly-to-near-dead tourists.

Boyd knocked back his first Bud.

"Pseudologia fantastica?" he said. "So what's that?"

"I told you, it's a disease. Same as mythomania."

"Right, but . . . those are big words."

Angie eyed him for a second. "If that's a comment on my education, you'd better watch it. Haven't you ever heard of self-improvement? That's what this whole country is *about*. Self-improvement and God."

Boyd nodded as quickly as he could, but she was already on the lecture circuit. Their food arrived, the dirty plates were taken away, two Bud bottles stood tantalizingly empty on the table, but Angie was only then gliding through the *J*s in an alphabetized menu of all the awesome words she had picked up over twenty-nine years.

"Jabberwocky, jacinth, jaculate," she said. "Jailbait—I bet you know that one."

"Uxorial," said Boyd, hoping to jump ahead.

"Sure, that one was on my very first list, years and years and years ago. I get these lists in the mail, fifty words every month, guaranteed to make you a more exciting and alluring person." She looked at him expectantly. "Well?"

"Well what?"

"You know what. Alluring. Say something."

"Oh, right. Should we go find Dooney?"

Just before dawn, Randy pulled into the parking lot of the Days Inn he'd checked into about fifty thousand years ago. After two and a half hours on I-10 East, another two and a half hours on I-10 West, he was in no mood for people messing with him, not anybody, for sure not midget redheads, so when he locked up the Cutlass and headed for his room, which he'd paid good money for and barely even used, he didn't care at all for a hand grabbing his elbow about thirty seconds from his pillow, and he didn't care for how the elbow went up behind his shoulder blades, or for how Cyrus said, "Welcome home, Zipper."

Not forty feet away, in his black-and-white FPD squad car, Toby Van Der Kellen had a good look at the parking lot, mainly because he was parked in the very same parking lot, and right now, after a dull and lengthy wait, it was good to have a ringside seat at some interesting action. As far as Toby was concerned, Randy Zapf was the next best thing to a Mexican, or maybe the next worst thing, so he enjoyed watching that elbow slide up behind the shoulder blades, nice and tidy, and he enjoyed watching the big Black dude give the elbow a little extra nudge just past uncomfortable.

Another guy, skinny and prison white and grandpa old, was giving the Black fella a helping hand, showing Randy the business end of what looked like a javelin, or maybe a garden hoe, hard to tell in the dark.

A one-way conversation was in progress. Could have been the Black guy was delivering a sales pitch, like for encyclopedias or something, but it was pretty clear that encyclopedias scared the shit out of Randy, who was having trouble with that elbow sliding up to where elbows can't go.

Maybe, Toby thought, it was time for law enforcement.

Or maybe not.

The long drive from Fulda had kicked Toby's ass, plus all that dead time monitoring Randy's cell pings, plus the fact that Toby was developing some professional interest in how far an elbow could go before it wasn't an elbow anymore.

Eeny, meeny, Toby thought.

Then he thought about what Lois might want, and that made him remember some stuff he might want from Lois.

Toby opened his door with a cop's here-we-go-again sigh.

In a safer part of town, Evelyn awakened from what at first seemed a bizarre dream but that instantly dissolved into a considerably more bizarre recollection of her encounter yesterday with Junius's CFO.

Beside her, Junius's side of the bed was vacant. It was always vacant these days.

She put on a robe, rode one of the mansion's elevators down to the kitchen, made coffee, and carried a large steaming mug out to the pool. It was here, as she lay sunning yesterday, that Henry Speck had popped up like a suave jack-in-the-box, all smiles and silk, full of that look-at-my-muscles confidence she'd despised from day one. Despised, but . . . oh well.

She drank the coffee fast.

Despised, but what? She folded her hands in her lap, sat very still for a minute or two, then laughed at herself.

Despised, for sure, but what amused her was that she hadn't sent him packing right off, instead pulling up her halter straps and smiling like a cotton-brain and telling him what a surprise this was, his showing up like this—a *pleasant* surprise, for God's sake—and how, on top of that, she hadn't told him to get lost when he stripped off his tie and shirt and sprawled down on the deck chair beside her.

Despised. But, of course, she would sleep with him. Probably soon.

Now, trying to push away these thoughts, Evelyn grunted an obscenity, took off her robe, swam a dozen laps, then air-dried herself on what was already a hot morning. She lay for a long while on her wicker lounger, just drifting.

Don't think, she thought.

Forget yesterday. Forget Henry Speck.

Then she was thinking again: how they had chatted about Junius's pool party, what a success it had been, and how Speck had eventually, ever so casually, mentioned that Junius had given him a little task to handle. He needed to track down Boyd Halverson. Did she have ideas? "Now mind you," Speck had murmured pleasantly, "I don't give a hoot about ex-husbands. Or even current husbands. But I'm afraid Junius gives a pretty big hoot. Seems he wants to discourage a meddling ex-husband. Can't blame him."

"Discourage?" Evelyn had said.

"Discourage, yes."

"And I'm to assist?"

"So I'm hoping."

"Put your shirt on," Evelyn said. "And knock off the pec flex. Doesn't impress me."

Speck chuckled. "Just a tiny hint, okay? Where would I find the unwanted ex? The world will be a better place."

"Boyd's no threat to anyone," said Evelyn, instantly thinking it wasn't quite true. "He wants my father, not me. Tell Junius to back off."

"*You* tell Junius. He commands, I get paid."

"Did he command you to massage butts in a swimming pool?"

"No. Probably not. That was the pecs talking."

"Well, fine. Next time it happens, I grab you by the ears, yank your nose up my ass."

Henry Speck laughed, put his shirt back on, rose from his deck chair, and said, "Actually, lover, you've helped a little. Sounds like what I do is find Dooney, stick close, wait for Halverson to show."

"I didn't—"

"One last question. Mind if I stop by again?"

"You're a creep, aren't you?"

"Yeah, but do you mind?"

Lois and Douglas Cutterby had convened in Community National's boardroom, which was a concrete table and two rusty chairs on the patio outside their home in Fulda, California. Douglas was working on his second croissant of the morning; Lois was updating him on a number of remedial measures she'd put in place.

"Bravo!" said Douglas when she concluded. "A loan! I married a wizard!"

"That's how it's entered on the books, in any case," said Lois. She glanced down at the bound ledger in front of her. "A high-interest loan, of course, for when Mr. Halverson's note comes due."

"High interest would be . . . ?"

"Fucking high," she said.

Douglas beamed and buttered his croissant.

"In other words," he said, "no stickup, just a civic-minded service to the community. And that's what we're here for, right? Loaning capital."

"Absolutely," said Lois. "Not to mention covering our tracks with the auditors. An eighty-one-thousand-dollar loan, who can complain?"

"That, too," said Douglas.

"There remains some paperwork."

"Oh, yes. And I assume—"

"In progress."

Douglas nodded abstractly. He buttered and took a bite from his third croissant.

"The documentation?" he said. "The *t*'s and the *i*'s?"

"For the time being," said Lois, "I've gone the straight-out forgery route, just scribbled Halverson's signature. Later on, I guess, we'll need to clean that up." She drew a breath, took the plunge. "I've engaged a debt collector—professional, very discreet. He'll see to both things at once, the paperwork and repayment of principal."

"Plus interest, don't forget."

"I haven't forgotten."

"Excellent. Would you care for coffee?"

"No thanks," said Lois, "but I'd love a two-week trip to where croissants were invented."

"Vienna?" Douglas said.

"Paris," said Lois.

"Forgive me, but I'm quite positive the croissant was invented in Vienna. Though, of course, it does *thrive* in Paris."

"Vienna, huh?"

"I believe so."

"Okay, we'll split the difference," Lois said. "Make it Monte Carlo."

"Done," Douglas said. "One other question."

Lois closed her ledger with a sigh. She knew what was coming.

"Your professional debt collector?" Douglas said with a gentle, almost comforting smile. "His name would not be Wife Banger, would it?"

* * *

The four of them, Cyrus, Carl, Randy, and Toby, had adjourned to room 204 in the Days Inn, which had once been Randy's room but which now belonged mostly to the other three. Cyrus and Carl had the twin beds, Toby had the imitation leather armchair, and Randy had the not-all-that-filthy wall-to-wall carpet. Actually, Randy was thinking, the carpet was probably the fat end of the stick. Dimensionwise, wall-to-wall beats a bed two to one, maybe three to one, no sweat.

All four of them were holding moist bottles of Coors, courtesy of the cooler that used to sit nice and comfy on the passenger seat of Randy's Cutlass. Toby had just been asking, more or less, what the heck was going on, and Cyrus was saying, "To begin with, Zipper stole my underpants," and Carl said, "Mine, too, and my shoes and socks," and Cyrus snorted, and said, "And my dignity, know what I'm sayin'?"

"Yeah, dignity," Carl said.

"Human pride," said Cyrus.

"Mostly dignity," said Carl. "And it stings."

Toby looked down at Randy and said, "That true? You an underwear thief?"

"Borrowed 'em," Randy said.

"You borrowed underwear?"

"Well, sure. If it's a big deal, everything's in the trunk. It's not like I went and pawned some underpants."

"Let's take a look at that trunk of yours," Cyrus said.

They put down their beers and trooped outside to where Randy's Cutlass was looking sharp next to Toby's black-and-white. Randy opened the trunk and stepped back. "Okay, so there's the underpants," he said cheerfully. "Shoes, too. I hope everybody's friends again."

Cyrus sat on the pavement and pulled on his shoes. Carl wiggled his nose and said, "Man, you gotta do something about that trunk. What you been keepin' in there?"

"Rodeo poop," Cyrus said.

They trooped back inside.

For a while, they worked their way through Randy's personal Coors stash. There was acrimony at work. The room, already cramped and small, seemed to be squeezing itself toward hostilities. Toby finally addressed the situation. "All right, fuck it, cards on the table," he said abruptly. His voice was ragged with beer and nasal impurities. "Truth is, I don't care much for Negroes. I don't care for Mexicans, Communists, Democrats, old people, and Randy Zapf. What I care for is eighty-one thou."

"S'cuse me," Cyrus said. "You an actual cop?"

Toby shifted in his chair. "Sure am. You an actual Negro?"

Cyrus looked himself over and said, "Yep."

"Well, me too, I'm actual. Uniform, badge, the works. And you know what my wet-dream fantasy is?"

"Believe I do," said Cyrus.

"My fantasy," Toby said, "is pollution control."

Randy said, "Anybody want to watch some TV?"

"What I'm saying is," said Toby. "I'm saying that Don's wall is fine and dandy—A-plus to that—but what this country needs is reservations, a place to stick the pollution we already got. Live and let live, I say. Long as it's on a reservation."

"How you vote in the last election?" Carl asked.

Toby gave him a cop stare. "Election?"

"You a liberal?"

"Watch your mouth," said Toby, putting steel in it. "Ain't no election when eighty million Demo-fuckin'-crats get to vote, half of them spades, other half Pedros. That's cheating, my friend. On top of that, I guess you heard how they got this DNA test on ballots, on voting machines? Mexican votes, Black votes, they get counted triple."

"I heard that," said Carl, "from an idiot."

"Who's the law here?" Toby said.

"Beats the hell out of me," said Cyrus. "What exactly you want?"

"Already explained. Eighty-one thousand dollars," said Toby.

For a while, once money was firmly the bottom line, things calmed down. Randy sat listening, mostly bewildered. He was dead tired after five wasted hours of night driving. He lay back on the carpet, briefly zoned out, then sat up again when his spine went stiff and prickly. Cyrus was saying, "So there's official and there's unofficial? Bank job happened, but then again, it didn't happen?"

"That's pretty sharp," said Toby, "for an African."

"And who's this Lois again?"

"Well, for starters," Toby said, "Lois is a white gal. She's the one hired me, made me her debt collector. So what I figured was, I figured I'd begin with Randy here, get a line on his girl-friend, who, by the way, is a nice piece of action if you go for pygmies. Lois thinks maybe she's hanging close to the eighty-one thou. Maybe she was even in on the whole bank job."

"Ever go Black?" said Carl.

"You asking something?" said Toby.

"Didn't you just say this Lois floozy is white? I'm asking if you ever went Black."

Toby hiked up his cop belt. "Buddy, you're already about a thousand years old. How old you want to get?"

"Tone it down, let's everybody be gents here," said Cyrus. He smiled but his voice didn't. "There's cash money up for grabs. Negro, honky—who cares? This is the USA. Opportunity knocks."

Again, Randy slipped away, daydreaming about a rubber thong that never got put to good use, and a good while later, when he tuned in, Toby was telling Cyrus and Carl that the Community National stickup was off the books, nonhistory, never happened, mainly because the bank had been robbing itself for a couple dozen years or so, and because his gal Lois didn't want the law poking around till things got settled with Boyd Halverson. "That's where I come in," Toby said. "I got loan papers for the guy to sign. Some basic debt collecting to do."

Cyrus whistled and said, "Man, I gotta buy me a bank to rob."

Carl said, "Why buy it? I know just the bank."

Toby looked at Carl for a second, then he looked at Cyrus, then back at Carl. "Are you peckers thinking—?"

Cyrus grinned. "How come we chasin' a lousy eighty-one when we know a whole bank that don't report bank robberies?"

"Where's Fulda again?" said Carl.

Randy had had enough. He stood up, went to the cooler, and fetched himself a Coors nightcap. "You oughta be ashamed," he said to Toby.

"About what?" Toby said.

"These two peckers—good word you used, *peckers*—these two peckers are gonna rob a bank. Isn't that illegal or something?"

"So?" Toby said.

"So I thought you were a cop."

"So?"

"So how come you're, like . . . How come you're all smiley like that?"

Toby and Carl and Cyrus did some eyeball Ping-Pong, then Carl reached to the floor and picked up his garden hoe.

"You got something else to say?" Carl said.

"Well, now you mention it, I sure do," said Randy. He looked over at Cyrus. "Remember a while back, half hour ago, you said, 'Know what I'm sayin'?' Remember that? You said I stole your underpants, then you said, 'Know what I'm sayin'?' Now, I don't want to step on toes here—maybe it's a brother thing—but you folks always say stuff and then a second later you say, 'Know what I'm sayin',' like you never even said it in the first place. Know what I'm sayin'?"

Cyrus turned to Carl and said, "How we gonna kill this moron?"

"Not sure," Carl said. "String him up by the mouth?"

"Another thing," Randy said. "Doesn't anybody here want breakfast?"

18

THE LYING CONTAGION HAD SWEPT ACROSS THE American heartland, barreling across the cornfields of Nebraska westward into Wyoming, southward into Kansas and Colorado, eastward into Iowa, hooking up with the Mississippi at Davenport and traveling aboard tongues and lungs down the Father of Waters into the cotton fields of a resurgent Confederacy. In Hannibal, Missouri, mythomania claimed the town's Truth Teller historian, who denounced the "God-hating Sam Clemens" as a "Jew and closet Muslim." The ahistorical, antihistorical historian informed tourists and schoolchildren that the pen name Mark Twain was plainly Semitic, plainly mongrelized, and that Sam's "so-called masterpiece" amounted to little more than an "instructional booklet on miscegenation."

The Hannibal historian's psychiatrist lied about his patient's mental health. The psychiatrist's Truth Teller congressman lied about psychiatrists, claiming he didn't need one.

Conceived as a personality disorder in the late nineteenth century, mythomania proved as catchy as the latest chart-topping pop song. Like music, the disease was transmitted by the quake and quiver of vocal cords, by the twang of guitar strings and the rhythms of human expression; like the fairy tale, it was received as an improvement on tiresome reality; like the daydream, it appealed to a craving for the impossible or the unlikely or the deferred or the unfulfilled and unfulfillable.

The term *mythomania* originally referred to a passion for, or obsession with, myth itself—the hero myth, the journey myth, the redemption myth, the broad-stroked, larger-than-life, happy-ever-after myth. Not only individuals but also whole cultures were ripe for infection. The fabulous and the fantastic—the wildly outlandish lies—were typically questioned by the intellect yet wholly absorbed by the heart. Almost always, mythomaniacs lied to reinforce fragile egos, decorating their lives with unearned grandeur.

Thus, in Concord, Massachusetts, the Minuteman Truth Teller Seed decorated its website with an American flag unfurled just above a headline announcing its intent to reoccupy Old North Bridge, this time with AR-15s. "The Mexicans are coming!" cried a Truth Telling ancestor of Paul Revere's grocer. Thus, too, not far northward, along the Connecticut River, the Walpole, New Hampshire, Truth Teller Seed tweeted the news that it had thrown up earthworks against an imminent invasion of "demented Democrats" massing in Putney, Vermont. And thus, in Fulda, California, Chamber of Commerce President Earl Fenstermacher had just completed a rewrite of Thornton Wilder's *Our Town*, peopling the cast with brave Truth Tellers, a jolly bank president, a socialist sugar beet farmer, a kindly neo-Nazi motorcyclist, and a narrator resembling Earl Fenstermacher. "Well, jeez, I don't know," said Mayor Chub O'Neill. "What's the point?"

"It's *art*," Earl said defensively, a little hurt. "At the end, everybody gets together and bombs a courthouse. Perfect for a middle school's Easter pageant."

"No argument there," said Chub. He thought about it for a moment.

"I don't think 'kindly neo-Nazi' is four words. You could use an editor."

19

PORT ARANSAS WAS FLAT AND GETTING FLATTER by the hour, or so it seemed to Boyd Halverson. The ferocious midday heat had apparently paralyzed what few human beings he'd detected along the town's sidewalks and docks and beaches. Now, dead ahead, a great mass of clouds squatted on the horizon, motionless and dull, almost unreal, as if painted against the sky by a depressed watercolorist. Stuporous humidity thickened by blast-furnace heat seemed to cause everything in these latitudes to move in painful slow motion—the waterfowl, the RVs, the poached tourists in their straw hats and sandals.

Boyd and Angie had checked into a decent motel. Decent, at least, in the sense that their window air conditioner coughed reluctant puffs of clammy, salt-scented vapor that instantly condensed against the room's lamps and walls and bedding.

They had each showered twice, changed clothes twice, and now, back in his mother's ancient Eldorado, they rolled along at six miles an hour behind still another RV, this one captained by the Lost Mariner.

"I think it's the next right," Angie said, holding a slip of paper in one hand, a map in the other. "Or—wait—maybe the next left and then the next right. I flunked Girl Scouts."

"What's the street number?" Boyd asked.

"That's what confuses me."

"How can a number confuse you? It's a number. They're all different."

"Don't be so cranky, Boyd. The guy who wrote this address down for me, the guy in Dooney's office, I can't help it that his twos look like eights. Or the other way around, it's impossible to tell. And besides, you should be showering me with flowers and chocolates for getting the address in the first place. I had to show skin for it; I had to pretend to bump into the guy's desk and go all gimpy, like I needed an amputation or something, and the guy even . . ."

"Right or left?" Boyd said.

"Let's try left," she said.

The RV ahead of them turned left.

"Let's try right," said Boyd.

They turned onto Sunset Years Drive, and Angie began squinting through the humidity in search of street numbers.

"I think it's 25388," Angie said, "or else it's 85322. Except the five sort of looks like a three, so that means the three is probably a five."

"You sure the street name is right?"

"Pretty sure," she said. "The *Y* sort of looks like an *F*."

"Who'd name a street Sunset Fear Drive?" said Boyd.

"You'd be surprised."

"Fearing sunsets?"

"Are you kidding me? People fear lots of stuff. There's probably a name for fearing sunsets, a whole psychological profile, like with you and your pseudologia fantastica."

Boyd pulled to the curb and stopped.

"Let's knock on doors," he said.

"Walk? In this heat?"

"Yeah," he said.

"No can do, Tonto. I weigh a hundred and ten pounds, and most of it used to be water."

"And mouth," Boyd said.

They knocked on thirteen doors with no luck, but on the fourteenth, they spoke with a plump, middle-aged gentleman who may or may not have recognized the name Dooney. The man wore swimming trunks, flip-flops, no shirt, and a cap that said GULF VET in ornate gold stitching.

"Yes sir," the man said thoughtfully. "Dooney? Older fella? Small town, you know, especially off-season, but . . . Big white head of hair? Thinks his shit don't stink?"

"That's him," said Boyd.

The man nodded. "Okay, good, but I'm not sure he lives on this street. Maybe across town, west side, where all the fancy boys hang their Speedos." He looked at Angie with a grin. "You and your granddad Speedo shopping?"

Angie hooked Boyd's arm and leaned in close to him.

"Boyd's my fiancé," she said stiffly. "And I bet he's younger than you are."

"Could be," the man said.

"Boyd's forty-nine; what are you?"

"Fifty-one, ma'am, but full of vinegar." He kept looking her over. "What say we step inside, have a bourbon lemonade?"

"No," Angie said.

"Yes," Boyd said, "and we thank you."

The man's cottage was immaculately neat, almost spit shined. They sat around a Formica-topped table, a pitcher of lemonade at its center, a bottle of Jack Daniel's flanking the pitcher, three spotless glasses standing at attention.

"This Dooney fella," the man said, "if I've got the right guy in mind, he's a part-timer in Aransas, sticks to himself mostly, comes in for a week, maybe two, then off to greener pastures. Never talked with him. Seen him in town a few times, bars, restaurants, that kind of thing. If I were you, I'd try the post office." He paused, grinned again at Angie. "Oh, yeah, I'm Jon without the *h*, and I bet you're . . . Lemme guess. You're Spunky?"

"That's me to a T," she said. "What's with the cap?"

"Which cap is that?"

"The one on your head."

"Oh, yeah." He took off the cap, looked at it, then put it back on. "Kind of a play on words, you know? We're on the Gulf here, Gulf of Mexico, and you could say I've lived in these parts a long time, all fifty-one years to be accurate. I guess that makes me a Gulf vet."

Nobody had yet dispensed the lemonade. Boyd mumbled something, reached out, poured a glass half full, and topped it off with bourbon.

"Delicious," he said. "And thank you again, Jon."

The man nodded without taking his eyes off Angie, a moist grin still sliding along his thick, fleshy lips.

"How tall are you, hon?" he asked.

"You mean how short am I?" said Angie.

"Well now, darlin', if that's the way you want to compute it."

Angie gave Boyd a let's-get-out-of-here look.

Boyd shrugged.

"In other words," she said, now with some brittleness in her voice, "you're asking a total stranger, a *girl* stranger, for her private statistics?"

"You betcha," Jon said.

"With my fiancé sitting right here?"

"Makes it interesting."

Angie turned to Boyd and said, "You still have that gun in your pocket?"

"I do. The lemonade's amazing."

Their host leaned back in his chair, not bothering to look Boyd's way. "My guess," he said, "is four nine? Four ten?"

"Show Jon your gun," said Angie. "Right now."

Boyd put down his mostly empty glass, took out the Temptation, looked at it briefly, then placed it on the red and white Formica tabletop.

"Any more measurements you need?" Angie said.

The man laughed. "Guess I'll manage on my own. Let me fill up that glass of yours, Spunky."

"Mine, too, while you're at it," said Boyd.

At that instant, a crack of thunder seemed to pick up the man's kitchen and give it a shake. Lightning burned across the windows, vanished, then burned again, and the Gulf of Mexico lifted itself over Port Aransas and began depositing its contents in a single vengeful onslaught.

The kitchen lights went out.

"We don't get rain here," the man said, "but sometimes we do get whatever you call this." He paused for a second. "That gun on my table, is that for real?"

"Sort of," Boyd said, and smiled pleasantly. "Could I change the subject for a second?"

The man licked his lips.

"Your cap, Jon," said Boyd. "I'm interested in that."

"My cap, you say?"

"Where it says Gulf vet. You ever hear the phrase 'stolen valor'?"

The downpour was deafening, and Boyd had to raise his voice.

"See, here's the deal," he said. "I don't mind you funning with my fiancée, she could use it, and your hospitality, it's fault-less. The cap, though. The cap is a problem."

Boyd sighed, drained his glass of lemonade, prepared an-other, smiled down at the gun before him, smiled again at his host, then unbuttoned his shirt and displayed a ragged scar on his shoulder.

"Fun's a good thing," he said. "But the Hindu Kush . . . the Kush wasn't fun. Fallujah, that was a whole bunch less fun. You understand the cap problem?"

"It's a joke," the man said. "I explained, didn't I?"

Boyd smiled and pointed at his own forehead.

"Inside here," he said, "you'll find a sliver of steel, not even an inch long, weighs less than a mouthful of Wheaties."

"You a Gulf vet?"

"One and two, both," said Boyd.

"Well, jeez, I didn't mean—"

"So here's the issue, Jon. That itty-bitty sliver of steel, it makes me not care for caps that say Gulf vet, at least not when the civilian with the Gulf vet cap is messing with my fiancée like I'm not even there, like I'm over in the Kush getting steel in my head."

Boyd gave the man a big wide smile.

"You got a couple raincoats we could borrow?"

"Yeah," the man said. "I sure do."

"And do you mind if I shoot your table?"

"You want to shoot it?"

"If it's no trouble."

A minute or two later, Angie took Boyd's hand as they trotted toward the Eldorado in a wet and heavy rain.

"Fiancée!" she squealed.

"Don't count on it," Boyd said.

20

THE RAIN ENDED, THE NIGHT BLAZED WITH STARS, and they splurged on an expensive surfside restaurant specializing in white linen, candlelight, and Cajun cuisine. Boyd was still riding his Formica high; Angie was riding her own premature uxorial high.

Port Aransas, they concluded, was okay.

The remaining difficulty was that Jim Dooney was no longer in residence. He had fled north to Minnesota, to Bemidji, Minnesota, wherever that might be, a place described by the Port Aransas postmaster as hell on earth, unless you enjoyed flies substituting for raisins in your Waldorf salad. Angie had done the talking—trailer parks, gymnastics, Pentecostal soteriology—and the kindly old postmaster had eventually declared a TKO and handed her the forwarding address, a Bemidji PO box.

Now, over a shared course of piment doux and celery shrimp, Angie suggested they defer Minnesota, defer Jim Dooney, and see about getting pregnant. "It's how we do things Pentecostally," she said. "It's a direct deal with God, one-on-one, you don't need red tape."

"What about your boyfriend?" Boyd asked.

"More red tape," said Angie.

"Meaning what?"

"Meaning once I'm good and pregnant, I'll drop the bad news on him."

Boyd looked around the restaurant for rescue. The place was nearly empty: a foursome at one table, a guy sitting alone with his cell phone at a table near the bar.

"Look," he said, "you're the one who brought up the fiancé stuff. All I did was, I jumped on the bandwagon, played along."

"And boy did I get the shivers!"

Angie rose, moved her chair closer to him, took his hand, and kissed it.

"The way you stood up for me with Jon," she said, "it was really something special. It made me think, Okay, Angie, this is for real, this is the guy for you, even if he's almost retired or almost in a wheelchair or something. I mean, shooting tables, I could've done without that—I'm basically antigun from the get-go except to defend your own castle, and except if somebody's dog keeps you awake at night, or unless some jerk starts putting moves on your betrothed like Jon did—so I guess one time is okay—shooting one table, I mean—but I don't want guns around our kids except if some shady character comes up and starts giving our kids candy and talks about the devil and evolution and all that. Bang! You shot that table for me! My whole life, nobody else ever did that, not even Randy, but just so you know, Randy could be pretty generous, like with flowers and horseshoes and these two Wrensilva stereo consoles he brought home one night. Not that we ever . . . You know. We never consecrated anything."

"Consummated," Boyd said.

"That either," said Angie.

She stopped a waiter, handed him her phone, and asked him to take a snapshot of the two of them.

"Boyd and I, we just got engaged," she said. "So after you

take the picture, we'll need one of those complimentary desserts, those ones for anniversaries and funerals. And maybe you should make an announcement, too. So everybody can clap."

The waiter presented them with Cajun rice pudding and a half bottle of Louisiana pinot noir. The foursome and the solitary diner stood and applauded.

"One last thing," Angie said when the pudding was gone. "That piece of steel in your brain. The lying has to stop."

"It was almost true," Boyd said. "A tumor."

"And that scar on your shoulder."

"Racquetball. It's a real scar, though."

"Boyd, I'm serious."

"Yeah, well, so am I," said Boyd. "Your lover boy with the fat lips, he was lying with that cap of his. I called him on it. *You* lied—the fiancé comment, remember? Dooney lied. Evelyn lied. Half this country, they worship a monster who can't do anything *except* lie. That God of yours, he *is* a lie. Getting pregnant—a lie. Happy ever after—a whopper."

"Are you finished?" Angie said.

"No," said Boyd, but nothing else came to him.

"In that case, I have two things to say."

"All right, but I'm counting."

"Number one, our kids need a good example. Number two, put down the bottle this instant. Number three—I forgot—I love you anyway."

Henry Speck stood to applaud the newly engaged couple across the room, then resumed his phone conversation with Junius Kirakossian.

"What I'm trying to explain," Henry said, "is I need you to

email me three or four decent photos, up-to-date ones, otherwise I have no idea what to look for, or how to . . . Yes, sir, I
did fly coach."

In the rearmost seat of their polished black Town Car, a dis-
continued stretch model, Junius and Evelyn gazed out opposite
windows as Sunset Boulevard presented its slideshow of evening
riches: the lawns of Bel Air, the twinkling glitz of Hollywood,
the beachy baronies of Malibu and Pacific Palisades. When Junius punched out of his call, Evelyn said, without turning away
from her window, "Was that Henry?"

"It was," said Junius. "I pay him way too much."

"No doubt. Except he has his virtues, yes?"

"Virtues? He does what I tell him to do. Mostly."

Junius was flipping through photos on his cell phone.

"The problem with Henry," he said after a moment, "is it
would cost more to fire his ass than keep him on. That's how
it is these days. Fire somebody, bam, you automatically got
pensions, severance, medical for eternity, and that's without
unions, and believe me, I've got unions, seven of the suckers,
twelve thousand three hundred employees worldwide. Thing
is, with unions, you can't fire a single one of them, ever, period.
Not without dicking around with shit like good cause, which
is impossible to prove without hiring your own police force,
which I do, and which also sets me back a million or two." He
paused and stared at one of the photos on his phone. "I got a
baseball team—I tell you this?—I got a baseball team can't beat
the peewees, but you think I can fire these spastic morons?
Know what I want to do? I want to bench the whole pathetic
team, if you call it a team, and I don't, I call it a clusterfuck.

Makes me want to put on a uniform and go out there and play the Phillies one-on-nine, just me against the Phillies, see who comes out on top."

"Do it," said Evelyn.

"You think?"

"It's your team, isn't it? Have fun."

Junius typed a short message, attached a few photos, and hit send.

"I'd get fined," he said morosely. "Having fun, even *that* would cost me."

"Do I cost you?" Evelyn said.

"Well, certainly. But not a bundle."

Evelyn looked out on Malibu, thinking about Henry Speck.

"Whose party is it tonight?" she said.

"Kim."

"Oh God."

"Not that one. The other one."

"What do I talk about?"

"Talk about money," Junius said.

Henry Speck jerked up from the photos on his phone, swiftly surveyed the restaurant, tossed down his napkin, muttered something profane, and hurried past Boyd and Angie's vacated table. Outside, there was no sign of them.

A young hostess tapped Henry's shoulder.

"Did we forget something?" the girl said.

"Did we?" said Henry.

The hostess laughed. "We aren't a food kitchen, handsome."

"Oh, yeah. Sorry."

Henry dug out a hundred-dollar bill, absently passed it over to her, and peered up and down the deserted street.

When he turned back, the hostess stood beaming at him.

"What?" he said.

She fluttered the hundred at him.

"We're halfway there," she said.

"For shrimp and hot sauce?"

The hostess, whose expression remained radiant, escorted him back inside to the cash register, where their transaction was completed.

"If you'd like," she said, "our sauce is on sale by the bottle."

"I'm afraid to ask how much."

"The price, you mean?"

"Yeah," said Henry. "And what'll I do with hot sauce?"

"Put it on me," she said.

Randy was at the wheel of his Cutlass, thumb driving, Cyrus and Carl in the backseat, Carl with his hoe, Toby about a quarter mile behind in his black-and-white, clocking Randy's speed to make sure nobody got arrested on the way to rob Community National up in Fulda.

They were closing in on Stockton now, doing a smooth seventy, and Randy was asking Cyrus how they'd tracked him to the Days Inn, which seemed like a magic trick, like a mind-reading act, and Cyrus was being coy, asking Randy if he'd ever heard about these inventions called cell phones, and Randy said, "Sure as heck have."

There was some silence in the backseat.

"These new inventions," Carl said, "all you do is, you push some buttons and talk into it, like with a walkie-talkie, and somebody says, 'Days Inn,' and you say, 'Hi, Days Inn,' and pretty soon you find out there's this rodeo nincompoop named Zapf on the register."

"Huh," said Randy. "That's slick."

Five or ten more miles down the road, Randy said, "So you figured me for a Days Inn man?"

"Mostly what we did," said Cyrus, "is we figured you for a half-wit."

"That so?" Randy said.

"A dipstick," Carl said, "who'd register under his real name."

"That so?" Randy said again, keeping it friendly, along the lines of Val Kilmer, a guy who takes shit for a while and then sort of smiles and shoves a pool cue through somebody's ears. Fact was, Randy was getting fed up with these two parasites in the backseat. No respect at all. Thinking they could outbadass him. Just a half hour ago, they'd been dissing his thumb-driving style, Carl calling it sissy driving, Cyrus laughing in that deep-throated way of his, like Uncle Remus or somebody, like he was smarter and tougher and a better all-around criminal than anybody else. It was an attitude issue, Randy thought, and it would be a cold day in Oregon if anybody outcriminalized or out–thumb drove Randy Zapf. "So, Carl, I've been wondering," he said after another mile or two, "what's up with the hoe? Bet there's a story there."

"No story," Carl said.

"Bet there's a garden story."

"There ain't. Found it outside the Super 8, just lying there, figured it was my destiny."

"Gotcha. Destiny, man. And I guess that means you're gonna rob a bank with a hoe?"

In the rearview mirror Randy watched Carl turn and look at Cyrus for a second.

"If you want to pull over," Carl said, "I'll show you what the hoe's for."

"Just sayin'," said Randy.

"Cut the crap," said Cyrus. "Unless you want—"

"No, man, it might be cool. Stroll real scarylike into a bank, and say, 'Stick 'em up,' then show everybody your hoe and watch all the freaked-out faces. Know what I'm sayin'?"

"Pull over," Carl said.

Randy shrugged and said, "Later, maybe."

Past Stockton, pushing the needle up to seventy-five, Randy put his mind to how he'd wiggle out of pulling an actual bank job, which wasn't his specialty and which could lead to problems down the line. Main thing, he thought, was to lose Carl and Cyrus, permanently this time, but the more he chewed on it, the more impossible it seemed. They were on him like . . . well, like underwear, come to think of it. He moved, they moved. An hour ago, when he'd stopped for gas, Carl had tailed him with his hoe all the way to the men's room, then all the way to the checkout counter, just sort of helicoptering there while Randy paid for the gas and a few minipacks of Cheetos and some pretty fair beef jerky, then all the way back to the Cutlass. What it was, Randy thought, it was privacy invasion. And who needed help robbing a bank that didn't mind getting robbed?

Twenty miles later, with Sacramento dead ahead, Randy was at the bottom of the idea barrel, getting frustrated, imagining how he'd install one of those backseats where you push an eject button and a couple of prison flunkies go airborne.

He glanced in the rearview mirror.

Behind him, there was nothing but Toby's squad car. The

road ahead twisted through shaggy, deserted, rolling grassland—no farms, no traffic.

A lock clicked open in Randy's head. He could've slapped himself. So simple it had been staring at him for two hundred miles.

He tapped the accelerator, pinned the needle on max.

In the backseat, Cyrus said, "Whoa."

Carl said, "Slow down, pinhead, or I'll stick you in a pretzel bag."

Randy jammed the Cutlass down a sharp descending curve—excellent velocity, he thought—then braked hard, pulled off the road, threw the car into reverse, and backed into a clump of high brush and orphan pines. Toby's black-and-white peeled by doing a hundred easy.

"What the fuck?" Cyrus said.

Randy hopped out, opened Carl's back door, grabbed the hoe, and gave the scrawny old-timer a good fast hoeing.

One, Mississippi, two, Mississippi.

A little giggly, a little amazed, Randy rolled across the trunk and was there waiting when Cyrus's door swung open. Cyrus was big and strong, so Randy had to hoe him up to twelve Mississippi, face mostly, a bunch of other places.

He crossed back to Carl, who wasn't in good shape, and gave him more garden work until the screeching stopped, then he trotted back to Cyrus and did another five or ten Mississippis to make sure. He dragged Cyrus into the brush, dumped Carl alongside his buddy, and took a breather.

The day was mild and quiet. There was a nice breeze. Weird, Randy thought, how good ideas just come to you.

He looked down at Carl and said, "You're dead, Carl."

He looked at Cyrus and said, "You're deader."

Weird, he kept thinking.

He stashed the hoe in his trunk, remounted the Cutlass, bumped back onto the highway, and floored it north toward Fulda.

He opened up a pack of Cheetos.

Okay, he thought. Maybe I can't stay on a bronc all that long, and maybe my girl's messing with me, but, man oh man, I can hoe the hell out of things. Yes, sir. And I wonder who's in the pretzel bag. Just sayin'.

21

"WE'VE DISCUSSED CORPORATE VERTICALITY," JIM Dooney told Calvin, "but if you want to understand our current problem—what we'll call the Halverson problem—you need to grasp a few other concepts."

Calvin sighed. "Jimmy, can't we skip the MBA degree? All I care about is keeping you alive."

"Pacific Ships and Shipping," Dooney went on crisply, "is also organized on a horizontal axis, meaning that our holdings go way beyond ships and shipping. Candy, for instance. We make candy, lots of it. Parachutes, for another instance. Paint. Indoor-outdoor carpeting. Recording studios—six of them. Cigarette lighters. Blood monitors. A baseball team. Temptation handguns. Artillery pieces. Toasters. Machine guns. Twist ties. Would you care for a hit? Don't sneeze."

Calvin bent down, pinched a nostril, inhaled through his embossed glass straw, and waited a few moments before saying, "How long is this list, Jimmy?"

"Long," said Dooney.

"Is there a point to it all?"

"There surely is a point."

Dooney used his thumb to squash a trespassing ladybug, then gazed out at his four hundred acres of lakeside property, a property that encompassed many thousand birch and maples and conifers, many thousand species of northern flora and fauna, and many trillion flesh-eating flies. At the moment, seated inside a double-screened gazebo, Dooney and Calvin were enjoying the outdoors without hazarding the actual outdoors.

"Now, what the horizontal axis does," Dooney said. "It hedges, it diversifies, it protects the core business—in our case, ships and shipping—protects us against the downturns, spreads out risk. Take Amazon, for example. Vertical and horizontal, right? Started out as a book peddler. Core business. Then goes vertical, begins publishing and manufacturing the very same product they're peddling—books, that is—then they scoop up Audible, another kind of publisher, but at the same time they're going horizontal, understand? A movie studio to make the movies they're streaming. Before you know it, they're selling everything there is to sell—forget books—they're selling applesauce, they're selling birthday candles, they're selling scissors and water fountains—this is horizontal gone infinite, Cal—and here's the nifty thing, the whole time they're also going vertical, trucks and hybrids to *deliver* the horizontal stuff, distribution centers the size of Delaware, their own postal codes. And if you think—"

"A question," Calvin said, and raised his hand.

"Yes?"

"Where do you think this coke comes from?"

Dooney frowned. "Amazon? You're kidding?"

"Well, not Amazon exactly. One of their delivery guys."

"Wow," Dooney said.

"So why are you criticizing Amazon?"

"Who's criticizing? I'm on my feet, for Chrissake. I'm yelling encore. Talk about horizontal."

"Okay," Calvin said. "But I still don't see—"

"I'm *getting* there!"

"Please don't snap at me, Jimmy."

"I wasn't snapping, I was excited, I was . . . All right, sorry."

"That's better."

"One last hit?"

"Just one," said Calvin. "But make it a foot long."

At that instant a breeze came up, threatening their woodsy fun; together they rigged a little tent over the picnic table. As Calvin broke out a fresh pack of blades, Dooney said, "If you want, I can wait on explaining all this. I mean, you keep asking about Halverson, so I thought . . ."

"Go ahead," Calvin said, "but maybe—just a suggestion—maybe we should call it quits with the coke. I've got some nice, up-to-date oxy in my shaving kit." He reached out and wiped Dooney's nose. "It's your birthday, you're seventy-five—branch out!"

Dooney shook his head, took a hit, and said, "So where was I? Adam Smith had it dead wrong. You want competition, play lacrosse. Play . . . What's the most popular board game in America?"

"Monopoly," Calvin said.

"Bet your sweet tush. Monopoly. USA game of choice. Monopoly's what keeps families together all night: setting up hotels, everybody screwing everybody else, Mom screwing little Sis, Pa screwing Uncle George. You ever see any antitrust squares on a Monopoly board? You see any Monopoly politicians bellyaching about one guy having too many houses, too many hotels, too many railroads? You ever draw a Chance card that says, 'Go to Jail, You've Got a Monopoly'? A Community

Chest card that says, 'Fuck You, You're Anticompetitive'? We're talking about the American pastime here, we're not—"

"I love you," Calvin said, "when you get passionate."

"I love me like that, too," said Dooney, and for a moment he sank into remembrance. "No joke, Cal, I was one fine CEO. Best of the best of the best. Truth is, I should never have retired, never passed the money torch to that cost-cutting, no-imagination, no-ambition son-in-law of mine. Far as I'm concerned, the man should still be making candy."

"Junius? I thought you handpicked him?"

"Oh, yeah, I did. Handpicked him for Evelyn, too."

"Jimmy?"

"Huh?"

"Do I have a face?"

"You do, my love, and a pretty one. Should I go on?"

"Of course you should," said Calvin. "But I need to mention something. At our age—and don't take this the wrong way—at our age I'm not sure this birthday party of ours is medically advised."

"Could be," said Dooney. "How old are you again?"

"Sixty-nine," Calvin said.

"*How* old?"

"Seventy-one."

"Cal."

"Seventy-two," said Calvin. "Stop me when you're convinced."

Dooney laughed, did a line, held his breath briefly, expelled it, and said, "Sixty-nine convinced me. You don't look a day older."

They kissed.

"Okay," Dooney said. "Now pay attention. Evil number one, competition. Evil number two, government. So let's say you're a respectable, all-American robber baron; you're sick and tired of all the save-the-water, save-the-whatever EPA types, IRS types, SEC types, DNC types, name your traitor. How can you be a robber baron if you can't rob anybody?"

"Got me," said Cal. "Retire?"

"Uh-uh," said Dooney. "Think vertical. If you're fed up with government, you hike up your trousers and throw your hat in the ring. You *become* the government. You go vertical. You install yourself right up there at the tippy-top of the pyramid. Corporations, Cal—they're *people*. Law of the land. Therefore you nominate your corporation for president of the United Capitalist States of America, that's what you do, you do an acquisition, you buy a subsidiary called the presidency, you install yourself as commander in chief—you install Amazon, you install PS&S and yours truly—because PS&S is a living, breathing, bona fide human being just like you and me and Jeff Bezos—human rights, legal rights—and, bingo, the IRS is your errand boy, the SEC is your own personal masseuse, the EPA is the groundskeeper on that golf course of yours down in Florida, and, hey, if you catch any flack, tough shit, you fire the whistleblower and hire somebody with the sense to do exactly what you want, what PS&S wants, what Amazon and the USA want. You make this country great again. Because you *are* this country. Because you *are* great. And if anybody thinks you're not, fair enough, you buy yourself another subsidiary, you buy a Congress, so then it's *your* Congress, the PS&S Congress, and you scare the shit out of anybody who thinks differently. That's vertical. That's king of the Monopoly board. That's queen of Sheba. That's why the Pilgrims showed up."

"Jimmy?" said Calvin.

"What?"

"Why does Halverson want to kill you?"

Dooney's heart was racing.

"Brass tacks?" he said. "I acquired a newspaper. Went horizontal—the L.A. *Trib*. Halverson's newspaper."

"Newspapers leak money, I thought."

Dooney nodded. "Like a colander, you're right. But imagine your daughter is married to a go-getter *Trib* fake-newshound. And then imagine that this go-getter fake-newshound hears some crap he shouldn't hear—like a couple of ships sinking, cheap steel, no inspections—and imagine that he plans to plaster that same semi-illegal crap across the front page. Imagine you don't want to end up like Bernie Madoff, eating SpaghettiOs and staring at concrete."

"Uh-oh," Calvin said. "You stretched the rules?"

"No, sir. I *made* the rules. I mean, if Congress can't understand what 'business friendly' means, you pass a few laws of your own. Ollie North's kind of laws. Sell a few machine guns, sell some nerve gas, sell a few artillery pieces. What's the harm in that?"

"I don't know," said Calvin. "Jail?"

"Right. Except for that. Excuse me a moment."

Dooney's blood was boiling. He knocked back half a line.

"Okay," he went on. "So I had to deal with Halverson—he's the fake-newshound, right?—and step number one was pretty obvious. Go horizontal, buy his fleabag newspaper, deep-six a few editors, hire my own, just like Rupert. Temporarily, at least, that solves the problem. No headlines. But I've still got Halverson on my hands. He wants his Pulitzer. He's out there raising hell, claiming censorship bullshit, all that, so of course

I had to take step number two. Got a few dozen PS&S lawyers on the case. They dig around, do background checks, hand me a Halverson file two inches thick. Presto, I've got my own front-page scandal, only this time it's Mr. Fake-Newshound who's in deep doo-doo."

"Fight crap with crap?" Calvin asked.

"Bingo. Well said. Only difference, the Halverson crap is *unfake* crap; it's *real* crap, the kind that makes me look like Our Lady of Saints."

"Was he gay?"

Dooney scowled and said, "Don't get cute, Cal."

"Just teasing. What did the guy do?"

"What didn't he do?" said Dooney. "Padded résumé, we'll start there. And by 'padded,' I mean *everything*. Weight, height, date of birth. Exeter? Nope. Princeton? Nope. Polo team? Nope. Summa cum laude? Nope. U.S. Army? Nope. Kuwait, Iraq, Afghanistan? Nope, nope, nope. Purple Heart? Nope. Silver Star? Nope. Letters of recommendation? Four of them: Rosemary Clooney, Robert Stack, Pat Hitchcock, Cecil B. DeMille. Forgeries, of course. You think I'm kidding? I am not. This weasel makes Pinocchio look like a pug-nosed beginner."

"Who's Pat Hitchcock?" Calvin asked.

"Take a guess."

For several moments, Calvin fell silent as he contemplated the big blue lake, the dusty picnic table before him, and finally Jim Dooney, whose nose was trickling blood. "Well, then," he said at last. "I imagine you dropped this research on him? Showed him a credibility problem?"

"No, I dropped it on Evelyn," said Dooney. "She married the liar, I didn't."

"And the Pulitzer?"

"I might've said a word to my *Trib* editors. Halverson ended up selling sweaters."

"Happy birthday," said Calvin.

"Thank you," Dooney said, "but I believe it's yours."

22

WHEN EVELYN THOUGHT ABOUT JAKARTA, SHE AL-most always thought first about LAX: the crowded, steamy-hot gate area, the delayed flight, and how at one point she had taken notice of a slim, mop-haired, youthful-looking man pecking away at his laptop, how completely inside himself the man was, as if he were alone on the moon, as if he were locked in a closet. How his lips moved as he typed. How he'd occasionally glance at his wristwatch and frown and then slide back inside himself.

When she thought about Jakarta, she then thought about a heart-skipping moment when she'd settled into seat 3-A next to the mop-haired man in 3-B.

She was twenty-six then.

She was expecting miracles.

They had chatted off and on during the long flight to Tokyo. And then later, on the flight to Jakarta, she had exchanged seats with another passenger so as to continue chatting.

Now, when those first thrilling weeks came to mind, Evelyn sometimes allowed herself to feel the vague aftersensations of what had once been love, its flavor on her tongue, its touch against her skin, its ferocious, almost painful voltage sizzling not only through her bones but through the inanimate objects all around her, through the pavement of a city that was new to her, through the pushcarts heaped with banana leaves, through the fish stalls and silk *kebayas* and black-felt *pecis*, through diesel fumes and blaring horns, and, of course, through those bluish evenings when she and Boyd sampled octopus in the Pasar Baru or walked to his apartment on the waterfront.

It was not, for Evelyn, a first love. It was a third or fourth. At Deerfield there had been Anders, the shy German boy, and at Stanford there had been Bobby and then Phillip, both talented with a tennis racket, both too smugly handsome for their own well-being, and later there had been the physicist, another Phillip, a maybe love. But never had there been the tingling, terrified feel of forever love, the elevation and the transport, that Boyd had delivered to her in Jakarta. Until then, her life had been . . . she didn't have words for it . . . Securely pleasant. Pleasantly dull. Not that she had suffered in the least. Evelyn had pedigree, privilege, beauty, and enough money that money was meaningless—Dooney had seen to that. Back then, in those early days, Boyd used to call her his Audrey Hepburn, his Kim Novak. At times this had alarmed her. But more often she'd been comforted by the certainty that Boyd found their love as magical as she did, like the love in those fading old movies he admired.

And so now, when she daydreamed, Evelyn dreamed two dreams simultaneously, the dream of how things had seemed and the dream of how things were. One was a fairy tale; the other was not. "If it sounds true," Boyd used to say, "it *is* true." Either way, Jakarta had seemed and sounded and felt electric.

He had proposed swiftly. Evelyn had accepted two months later, after convincing Dooney he had no choice but to accede.

The wedding itself—a welter of executive charm and blue business suits—took place in the seventeenth-floor lobby of the PS&S East Asian headquarters in Sudirman Central. For Evelyn, the sterile, high-finance wedding had been a concession, a necessary bruise on the fairy tale. For Dooney, it had been an occasion ripe for horse trading. And for Boyd, it had been a wide-screen triumph, a Charlton Heston moment, a spectacle for which he had been rehearsing since his days as a Santa Monica paperboy.

They had honeymooned on Borneo.

Afterward they had moved into Dooney's wedding gift, eleven rooms of Franco-Indonesian luxury that had once housed Suharto's third oil minister.

There, on the floor of their drawing room, scrawling thank-you notes, they had opened another of Dooney's wedding gifts, this one a .38-caliber handgun that had been manufactured in Lowell, Massachusetts, by Dooney's Temptation Munitions subsidiary and that bore the engraved legend: TO MY SON-IN-LAW, SHOULD HE FUCK AROUND ON MY DAUGHTER.

Boyd had chuckled. Evelyn had not spoken to her father for a month afterward.

But faithfulness was never the issue.

Or, more exactly, romantic faithfulness was never the issue.

The issue was ambition—insatiable and compulsive ambition—a quality that for the first year or so had seemed to her almost endearing: another reason to adore her hardworking, laptop-pecking ex-newsboy. The fun times were splendid, yes, but slowly at first, then rapidly, Boyd's betrothal to the journalistic big leagues began to draw him quite literally away from her—always packing for six days in Hanoi, four days in Bangkok, two weeks in Taipei. Like newspapers everywhere, the *Trib* had cut back on its independent foreign coverage, closing bureaus in Hong Kong, Manila, and Singapore, relying for its breaking news on the AP and a network of part-time stringers, and so it happened that at age thirty-two Boyd became the paper's one and only Pacific Basin correspondent. There was pressure to produce; the workload was crushing: typhoons on Bali, insurgencies on Mindanao, decaying coral reefs, sexual slavery, economic slavery, the rise of Islamic fundamentalism, power grabs in Kuala Lumpur, the transfer of sovereignty in Hong Kong, crop failures in the Mekong Delta, poverty abutting riches, centuries of exploitation, oligarchs and coups and autocrats and terrorists and gold-braided military strongmen puffing out their chests inside fortified palaces.

A thousand *Trib* correspondents, even ten thousand, could not have covered the sheer scale and variety of it all. But Boyd thrived. More than thrived. He was making a name for himself. His earnest, long-winded think pieces, which sometimes substituted for actual reporting, kept him up late into the night. His unnamed sources began to outnumber those with names. Too often, their intimate evenings became obligatory evenings at the Merdeka Palace, or receptions at the U.S. embassy, or diplomatic cocktails in diplomatic ballrooms, where her teeth ached as Boyd exchanged confidences with an ambassador's deputy's deputy. Though way out of his depth, Boyd had cultivated a knowing, secretive, wise-man smile. And, of course, Boyd lied. He lied about big things and small things. He lied with humble, self-deprecating grace. He lied when there was no reason to lie. Oddly, it hadn't occurred to her that she might be the recipient of even bolder lies.

Did he love her? Yes, he did.

And she loved him.

Now, when she found herself contemplating those years, Evelyn was no longer shocked by Boyd's serial deceit or by her own naïveté. Both made sense to her. He had lied for love; she had believed for love. Crippling, yes. Corrosive, for sure. But no longer shocking. The opposite, in fact. Her mop-haired boy *was* a boy. An eight-year-old stunted by CinemaScope. A boy whose reflexes went instantly and automatically to the fantastic, to what should be but was not, to what he coveted but did not have, to a late-night movie version of happiness and aspiration, to a dead father who turned up alive and well, to a mother who dated Cesar Romero, to a pile of military medals he'd won the hard way—for gallantry in a pawn shop, for gallantry in his imagination, for the gallantry of a boy dreaming Burt Lancaster's heroic dreams. When Evelyn looked back on those early years, when she sometimes cried in the shower, she couldn't help wondering if Boyd's marriage to the daughter of a billionaire had somehow become one more notch on his belt of golden fantasies.

In a way, of course, she had blinded herself to the obvious, pretending she was immune to deceit, vaccinated by romance, imagining that she had access to the real Boyd Halverson, the true Boyd Halverson, the man, not the insecure little boy. Part of her blindness, perhaps, could be chalked up to the smooth surface of their lives. No confrontations, no slammed doors. True, Boyd traveled constantly, and true, he was sometimes moody, sometimes distracted by his precious byline. But they were adults and they had obligations, and it seemed unfair to cast blame on him for simply doing his job and doing it well. On top of that, she'd had her own distractions, teaching algebra to rich Catholic girls, a job Dooney had arranged after her breakup with Phillip the physicist. Algebra was hardly her obsession, and teaching held little appeal, but it beat the hell out of physics, and the prospect of Jakarta had seemed exciting to a superbly educated, overindulged young woman with time on her hands.

And it *was* exciting.

That was what now made the sadness so sad.

She'd been married to a man she loved—it was intoxicating. It was rocketry. It was coming home from a day of algebra, a day of rich, bored Catholic girls, and seeing Boyd look up from his laptop and smile at her almost shyly, almost embarrassed by his own rocketry. It was how, after some stiff diplomatic party, they would change into jeans and T-shirts, and walk the eight blocks to a little family-run *warung*, where they would eat bowls of rice and spicy vegetables and breathe the diesel fumes and watch the nighttime bustle and banalities of people doing more or less what people everywhere were doing. It was getting pregnant. It was giving birth. It was Boyd on the parquet floor of their bedroom wrestling with a diaper and a two-month-old boy they called Teddy, named ridiculously for the fluffy blue teddy bear the boy clutched in his sleep.

That, too, was what made the sadness so excruciating on the morning when Dooney dropped a thick dossier on her kitchen table. "I'd like to introduce you," he said, "to your husband."

23

HENRY SPECK WAS ON THE PHONE WITH JUNIUS, explaining how close he had come, how he'd missed them by only a minute or two, but how, no problem, he'd done his leg-work. Halverson and Bing were driving an old neon-orange Eldorado, property of Halverson's deceased mother. According to the Port Aransas postmaster, it was a pretty sure bet they were headed north toward Minnesota.

"Wherever Minnesota is," Henry said. "You want me to quit or keep going?"

In the background there was a clatter of sound Henry couldn't place. Loudspeakers maybe. Then the national anthem.

"Keep going," said Junius. "And don't call again until it's good news. I got baseball to play."

"Sir?"

"Me against the Phillies."

"You?" said Henry.

"Look, I gotta run, but those expenses you phoned in—what's with the hot sauce?"

"Oh, right," Henry said.

"Eight bottles?"

"Terrific discount, sir."

Junius grunted. "Okay, hot sauce, but pay for it on your own dime. Right now I own a baseball team that couldn't . . . couldn't beat itself, not to mention a wife crying in the shower every night. Minnesota, Montana, I don't give a shit. Find Halverson. Make sure he's on disability and stays that way."

"Will do," said Henry. "Lots of luck with those Phillies."

"Yeah," said Junius. "Could be a long game."

In Corpus Christi, Boyd traded in the Eldorado for a second-hand 2001 Pleasure-Way camper van, plus twenty-six thousand in cash, a transaction that ate up almost half of Community National's remaining money.

Around ten that evening, they pulled into an RV park off I-37. Angie helped him put up the awning, connect the electricity, fill the water tank, and prepare a light supper of baked beans and sausages. Later, sitting in the dark beneath their awning, Angie said, "I feel like we're an old married couple, don't you? Off on a big adventure, seeing the country, just you and me and nobody else. No itinerary either. Go where we want, stop where we want. That's what RVs are for. That's the American dream for an old married couple like us, even if you're the only old one. You're pretty lucky I'm Angie Bing. Not an ageist, I mean—*ageist*, that's one of the words in my self-improvement program. An ageist is somebody who discriminates against feeble, gray-haired people like you—but I barely even notice except when you start yawning like that. And by the way, it's hard to get pregnant when people don't even sleep together. I figure, well, you're probably old-fashioned when it comes to making babies. Problem is, I don't know any other way to do it. So maybe we should get you some vitamin D and a big fat jar of mushroom extract, which does wonders with things like sperm count and complexion. My dad actually farmed mushrooms—did I ever tell you that? Mushrooms and spinach, that's why I've got this perfect complexion. When I was a little girl, there was a kind of woodsy, shady area out behind our trailer, ideal for mushrooms and spinach, so I guess it wasn't really a farm, more like somebody else's woods, but my dad called it his farm, at least until he got busted for a certain mushroom he specialized in—you know what I mean, right?—the one that gets you closer to God. He was a Shaker then, my dad was. He was Pentecostal, too, but a Shaker-Pentecostal, the kind they have in Idaho, which meant you don't pay income taxes and you stockpile canned goods for the end of the world and you carry around laundry detergent in case somebody accidentally cusses. The important thing, though, is salvation. And that's what's going on here, right? I'm saving you. Right now, just sitting here, you're not shooting anybody, you're not sticking up banks, and you've got your own little house on wheels and you've got a supercute fiancée and, believe it or not, things aren't even half as bad as they used to be back when you first kidnapped me. You know what the word *soteriology* means?"

Boyd started to say yes, more or less, but Angie had already refilled her lungs.

"It's the whole doctrine of salvation," she said, her voice sliding into whispery diminuendo. "Or all the different doctrines. Like how sometimes you have to hit rock bottom before you can even think about getting saved. That's where I figure in. I mean, what if somebody *else* had been at the teller cage that morning? What if you were stuck with a Lutheran or a Methodist? You'd be up a creek right now. Rock bottom, Boyd, that's exactly where you were, but now you're sitting here under the stars—God's stars—and you're not even drinking, and you don't have to tie me up or anything because I'm not going anywhere, I'm barely even kidnapped now, I'm your miracle, I'm that bright silver light Saul saw when he was at rock bottom on the road to Damascus and, boy, did you get lucky. And you know something else? What salvation really means is you just sort of surrender. It's not all that complicated. You take a nice deep breath and say, 'All right, Angie, let's make a few babies. Let's get in our RV and go see the Grand Canyon and wipe the fingerprints off that stupid gun and throw it about a mile down into the river,' then we drive up to Vegas and get married in one of those romantic chapels where anybody's welcome, even atheists like you. I'll tell you a secret, Boyd. Even atheists help old ladies across the road. It's the Boy Scouts you can't trust. And the Methodists, and the Lutherans and Catholics. For example, my dad didn't know the first thing about Shakers, he just shook a lot, but I guess that's all he *had* to know, because when you're shaking, you're sort of cleaning yourself—like with a dog, you know?—you're shaking off all the bad stuff, you're shaking off your sins and your mistakes, you're shaking off FBI agents trying to take away your mushrooms and your basic human right to throw staplers at your kids if you want. See what I'm saying, Boyd? Surrender. Shake it all off. Get clean. Hey, where you going?"

By noon the next day, they had picked up I-35 outside San Antonio. The Pleasure-Way balked at speeds over fifty-three miles an hour, and as they lumbered north toward Waco, Boyd regretted agreeing to Angie's idea about trading in the Eldorado.

They spent the night in a grassy pasture outside Denton.

In the morning, rolling toward Oklahoma, Angie elaborated on Boyd's good fortune, pointing out that he might be the only bank robber in world history not to have the police on his trail; in fact the only bank robber who never even robbed a bank, at least not officially. Later, two hundred miles up the road, just south of Stillwater, she had looped back to the theme of salvation, which fed without a hiccup into a discussion of her addiction to bubble gum back in middle school and how the only way to save herself was to spend forty days and forty nights out in the woods behind her trailer, except it was forty minutes, because numbers weren't the issue, the issue was commitment to your own salvation.

"*Pertinacity,*" she said, as they dined in a Wendy's that evening, "that's another really good self-improvement word."

"Yes," said Boyd. "I know that one."

"Well, knowing it and doing it are two different things. You can know you should stop chewing bubble gum, but then you actually have to stop." She looked at him with radiant expectation. "Don't be a glum-bum. Salvation's sitting right across the table from you."

Through the flatlands of Oklahoma and Kansas, Angie kept talking, her voice gliding up and down the scales of rhetorical musicality. She recounted her embarrassing brush with child welfare services, her family's eviction from two different trailer parks, her determination to make something of herself, her irreducible belief in the divinity of all things animate—which included water and fire and Boyd Halverson—her faith in some indeterminate but glorious future, her on-and-off relationship with Randy Zapf, who plied her with stolen stereos, who defended her honor in pool halls against sharpies and defilers, and who may not, in all likelihood, take it too well once she was pregnant and happily married to an old man.

"I'm fifty-three," Boyd said. "I'm not an old man."

"Wow," said Angie. "You *said* something."

"And I'm not married."

"Yeah?" she said. "Not yet."

Midway between Wichita and the Iowa-Missouri border, Angie's voice at last sputtered and died away. She crawled into the back of the Pleasure-Way and slept for seven silent hours, not awakening until they approached the Minnesota state line a few miles south of Albert Lea.

Five hours later, when they stopped for the night outside the resort town of Brainerd, Minnesota, Angie had nearly wrapped up Boyd's psychological profile. "The upshot," she was saying as they hooked up the RV's electricity, "is you need to change pretty much everything about yourself. Start by telling the truth. Start showing me some personal attention, like asking what I want for my birthday in a few days, which I've already mentioned about a thousand times. Seriously, turning thirty's a big deal, Boyd, and you should be dropping hints about engagement rings, what size I wear, do I want it inscribed, that sort of thing. And you should start calling me stuff like 'honey' or 'sweetheart' or 'baby,' not just saying, 'Pass the mustard,' and not even saying please, not even half polite like any other fiancé on the whole planet. And, by the way, you should forget this vendetta of yours, whatever the heck it is—this Dooney thing, which I still don't understand—because it's totally unhealthy and totally selfish. What if I did that? What if I started chasing some ex-boyfriend all over God's creation? How would you like *that*? Not much, I bet. I bet you'd tie me up again, or make me get down on my knees and beg for forgiveness, something like that, because you'd be so jealous you couldn't even stand it. And if you really want to know, I think we should probably do our honeymoon somewhere special, probably Niagara Falls, or else Paris, which would be a good place to practice some French words I know, like, for example, *amour* and *enceinte* and *framboises* and *entrée* and *salut* and *fromage* and *courtesan* and *bon vivant* and *cher*, and a bunch of other ones. Did you ever see that movie *Gigi*? It's a super-super old one, so you probably saw it about a hundred years ago. Anyway, there's this girl, Gigi, who's a lot like me, nice and slender like a ballerina, with this cute little nose that turns up at the tip, and she's really pretty, really sweet, except everybody treats her like dirt, like she can only be somebody's mistress, but then finally she wins the heart of this older gentleman, this *bon vivant* Gaston, because Gigi is just so awesome and so beautiful he can't resist. I guess you see the similarities, right? At the end, this old French guy sings 'Thank Heaven for Little Girls,' which is exactly what you should be singing right this minute. I can teach you the words if you want. But the point is . . . Boyd, are you even listening?"

"No," he said.

"How can you say no if you didn't hear what I just said?"

"Got me," Boyd said. "No covers everything."

Angie looked at him grimly. "Well, mister, there's one more example of your personality problems."

They bought groceries at a mini-mart on the RV campground, battled flies for the rights to their undercooked hamburgers, then sealed themselves inside the Pleasure-Way for the night.

In the morning, well before sunrise, Boyd got dressed and walked down to the shoreline of a little lake at the foot of the RV park. There was the chill of early autumn in the air. For several minutes, he stood listening to the rustlings and stirrings of dawn, thinking of the day to come, partly fearful, partly full of promise. Bemidji was only a couple of hours up the road.

Boyd pulled the Temptation from his pocket, looked at it for a few seconds, then test-fired it in the direction of what he took to be a bird of some sort, possibly a loon, bobbing twenty yards offshore. The handgun worked fine. He had four remaining bullets—three too many.

Toby Van Der Kellen, Lois Cutterby, and Douglas Cutterby sat uncomfortably in Toby's squad car outside the Fulda PD building on North Spruce Street. Lois was scowling, Douglas was beaming, and Toby didn't know what to think. On the one hand, he'd explained why he was back in town, how he'd lost his one and only lead on tracing Halverson, but how he'd already ordered up cell phone pings. Give it twenty-four hours, he'd said, and Halverson was dead meat.

On the other hand, Lois was busy unloading on him about sloppy cop work.

"In a nutshell," she was grousing, "you let an airhead dweeb with an IQ of four outsmart you. Do I have that right? You were on his tail and then he's gone?"

"Sort of," Toby said. "But I wouldn't call it outsmarting."

"What would you call it?" asked Lois.

"Luck," said Toby. "Bad for me, good for Zapf."

Douglas kept beaming in the backseat. Lois, who sat up front beside Toby, wagged her head.

"You're a cop," she said spitefully. "That's your job, right? You find people and intimidate them. Isn't that what you get paid for?"

"Sweetheart," Douglas murmured. "Be nice."

Toby squirmed. He didn't care for the way Douglas beamed at him.

"What I don't understand," Lois went on, "is how it happened. You drive seven hundred miles, you track down this Randy bozo, then you drive all the way back here. I don't get it."

"I told you already," Toby said.

"Told me what?"

"You know—I was tailing my contact, the cowboy; I figured he'd lead me to the Bing woman, which would lead me to Halverson. Basic police stuff. If you want your eighty-one thou back, you're gonna have to be patient."

Toby paused there, thinking it would be best not to mention rerobbing Community National.

For a few moments, no one spoke.

"If you don't mind," Douglas finally said from the backseat, "I have a question."

"Sure," said Toby.

"How much is Lois paying you to sort out our difficulties?"

"Not enough by half," said Toby.

"And that would be how much exactly?"

Toby glanced over at Lois.

"How much you paying me?" he said, keeping it flat and straight. "I forget."

Lois glared at him and said, "More than you're worth."

Douglas said, "My, my," and kept beaming. After a second, he chuckled, and said, "We're all adults here. Let's settle on a good wage. What would you suggest, my pumpkin?"

"Don't know," Lois said.

"Well then," Douglas chirped jovially, "let me propose a month's cop salary. Plus expenses, obviously. Plus maybe seven or eight wife bangs. Would that satisfy everyone?"

"Okay by me," Toby said.

"Darling?" said Douglas.

Lois said nothing.

Douglas let out a hearty laugh. "No dissenting votes! Therefore onward and upward. Officer Van Der Kellen—may I call you Hubcap?—will proceed as planned. Ping cell phones, locate

our missing funds, get a John Hancock on those loan documents, then chastise the thieves. Sound good?"

"Screw you, too," said Lois.

"Wonderful," said Douglas.

Toby raised a hand.

"Hubcap?" he said. "What's *that* mean?"

Douglas winked cheerfully and said, "An affectionate nickname."

"You saying I swipe hubcaps?"

"Well, I suppose I am, but we're brothers in crime, are we
not?" Douglas winked at Lois. "Brothers and sisters, I should
say."

Douglas stepped out of the squad car. He was a tall, over-
weight man, a former athlete who had executed his last sit-up
in the previous century.

He moved to Toby's open window and leaned down.

"You two bangers have fun," he said.

"Thanks," said Toby.

"My pleasure," said Douglas. "We'll tally it up as an advance
on wages."

Buttoning his suit coat, Douglas strode like a country squire
up North Spruce, humming to himself, nodding at passersby.

Lois watched him for a few thoughtful seconds.

"If I were you," she told Toby, "I'd watch my step. That man's
dangerous."

"Doug?"

"Yes, Doug."

"What about you?"

"Me?" Lois said. "I'm the snake in Doug's dreams."

24

JUNIUS KIRAKOSSIAN COULD NOT REMEMBER A MORE thrilling few hours in his long and not so memorable life. He had lost to the Phillies 43–zip in a game that had been called after not quite half an inning. But the fans had been with him from his first two-hop pitch. Even now, gliding home toward Bel Air in his chauffeured Bentley, Junius was shivering with excitement, reliving his first miraculous putout after two hours and twenty minutes.

It was true, he thought, that the million-dollar fine stung a little. And there was a better than even chance he'd end up barred from baseball, probably forced to unload the team. All the same, what a magnificent career-ender for a sixty-three-year-old ex-candymaker from Toledo, and what a life lesson for those overpaid, undertalented losers who had to sit on the bench and endure what he had been enduring for nine excruciating years.

Next to him, even Evelyn seemed elated.

"You know," Junius was telling her, "when your dad first offered me this crummy job, I almost turned him down flat, almost said, 'Thank you, sir, but I'll stick to candy, who needs shipyards and swivel chairs?' But tonight . . . Me against the Phillies! Like Steinbrenner taking on the Sox, Autry tackling the Yanks. And you know what?"

"What?" Evelyn asked.

"It was fun."

"I'll bet it was." To her surprise, she reached out and took his hand and held it without letting go.

"Fun," Junius said. "It's underrated."

"Yes, it is," said Evelyn.

Junius laughed.

"I'll admit the game slowed down after a couple minutes. No catcher, I mean. Christ, I must've walked twenty miles tonight, mound to backstop, backstop to mound. What I should've done, I should've named myself visiting team. At least given myself a few whacks with the bat."

"Next time," said Evelyn.

For a while they watched nighttime L.A. pass by: Santa Monica, Westwood, then up into Bel Air.

Junius released her hand. He was a small, emaciated man, eighteen years Evelyn's senior. At times he could look dapper. Now he looked old.

"Couple things we need to clear up," he said, then hesitated. "I don't want to be nosy about this—we all deserve privacy—but that ex-husband of yours, the way he shows up after ten years." He hesitated again. "I hear you in the shower, Evelyn."

"You hear me?"

"I do. It's not crying. It's weeping."

Evelyn blew out a breath. She had guessed this might be coming.

"Correct, it's weeping all right," she said, "but not the way you're taking it."

"How am I taking it?"

"The wrong way. I spoke with Henry a few days ago. He paid me a visit. I know you've decided I'm still—what's the word?—still yearning for Boyd, still in love, still something, and I know you've sent your fixer, your Mr. Speck, to make Boyd disappear, make him lay off, whatever it is you've told him to do. But it's not Boyd I'm weeping over. It's not lost love or romance or anything of the sort."

"No?"

"Not even a little. Siccing your thug on Boyd won't stop what's happening in the shower."

"Henry visited you? When was this?"

"Doesn't matter—a few days ago—but I wish you'd call him off. All I want is peace. A nice, dull, rich-lady life."

"No hot sauce?"

"Hot sauce?"

"An expression."

Evelyn took his hand again, laced his fingers into hers. "Look, Junius," she said quietly. "These last eight or nine years together, you and me, I realize there hasn't been much in the way of fireworks. But haven't we been—you know—*content* in our own so-so way? We laugh, don't we? Like tonight: we *laughed*. We don't fight, we don't throw scenes. That's not so terrible, is it? I can't fake happy ever after."

"I know," Junius said.

"There's nothing wrong with peace, is there?"

"No. That's what Henry's for. Restore the peace."

"Will you call him off?"

"You want that?"

"Boyd's sick, Junius. A disease. He's not a threat."

"Well," he said, "if that's what you need."

"You're a good man."

"Am I?"

They pulled into their long semicircular driveway. It was

a little after two in the morning. Their driver, an elderly man named Russell, opened the Bentley's doors and escorted them up the white marble steps.

"If you don't mind my saying, sir," said the driver, "you made an old man happy tonight. Taking on the Phillies, sir, it's every kid's fantasy."

"That right?" said Junius.

"Not baseball necessarily—anything—amateurs taking on the hotshots. This whole drive tonight, I'm fantasizing I'm you."

Junius found himself giving Russell a hug. "Next game," he said, "it'll be me and you against the Yankees. You're my catcher."

"Yes, sir. We'll kick butt."

At 4:00 a.m. Henry Speck's cell phone buzzed.

"You see the game tonight?" Junius asked.

"Afraid not. You won, I hope?"

"Hell no I didn't win. What's wrong with you? Your boss plays the Phillies; you don't bother to tune in?"

"Sorry, sir." Henry pushed away the sauce-stained sheets and sat up against a sauce-stained pillow. "Early flight today. Bemidji, remember?"

"Yeah, I remember. Four items. Item one, don't go breaking Halverson's legs, I promised Evelyn. Fingers. Couple toes. Item two, if you come near my wife one more time, you'll be getting a visit from a guy just like you."

"All I did—"

"Item three, I want to see some pay stubs."

"Well, sir—"

"Item four. That airplane ride? Fly coach."

* * *

At 4:03 a.m. Jim Dooney's cell phone chimed. He picked up, listened to Evelyn for ten minutes, then shook Calvin awake. Forty-two minutes later they were in a cab headed for Bemidji Regional Airport.

By 4:20 a.m. Boyd had test-fired his Temptation .38 Special, given himself a sponge bath, and was now pouring his first mug of coffee of the day. He carried it outside along with an unbuttered bagel and sat beneath the Pleasure-Way's awning to watch the sun rise.

After a bit, Angie joined him. Neither of them had slept well, and for once Angie had little to say.

They hit the road just before 6:30 a.m., chuffing slowly up State Highway 371 toward Leech Lake, then connecting with U.S. Highway 2 into Bemidji. At the local post office, Boyd stayed in the camper while Angie went inside. Fifteen minutes ticked by before she emerged in the company of a tall, Nordic-looking young man of about twenty-five, lushly bearded, dressed for a Paul Bunyan festival. The guy's lumberjack looks were modulated by a street punk's saucy hairdo, a top knot holding aloft a pound or two of frosted Prince Valiant overgrowth.

The two of them stood talking outside the post office for a few minutes, then Angie led him over to the Pleasure-Way and rapped on Boyd's window.

"This is Alvin," she said, "and I just hired him. He's our guide. Alvin, this is my dad, but you can call him Boyd the way I do."

The man grinned and shook Boyd's hand through the open window.

"Pleasure," he said.

"Me, too, and I love the coif," said Boyd. "But listen, my daughter here—I forget the nice way to say this—she's erratic, a little nuts. We don't need any guides."

Angie shot him a glare.

"I'm not erratic, I'm *gifted*," she snapped. "And we *do* need a guide. The post office people, they won't give out addresses, like it's a crime or something. You can thank your lucky stars Alvin was right there. We got to flirting and he knows this whole area; he almost grew up here." She gave the lumberjack a swish of the eyelashes and turned back to Boyd. "So stop being an ungrateful, jealous juvenile and act your age . . . if you can even remember it. Alvin knows exactly where to find Dooney. Isn't that right, Alvin?"

"Not exactly," the young man said, his eyes roaming all over Angie. "But I've got some ideas."

"So, there you go, Dad," Angie said. "Now give Alvin four hundred dollars."

"Four hundred?"

Angie sighed. "That's for the whole day. In case we need to drive around a bunch, or in case we need more guiding tonight or tomorrow or next week."

"Did he bring pajamas?"

"Pay him."

Boyd unlocked the glove compartment, took out four of Community National's dwindling bills, and passed them through the window to Angie's lumberjack. The young man inspected the cash skeptically, then shrugged and gave Angie a wide, bushy smile. "Let's roll," he said.

Angie and Alvin climbed into the camper, sitting side by side on a fold-down bench behind Boyd. For well over an hour, they bumped up and down all four points of the compass, north for a time, then due west, then down a dirt road that eventually dead-ended against a wall of birch and pine. "Dooney, have I got that right?" Alvin was muttering. "Maybe I'm thinking of Donny or Danny or somebody. You're positive the name's Dooney?"

"Pretty positive," Boyd said. "Where's almost?"

"Sorry?"

"Angie said you almost grew up here. Where's almost?"

"Chicago, man. Tell you what, let's try our luck out by Turtle River, other side of Little Bass Lake."

By midafternoon they were back in Bemidji, refueling. Afterward, heading southeast toward Grace Lake, Boyd resolved to give it another ten minutes, twenty tops, but an instant later Alvin released a throaty cry from the rear of the camper. "Dooney!" he yelled. "Rich-rich-rich guy, am I right? This buddy of mine, he gave them a tow last week. Lake Larceny, man—turn around!"

"You're sure?" Boyd asked.

"Yeah, man. Almost!"

It took Boyd forty minutes to reverse direction, return to Bemidji, and make the winding drive north to Lake Larceny, a modest-size body of water that was already going steel gray in the shadows of late afternoon. Though barely fourteen miles outside Bemidji, the lake seemed deserted and half forgotten, with only a half-dozen cabins scattered along its shoreline.

A narrow tar road, broken with frost heaves, encircled the lake, and at times thick growths of maple and birch and pine pressed up against both sides of the camper, making sharp scratching sounds. After twenty minutes, Boyd switched on the headlights.

Angie and Alvin peered out at what had now become twilight.

"These cabins," Alvin was saying, "they usually have signs
out front—those wood shingles that say HANS'S HIDEAWAY,
stuff like that. It's getting pretty dark, though. Maybe in the
morning we can—"

"Boyd, give me my cell phone," Angie said.

"Forget it."

"No, *really*. A quick web search, I can do this."

"No," Boyd said.

"You want to find Dooney? We've got a location now, an
actual lake, something I can search. Give me the phone."

"No."

Boyd exhaled a sour breath of distemper. After a moment,
he stopped, unlocked the glove compartment, and handed
Angie her phone. Twilight had crossed over into full dark.

"More like it," Angie muttered, and began tapping keys. A
few minutes passed before she said, "Okay, maybe I've got it,
maybe not. Straight ahead. Another five hundred yards, there'll
be a long driveway down to the lake. Try not to kill us, Dad."

She laughed and snuggled closer to Alvin.

Slowly, just nudging the accelerator, Boyd turned onto a
rutted, tree-lined gravel driveway that after a hundred yards
opened up into a sprawling lakeside arboretum. A quartet of
pole-mounted farm lights illuminated lawns and gardens and
ghostly silver birches meandering down to the lake's shoreline.
Directly ahead were a pair of tennis courts and a canvas-covered
swimming pool; off to the right, fifty or sixty yards from the
lake, loomed what appeared to be a massive frontier castle—
what the Irish would call a Grand House—a multichimneyed,

multiporched, multiturreted mansion constructed in the style, though not with the dimensions, of a log cabin. Boyd parked in front of an enormous garage.

"Well," Angie muttered. "Cozy."

Alvin gave her thigh a slap.

The log castle stood completely dark. Boyd turned off the camper's engine, got out, and made his way to one of four windows set into the sides of the garage. Assembled inside like members of a gentleman's dining club were a Bugatti, a Ferrari 812 Superfast, a Ford pickup, two identical Teslas, a BMW SUV, a snowmobile, and what was probably a Porsche Spyder beneath its plastic car cover. The ninth parking slot, double size, was occupied by the servants, a John Deere tractor and a boat trailer.

Dooney, for sure.

Half smiling to himself, Boyd swung around and moved swiftly across a stone terrace to the castle's front doors. He pulled the Temptation from his pocket, let it dangle at his side. Curiously, he felt a calm unlike anything he'd ever known.

Here, he realized, was where he belonged.

If there was a doorbell, he couldn't find it, and he used the butt of the pistol to pound on the door. He had no fear. He was aware of his breathing, his history, the gun in his hand. He cocked the pistol's hammer with both thumbs. He wanted to laugh. He pressed the gun's muzzle square against his temple. Here was what he deserved. The shame and the revulsion. A twitch in his trigger finger. His punishment, his reward, his happy oblivion.

"Open up!" he yelled.

"Nobody home," said Angie from the dark behind him.

25

"BOTTOM LINE, HALVERSON TRIED TO CRUCIFY ME,"
Jim Dooney was telling Calvin. "Somehow—and I think I *know*
how—he got tipped off that PS&S stretched a few legalities here
and there. But what's *new* about that? He never heard of Rocke-
feller? Never heard of Gould, Vanderbilt, Ford, Frick, Morgan?
I mean, if it's not new, for Chrissake, how can it be news, and
if it's not news, what's it doing in a *newspaper*? They don't call
them oldspapers, do they? Fake news—am I right?"

"You're always right," said Calvin.

"Not always. I let him marry my daughter."

It had been a hectic few days: the hurried departure from
Bemidji, the flight to Chicago, the bumpy connecting flight to
LAX. Now, they were safely inside Dooney's primary residence
in the hills above Los Angeles, behind gated walls a stone's
throw from Elton John, not twenty minutes from Junius and
Evelyn's digs in Bel Air. Security here was tight. Dooney em-
ployed a firm that provided twenty-four-hour on-site patrols of
the grounds—burly gentlemen with clubs and tasers. Dogs, too.
Three of them, 126 teeth total.

Even so, the doors and windows were locked.

"So you bought the newspaper," Calvin said. "Problem
solved, yes?"

"Temporarily, yes. Permanently, no." Dooney stepped out of
the shower, toweled off, slipped on a robe, and sat on the edge

of the fossilized-wood tub where Calvin lay soaking. "Remember, this was—what?—ten years ago. I'm in Jakarta, that's where our Pacific operation is based, the meat and potatoes, and so obviously I can't trot around buying up every crummy website, every crybaby oldspaper rag—it'd be like acquiring fleas. You buy one, a million more pop up. See the problem? Halverson can peddle his old news wherever he wants."

"I assume you took other steps?" said Calvin. "Drastic, I'll bet."

"Bet your life I did. Can you imagine me in one of those prison jumpsuits?"

"Well—"

"Don't say it. I look good in anything."

"You do!" said Calvin.

"Not orange," Dooney grunted, then grinned. "So I took a page out of the Corny Vanderbilt handbook. I quote: 'I won't sue you, because the law is too slow. I'll ruin you.'"

"Elegant," Calvin said.

Dooney ran a hand across the silver stubble on his jaw. "At any rate, Halverson intended to nail me to a cross, publish this giant exposé of so-called corporate malfeasance. Two or three ships go down? Where's the crime in that? All I did was, I got the jump on him. Arranged my own exposé."

"The lying, you mean?"

"A gazillion lies," said Dooney. "Who's gonna believe a newspaper rat who can't tell the truth about his own name? Boyd Birdsong. Actual name."

"Birdsong?"

Dooney laughed. "Yeah, I'll tell you more if you hop out of the tub. I could use a shave, Cal."

"You love me for my shaves."

"No, no," teased Dooney. "Your haircuts."

On the mansion's second floor, in a replica of a 1930s Art Deco barbershop, Dooney relaxed under the strokes of Cal's straight razor. It was a ritual for them. Sometimes they'd sit chatting, or quietly reading, in Calvin's two hydraulic barber's chairs, afloat in the fragrances of Redstone's hair tonic and talc and mint-spiced shaving soap. Years ago, they had met this way—Dooney the client, Calvin the West Hollywood hair therapist. Gradually at first, then swiftly, a casual friendship had evolved into the rich and surprising love it now was.

Eyes closed, listening to the scrape of the razor at his ear, Dooney wondered how he'd made it through seventy-five years without Cal at his side.

"Boyd Birdsong," Calvin was saying, "it's a . . . it's a perfectly *gorgeous* name. I wish it were mine. Why would he change it?"

"No idea," said Dooney. "Too exotic? Took some teasing, maybe?"

"Well, yes, I can see that in an eight-year-old, but—"

"Halverson *is* an eight-year-old, Cal. Lives inside a Disney movie—*Fantasia*, maybe. Something got stunted."

Calvin released a quick little laugh and said, "We have our own *Fantasia*, don't we? You and me?"

"Don't be crude. We're people, not fairies."

"Jimmy, it was a joke."

"Halverson's the freaking fairy. Not even a real person. If he doesn't like facts, he invents them. Apparently the name change broke his father's heart, so Evelyn says. Like some sort of . . ."

"Repudiation," said Calvin.

"Yeah. Like that."

For a time, Calvin worked his razor along the back of Dooney's neck, humming to himself, then stopped in midhum and said, "You mind if I ask something impertinent?"

"If I mind, I'll let you know."

Calvin studied his partner in the big wall mirrors behind the barber's chairs. "This exposé of Halverson's—or Birdsong's—was it factual? Corporate malfeasance? All that?"

"I mind," Dooney said sharply.

"Jimmy—"

"We had a deal. No more legal questions."

"I'm just asking—"

"If I volunteer something, fine, but legal's off-limits. Anybody runs a multinational, he's playing with vipers. But all that's history. I'm retired. No. More. Questions."

"Sorry," Calvin murmured.

He unclipped the barber's apron, brushed Dooney's neck, patted on some aftershave, then turned away and quietly left the room.

Dinner that evening was a festival of monosyllables.

Bedtime was worse.

Calvin carried a pillow and his pajamas down to the theater room. At dawn Dooney finally joined him.

"You're sulking," he whispered.

"I certainly am," said Calvin. "I thought we were beyond secrets."

On the big TV screen across the room, a muted Ginger Rogers was scolding a muted Fred Astaire. In a moment they would break into dance.

Dooney watched for a while.

"All right," he said quietly, "Halverson's fake news wasn't completely fake. Do you really want to hear this?"

"Yes," said Calvin.

Dooney drew a breath and uttered the first syllables of a recitation that lasted well into the morning. Occasionally, Calvin stopped him, asking for clarification. By and large it was a blunt lesson in profiteering, price manipulation, tax evasion, embargo noncompliance, insider trading, conspiracy to defraud, violations of the Arms Export Control Act, and a half-dozen other imprisonable offenses. "I told you I was a son of a bitch," said Dooney. "But I was a son of a bitch looking at three hundred years in lockup. That's Bernie Madoff times two. And my own son-in-law planned to put me there."

"Well," Calvin said.

"Yeah, well."

"He had evidence?"

"A ton."

"So how—?"

"Evelyn, I'm pretty sure. Enough to put him on my trail anyway. The sensitive stuff I kept at home. She had access to it."

Calvin pinched the bridge of his nose.

"I have a headache," he said, avoiding Dooney's gaze. "Basically, you saved your neck by destroying somebody who was just . . . telling the truth."

"Not just," Dooney said. "In print. Front page."

"Even so."

"Cal, for God's sake, it was war. I fought *his* truth with *my* truth. So what? Okay, I discredited him, ruined him, however you want to pitch it, but I didn't invent that pitiful Pinocchio."

"Birdsong, you mean. You destroyed Birdsong."

"Yes, I did."

"And no regrets?"

"Not even a little," said Dooney. "Let's have breakfast."

* * *

A half mile away, in Bel Air, Evelyn Kirakossian, who was once Evelyn Halverson, or once Evelyn Birdsong, or possibly some other Evelyn she didn't know, had just made reservations for a midmorning flight to Bemidji, Minnesota, a place her travel agent had never heard of.

Evelyn packed, carried her suitcase down to the foyer, and went looking for Junius. It was a sizable house, but after a few minutes, she found him mixing up a protein shake in the kitchen. He was still beaming from his rendezvous with the Phillies.

Evelyn waited only a moment. She blurted it out and watched Junius lick his spoon and place it carefully on a paper towel.

He didn't ask why, but she told him anyway: Boyd was sick. He could hurt somebody, probably himself.

"It's not you," she said, "and it's not even me. It's just the right thing. Really, I need to do *something*. Make peace. Boyd and I. Talking might help."

"Any other reasons?" said Junius.

"No, except . . ." Evelyn drew a breath. "I know you promised not to hurt Boyd, not to let Henry hurt him. But that so-called CFO of yours, he's a psychopath—loose screws—violence screws. I don't want something terrible to happen."

"Well," Junius said. "I'll try to reach him. Have a good trip."

"That's it?"

"What can I do? Say no? Issue orders?"

They looked at each other.

"Not orders," Evelyn said. "But maybe a kiss?"

PART II

CARS, GUNS, CRIME, CASINOS,
CONSPIRACY, MOVIES, MONEY, ROAD TRIPS, REMODELING,
ICE FISHING, FAST FOOD, VENGEANCE, REUNIONS,
BIRD WATCHING, GOD, MARRIAGE, SHOPPING, OPIOIDS,
AND LIARS IN PUBLIC PLACES

26

IN TALLAHASSEE, FLORIDA; IN CASPER, WYOMING; in Storm Lake, Iowa; and in Fulda, California, America's Truth Teller Seeds were having trouble keeping up with the reality of unreality slithering off the tonsils of far more practiced, far more brazen, and far more earnest mythomaniacs who were multiplying like rabbits across the great North American continent. In Wimberley, Texas, a middle school English teacher lied about the authorship of *Mein Kampf,* assigning credit to his twenty-eight-year-old wife, who would soon be producing "absolute proof" that the struggle had been hers and hers alone. Northward, in Chicago, a candidate for city council lied about the score of a recent Bears-Lions game. On Block Island, just off the Rhode Island coast, a honeymooning couple lied about their weekend aboard a sunken Soviet-era submarine accompanied by a skeletal crew and "better than ever" kegs of caviar. In the nation's capital, POTUS claimed he had just spoken before the most "massive crowd" in American history, ignoring fifty-three Super Bowls and the crowds of his predecessor. "We're getting our asses outlied," Chub O'Neill was telling his brother Dink. "And it's time to double down. We gotta lie about our lies, then we lie about *those* lies, understood?"

"I need an example," said Dink.

"Well, like that swastika on your arm. Let's say we take a snapshot and photoshop it on somebody like, you know, like Joe

Biden, some stinking Democrat, then we put it up on the web with a caption like—I'm winging this—like 'Biden Surrenders City of Phoenix to Red China.' If we get called on it, big deal, we double down and stick a red star on his arm. Somebody calls us on *that*? We photoshop Biden holding up a sign that says BLACK LIVES MATTER? Amazing what punctuation can do."

"What's punctuation?" Dink said.

"Boy oh boy," said Chub. "Do I miss Boyd Halverson."

27

ON DOONEY'S FRONT DOORSTEP, ANGIE HAD COME up behind Boyd. She had whispered, "Nobody home," and pried the pistol from his hand.

Boyd squatted on his heels.

In the dark he heard himself laughing, which made him choke. He tried to speak, then tried to laugh again. All he could manage were bleating sounds.

"It's okay," Angie said. "It's your moment with God."

Later Boyd found himself soaking in a large cast-iron bathtub, probably Dooney's. A few feet away, Angie and Alvin sat conversing in a pair of barber's chairs, their voices subdued and oddly distant. Though Boyd couldn't be sure, it seemed only minutes had ticked by, or maybe a few hours. Not that time meant much to somebody who had just tried to stop time. For months now he'd been living with a single driving thought: my last burger ever, my last tied shoe, my last bad dream, my last "I'm sorry," my last pitiful gasp. Everything had been last. Last "Good morning," last "So long." Last yesterday.

Angie slipped out of her barber's chair and kneeled down beside the tub. "Welcome back, Mister Naked. What did God have to say?"

Boyd smiled weakly and let himself slide beneath the suds.

Later still, possibly after a full day or more, Boyd blinked and realized he was swallowing something delicious. A plate

of fried fish was before him. In the balmy quiet of late afternoon, Angie and Alvin sat across from him at a picnic table that
overlooked a lovely blue lake framed by pines and birch and red
sumac. By daylight, Dooney's lakeside estate seemed to stretch
out for three or four hundred yards in every direction except
lakeward, where the land sloped abruptly and steeply down
to the water. The expansive and expensive-looking grounds
brought to mind an English squirearchy, with boxwoods and
overgrown gardens and a duck pond and the labor of others to
keep it all shipshape.

There was the sun's heat and the turpentine scent of conifers. There were birds—living, chirping birds. Amazing, Boyd
thought.

After a time, Alvin excused himself and sauntered away
into Dooney's big manor house.

"Well," Angie said. "Are we back on earth?"

Boyd said nothing.

Ten minutes passed before Angie sighed and said, "Last
night it dawned on me, Boyd. You didn't ever plan to shoot
anybody, did you? Except yourself. And make Dooney watch.
Right from the start—day one, when you robbed the bank—
that was always the plan, wasn't it?"

Boyd had to teach himself how to say, "Pretty much."

Angie nodded. "And that's what all this has been about? Put
on a suicide show."

"It seemed amusing."

"Amusing. And did God have any advice about that?"

"God laughed at me. Nobody home, remember?"

For a few moments, Angie studied him. She shook her head,
stacked the dinner plates, carried them into the house, then
returned and sat down again.

"God doesn't laugh at us," she said stiffly.

"No?"

"No. God isn't a laugher, my friend."

More bitterly than he'd expected, Boyd stared at her. "If God wants to laugh, God laughs. Who are you to decide what God can't do?"

"I'm Angie Bing. I go to church. I know how to pray."

They fell silent. Several dozen outdoor lights clicked on; purply-blue shadows came creeping toward them from across the lake. "The way I learned it," Boyd finally said, "God does whatever God wants to do. My big moment, the finale, and God slaps his knee, and says, 'Sorry, asshole, nobody home.'"

"God doesn't swear either," Angie snapped. "That was the devil talking."

"Same difference," said Boyd.

They didn't speak again until the next morning when Alvin appeared at the breakfast table to report that he'd done some exploring. As far as he could tell, the huge house had been very recently occupied and very swiftly evacuated. He'd counted eleven bedrooms, one unmade bed. There were dirty dishes in both dishwashers, tons of food in both Sub-Zeros. In the east wing, a two-lane bowling alley had been left brightly illuminated, the pin-setting machines still humming, and in the library he'd found a turkey platter piled high with coke.

"Excellent quality, I'll add," he said, and flashed a smile through his beard. "Anyway, I'm not really sure why we're even here, but if you want, I can stick around for a while."

"Yes, maybe," Angie said.

"Or maybe not," said Boyd.

"Or maybe forever and ever," Angie snapped. "Right now,

my daddy needs to figure out an afterlife for himself." She leaned back, not quite looking at Boyd. "Obviously suicide is a mortal sin—you'd roast in hell—so that option is off the table. Question is: Now what?"

She smiled at Alvin, scowled at Boyd.

"You two have fun," Alvin said. He walked to the door. "I'll check out the Ferrari, maybe bowl a line or two. Man, I gotta be honest, this place is paradise."

Twelve miles outside Fulda, California, heading home, Randy Zapf began to entertain second thoughts about hoeing Carl and Cyrus. Surprise, but he sort of missed them. Okay, sure, they deserved a good, expert hoe job, always dissing him, acting like he wasn't the professional operator he was. But they'd been pretty fair company. Excellent prison stories—shankings and watch your step in the shower and Charlie Manson's spaghetti-eating technique, one strand at a time, wrapping it around his pinkie and dipping it in the sauce and taking his time sucking it off the spindle. Cool stuff like that. It wasn't achy-breaky-heart missing, not that kind, just too much emptiness in the backseat.

Too bad, he thought. On the other hand, Carl and Cyrus probably respected him now.

Taking his last slow turn eastward into Fulda, Randy figured you couldn't cry over spilt milk, and for a few minutes he tried singing "Achy Breaky Heart" like Billy Ray, except all he remembered was half the first line, so he whistled it, and soon enough he was cruising into town past some dried-up onion fields, then straight down South Spruce Street, where all the spruce trees were ancient history, past the farm implement warehouse and the JCPenney store and Community National

Bank, which he figured he'd case after a hot turkey sandwich and a heart-to-heart with Toby Van Der Kellen.

First thing, though, was all that blood caking up on his best rodeo shirt, the red, white, and blue one with patriotic spangles. Say what you want, Carl and Cyrus knew how to bleed. Especially Cyrus. The guy was one Olympic-caliber bleeder's bleeder.

Randy turned onto Cutterby Boulevard, parked in a vacant lot across from his rented room, and trudged up two flights of stairs with his duffel and hoe. The room was on the smallish side, twelve by fourteen, but Randy had done wonders with it—walls lacquered glossy black, strobe lights, framed wanted posters from a buddy over at the post office, a couple of I Support Law Enforcement posters for balance, a stereo system he'd swiped up in Portland, three more stereo systems still boxed up and ready to go in the room's only closet, a horseshoe nailed over the toilet, his prized Malian *takoba* sword hanging over the TV, a black-and-white mug shot of yours truly mounted on the wall next to a much larger full-color photograph of Angie Bing looking sharp in an Arby's booth on their very first date.

At the moment, Randy was pretty peeved at Angie—more than pretty—and he didn't give the photo the usual touchy-feely on his way to hit the shower.

He lathered up, rinsed out the rodeo shirt, tried singing "Achy Breaky Heart" again, toweled off, put on almost-clean jeans and his second-favorite shirt, stashed the hoe under his bed, checked himself out in a mirror, and took off to visit a hot turkey sandwich and the Fulda PD.

The sandwich ended up A-okay, but when Randy arrived at PD headquarters, it turned out that Toby was busy hassling

Mexicans or plunking Lois Cutterby or doing whatever else he did to keep the streets safe.

For a police department, Randy thought as he walked in, the place was a joke. Even though Fulda was a small town, not even four thousand bored-silly souls, this little two-cell dump made the town's commitment to law enforcement look more pathetic than it actually was, which was pretty pathetic. One full-time cop, one part-timer, and Wanda Jane Epstein at the dispatch console.

Randy gave Wanda Jane his usual surprise squeeze from behind, licked her ear, and made himself comfortable in one of the cells. For a good forty-five minutes, he chatted the girl up from behind bars. Way back in high school she'd had a thing for him. Always had, even in middle school, and they'd stayed in touch whenever Randy spent a few free-of-charge nights here. He liked Wanda Jane's sense of humor. He liked how she had a bunch of pet names for him, like Shithead and Stupid, and how she tried her best to look pissed off when he oiled her up with subtle compliments about her excellent dual mufflers up front. Right now, he was telling her how great she'd look bending over a bank shot at Elmo's. "Play your cards right," he was saying, "I can probably get there around, I don't know, let's say ten o'clock. We'll rack 'em up, okay?"

Wanda Jane laughed.

"You," she said, "are a moron."

"Tar and feather me—tie me to your torture rack," said Randy.

"You have a girlfriend, I thought."

"Nope, not no more. Angie and me, we're on the outs. Un-reversible differences."

"Irreconcilable," said Wanda Jane.

"Ir-what?"

"It's a word. You know what words are?"

"I know me a couple," Randy said cheerfully. "Anyhow, when the mouse is away, this cat's gonna play some eight ball with Wanda Jane."

"Other way around, Stupid."

"What is?"

"The mouse and the cat," said Wanda Jane. "You've got it backward, like everything else." She yawned and stretched. "So Angie finally figured out you're a dumb, immoral waste of time? Took me like half a second. Seventh grade, remember? Standing in the lunch line, the way you kept bumping me—whatever you could find to bump. Remember that?"

"Sorta," said Randy.

"I used a fork on you, didn't I?"

"Yeah, a fork."

"And where did the fork go?"

"You know where," Randy said. "So are we gonna shoot some pool or sit here flirting?"

Wanda Jane stared at him.

"You're so stupid," she said, "it's impressive."

"Gotcha," said Randy. "What time tonight?"

The door swung open and Toby walked in. Rotten coincidence, Randy thought—he was rounding third.

Toby hooked his thumbs to his belt and stared.

"Where the hell've *you* been?" he said, definitely not to Wanda Jane.

"Delayed," said Randy. "Gardening to do."

"Step outside," said Toby.

Randy made a show of grinning at Wanda Jane, taking his time following Toby out the door.

"Get in the car," Toby said. "Backseat."

"I thought we were—"

"Car. Backseat."

Randy shrugged. He slid in and waited for Toby to sit up front and open the little bulletproof window in the partition between them.

"All right, talk," said Toby. "This better be good."

Randy widened his eyes, gave Toby the who-me expression he saved for cops and rodeo judges and Angie Bing after he'd forgotten it was Christmas.

"Talk how?" he said.

"I asked where you been. One minute you're up ahead of me on the highway, next minute you're Houdini, that cute vanishing trick."

"Is that so?"

"Yeah, it's so. What happened to your convict pals?"

Randy took a little steam out of the who-me look, brightened it up with a grin. "Okay, Toby, maybe I was late getting—"

"Don't Toby me," Toby said. "It's Officer."

"Right, I forgot," said Randy. "What happened is, Carl and Cyrus, they chickened out. Made me drive all the way over to Redding, dump them at the bus depot there. Good riddance, I figure. So there I am, I'm in Redding, next thing you know the Cutlass gets itself a fan belt hiccup, so I spend half a day drinking crappy coffee while this mechanic tries to remember what a fan belt is, then finally I go to pay the guy and guess what? No wallet. You believe it?"

"Not a word," said Toby.

"Yeah, and I'll tell you what, I had to do me some fancy talking. This mechanic, he won't give me back my Cutlass, so

I wait around till like, you know, like till almost two in the morning, finally had to break into the shop, swipe back my own car."

Randy kept the grin on, looking to see how Toby was taking the story. Not all that well, it seemed, which ticked Randy off, mainly because some of it was true, at least the part about the wallet, which had popped out of his back pocket while he was busy hoeing the boys. He'd had to turn around and drive all the way back to the scene of the crime, stomp around in the weeds for a good ten minutes till he finally found the wallet not three feet from big ol' Cyrus, who looked pretty goofy with his mouth open like that, except he looked a lot deader after a few hours in the sun.

The truth was a better story than the one he'd invented, Randy realized, except it probably wasn't the kind of thing you bragged about to a cop.

"So that's that," Randy said. "No Carl, no Cyrus. A two-way split now, just you and me." He grinned again at Toby. "We gonna rob a bank or aren't we?"

Toby looked at him skeptically. "Yeah, maybe. I'll talk to Lois."

"You're asking permission?"

"More or less," Toby said.

Community National's vault was a far cry from state of the art, a former storage room with a thin steel door and a combination lock that looked like something off a toy. Even so, with its door closed, the vault had an eerie, sinister feel, especially at 11:15 p.m. with a stubby candle burning on the linoleum floor. "Look, I'm sorry about L.A.," Toby was telling Lois, "but

Halverson and Bing, they'd already taken off for who knows where. Waste of time. That's the bad news. But there's good news, too."

"Let's hope so," said Lois. She bent back Toby's thumb, levering his hand from her thigh. "Go on, cheer me up."

When he'd finished his pitch, Lois looked down at the linoleum for a while, then clicked her tongue and said, "Not a bad idea."

"I thought so, too," said Toby.

"You and your idiot brother rob us, right?"

"Right. Except he's not—"

"And your cut's a third. Doug and I, we get two-thirds."

"Well, see, that's not exactly how I explained it."

Lois gave him a stare. "Listen, Hubcap, this is America. Reward goes to the risk-taker. Doug and I, we'll be bankrolling things, putting up the hundred K for you to rob."

"True," Toby said.

"You bet true," said Lois.

"All I mean is," said Toby, trying not to whine, "I've got my own risks. Like walking in and sticking up the place. What if . . . I don't know. What if somebody hits the alarm? Cops bust in and shoot me dead?"

"Toby," Lois said slowly, "you *are* the cops."

"Oh, yeah."

"So there you go. I'll be the only person in the bank. No alarms. Just in and out." She paused, thinking. "You can put your hand back now."

"Thanks," Toby said.

"No problem," said Lois. "Let's talk specifics. What we'll do, we'll order up the green this coming Thursday, have it ready by

Friday noon. You and your brother show up around . . . let's say a half hour before closing time. Agreed?"

"He's not my brother."

"Whatever. The idiot. What's his name?"

"Randy."

"Right. Can we erase him afterward?"

"You mean erase-erase?"

"Yes, sir, that's what I mean. Stop pinching."

"I was massaging."

"Fine, but easy does it. So after you stick us up, you'll plant the idiot brother in some sugar beet field, keep this in the immediate family."

"Plant him, huh?"

"Medium deep. Sweeten up the sugar beets."

Toby stopped massaging. It wasn't that he minded giving Randy the chance to do something useful, like become fertilizer, but the thought occurred to him that he, too, was not a member of the immediate family.

"I don't know," he said cautiously. "Erasing, I mean. That's more up your alley."

"You think?" said Lois.

"I sort of do."

"All right, maybe. Let me think about it." She lay back, shivered, and gazed up at twenty rows of safe-deposit boxes. The vault was fun, but after hours it got chilly. "You realize," she said, "that I'll have to run all this by Douglas."

"I figured."

"He'll go for it, I'm pretty sure. Two-thirds of a hundred grand right off the top, and if the feds come poking around, who cares? Just transfer personal funds over to the bank—

presto, everything balances—then later we transfer the money right back again. I mean, it's *ours*. We robbed it in the first place, didn't we? Basically, we're the bank behind our bank. Follow me?"

"I guess," Toby said, though he didn't.

His mind kept wandering. Erasing was not his MO. And there was something about that word, or the way she'd used it, that made him wonder if he should forget banks and go back to checking tire pressures. On the other hand, there were those pantyhose sliding down.

"Also, just to fill you in," Lois was saying, "I've taken care of the Halverson issue. Turns out he had seventy-two thousand on deposit with us, which naturally I confiscated. We're still out nine grand, true enough, but it's like when a loan defaults, cost of doing business . . . Wow, it's freezing in here. Aren't you cold?"

"I wouldn't say cold," Toby told her. "I'd say busy."

"Any questions?"

"Yeah, one. I'll ask it in a minute."

"A minute?"

"Not even that," said Toby.

A dozen or so heartbeats later, Toby said, "Man, you're right, it *is* cold in here."

"What's the question?" said Lois.

"Just paint me a picture. What happens exactly after I walk in and say stick 'em up?"

"What do you think happens?" Lois said tartly. She was wiggling back into her pantyhose. "No dawdling. Wear a mask. Shove a gun in my face, grab the cash, and get out." She smiled, then laughed. "You see the beauty of this? You're not just the robber, you're the cop I call right afterward. It's like I'll be reporting you to yourself. You say to me, 'Tell me about these robbers, ma'am,' and I say, 'Well, one of them had a pretty fair-size dick,' and you say, 'Can you describe it?' and I say, 'It's indescribable,' and you say, 'Yes, ma'am,' and write down 'indescribable dick' in your cop notes. It'll be fun."

"Good plan," said Toby.

"Friday then. I'll talk to Doug and let you know if it's a go."

"Roger that," Toby said.

He pulled up his pants and followed her out of the vault.

In the dark, as Lois locked up, Toby was struck by a pang of apprehension, something final, as though the vault door had just closed on the rest of his life.

To cover up, he said, "Let's do that again sometime."

"Oh, we will," Lois murmured.

"Right now?"

"No, but very soon. I promise."

At their board meeting the next morning, Douglas signed off on the plan.

"Just two questions," he said. "Isn't one hundred percent better than two-thirds?"

"Quite a bit better," said Lois.

"And do you know how to use my shotgun?"

"I can certainly learn."

28

OVER THE NEXT DAYS, ON THE DOCK BELOW DOONEY'S log mansion, Boyd Halverson found himself dwelling not in actualities but amid the remote wanderings of a man who had pressed the muzzle of a Temptation .38 to his temple.

He slept alone in the camper. He spent his days in conversation with himself, explaining the inexplicable, how the issuance of big bald lies had become as automatic as breathing, without malice, without intent, without foreknowledge, and—he admitted it—without the sting of moral compunction. At various times, on various occasions, he had lied about books he'd never read, foods he'd never tasted, cities he'd never visited, celebrities he'd never encountered, diseases he'd never contracted, war wounds he'd never suffered, medals he'd never won, hotel rooms he'd never occupied, high school proms he'd never attended, double plays he'd never turned, paintings he'd never painted, schoolyard bullies he'd never confronted, cool ripostes he'd never been quick enough to frame with words. And plenty more. He'd lied about his age, his height, his digestion, and his name. He'd lied for no reason. He'd lied for sport. He'd lied to hear the sound of the lie. He'd lied for convenience. He'd lied for the thrill. He'd lied to get the job he wanted, the respect he wanted, the love he wanted, the wife he wanted. He'd lied to escape a twelve-year-old paperboy named Otis Birdsong Junior.

No wonder God laughed.

No wonder God had just sent a pair of enormous glossy-black crows crashing into the whitecaps on Lake Larceny.

On the nineteenth day of October, Boyd was summoned to a conference on Dooney's terrace overlooking the lake. Angie presided. Alvin and Boyd sat mostly mute.

"Since nobody else is in charge here," Angie began, "I've made some decisions about what happens next. Most important, we'll be staying here awhile. Nice scenery, a house the size of Algeria, so why not make ourselves comfortable? One of us—I won't name names but it rhymes with Boyd—one of us needs time to figure out a future for himself. Life after suicide, sort of. Second thing, we're low on cash. The camper set us back big time, not to mention gas and food and those hotels down in Mexico and a whole bunch else. The point is, we can't ignore reality. What if one of us needs a nursing home? What if I have a baby?" She rotated her eyes toward Boyd as if daring him to speak. "Anyhow, in case you haven't noticed, Alvin and I have been busy selling a few things. Dooney's things, I mean."

"You and Alvin?" said Boyd. "Sounds cozy."

"Sarcasm doesn't work on me. I told you a long time ago, I attract criminal types, don't ask me why. But Alvin's a sweetheart. He can't hardly keep his hands off me, and he's definitely helping with the cash problem, fixing us up with buyers. He knows the ropes. Isn't that right, Alvin?"

"Absolutely," Alvin said, grinning modestly. "All the above."

"Lucky us," said Boyd.

"You *bet* lucky us," Angie said. "Mostly lucky you. I mean, if it's revenge you want, wait'll Dooney sees an empty garage. Empty house, empty everything. In a couple of weeks, maybe less, we can unload skylights, hot tub, billiard table, both bowling lanes—we clean him out. The boat, too. And the tennis nets. And the gazebo. And the greenhouse. Alvin thinks we can hire somebody to strip off the roof shingles, then we go to work on the small stuff. Linens. Dishwashers. Computers. TVs. Silverware—real silver." Again, she looked at Boyd, this time with a flat, end-of-the-road expression. "Beats suicide, doesn't it?"

"I guess it does," Boyd said.

"Better stop guessing, Gunslinger. After that crackup of yours, whatever you call it, I recommend you start sorting out priorities. No offense, but you look terrible. Old and sick and feeble and lost and half dead."

Angie challenged him with her eyebrows.

"All right, that's settled," she said. "Now here's how I see things—"

She leaned back in her chair, took a sip of Dooney's Bordeaux, and slipped into a long, somewhat rambling synopsis of the situation. Life on the road was getting old. She hadn't had a manicure since Mexico. Nobody had baked her a birthday cake. She needed a vacation. Also, with three people now, the Pleasure-Way was way too cramped, therefore from here on they would be the temporary guests of Jim Dooney, like caretakers, making sure the place didn't get too cluttered, getting rid of stuff like Sub-Zeros and Teslas and a bowling alley. "Speaking of which," she said, "I'm a pretty good bowler. One time Randy and I, we joined a bowling league. He bought us these matching shirts that said HE-MAN and SHE-GIRL on the back, or probably he stole them somewhere, but then he got upset about throwing gutter balls all the time, so one night he broke in and mixed up a bunch of cement and poured it in the gutters. We stopped bowling then, even if I was getting really good at it, even if Randy couldn't—"

"Who's Randy?" Alvin said.

"Don't interrupt," said Angie. "Randy's one of my options."

Alvin thought about it and said, "Roger that. One more question: What about the bedroom situation? Does Dad mind if you and me bunk together?"

"Gee," Angie said. "What about it, Daddy?"

They turned and looked at Boyd.

He started to speak—"You and I," he almost said—but it didn't seem worth the trouble. A disconnected sensation came over him. All he wanted was to find the Temptation and try again.

"Sleep where you want," he said. "I hope you trust him."

"Who? Alvin?"

"Who else?"

Alvin waved a hand and said, "Hey, Dad, I'm right here. I'm an Alvin expert."

"He's a wounded bird," Angie said. "And I'm in the salvage business, so leave all that to me." She started to say something more, but then she jerked her head at Alvin, who nodded and stood and walked away, whistling to himself.

"That was rude," Angie muttered when he was gone. "Rude and embarrassing. What you need to worry about, Boyd, is your own soul. Getting one, I mean."

Boyd shrugged. His head had gone empty.

For some time, he looked out on Dooney's expansive green lawn, at the lake beyond, at the unfolding layers of forest along the far shore. To be unexpectedly alive, he thought, was not without pleasures. A clean, scrubbed-out sensation. As if a plug had been pulled inside him.

When he looked back, Angie was gone.

Later, as he contemplated getting a bite to eat, his gaze

idly fell on her cell phone, which lay on the deck chair beside him. He opened it and took a look at her messages. There was only one.

> Hi Awesome Randy—I'm here in Bemidji, Minnesota, which you can probably find on a map, but don't even think about coming to get me. (I'm engaged!) If you do come, my birthday was almost a week ago.
>
> P.S. Boyd almost shot his head off.
>
> P.S.S. I need a good winter coat, snow boots, and a hairbrush with a silver handle. No fakes!

Boyd pocketed the phone.

Strange, how he'd ended up like this. So completely alone.

After an hour or so, Alvin reappeared beside him. He handed Boyd a glass of Dooney's wine and said, "Don't tell your daughter I gave you that. She'll burn me alive."

"Cheers," Boyd said.

"Mind if I sit?"

"Not at all," said Boyd. He drained the wine in a single agreeable swallow. "One thing, though."

"Sir?"

"She's not my daughter. She's my fiancée."

"Oh, yeah?" said Alvin.

"Yeah," said Boyd.

They were quiet for a moment.

"Does that mean I can't call you Dad?"

29

HENRY SPECK DID NOT CARE MUCH FOR MINNESO-
ta's lakes and forests. He was a city boy with city tastes. Therefore he had spent seven nights and eight days in the sealed
rooms of his rented cabin on Lake Larceny in the company of
a young casino hostess he'd encountered on his second night
in Bemidji. Her name, he was pretty sure, was Enni. Or maybe
Anekie. Or something else. As far as he could tell, she was
Finnish, though possibly not. The girl's command of English
was at best barely passable, and Henry had absorbed only bits
and pieces of the young lady's garbled life story: a veteran
of youth hostels and YMCAs, a former nanny, a cruise ship
laundress, a mountaineer, a tap-dance instructor, a tour guide
in Borneo, a pest control officer in Brooklyn, a zookeeper in
Bangkok, an icy-eyed, fresh-faced vagabond in pursuit of new
sights and sounds. At present, she was enrolled as a part-time
business student at Bemidji State, making ends meet out at the
Blue Fly Resort and Casino.

The romance, if that was the word for it, had been swift
and effortless. She had admired his physique, his tan, and his
credit card. Henry admired exactly what Enni admired, along
with her appetite for anything.

Finnish or Flemish, she was a find—a well-earned busman's
holiday.

For all practical purposes, Henry had already wrapped up

his essential business here in Bemidji. A brief stop at the county courthouse had yielded the address of Dooney's estate on the eastern shore of Lake Larceny. After a twenty-minute drive, and after an hour of woodsy surveillance, he had located Halverson and Angie Bing, reported back to Junius, and started mapping out his final few moves. A hardware store, he decided. Hammer and pliers. Monkey wrench for a bit of fun. All this had been accomplished in a single industrious morning. Later in the day, as he'd celebrated over a nightcap in the Blue Fly, young Enni had come striding across his field of vision, hips first, award-winning torso not far behind. *Voluptuous* was not a word Henry would've, or even could've, used—he suspected the term referred to indoor plumbing—but the general idea of a wholly animate, flesh-and-blood fantasy had instantly crossed his mind. With her sparkling arctic eyes and glacier-white hair, the girl reminded him of those well-muscled Olympic ski jumpers he'd admired on ESPN, at least some of whom seemed to be batting from his own side of the plate. This had led to an impulsive that. The following afternoon he'd rented a tourist cabin three properties to the south of Dooney's place, stocked up on hot sauce, and settled in with Enni to await developments.

Now, exhausted and bed sore, Henry wondered if he had bitten off more than a grown man could chew.

At breakfast that morning, young Enni—if that was her name—had been complaining about what she called "fever of the cabin." She needed sunshine; she needed exercise. To keep the peace, Henry reluctantly allowed himself to be led into the glaring brightness of a mid-October morning. "What we do," Enni informed him, swatting his hand away, "is we make a nice long job around water."

"Which job is that?" said Henry.

"To clean the lung. Job the lake circle."

She laughed, drew a breath, and set off at a bouncy sprint down the shoreline. Henry followed, though not sprinting.

Not an hour later, pressing through a thicket of brambles, he was struck by a flurry of intersecting insights: he was thirty-three years of age, jobbing was not his strong suit, nature was a pain in the ass, and he was almost certainly in love. He settled into a slow, uncertain walk. By Minnesota standards, Lake Larceny was not a huge body of water, yet neither was it small, and Henry found himself daydreaming about the flat, firm sidewalks of L.A.

He eventually struggled down the final exhausting yards of shoreline. Enni sat waiting for him on Jim Dooney's dock, still fresh-faced, her feet stirring the water next to an expensive-looking yacht.

Henry sat beside her and said, "Jog. Not job."

"I *said* job."

"The word is *jog*. Work on your *g's*."

"Job, jog," she said enthusiastically. "Now we have a big clean lung, okey-dokey? Tonight I think we dance and eat good foods and maybe use the credit card."

"I don't know," said Henry. "My boss, he doesn't—"

"Boss! Enni is your boss." The girl stood, stripped off her clothes, and dove in. "Swim now!"

For some time, Henry sat watching her arrow through the water, sleek and robust, way out of his nightclub comfort zone. After she had dwindled to a speck of foam, he turned and let his gaze follow a slope of green lawn that led to a pair of tennis courts, a gazebo, a beat-up old camper, and an impressive log mansion. A U-Haul truck was parked in the driveway. Two figures had emerged from the house, a brawny guy with a blond beard and behind him the improbably tiny Angie Bing. They carried what appeared to be a load of pine flooring, which, after a struggle, they hoisted into the truck.

They went back inside and returned with a rolled-up carpet. Persian, Henry thought. This, too, went into the trailer. Then three smaller carpets. Then another load of flooring.

Hesitating, not sure what to do with himself, Henry slipped off the dock into frigid Lake Larceny. The fact was, Henry was no swimmer—he was a tanner—sunlamps, not the actual sun—and he found himself bouncing on his toes to keep his head above water.

Junius, he told himself, would pay cash for this.

Over the next many minutes, as his bones iced up, Henry looked on while Angie and the blond-bearded guy made repetitive trips from house to truck. For a dwarf, Henry reflected, Angie handled herself well. She muscled TVs and drapes and computers and bowling balls and what seemed to be miles of wainscoting. The bearded guy occasionally gave her a hand with the heaviest stuff—sofas, two massive desks—but for the most part, Angie worked alone, with the determination of a woman born to plunder.

At one point, an enfeebled facsimile of Boyd Halverson stepped out of the camper and stood watching as Angie lifted a microwave into the truck. Halverson's posture was stooped and unsteady, his expression bewildered, as if senility had grabbed him by the throat halfway into middle age. Henry had seen Junius's photographs of the guy, but this was not the same man. This was decay.

After a moment, Halverson turned without a word and wobbled back into the camper. Pitiful, Henry thought. Maybe lose the monkey wrench. Maybe just a good spanking.

Then he shook his head. He was a Speck and Specks did what Specks do.

For an uncomfortable stretch of time, Henry observed more of the same, the slow but efficient dismantling of what had been a state-of-the-art lakeside compound. Item by item, the U-Haul truck was topped off with chandeliers, candle sconces, a fuse box, a banquet-size dining table, twelve upholstered chairs, coils of copper wiring, eight boxes of bowling pins, an automatic pinsetter, a jukebox, mirrors, a wicker love seat, a washer and drier, shower fixtures, light fixtures, doorknobs, two water heaters, granite countertops, a waterbed, two matching walnut nightstands, and a life-size statue of the reigning president of the United States of America.

Larceny fucking Lake, Henry almost muttered, not without admiration, and in the midst of that reflection, Enni surfaced at his side.

"What is this?" she said, too loudly.

Henry shushed her, but the blond-bearded guy had swung around and was moving down toward the dock, Angie trailing behind him.

"Okay, listen," Henry said quietly. "We're the new neighbors. Be friendly."

Enni gave him a teasing, almost taunting look.

"Okey-dokey," she said.

The girl seemed at ease with her own nudity. Wading ashore, she flung back her hair, approached the bearded guy, vigorously shook his hand, and said, "Friendly neighbor!"

"No question about it," said the bearded guy.

"Sorry, no clothes," Enni chirped gaily. "Maybe now I get dressed."

"Yeah," said Angie Bing. "I was thinking along those same lines."

A few minutes ticked by as Enni trotted over to the dock and wiggled into a halter top and a pair of Bemidji State running shorts. Henry seized the moment to apologize.

The bearded guy said, "No problem, man."

Angie Bing said, "How old is she?"

"Who?" said Henry.

"The floatation device. The friendly one."

"Oh, yeah, she's . . . thirty?"

"Nineteen," Angie said flatly.

Henry glanced over at Enni. "You think? I mean, she's been around the world like, I don't know, a thousand times. Climbs mountains, grown-up stuff."

"Nineteen," Angie said again. "Maybe not even."

"Well, she's Finnish, and over there . . ."

Henry stopped. Enough of this, he thought. He could fall in love with anybody he wanted to fall in love with, or anybody he *did* fall in love with, and besides, love was a falling thing, not a counting thing.

"Maybe she's Flemish, I'm not sure," he finished lamely.

"Climbs mountains?" Angie said.

"So she says. It's hard to follow every single word."

Angie looked at her bearded friend, who gazed studiously at Enni as she slithered up to Henry and hooked his arm.

"All right, bad luck, we're neighbors," Angie said, an edge in her voice. "I'm Angie. This is Alvin—my second or third fiancé." She gave Enni a defiant look. "Right now, we're busy."

"Not so fast," said Alvin. "Be polite."

"That *was* polite," Angie said, and turned away.

On the short walk back to their rental cabin, Henry found himself intensely disliking Angie Bing, the piety and spoil-sport morality. She hadn't so much as glanced at his excellent pecs. It occurred to him that he might offer Junius a two-for-one, first Halverson, then Bing. A freebie with the monkey wrench.

Even so, after lunch and a romantic three minutes in the shower, he asked to see Enni's passport. "A formality," he said.

"Passport after sex?" Enni said.

"This isn't Finland. We have rules here."

Enni nodded doubtfully and went off to retrieve her passport.

As it turned out, Angie Bing wasn't far off: Enni was twenty, barely. Henry had no problem with that, but he sat her down to set the record straight. He began with his own name, Henry Speck, of the Speck Specks, the famous ones.

The girl looked at him blankly.

"Speck," he said. "In Finland it's like . . . Don't you have spree killers over there?"

"What is the 'spree'?" asked Enni.

"It's when somebody . . ." He regathered himself. "Okay, pay attention. There was this *other* Speck—distant relation, same last name—I wasn't even born yet—but the guy butchered eight innocent nurses. Raped one of them, slit their throats. A hard thing to live down, right? Imagine I go to a nightclub, chat up a cute young babe like you, first thing I'm doing is explaining how peaceful I am, how I don't eat meat products, how I can't look at a stupid roller coaster without getting all seasick. It's embarrassing. What if your name was, like, I don't know, like Hitler or something? How would you feel?"

Enni sat on his lap and frowned at him. "Babe, you said?"

"Sorry?"

"You say I am the babe."

"Well, yeah. It's an expression. In English it means—"

"I *know* what this means. You love only the flesh body."

"Hey," Henry said snappishly. "I'm talking murder here. You're worried about words?"

"I worry *babe* is no respect."

He let out a breath of exasperation. "Don't you modern babes—girls—don't you sit around calling men hunks and studs and all that? Babe, hunk—what's the difference?"

"But Mister Henry, I am not this babe."

"Okay, but what I'm getting at—"

"When a woman say 'hunk,' she will maybe giggle, but she will not make the big bragging donkey noise. It is different."

"Donkey? What are you talking about?"

"The man sound—*Hffmmmgh!* In sex you make that noise."

"You're kidding."

"*Hffmmmgh!* Like that."

"Well, I'll tell you something," Henry said sternly, "that's not a donkey noise, that's a Speck noise. There's homicide in my family tree, cutthroat stuff, so maybe I overcompensate."

"The naughty donkey," said Enni.

Henry shook his head in confusion. She was throwing him off his game with crap that didn't belong. "Listen," he said. "If you look like I do, like Superman or Burt Reynolds or somebody, what the hell, you go with what works. I'm a hunk, so what? Do I complain?"

"But why donkey?" said Enni.

"Donkey! I'm in love with you!"

"With Enni?"

"Obvious, isn't it?" Henry gave her a romantic pat on the rump. "That's why I'm being straight with you about this Speck problem. People get the wrong idea; they think I'm carrying some kind of—I don't know—a murder disease or something. I'm harmless. I get a blood test, I faint. No joke. Down I go." He looked at her to see if he was making headway. "Besides, the old great-haircut, great-tan guy, he's history. I'm a new me."

Enni laughed.

"All you like is squeeze on Enni."

"Well, okay. That, too."

She rearranged herself on his lap, partly a straddle, partly a cuddle, and said, "If this Speck name is problem, why not change it like Enni do? I am born Eau Claire, Wisconsin. Peggy Shaughnessy."

"You're a Peggy?"

"Was Peggy, long time ago. You like this new Enni, yes?"

"What about Finland? You showed me a passport."

"Easy! Ask Alvin to get. Total not real passport."

"Alvin?"

"Friendly neighbor, yes. Small town, meet in Blue Fly. Hunky-dory."

Henry lifted her off his lap and deposited her on the sofa.

"We make love?" she said.

"No," said Henry, "we make *sense*. Alvin's the guy I just met, right? The guy with the beard?"

"Old, old boyfriend. No worry, okey-dokey?"

"Stop talking like that. You're from Eau Claire, for Chris-sake."

"Talk how?"

"Like Greta Garbo. Skipping every other word."

The girl pulled her knees to her chest, sulking.

"Cut it out," Henry said. "This whole time, I'm in love with a fake Finn. You should be ashamed."

"You want I should be plain Peggy?"

"I don't know what I want," said Henry, "except it's like I've run into some freaky actress." He paused. "Do you actually climb mountains?"

"Sorry, no."

"Is anything real? Cruise ships? Pest control?"

She shook her head.

"Tap dance?"

"Tap dance! I show you!"

She brightened, pushed to her feet, and tap-danced. "It would be better," she said, "not in bare feet."

"Probably," said Henry.

Enni flopped back on the sofa.

"I think we stop now," she said. "You love Enni, not so much love Peggy. Our secret, yes?"

"Yeah, okay. Let me think a minute." Henry looked at his wristwatch, not that he cared about time, except to buy some. "Here's the deal. Let's hear you say just one Peggy thing. Then we'll go back to Enni."

"You are sure?"

"Yeah. Do Peggy talk."

"Okey-dokey." She put her lips to his ear, and whispered, "Get out the credit card, bubba, and let's drain that mother-fucker." She leaned back and looked at him. "Good Peggy talk?"

"Pretty good, yeah," said Henry. "How old is Peggy?"

"Enni?"

"No, the other one. Peggy."

"Ah, yes. Peggy will be almost eighteen."

"You're seventeen?"

"*Peggy* is seventeen," she said. "Enni is twenty. Enni travels whole world, teaches the lap dance."

"Lap?"

"Tap," she said. "No sweat."

"You said 'lap.'"

"Lap and tap. You see some problem?"

A sour taste rose into Henry's throat.

"Yeah, I see a problem," he said. "A seventeen-year-old lap dancer? People will think—" The word came to him, but there was no reason to put ideas in her head. "You could've told me all this before . . . Stay there, I'll be back in a second."

He hurried into the bedroom, dug through his suitcase, and returned to the sofa with his standard consent form.

"Read it and sign," he said. "Both of you."

30

EVELYN'S FLIGHT TO MINNESOTA HAD BEEN DELAYED by more than a week. Twice she had cancelled; twice she had rebooked. Don't do this, she'd think, then she'd think, Do it, then she'd think, Don't! Even in late October, after her plane had touched down in the Twin Cities, Evelyn spent a restless night in a hotel near the airport, waking often, quarreling with herself, at one point sitting frozen and indecisive on her midnight-dark balcony.

At daybreak she boarded a shuttle back to the airport, had coffee, then booked an immediate return flight to L.A.

Ten minutes later she muttered, "Coward."

Undoing the flight changes consumed the better part of the morning. Nevertheless, Evelyn hesitated when her boarding number was called. During the turbulent forty-six-minute hop northward, she consumed two and a half vodka tonics, which did her little good as she walked into a bleak, nearly deserted Bemidji Regional Airport. She almost turned back again. If there was a sensible purpose for all this, she had forgotten it. Boyd was Boyd. You couldn't talk away heartbreak.

She sent a short text to Junius—*I'm here, please don't worry*—and caught an old, fish-smelling cab to Windy Point Resort just outside Bemidji. Here, at least, was something familiar.

Evelyn checked in, showered, napped, and later awoke to a jet-lag headache with a vodka kicker.

Well, she wondered, what now?

Outside, the day had gone from autumn gold to an almost blackish gray, the sky thickened by dangerous-looking clouds that somehow comforted her. As a girl, Evelyn had spent summers a few miles from here, out on Lake Larceny with Dooney and her mother, and although their divorce was already in the cards—forced gaiety, late-night bitterness—the memories were mostly happy, or happy in the way ignorance softens remembrance. Dooney was more than a decade away from stepping out of his locked closet. Her mother was thirteen years away from a separate beach house, a succession of gentleman escorts, lung cancer, and St. Ursula's Crematorium in Thousand Oaks.

For Evelyn, who had been spared those tumultuous years by boarding school and then by Stanford, the lakes and forests of her girlhood seemed both wondrously magical and completely illusory, a pleasant summertime lie. Not unlike, she now realized, her years with Boyd Halverson Otis Birdsong Whoever.

She closed the room's drapes and slept again, deeply this time, awakening late in the night to the sounds of thunder and heavy rain and the ping of her cell phone. A message from Junius: *Who's worried? I play the Yankees tomorrow. Love you too much.*

Win, Evelyn texted back, then ordered room service.

Eighteen hundred miles westward, in Fulda, California, Randy Zapf and Toby Van Der Kellen had completed a bank-robbing dress rehearsal and were now comparing notes over a six-pack in Randy's getaway Cutlass. Out of cop uniform, Toby wore a disguise of tights, tail, and a Lady Gaga mask. "Yes, ma'am," Randy kept saying whenever Toby opened his mouth, which was putting the boil to Toby's temper.

"Listen," the cop grunted. "One more 'ma'am' and you're sugar beet fertilizer. And that disguise of yours isn't what I'd call macho."

"It's Matt Dillon," said Randy. "*Gunsmoke*, man."

"Matt Dillon didn't carry a friggin' hoe."

Randy popped open a Schlitz, sipped the overflow, and briefly wondered how Toby might look after a nice professional hoeing. The fertilizer comment had come too quickly, as if Toby had been practicing in front of a mirror.

Randy told himself to keep it friendly.

"Well, looky here," he said. "It's barely midnight, what say you get out of them tights and we shoot some pool, you and me and Wanda Jane?"

"I don't fraternize with criminals. And tomorrow we got a bank to rob."

"Yeah, right. What time was that again?"

Toby crushed his beer can and opened his door. "You really are an idiot, aren't you?"

"Some think so, some don't," said Randy.

"Who doesn't?"

"Cyrus doesn't. Carl doesn't. They don't think much of anything."

Toby stepped out of the Cutlass, slammed the door, and waddled over to his squad car. Erasing, Toby decided, was not out of the question.

Randy watched him go, thinking almost exactly the same thought.

A half block away, in Community National's chilly vault, Lois Cutterby slipped Douglas's shotgun under two pillowcases stuffed with a hundred thousand dollars in crisp, freshly delivered bills.

Douglas, who watched, said, "Tomorrow will be fun, don't you think?"

"So-so," said Lois. "Another day at the office."

Douglas chuckled. "You know something, lovebug? I wonder why everybody on the planet doesn't get into the banking business. Not enough greed maybe."

Lois nodded and looked at him with an affectionate smile.

Lardass, she was thinking.

Seven hundred miles south, Calvin said, "Okay, Jimmy, I understand the big business stuff, vertical, horizontal, all that, but didn't you mention something about a child? A dead one?"

"I don't talk about that," Dooney said.

"Was it your fault?"

"No," Dooney said. "But I don't talk about it."

And on Lake Larceny, Angie Bing was saying, "Obviously, suicide is a sin, so we'll automatically ignore that possibility. God gives life, God takes life, it's super simple. You need to get your act together, Boyd. Snap out of your dream world, figure out what you want for the rest of your life. At your age there isn't a whole lot of time to waste. And I'm still waiting on a birthday present."

31

ANGIE AND ALVIN WERE GETTING ALONG NICELY. Most days, after looting Dooney's compound, they swam or took the boat out or lay sunning themselves on Dooney's dock. In the evenings, which were growing chilly, Boyd sometimes sat with them before a fire in the mansion's oversize great room, its ceiling high and vaulted, the walls a menagerie of deceased deer and fish and wolves and waterfowl.

Sometimes they played cards, sometimes they watched the fire, sometimes they listened to talk radio tearing apart the last shreds of American civility. A political season had opened; rhetorical artillery was booming; Boyd found himself impressed by the scale and grandeur and daring of it all, like a proud father, like Edison watching whole cities light up in the glare of phosphorescent new lies. Occasionally, Boyd chuckled. Most often he cringed. He was culpable, of course. He was ashamed. He should've blown his head off.

The warm days and chilly nights had the feel of halftime at a lopsided sporting event, an intermission crying out for departure, but there was little to do but hang on and see what developed. Neither Angie nor Alvin seemed in the least concerned about occupying the place. Angie had made use of Jim Dooney's embossed stationery, dispatching letters of dismissal to a lawn maintenance firm, a housecleaning service, a handyman, and the car dealership charged with caring for Dooney's vehicles. Under the same letterhead, Angie had informed the Bemidji Police Department of the property's three new live-in caretakers. "These hardworking Christians have my absolute confidence," wrote Angie-Dooney. "And as they undertake major renovations, I would reward any assistance your men in blue might offer. Your loyal (and wealthiest) taxpayer, James Dooney."

There were few visitors. No awkward questions.

Through the crisp, cooling days of late October, Boyd paid little attention to practical matters. Dazed and empty-headed, he drifted from hour to hour with the sensation of a man who had outlived his usefulness. He felt hollow and weightless. For the most part, he lived in his head, replaying history. Occasionally, as if emerging from a dream, he'd catch bits and pieces of the here and now. He learned that Alvin was a native of south-side, Blackstone Ranger Chicago. He was an unemployed plumber, a three-tour veteran of Iraq and Afghanistan, a Bemidji State dropout, a lover of Bach, a cheerful thief, and a dealer in whatever illegal commodities came his way, which now included a garage full of handsome vehicles. He had already sold Dooney's snowmobile and Ford pickup; he was entertaining offers on the Ferrari and Porsche, or so Boyd surmised, and he had—with self-satisfied ceremony—presented the Bugatti to Angie as a tardy birthday gift.

The guy was a crook, Boyd concluded, but a friendly crook— almost likable.

Day by day, over meals or while fishing from Dooney's dock, Alvin attended Boyd with the brisk efficiency of a nurse, clucking words of encouragement, entertaining him with war stories and tales of the north woods. Lake Larceny, Alvin explained one afternoon, had once been called Zaaga'igan Waagosh, which in Ojibwe meant Lake Fox; later, the wife of a

Norwegian farmer rechristened it Blueberry Pond; and later still, after the lake's theft by treaty in the 1870s, a clever St. Paul cartographer came up with the alliterative and enduring Lake Larceny. Alvin—whose surname, Boyd discovered, was either Grable or Graybull—had a habit of laughing at his own stories, qualifying or ridiculing almost everything that came out of his own mouth. Grinning amiably behind his bushy blond beard, Alvin told Fallujah stories, Kandahar stories, near-miss stories, funny stories, scary stories, but always with a don't-take-this-too-literally twist of the tongue, as if signaling that he and Boyd were members of the same truth-stretching tribe.

Alvin was not bad company. He was affable to a fault. Yet Boyd kept mostly to himself. He looked on with only mild interest as Angie and Alvin pushed ahead with their dismemberment of Dooney's lakeside estate, carting away cars and hot tubs and whatever else could be profitably fenced or otherwise liquidated for cash. On weekends they held yard sales. Each Tuesday, Alvin drove a load of furniture down to Minneapolis, returning with an empty U-Haul truck and a pocketful of hundred-dollar bills. Plainly enough, Angie and Alvin had become partners not only in crime, but also partners in something more intimate. Angie was the brains of the operation, Alvin the infatuated brawn. They had discovered a pair of antique pinball machines in an attached guesthouse, and the two of them spent late-night hours slapping silver balls into tiny holes, taking turns praising each other's marksmanship. Angie kept up her usual chatter, infusing it with sappy endearments. She called Alvin Tiger. Or Monster. On his part, Alvin gazed back at her with gooey adoration.

It was astonishing, Boyd reflected, how swiftly she had

traded him in on the latest model. Astonishing, but mostly a relief.

Now it was Alvin who endured Angie's topic-jumping disquisitions on whatever popped into her hyperactive mind—religion, of course, but also the evils of fountain pens, floor polish, canned vegetables, bunk beds, cheapie engagement rings, public nudity, and—glancing at Boyd—wishy-washy men. All of this Alvin tolerated with superhuman patience. Stroking his beard, nodding to prime her pump, the guy's staying power was spectacular.

Slowly at first, then decisively, Boyd concluded it was a scam, but he was content to let the days slide by.

One morning, he found himself lying faceup on Dooney's tennis court—no memory of before or after or why.

The same afternoon, he awakened from a thick, swampy nap, only to realize he was standing knee-deep in Lake Larceny, Alvin at his side, Angie on the dock a few feet away, and Boyd himself in midsentence as he struggled to complete a thought about his days as a paperboy to the stars.

"Well," Angie said when he fell silent. "My seventh boyfriend was a paperboy."

Randy Zapf sat over an atlas in the Fulda public library, impatiently searching for the word *Bemidji* on a map of Minnesota. Geography was not his strong suit, nor was spelling, nor was keeping a lid on his temper.

How does a guy read a map, he was thinking, when all you can do is cuss to yourself about the message that popped up on your cell phone a few nights ago, all about engagements and hairbrushes and guys you don't even know? How do you concentrate?

Randy was pretty sure the letter *e* came after *i* in the alphabet, which caused some delay, and he was ready to bust a gasket when his eye accidentally fell on a word that looked like Bemidji, except it obviously wasn't even an American word, probably Canadian or something, probably invented by some wee-wee who wouldn't know a Cutlass from a Peterbilt.

Randy tore out the atlas page, stuffed it in his pocket, chatted up the not-so-hot librarian, then ambled down to the Mobil station to steal a book of road maps.

Thirty minutes later, after polishing off a plate of hush puppies, he headed back to his rented room, pulled his *takoba* sword off the wall, took a good long pee, hustled down to the Cutlass, stashed the sword in the trunk under a pile of comic books, then went looking for Toby Van Der Kellen. They had a bank to rob in a few hours, but first things first.

He found Toby where he thought he'd find him, a half mile outside town, parked behind a Wendy's billboard with his radar gun. "What I need to do," Randy explained, "is hit the road ASAP, postpone the stickup for a week or two. Or else you can do the job yourself and grease my pockets later."

Toby sat smoking, blowing cancer at Randy's nose. At first, Toby seemed miffed. Then a thoughtful expression crossed his face.

"Postpone," he said, almost slyly. "That sounds like scaredy-cat talk. You afraid of a bank caper?"

Randy shook his head. "Nah, it's Angie trouble, I gotta hit the road. Long drive. You happen to know where I can pick up a hairbrush with a silver handle?"

"Not offhand. Might try JCPenney."

"Been there, no luck. Speaking of handles, how about you

handle the bank, then we split the take after I get back?" Randy winked. "I'll lend you my hoe."

There was still that thoughtful look on Toby's face, as if he were busy counting something, a pile of money maybe.

"Yeah, I guess," he said. "Where's the hoe?"

"At home. Under my bed."

"What about the *Gunsmoke* getup? Matt Dillon. Can I borrow it?"

"All yours," said Randy. "Might be tight around the tummy."

"Is that a wisecrack?"

"Sorta. Between pals."

Toby exhaled cancer again. "Go get the stuff. Then take off. Forever, if you're smart."

"Smart enough," said Randy.

On the evening of October 25, Alvin whipped up a mushroom, spinach, and walleye casserole, and over dinner Boyd felt the painful stirrings of an appetite that had mostly abandoned him for many days. He ate and ate. First the casserole, then a salad, then a half row of Oreos out of the package. He pulled a left-over sandwich from the refrigerator and went to work on it while Angie drew a breath and stormed into the second half of a forty-minute monologue about relationships, her own in particular, how in sixth grade a boy named Cecil had stolen her lunch pail at school and not ten minutes later she'd found him feasting on her Twinkies in the boy's lavatory, which naturally led to a first kiss—actually her fourth or fifth, but this one was tongue in mouth, which counted as a first. Cecil had been succeeded in seventh grade by Dorian and Everett and Devon, but those three were Mormons and Angie didn't believe in mixed relationships, so they went on a completely different list, not the relationship list, although tongue in mouth still counted as an actual first kiss, even if she had to pray for forgiveness every night until Brandon came along in eighth grade when she'd taken pity on him for getting expelled after cooking a live frog in chemistry class, but unfortunately Brandon wasn't all that romantic and kissing wasn't his main interest, so she'd dumped him for the paperboy, Luther, except the paperboy relationship lasted only four or five hours because Brandon got jealous and scratched Luther up pretty bad with a nail file and ended up getting expelled again, which seemed totally unfair, especially since Brandon was being gallant and exciting, which was what relationships needed—romantic backbone—like with Randy Zapf, who everybody treated like a loser, a nobody, but who almost always gave her first dibs on everything he stole, except for all that rodeo stuff she didn't care about.

Alvin gazed at her with heroic concentration, a frozen smile at his lips.

As a test, Boyd lifted his fork and said, "Could you repeat that?"

"Repeat what?" Angie asked.

"Everything. All of it."

Angie squinted at him. "What does 'everything' mean?"

"The whole spiel," said Boyd. "What you've been talking about for the last twenty years or so. I think Alvin might've dozed off."

For a moment, Angie's eyes shifted toward Alvin, then slid back toward Boyd.

"He has this smiling trick," Boyd explained. "It makes him look . . . sort of interested. Like he's enjoying it."

Alvin mumbled something, chuckled, and walked away.

"Well," Angie said, "that was probably the rudest thing I've ever heard. Just when Alvin's starting to find his way."

"Is he lost?"

"Of course he's lost. Are you blind?"

Boyd shook his head. "All that smiley stuff, he was faking it. He didn't hear even a single—"

"Just because you're jealous," Angie said softly, too softly, "doesn't give you the right to tear down somebody's psyche. Alvin was in a *war*—a *real* one. Haven't you ever heard of PTSD? The last thing he needed was that comment of yours."

"He's a thief," Boyd said.

"We're working on that."

"How? With talk therapy?"

Angie's face tightened. She seemed ready to cry, or ready to scream, but her voice dropped into something like a stage whisper. "In case you haven't noticed, Alvin loves me. Real love. Passion. Devotion. That kind. The kind I need and you need and everybody else needs."

"He loves you? Does that mean I'm off the hook?"

"No, it does not," she said. "It means I've got this theory about why you keep trying to get rid of me, why you wouldn't consecrate our relationship that night in L.A. Remember that? When I almost unzipped your pants? Back then I thought, Well, Boyd's being a gentleman, or else he's saving it for the honeymoon, or else he's bashful because he's old and decrepit and fat, or else it's been so long that he forgot how. But now I've figured it out." She studied him as though expecting something. "Do you want to hear my theory or not?"

"No," Boyd said.

"It's because you didn't want me to be a single mom."

"It is?"

"Sure, it is. You didn't want me alone in the world, stranded and bereft, probably suckling a fatherless child and weeping a widow's tears on your godless coffin."

"Shakespeare?" said Boyd.

"It's *me*!" Angie yelped. "You pushed me away, rejected me, because you thought you'd be dead and gone by now. Because the entire time we've been together, every single second, all you could think about was putting a hole in your thick head, and because you knew we wouldn't have a future together and you didn't want me to feel like a sex toy, like a used-up woman. Am I right? Of course I'm right! Tell me I'm right!"

Boyd thought about disagreeing, or just walking away, but in fact she *was* right, or partly right.

"Okay," he said.

"So there you *are*! And now that suicide is ruled out—which, by the way, was off the charts on the stupid scale—now we can move forward with this relationship, see if you can treat me like a real human being. Now there *is* a future! You're redeemed. Open your arms, for Pete's sake. Open that miserable, hard heart of yours."

Boyd felt something jerk across his thoughts, a mental hiccup.

The truth, he realized, was that he had no idea what to do with himself. Not now, not ever.

He grinned stupidly at Angie.

"You don't give up, do you?"

"No, I don't," she said.

"May I have my gun back?"

32

IN FULDA, CALIFORNIA, THERE WAS THE PROBLEM
of water, or the absence of water, and as a consequence, Douglas Cutterby carried the heavy, sometimes contradictory burdens of obligation to his community and obligation to the
health and stability of Community National Bank. It was Douglas who kept the farmers afloat through five and a half years
of killer drought. It was Douglas who fed the cattle. It was
Douglas who issued second and third mortgages on bone-dry
onion and sugar beet fields, bone-dry grazing land, bone-
dry irrigation systems, bone-dry wells, and bone-dry savings
accounts.

On the other hand, only a solvent and prospering Community National Bank allowed him to continue his benevo-
lence toward the town and environs of Fulda, California. A
bankrupt bank wasn't a bank. A bankrupt bank made no loans,
supported no families, rescued no businesses. There lay the
contradiction. On occasion, foreclosure was necessary. Many
occasions, in fact. Forty-three occasions at last count. Community National now owned just under eleven thousand acres
of California, another six thousand acres of southern Oregon.
And, of course, Douglas owned Community National. Already,
after some speedy rezoning, he had unloaded three thousand
acres to a grocery distributor, an express package service, an oil

conglomerate, a shopping mall developer, and—still pending—
a foreign manufacturer of very popular automobiles. The original mortgage losses had been recouped in full. And Douglas's
portfolio still included a nice chunk of two states.

At the moment, as he waited for Fulda's mayor, Chub
O'Neill, to meet him on the first tee for nine holes of golf,
Douglas reviewed his upcoming transaction with a couple of
dumbbell bank robbers. Small potatoes, only a hundred grand,
but the potatoes added up. Like with bank fees—fifteen bucks
here, thirty bucks there, and pretty soon you're looking at two
nights at the Bellagio. The devil was in the details, and Douglas
prided himself on details.

This was a Friday, the twenty-fifth day of October, 10:30 a.m.,
and in precisely five hours he would be a hundred grand richer
than he was here on the first tee, loosening up with a few lazy
practice swings. Details: vault wide-open, cash bundled up and
ready to go, cameras on, audio on, shotgun loaded, Lois as
greedy as ever.

A pity, to be sure, that he'd be losing a wizard double bookkeeper. What could you do? Community service.

Douglas bagged his driver, took out his putter, moved to
the practice green, and dropped three eight-footers, no sweat.
Drive for show, putt for dough.

Randy Zapf was already thumb sore. Not even three hundred
miles under his belt, another fifteen hundred still ahead, and
his trucker's pal was full to the brim and the Cutlass was begging for another quart of oil and the scenery belonged in one
of those National Geographic videos guaranteed to send you
into dreamland or your money back. And his thumbs ached.

Not ached, exactly. Sort of numb, sort of tingly, as if he'd been sleeping on them all night.

He decided to switch thumbs every ten miles. Except right away he was fantasizing about how he'd handle the Angie situation, nifty ways to put her in her place once and for all—tell her she had twelve seconds to pack a suitcase, one Mississippi, two Mississippi—not to mention a bunch of interesting plans for the JCPenney dude, like that time over in Reno, a guy who wanted his computers back, and how Randy grinned, and said, "Sure thing," and how a week later he'd returned the computers in a navy duffel, everything miniaturized, about fifty thousand tiny, smashed-up pieces . . . then, bang, end of daydream, and he'd almost fly off the road because he forgot to thumb switch and his driving thumb felt like it belonged to somebody stone-dead, like Cyrus, like scrawny old Carl.

A few hours farther down the road, somewhere in northwest Nevada, Randy got to wondering if maybe he should've stuck around for the bank job. How many opportunities do you get to rob a bank that doesn't mind getting robbed? Probably not a whole bunch, he figured. Kind of hurt missing out on the fun. On top of that, handing over the hoe to Toby had probably been the third or fourth most depressing moment in his entire life, right behind getting kicked out of the boys' reformatory down in Sacramento, which, now that he thought about it, was probably the only school that ever taught him anything worth learning, like how to tape a window so you could cut it open in ten seconds, nice and clean, not even scratching yourself. The second most depressing moment had to be . . . He didn't want to think about it.

In Twin Falls he filled up the Cutlass again, bought another case of motor oil, emptied his trucker's pal, wiped up the spillage, then checked his wallet for spending money. He was down to seventeen bucks and two stolen credit cards. After stopping for a couple of Big Macs and a vanilla shake, and after both credit cards were declined, it occurred to Randy that by now Community National had already been robbed and Toby was squatting on Randy's share of a gold mine.

For a second he considered heading back to Fulda. On the other hand, there was that McDonald's forty feet away. Lights on, two old-lady customers, middle of the night, almost closing time. Should be a sign hanging on the door—*please stick me up.* Boy, Randy thought, what he'd give for his hoe.

In the trunk, his only choices were a tire iron, his *takoba* sword, and his electrician's kit. He went with the kit, mainly because it seemed cooler, partly because he didn't want to dirty up the sword.

After breakfast in the near-empty dining room of Windy Point Resort, Evelyn placed three phone calls. First, she ordered up a cab. Next, she spoke briefly with Junius, checking to be sure he'd called off his muscle. It turned out that he hadn't, or not entirely. "I want it entirely," said Evelyn, "and I want the entirely right now." She jabbed the end-call button on her phone, ordered another half pot of coffee, waited a few minutes, then dialed up a nursing home in Seattle, Washington. When the old man gave her a puzzled hello, Evelyn rose to her feet and walked outside to catch her cab and carried on a conversation with eighty-three-year-old Otis Birdsong that lasted halfway out to Lake Larceny.

"Well, I'm here if he wants me," the old man said. "But it would be a first."

* * *

An hour earlier, Henry Speck had dropped a two-pound monkey wrench into the pocket of his raincoat. He'd taken Enni's
arm and said, "What say we visit the neighbors?"

Enni had said, "Where is this rain?"

"On the way," Henry had said. "Might even be snow. Hey,
can I ask Peggy something?"

"Ask Peggy?"

"Right."

Enni thought about it. "You will still love to death Enni?"

"Sure I will."

"Okey-dokey, ask Peggy."

"Ever stub your toes?"

"Shit, yeah," said Peggy.

"Hurts, huh?"

"Fuckin' A."

"You're in for a treat."

In Fulda, California, Toby Van Der Kellen lay without much of a
stomach on the linoleum floor of Community National's vault.
Lois Cutterby was in no better shape. She slouched wantonly
on an iron love seat three blocks away. At her feet was what
looked like an empty trick-or-treat bag.

The sun had not quite risen as Douglas Cutterby sat at his
rosewood desk, taking a last satisfied look at the bank's camera clips. There was Lois with the trick-or-treat bag. There was
Matt Dillon stuffing it with a hundred grand. There was Matt
again—with a hoe, for Chrissake—giving Lois a quick love
peck on the cheek, and there was Lois giving Matt a quick
love peck in the stomach with a twelve gauge. There was Lois
heading for the door with the trick-or-treat bag. And there was

that cute outdoor shot of Lois hustling down South Spruce Street, heading for an iron love seat and an unpleasant few moments with her off-camera husband. Odd, he thought, that she had been careless with the second barrel of a double-barreled twelve gauge.

Douglas Cutterby congratulated himself. Tit for tat, he told himself. Bang bang to two bangers.

Boyd Halverson had been wide-awake since two in the morning. He'd taken a stroll along the shoreline of Lake Larceny, listened to the splash of waves against Dooney's dock, and found himself regretting the last few months of his life. He could not undo anything, could not unrob a bank. But managing a JCPenney store no longer seemed all that terrible, nor did Kiwanis, nor did falling asleep in the pompous company of Winston Churchill.

For some time, he watched a turtle make its patient way through the moonlight toward whatever a turtle's future might be. Boyd wasn't thinking, really. Just quick flashes of this and that: Evelyn hauling a crib out to the street; a dossier on the kitchen table; Jim Dooney's smirking blue eyes; an exquisite, handcrafted parrot casket on display in the Jalan Surabaya marketplace; an obscure paperboy pedaling for his life up Ocean Park Boulevard; his father looking at him with milky eyes and saying, "Changed your name?"

Empty time went by, the sun rose, and Boyd looked up to see a cab bumping down Jim Dooney's long gravel driveway.

33

WANDA JANE EPSTEIN WAS HAVING TROUBLE FIT-
ting the pieces together. There lay Toby on the vault floor, no
stomach to speak of, all duded up like a Halloween cowboy,
a bloody hoe at his side. Three blocks down the street, Lois
Cutterby looked no better, probably worse, her corpse sprawled
across an iron love seat. And there, sitting in grave silence at his
desk, Douglas Cutterby had just finished running video clips of
a holdup in progress.

It was a little after eight o'clock on a Saturday morning. After Douglas's call, Wanda Jane had taken a peek at the bodies,
jumped on the horn to call the county sheriff's department, then
sat down with Douglas to wait. Already they had been waiting
forty-five minutes.

"A hoe," said Wanda Jane. "What the heck's up with that?"

Douglas shrugged, switched off the video recorder, and
leaned forward with his head in his hands. He didn't speak.
Maybe grief, Wanda Jane thought, or maybe something else.

"Honest," she said, "I wish I could—you know—*do* something. I'm not a real cop. Not even close." She hesitated. "It looks
like . . . it looks like Lois shot him and then walked out of here
with a lot of money."

"It does look that way," Douglas murmured.

"Do you think—?"

"What else *can* I think? My wife was robbing me."

"You?"

"The bank. Same thing."

"But somebody shot her. She's deceased."

"I'll say," said Douglas.

Wanda Jane looked around for help. Officially, she was a police officer, except all she had ever policed was a dispatch microphone and a few file cabinets. Twenty or thirty seconds ticked by, then Douglas pushed to his feet, came around the desk, and rested his hands on her shoulders in a gesture of . . . Wanda Jane wasn't sure what.

"My dear," he said, too quietly. "I'm afraid we're up against the obvious. It's no secret that Lois and Officer Van Der Kellen were . . . I won't pull punches . . . they were involved, let's say. Intimately. What we have here is a bank robbery wrapped inside a lover's quarrel wrapped inside greed. Or in some other order."

"I guess. But how did Lois end up in heaven?"

"An accomplice, no doubt. Whoever has my money."

"An accomplice, you think?"

Douglas sighed a banker's windy sigh. "Three of them pulled it off. My wife, of course, and that dead cop in my vault, and somebody else." He squeezed her shoulders. "For what it's worth, I'm pretty certain I know who that somebody else is. I suggest you bag the hoe, check it for fingerprints. Same with the cowboy clothes. Unless I'm mistaken, you'll soon be looking for Randy Zapf."

"Randy?"

"A drifter. Burglar."

"I know who he is," said Wanda Jane, "but I don't—"

"Zapf has been in and out of your jail a dozen times, three dozen. You'll have his fingerprints on file." Douglas ran his

hands reassuringly downward along her spinal column, heading south. "May I ask a somewhat personal question, Wanda
Jane?"

"Well, sure."

"How old are you?"

"Thirty-four," she said.

"Attached or unattached?"

"Sir?"

"Best beau, life companion—that sort of thing? You're an
attractively structured young lady."

"My tits, you mean?"

"I do."

Wanda Jane sat still for a moment, then turned and faced him.

"Mr. Cutterby, here's the deal. Right now we've got Toby
stinking up your bank vault. And your wife looks like somebody dumped a smoothie on a park bench. What's up with the
structure talk?"

"Alas," said Douglas. "I'm not a sentimental man."

"Yeah. Noted. Right now, though, I'm all you've got for law
enforcement in this town. Best leave my tits out of it."

Douglas shrugged, smiled amiably, and returned to the
presidential chair behind his presidential desk.

"Very well," he said. "But no reason why we can't soon
negotiate—you know—some sort of merger."

"You'd need to lose the paunch."

"Done."

"And thirty years."

"Viagra."

"And that smug look on your face."

"It isn't smug. It's anticipation." Douglas worked his jaw in an expression of hopeful masculinity. "In any case, returning to our situation here, I'd like to recommend a course of action. Two words—drop it."

Wanda Jane laughed at him. "Bank robbery's a federal crime."

"No, my love, bank robbery can't be—and isn't—a crime, federal or otherwise, not if there has *been* no bank robbery. You need a victim, correct? Bear in mind, my disfigured late wife plainly walked out of here with the bank's funds in her possession, and, of course, she is—or was—a co-owner of the bank. Hence no victim, no robbery, and therefore no crime to report. What we do have is a shortfall of a hundred thousand dollars, a situation I'm sure the authorities will swiftly correct. Fingerprints, remember? Randy Zapf?"

Wanda Jane grunted and said, "Huh."

"'Huh' means you understand?"

"No, sir. It means I'm stuck with two corpses minus a whole bunch of stomach. And I'm supposed to drop it?"

"You misunderstand." The man's voice fell into patronizing slush. "Corpse number one, Officer Van Der Kellen, was shot dead by Lois—plain as day, we just watched the clip. Case closed. Corpse number two, my beloved Lois, met her fate at the hands of an accomplice by the name of Randolph Zapf. Again, case closed. All I'm saying, dear, is let's not push this past the obvious."

Wanda Jane studied him briefly. "You've got it pretty well thought out, don't you?"

"Every detail," said Douglas.

"Except only Lois and Toby show up in the camera clips. No Randy. No accomplice."

"Of course not. No doubt he was waiting for the loot, three blocks away."

"And where's the proof?"

"Proof?" said Douglas. "How about my gut-shot wife? How about Zapf's fingerprints on the hoe, on the cowboy outfit? How about the missing cash?"

"You seem awfully sure."

"Oh, I am. I'm sure."

Wanda Jane glanced at her wristwatch. "All right, I appreciate the theory. Let's lock up and wait for somebody who knows what the hell they're doing. Fair enough?"

"Certainly," said Douglas. "You're the law."

Outside, Wanda Jane pocketed the bank keys, told Douglas to stay put, and walked the half block to Elmo Hive's pool hall on North Spruce. The place hadn't opened yet, but she found Elmo out back, unloading a water heater from the bed of his Chevy pickup.

As best she could, Wanda Jane explained the situation.

"Old Toby, he was due," Elmo said. "Lois, too. I'm not surprised. What do you need?"

"Grab a tarp and go cover up what's left of Lois." Wanda Jane thought for a moment. She was winging this. "Hang loose till the sheriff's people show up. Should be twenty minutes, a half hour maybe. I'll see if I can dig up some crime scene tape."

"Well, jeez," said Elmo, "I've got this water heater; I can't drop everything just to—"

"Elmo."

"Yeah?"

"You rake in three hundred a month as Toby's backup. Last I heard, you worked three hours way back in August."

"Six," Elmo muttered. "But okay. Help me get this damned heater inside. One thing for sure—with Toby out of commission, we're gonna have a townful of happy Mexicans tonight."

Wanda Jane nodded. "I'm not all that torn up myself."

Together, they carried the water heater through a back door and up a flight of stairs. Elmo put on a clean shirt, clipped his constable's badge to the brim of a Seahawks cap, folded up a plastic pool table cover, and followed Wanda Jane out to the street. It was not yet 8:45 in the morning. Except for Douglas Cutterby pacing in front of Community National, nothing much was moving.

"So Doug did it?" Elmo said.

"I'm pretty sure. At least the Lois part."

The two of them stood watching Douglas Cutterby for a few seconds, then Wanda Jane sighed and said, "You know what?"

"What?" said Elmo.

"Forget the yellow tape. I'm taking a drive out to Dougie's place, see if I can scare up a shotgun and a hundred thousand dollars."

Elmo looked at her. "Be careful. The guy's mean."

"I'm meaner," said Wanda Jane.

34

EVELYN, ANGIE, ALVIN, AND BOYD SAT IN FOLDING chairs arranged hastily in the center of Jim Dooney's well-looted great room on the shore of Lake Larceny. Conversation was sparse and stilted. Except for a grand piano and a pair of wolf heads mounted on a wall, the place had been emptied of its furnishings, and now each clink of a coffee cup, each cleared throat and recrossing of the legs carried the strange, amplified echo of anxiety.

Boyd sat with his hands folded in his lap. He looked on with mild interest as Alvin did his best to smooth things out. To his credit, Alvin had prepared the coffee, found four mismatched cups and saucers, and he was now asking Evelyn about the wolf heads, their history and provenance. "Your father slew those critters, I assume?"

Evelyn carefully placed her coffee cup on what was now a plywood floor. The hardwood and pine flooring had been sold a week earlier.

"Slew?" she said.

"It means killed. It's one of Angie's words. She knows some awesome words."

"Does she?" said Evelyn. Her eyes slid toward Angie without quite reaching her. "Does she know the word *theft*?"

Alvin laughed. "What I meant was, I hear you grew up here, so I thought you might know how those wolves got slewn."

"*Slewn* isn't a word," Angie said. "The word is *slain*."

"Right," said Alvin.

Angie's lips had gone thin and tight. For ten minutes she had been shooting murderous thoughts at Evelyn. "And I know what *theft* means. It means fat cats with their own private barber's chairs and bowling alleys. And their fatter-cat daughters."

"Ah," said Evelyn.

"Ah what?" said Angie.

"I see you've been talking to Boyd."

"Boyd doesn't talk. Hardly at all. Not since he tried to put one of your daddy's bullets in his head."

Evelyn had the poise not to glance at Boyd. Poise was her default. She turned instead toward Alvin.

"Actually, I didn't grow up here," she said brightly. "I summered in Minnesota—two or three times, not all that often. And I doubt my father slew many wolves. Dooney *was* the wolf." She scanned the barren room without looking at any of them. "I'll admit, though, I remember the house being a bit more lavishly appointed. Furniture. That sort of thing."

"And a bowling alley," Angie muttered.

"Yes, and a bowling alley."

"And a boat you could use for a cruise ship."

"Should I apologize?"

"Yeah," Angie said. "Good idea."

"Well, then, forgive me," said Evelyn, casting a smile at not much of anything. She reached down for her cup, took a sip, and set it with ladylike precision back on the floor. "So then. Pardon begged. Now, if it's no trouble, I was hoping to spend a moment or two with my husband. Perhaps there's a spot where he and I might—"

"Husband?" Angie said. "You divorced him."

"Old habit, sorry. Dumb, fat-cat me."

Evelyn glossed the room with another smile. For the first time since she'd stepped out of her cab, she allowed her gaze to fall directly on Boyd. He looked up at her, partly dazzled, partly apprehensive.

He stood and said, "This way. My camper."

"After you," she said.

Sixty feet away, approaching from the shoreline, Henry Speck and Enni walked hand in hand up a grassy slope just as Boyd and Evelyn were stepping into the Pleasure-Way. Evelyn stopped and looked back.

"Stay here," she told Boyd. "I need to talk to that man."

Angie and Alvin watched through a window. Outside, a gentle, almost invisible snow was falling in the autumn sunlight.

"Any idea what's going on here?" Alvin said.

"Not exactly," said Angie. "But I can guess. Do me a favor, okay?"

"Make more coffee?"

"No. How much cash have we pulled in so far?"

"Counting the boat?"

"Counting everything."

"A lot. The place is pretty much stripped."

"Okay, good. Is the Bugatti gassed up?"

"I sold the Bugatti."

"Sold it? That was my birthday present."

"I can't help myself. PTSD."

"You were a typist, for God's sake."

"A disabled typist." He paused. "What's the favor?"

Angie turned away from the window.

"Listen, I've been thinking," she said. "This isn't working out the way I'd hoped. Our engagement's off. Really, really sorry."

"Yikes," Alvin said.

"Yikes is right. I need you to vacate."

"Vacate how?"

"We'll split up the money, then you hit the road. No hurry. Sometime in the next ten minutes."

"Afraid of the ex-wife?"

"How much?"

"Thirty-seven thousand each."

"That's all? It seems—"

"Stolen goods, Angie. You're lucky to get a nickel on the dollar. I explained that, didn't I?"

"You did. Go get it, then pack up."

Evelyn and Boyd sat across from each other at a tiny fold-down dining table in the cramped quarters of the Pleasure-Way. They had once loved each other with insane ferocity, which now made the twenty inches between them feel bizarre and falsely intimate. Twenty inches and ten years.

Small talk was out of the question. They looked at each other and remembered things. "The fact is, we shouldn't talk at all," Evelyn finally said. "We should sit here for a bit then go away."

She took his hand and held it to her lips. Nothing happened, because nothing could happen, and after a while, she returned his hand to him.

"That guy outside," Boyd said. "Who is he?"

"One of the reasons I'm here. He works for Junius."

"And who's Junius?"

"You know very well who Junius is. Be civil."

"Civil's my bedrock," said Boyd.

Evelyn leaned sharply forward, closing the distance between them. "That man out there, he gets paid for twisting
arms. Breaking arms. My husband wants you out of my life—
forever out, completely out—no more showing up like some
psycho Sir Lancelot."

"Right," Boyd said. "Sort of like you popping up here."

"I didn't come to score points, Boyd."

"Why then?"

"To help. I want to help you." She leaned back and looked
around the camper. "I told Henry—Henry's the thug out
there—I told him to lay off. But it's his job. He wants a word
with you."

Boyd nodded. "Fine. Is that all?"

"No," Evelyn said.

"What else?"

"Look, this is awkward. Why did you—?"

"Ten years, Evelyn. I ran out of ways to keep begging. In my
head, I mean. I used up all my words."

"I forgave you. I forgive you again."

"Yes, but it doesn't help. I thought a bullet might. Now it
seems silly."

"I *hope* it seems silly. It *is* silly."

Boyd tried to look at her but couldn't. All he wanted was to
crawl inside her and sleep there.

"Awkward, you're right," he said. "Should we take a walk?"

"Yes, let's," said Evelyn.

A scattering of snowflakes swirled in front of them as they
made their way down to Lake Larceny. The day had gone gray
and cold and windy. For some time, they followed the shoreline without speaking, neither of them feeling the need, then

Evelyn shivered and said, "Snow in October. Climate change, probably."

"Probably," Boyd said. "Or else Minnesota."

"So."

"So?"

"So you tried suicide?"

"In my own half-assed way. I wanted Dooney to watch."

"I see."

"Do you?"

"Not really. In fact, not at all. And did you actually rob a bank?"

To his surprise, Boyd laughed. "Yes, ma'am. Half-assed again. Picked the one and only bank that doesn't give a damn about getting robbed."

"I've wondered about that," she said. A frown, or maybe a wince, flickered across her face. "Not a word on the internet either. Are you sure you're not—"

"No, I'm not lying. And I'm not lying about not lying."

Her eyes shifted away from him.

"Why?" she said.

"You mean—?"

"Why rob a bank?"

Boyd thought about it. "No good answer. Curiosity. It's like if you see a plate-glass window, you keep looking at it, keep thinking how it would feel to hit it with a hammer, just smash away, so one day . . . I don't know. I guess maybe I needed this to happen. This. Right now."

"Should I pretend to understand that?"

"No. Don't pretend."

"I'm freezing. Take my arm, will you?"

"Sure."

"I don't hate you, Boyd."

"Is that so?"

"I don't. I'm scared for you."

He could think of nothing to say. Words wouldn't do it. Nothing would do it.

They walked a bit farther before Evelyn said, "Don't get angry with me, but I need to be sure this crazy suicide thing is finished now. Finished for good. I couldn't bear it, Boyd."

"You want me to promise? I'm a liar, don't forget."

"Promise anyway."

"Okay, I promise," he said.

"Are you saying that just for me?"

"For you, but not just for you. What I want is impossible—a rewind button. Start over. Do better. It's pure fantasy, I know, but right now I'd settle for JCPenney and a round of golf. Maybe a Lean Cuisine for dinner. I've scaled down the ambitions."

"Except there's a problem even with that. You rob banks."

"Only one bank. But, yeah, that's a problem."

"Boyd, may I kiss you?"

"To rewind?"

"No," she said. "Just to kiss."

They stopped and kissed the inconsequential kiss of the long divorced. A moment later they tried again, with even less consequence.

"Well," Evelyn sighed. "It beats fighting."

They walked for another forty-five minutes through a snowfall that had turned vigorous. They avoided history. They avoided Teddy and a dossier of lies and exotic nights in paradise. When they spoke, which was infrequently, it was to acknowledge the things that even now locked their lives together. Evelyn asked about stripping Dooney's log mansion—what was the point?—and Boyd shrugged and told her he was mostly uninvolved. "I'm a spectator," he said, "but I do get a kick out of watching the chandeliers disappear. I guess it's Angie's way of exacting revenge for me."

"It's grand larceny, Boyd."

"So it is and I admire the grandeur."

"People go to prison."

"Dooney didn't."

Evelyn gave him a sideways glance, partly irritation, partly a warning. "We're not going there," she said.

"You're right. Sorry."

"I'm not asking you to be sorry. I'm asking you not to go there." She took him by the arm again and fell silent for a while before releasing a sharp little breath, not quite a laugh. "This girl, Angie, she doesn't care for me, does she?"

"She does not."

"And you two have something going? I'm the enemy?"

"Kind of, but . . . She has a chip on her shoulder. You're the rich lady from the right side of the tracks."

"Understandable, I suppose. Sounds like the man I married."

"Now *you're* going there—that place you don't want to go."

Evelyn nodded. "It's hard, isn't it? Not talking about everything we should be talking about?"

"Not hard, just pointless," said Boyd.

"Of course. Pointless. But you know I adored you, yes?"

"Mostly I know it. Sometimes I have to make myself believe."

"Boyd?"

"Yes?"

"Why did you lie and lie to me?"

He hesitated for a second. "Because I'm a worthless shit. Because I loved you too much."

"Is that true?"

"Yes."

"Good. Let's be quiet."

Evelyn went inside herself for a while; then later, when they turned back toward Dooney's house, she apologized and said she was being ridiculous, she didn't mean to pile more guilt on him, didn't mean to dive back into the ugliness, didn't mean to do anything at all except help. "If you want," she said, "I can speak to my dad. Maybe there's a way to fix things."

"Fix which things?" said Boyd.

"Well, for starters, ripping his house apart. Selling everything that wasn't nailed down and a heap of stuff that *was* nailed down. It's a drop in Dooney's bucket—he owns nine houses, maybe ten, I've lost count. I can ask him not to press charges."

"Fat chance," Boyd said.

"Not if I push. Maybe he'll see the humor in it."

"Dooney has a sense of humor?"

Evelyn shrugged. "Boyd, this is the guy who peddled nerve gas to monsters. Of course he has a sense of humor—it's all a game. You're the one who caught him at it."

"True, but I don't remember any laughing. He fucking destroyed me."

"And he found that hilarious. Still does. The same would've happened if you'd dumped your brains all over his doorstep. Two seconds later, he'd be rehearsing how he'd tell the story to his buddies over cognac and cigars. Don't ask me to defend him, because I won't." She started to add something, stopped, then started again. "Be honest with me. How serious were you about wanting your old life back—Lean Cuisines and all that?"

"Not serious," said Boyd. "I robbed a bank."

"But if that hadn't happened?"

Boyd looked at her obliquely, pretending not to look. The skin at her cheekbones had been bitten by the day's cold. She was wearing only a thin cotton sweater and a pair of slacks designed for an afternoon on Catalina.

"Well, it did happen," he said, "and I'm not stupid. There won't be any happy endings."

"Not happy, you're right. What about peaceful?"

"That either."

"Maybe so, maybe not," said Evelyn. "You'd be amazed at what money can buy."

Angie Bing waited for them in Dooney's living room. "Three things," she said, directly to Evelyn. "He's mine. You lose. I've called you a cab." She turned to Boyd. "Make it four things—there's a guy with a monkey wrench waiting in the camper. Oh, yeah, and Alvin got called away, the engagement's off. Pretty soon we'll be hitting the road back to California. Everybody clear?"

Evelyn took a brave step toward Angie. "Come here, honey. I need a hug."

"He's *mine*," Angie said.

"Of course he is. That's why I need the hug."

35

BOYD MADE HIS WAY FROM THE HOUSE TO THE Pleasure-Way through what had become a serious October snowfall. At the camper's doorway, he stopped for a few seconds, taking notice of the snow, the cold, the quiet, the strange and very sudden apprehension that he was not entirely alone, not entirely despised, and not entirely without a future. It was not the future of his fantasies, true enough, but standing in the soft and silent snow, he understood that it was far better than he deserved.

He held out his hands, gathered a few snowflakes, watched them swiftly melt.

What a life, he thought.

As Boyd stepped inside the camper, there was a flurry of activity off to his left, where the bed was. "For Chrissake," Henry Speck snarled, "you got a problem with knocking?"

Clumsily, Speck disentangled himself from the limbs of an underdressed young lady whose smile was innocent, cheerful, and welcoming.

Speck yanked up his trousers.

"Just give us a goddamn second," he muttered. "Close your eyes or something."

Boyd closed his eyes and turned away. Behind him there was a girl's raspy laughter.

"All right," said Speck after a minute or two. "You can turn around now but, I kid you not, somebody's got to teach you manners. Sit down over there." Speck motioned at the narrow bed where the girl had draped herself in what appeared to be a dish towel. "Here's the deal. I'm Henry, this is Enni, and we've got business to do. It won't take long."

Boyd sat obediently on the edge of the bed, aware of the dish towel and a glowing smile next to him. He watched Speck tuck in his shirt, lock the camper's door, pick up a raincoat, and extract from its pocket a shiny new monkey wrench.

"This gadget weighs . . . what? Couple of pounds?" Speck gave it a thump against the palm of his hand. "Now, see, there's this nice married lady here; she's my boss's wife, right? I think you probably know her."

"I know her," Boyd said.

"Okay, good, you know her. So my boss, he wants you to *unknow* her. Unknow her, like, let's say you're sitting around trying to remember her name, right? But the name just won't come to you. It's frustrating, you try and try—zip—you go through a whole list of names, a million of them, two million—still zip. Can't remember her hair color, shoe size, if she talks in her sleep. Can't remember if she's black or white or yellow or albino like Enni here. Can't remember nothing. That's what 'unknow her' means. Are you following me?"

Enni giggled.

Boyd shook his head yes.

The guy was riffing, Boyd decided, mostly for the girl, dragging things out to amass clever points.

"Now, here's where it gets tricky," Speck said. "See, it's not just my boss who's pissed off. It's me, too. Because, man, I've been all over creation trying to nail you down, places I never want to see again, like this lousy RV you can't turn around in without breaking off your ears. My social life is zero. I'm losing my tan. If it wasn't for Enni, bless her heart, I'd be a snowman by now, I'd be an icicle dangling from one of those trillion pine trees out there." He took a breath, glanced at the girl to see how he was doing. "So, I got a question. You ever hear the name Speck?"

Boyd was unsure if he should speak or shake his head. He said, "No."

"Well, buddy, that's me, Henry Richard Speck, almost like my great-uncle except he wasn't a Henry. You should google it. Speck—S-P-E-C-K. You ever bump into a Speck, my friend, you'll be lucky to swallow the Cheerios oozing out of the slit in your throat. And that brings us back to this gadget." He wiggled the monkey wrench. "What'll it be? Toes or fingers?"

"You want me to talk?" Boyd said.

"Sure. This isn't Poland."

"Okay, thanks."

"No sweat. Fingers?"

Boyd shook his head, meaning no, and said, "The thing is, Evelyn mentioned—Evelyn's that nice lady I don't know— she mentioned you'd take it easy on me. She was under the impression . . ."

"That was almost an hour ago."

"Oh."

"Toes?"

Enni slipped off the bed and stood beside Speck, the dish towel suspended from a glossy brown shoulder. "I think toes," she said brightly, "because maybe not so hurt."

"She's from Finland," said Speck. "Or Eau Claire. We've been working on her English."

The girl winked at Boyd. Her voice dropped an octave. "Go on, bubba. Off with the shoes and socks."

Boyd looked at his shoes.

"You're serious?" he said.

"Forget the foreplay," Speck said. "Show us those tootsies. Five minutes and we're out of here."

Boyd glanced at the camper's door, calculated his chances, decided to be realistic. "Just so you know," he said, "I'm not a problem for your boss. Evelyn will vouch for that. I mean, right now we could all walk over to the house, she'll back me up, it wouldn't take twenty seconds."

"Evelyn doesn't write the checks," said Speck. "Shoes. Socks. Junius wants pictures."

Boyd pulled off his shoes and socks.

"Tiny pinch, not so bad," said Enni, back to light and flirty.

"Feet flat on the floor," Speck said.

The Pleasure-Way's floor was icy cold. Boyd had always feared medical instruments, even stethoscopes. For a few seconds, he went to a new place in his head, then the girl was saying, "Mister Henry promise me pinkie toe, okey-dokey?"

"Pinkie I can do," muttered Speck.

"Is this for real?" Boyd said.

"Good attitude. Keep hoping." Speck turned to Enni. "Put on some clothes and get the camera. Man, it's freezing in here."

It wasn't so bad.

Surreal, then afterward, real.

Speck handled the procedure like a mechanic, Enni with an explorer's wide-eyed delight. Big toe on one foot, baby toe on the other. All crushing, no cutting. Moments later they had him outside, barefoot in the snow.

Enni snapped two close-ups with a cell phone; Henry Speck dispatched the photographs westward to Junius.

"Numb yet?" Enni asked.

"Not yet," said Boyd.

"Good idea to choose toes, bubba."

Boyd thought about saying okey-dokey, but instead he watched Henry Speck walk off in the direction of Dooney's house. Who would believe it? Boyd shook his head, amazed, and wiped away some tears.

The girl laughed. "Kinda fun, wasn't it?"

"Kinda," Boyd said.

She helped him hobble back into the camper, told him to ice his feet for a day or two, then slipped him her Blue Fly calling card. "The name's Peggy," she whispered. "Peggy doesn't do orgies. Enni's the bad girl."

36

NIGHT HAD FALLEN WHEN ANGIE AND EVELYN FOUND him half dozing in the Pleasure-Way. Boyd asked to be left in peace, said he was fine, but after a number of stern words, they conveyed him through five inches of snow to Dooney's log mansion. In the great room, which was otherwise unheated, a fireplace threw out a few feet of inviting warmth. There, on the floor, they settled Boyd into a bed of cushions and quilts. Evelyn dispensed a pair of hydrocodone tablets—one for now, one for later; Angie heated up a bowl of tomato soup.

For Boyd, things were hazy—in and out—but apparently the two women had been mending fences. Evelyn's cab had been cancelled, wine had replaced coffee, and sisterhood seemed to have been secured. Maybe it was his swollen toes, maybe the hydrocodone, but Boyd surmised that Angie and Evelyn were far more content with each other than with him.

Once, while the fire was still burning, he awoke to a whispery list of Evelyn's dos and don'ts, a kind of Boyd Halverson user's manual, like a tip sheet or a warning label. The words *juvenile* and *grain of salt* and *ridiculous* and *morbid fear of failure* made him slip away into a seasick half slumber. And then later in the night, not long before dawn, he emerged to behold a single red ember twinkling in the fireplace. It took a moment to realize that he lay flanked by the forms of Evelyn to his left, Angie to his right, both wrapped in blankets, both perfectly still. He was struck again by the knowledge that he was not alone, not despised, and not without the bare bones of a future. Robbing a bank, he decided, was just the ticket. Without crime, none of this could have occurred, not the twinkling ember, not his aching toes, and not these two women at his side.

Boyd sat up, found the second hydrocodone, swallowed it. He rose cautiously to his feet.

Moving stiff-legged, he found he could keep his weight on his heels as he shuffled toward the front door with only occasional pain. He stepped outside and relieved himself on Dooney's doorstep.

Morbid fear of failure?

Probably so.

Ridiculous?

Pure rhetoric.

He stood for some time in his bare feet, listening to the icy cracklings of the night, dimly conscious of the snow at first stinging and then anesthetizing his toes. He had certainly failed, morbidly or not, with a Temptation .38 on this very doorstep. Failed Evelyn, of course. Failed pretty much everyone and everything he had encountered over a mismanaged half century. A lifetime of lies, no question, and yet, as the falsehoods slithered off his tongue, as the delusions shaped themselves into truths before his eyes, he had fervently believed every word, every unearned moment of an unlived life. Yes, he *was* a Princeton graduate. Yes, he *had* distinguished himself in the Hindu Kush, scaled Mount McKinley, survived brain cancer, scored near-perfect on his SATs.

But so what?

Why risk failure when a fib was always conveniently at hand?

For a few seconds, Boyd looked up at a sky full of stars. The snowfall had ended; the night sparkled like a silvered Christmas card; his feet seemed to have been disconnected and removed from beneath him. There was no pain, no sensation at all.

He turned back toward the door, took a step, and teetered sideways. He fell hard. His elbow struck stone. "Man," Alvin said from the dark, "that was a close one."

He lifted Boyd from under the armpits, propped him against the doorway, and dusted him off with a fuzzy white mitten.

Where Alvin had come from, or why he was there, Boyd had no idea. The guy was dressed for winter in a stocking cap, heavy boots, snowmobiler pants, and a Pompeian red parka.

"Nothing broken?"

"No," said Boyd. "My toes, I guess."

"Come on, let's get you someplace warm. Five more minutes, you'll be walking on stumps." Alvin turned and draped Boyd's arms over his shoulders. "Hop aboard; I'll piggyback you over to the camper. We need to talk."

"I thought Angie—"

"Yeah, she did. Booted me out. Nowhere to go, so I decided—you know—I'm hanging out in the garage. The Ferrari's got a pretty fair heater. Hold on tight now."

The sixty-foot ride to the Pleasure-Way concluded what had been an eventful twenty-four hours. Alvin got the camper's engine started, turned up the heater, and pulled his mittens over Boyd's feet. "In the morning, first thing, you better see a doctor," he said, and waited for Boyd to nod. "I know you're hurting—who wouldn't be—but there's a couple things you need to hear. You up for this?"

A filament of fire snaked its way from Boyd's toes to his knees. He sucked in a breath and said, "Make it quick."

"No problem." Alvin paused for a second. He seemed nervous and jumpy. "Here's the deal. A long story. Enni and me, we used to be . . . whatever the word is. A twosome, let's say. Ken and Barbie. Up here in rural Minnesota, it's mostly old folks—no offense—so naturally we spotted each other real quick. Better than swapping sixties stories down at the Elks club. Anyhow, both of us, Enni and me, we've got issues. I like stealing stuff, she likes messing with people." He paused again. He half grinned, shook his head hard. "Anger issues, you know? Match made in heaven, sort of, except the match ended up way too perfect, like making eyes at your sister, so now—you know—now we just help each other out. Look after each other, that kind of thing. Last night she calls me up, gives me the toe story. She's upset. This dude she's with right now, the Speck dude, he's George Hamilton with a monkey wrench. Follow me so far?"

"My feet are on fire," said Boyd. "What's the point?"

"Enni's conflicted—you probably noticed. Two different people. Loves the credit cards, only so-so with mangling people's feet. Speck scares her. Total psycho. Enni wants out. Wants to ask a favor."

"From me?" Boyd said.

"From you. That's why I hung around tonight."

"She crushed my pinkie toe. She *liked* crushing it."

"Right, and Enni feels terrible about that. She apologizes."

"What favor?"

"Your gun."

Boyd sighed, wagged his head, tried to stand, but gave up. "No gun, Alvin. She's dangerous enough."

Alvin chuckled. "Can't argue with that one, Papa. But it's not for Enni. She wants me to put a scare into the Speck fella—wave the gun around, tell him to get lost. She thinks he'll fold fast."

"Sorry," said Boyd. "No gun. At least not from me. Angie confiscated it."

"Right, except Angie won't barely speak to me. And I guess that's another thing we need to straighten out. All of it, man, start to finish, it was one big charade. Nothing between Angie and me, you know? A love con. She figured you'd freak out, thought you'd come begging. I told her it was teenybopper tactics."

"And?"

"And nothing. You barely noticed, then later . . . Later I wasn't acting anymore. That's when she gave me the heave-ho."

Boyd laughed.

"It's not funny," said Alvin.

"No, but it's Angie. Last night she called *me* juvenile."

Alvin looked at Boyd as if deciding whether to speak or walk away.

"Man, you're something else, aren't you? A rose falls in your lap, you can't yell hallelujah. What's wrong with you?"

"I'm a yo-yo," said Boyd.

"No argument there. A yo-yo with sore toes."

"Look, if you'll help me back to the house . . ."

"In a minute. Get me the gun, then I'm history. After that, lots of luck—go back to stinking up the rest of your life." Alvin stopped, tried to smile, but didn't. "You know which holiday is coming up?"

"No," Boyd said.

"Halloween. Just a couple more days."

"Yeah?"

"My favorite. Only day it's cool to soap windows, swipe lawn furniture. I was *born* for Halloween. One time down in Chicago—I'm eleven, twelve years old—I go trick-or-treating in this department store—Marshall Field's, I think—and I walk out of that place with junk I didn't even want, calculators and dustbusters, just for the thrill, you know? Like you robbing a bank, I guess. It's who I am. It's who I *want* to be." Alvin's eyes crinkled with what might have been amusement, possibly resignation. "Anyhow, after a couple of tours in Iraq, bingo, I've got this perfect alibi. I'm a wounded warrior, right? I'm damaged; I'm crammed to the gills with guilt. But see, the truth is, I *like* what I do for a living. Every day is Halloween."

Boyd shrugged and said, "Okay, you're a meanie. How about giving me a hand up to the house?"

"And the gun?"

"I'll see what I can do. But no bullets."

"None needed," said Alvin. "Leave the hardware in the garage. For old times' sake, okay?"

"We'll see."

Alvin pushed wearily to his feet. "You and me, Pops, we got some metaphysics in common. That end-of-the-line feeling. Only difference, I'm not a chicken. Not afraid to pull the fuckin' trigger. Understand?"

"No."

"Let's get you back to Angie. Make sure you give her my love."

On the morning of November 7 autumn returned. By noon, the roads were clear, the temperature had risen into the low fifties, and Evelyn's cab came grinding up the driveway under a sunny sky.

Her departure was as awkward as her arrival. Neither she nor Boyd knew what to say. Angie hugged her twice, once on the doorstep, again at the cab. Boyd had the feeling that important things had been decided out of his presence, although what exactly, and how exactly, he had no idea.

Evelyn handed him two vials of hydrocodone. "Four tablets a day and get some X-rays. Don't worry about me, I'll make it."

She stepped into the cab, shut the door, then opened it and stepped out and said, "I spoke with your father. Maybe if you two can . . . He's an old man. It couldn't hurt."

"Or it could," said Boyd.

"He's in Seattle."

"I know where he is."

"You're angry with me."

"Not angry. Hopeless."

Evelyn looked at him and got back into the cab.

"If it helps," she said, "I forgive you. Again."

"Ditto," said Boyd.

That evening another snowfall hammered Lake Larceny.

37

WAS MYTHOMANIA A VIRUS OR A CURSE OR ORIG-
inal sin or willful self-interest or egoism gone berserk or mean-
spirited arrogance or convulsive incivility or neurotic bullyism
or raw ignorance or pathological insecurity or a simple craving
to replace the humdrum with the fantastic? Or, instead, was it
no more than a child playing doctor or a draft-dodging hotelier
playing commander in chief? Mythomania appeared to be all
of these and more, both cause and effect, steamrolling its way
through PTA meetings and the House Judiciary Committee. By
midautumn of 2019, seventy-one million adult Americans had
been infected; another two hundred and twenty million schoolchildren exhibited symptoms in the classroom. Cheating was
epidemic. Absentee excuses read like science fiction. Teachers
retaliated.

Alarmingly, in late October of that year, a CDC field in-
vestigator detected the first demonstrable "genetic crossover"
from humans to European starlings and American crows. How
mythomania caused blackbirds to begin dropping from the sky
was a mystery. And how blackbirds lied to one another was
equally puzzling—feather configurations, maybe, or misleading cheeps and peeps. Whatever the explanation, there was no
dodging the deluge of crows and starlings crashing into wind-
shields and backyards across the Upper Midwest. Mythomania
had turned deadly.

In Fulda, California, where life was humdrum and where sins were more stale than original, the four-man Truth Teller Seed had exhausted its run-of-the-mill untrue truths and was now in search of fresh fake unfake news. "Aliens and UFOs, all that's ancient history, proven fact," Mayor Chub O'Neill explained to his confederates. "We're losing subscribers, can't compete with POTUS—the guy's killing us. What we need is something lunatic. I'm open to ideas." He waited for suggestions from his brother Dink, Earl Fenstermacher, and the grieving Doug Cutterby, all of whom had gathered in Earl's Chamber of Commerce offices for a Truth Teller's strategy session. It was Douglas who eventually released a profound sigh and said, "What about we go local? Zombies teaching second grade? Witches in the fire department? Personally, I can't contribute much—Lois's funeral, of course, is right around the corner. All the same, we should clean house around here. I know a couple Democrats."

"Where does Alec Baldwin live?" said Dink.

"Not local," Chub said. "And he's already on the ropes. Anyhow, I've said it before, I'll say it again, we need Boyd back in the game, somebody with imagination."

"Here, here," said Douglas.

For twenty minutes they batted around ideas, nothing catchy, then Douglas looked at his watch and said he had flowers to buy, a eulogy to write. "Keep plugging away, gentlemen," he said cheerfully. "See you at the cemetery."

When Douglas was gone, Chub said, "Guy's torn up."

"Shattered," said Earl Fenstermacher.

Across the room, a flight of five starlings thumped into the Chamber of Commerce's plate-glass window.

"Jews!" Dink snarled.

38

A FEW MILES OUTSIDE PARK RAPIDS, MINNESOTA,
the Cutlass jerked and coughed and decided its top speed was
twenty-seven miles an hour. The car's heater had failed back
in North Dakota, the radio hadn't worked in years, he'd spent
Halloween in a ditch east of Fargo, and his cash reserves would
not survive even a frugal stop at Wendy's. Not that there was
a Wendy's in sight, or anything else for that matter. It was
1:30 a.m., snowing hard again. The windshield wipers scraped
weakly across a sheet of half-opaque ice as Randy blinked at
the road.

Eighteen hundred boring miles, nine quarts of oil, and you
end up a popsicle.

What a world.

As he chugged up the main drag of Park Rapids, the first
order of business was thawing out. Nothing moved: no cars, no
people. The town, Randy thought, seemed to have flatlined under
some terrible arctic snow bomb. Two snow bombs. Now this.

For twenty minutes he drove randomly up and down the
streets, watching his gas needle hit pray, and at last he pulled
into the parking lot of a closed-down Walgreens. What this
burg needed, Randy decided, was a wake-up call. A mini crime
spree, for example.

One disarmed burglar alarm later, he was revving up the
Walgreens thermostat to a toasty ninety degrees.

He took his time surveying dinner possibilities, settled on M&M's and two packs of Chuckles, then swiped a couple of heating pads and plugged them in and bedded down in the home health care aisle right under the NyQuil.

Bemidji was barely fifty miles away. Once the Cutlass was tuned up, he'd be there in under an hour.

He slept soundly.

At dawn, when Randy awoke, the outside temperature squatted in the single digits. A steady snow was falling. He slipped out to the car and sat cranking the Cutlass's frozen engine until the battery died. Man oh man, he thought, this was not California. He grabbed his duffel, hustled back into the Walgreens, put on all three of his silk rodeo shirts, plugged in two heating pads, waited a few minutes, then slid both pads under the shirts. He used a roll of plastic packing tape to secure the pads forward and aft.

Outside again, he half walked, half trotted up the main drag to a café where six or seven survivors of the apocalypse sat thawing out in booths, drinking coffee and dreaming of Fort Lauderdale. Randy took a stool at the counter, asked for a menu, and checked his cash supply—two dollars even.

Charm time, he thought. Smooth. Not too smooth.

When the young waitress appeared, Randy delivered his crookedest grin and said, "These buttermilk pancakes. What's the story exactly?"

"They're pancakes," said the girl.

"Right as rain. But see, if you hold the buttermilk, abracadabra, you got a cheaper pancake."

The girl looked at him. "Drain the buttermilk?"

"Wouldn't say drain," Randy said. "Just plain old pancakes. They come with sausage?"

"Well, if you get the platter"—the waitress used her pencil to tap the menu. "Right here it says pancakes with sausage, bacon, or ham. And hash browns. That's the platter."

"How much is the whole kit an' caboodle?"

"Nine ninety-nine. Aren't you chilly, sir?"

"Chilly?"

"No coat, I mean. Just the shirt."

"Three shirts," Randy said. "All different colors. And a couple heating pads. Nine ninety-nine, you say?"

"Yes, sir," the girl said. "You're wearing heating pads?"

"Sure as the dickens am," said Randy. "Plug 'em in, give it twenty minutes, you're in Hawaii." He frowned at the menu. "Nine ninety-nine, but that's *with* the buttermilk."

The girl laughed. She was twenty, tops, not bad looking if you didn't mind Norwegian movie stars.

"Buttermilk or nothing," she said.

"Don't hardly seem fair." Randy sighed and put some extra crooked in his grin. "All righty, we'll go buttermilk. Got your pencil ready?"

"Ready and waiting, sport."

"Make it three complete platters. Tack on a donut. I'll be here a while."

In the end, all he could handle were two and a half platters, but Randy stretched things out well into midmorning, using the men's room three times, twice for real, once to adjust the heating pads. The bill had been lying in front of him for a couple of hours, almost thirty-nine unavailable bucks, but coffee refills were on the house, and Randy kept them coming as he worked his magic on the young waitress. Her name was Fran—a fact he squeezed out of her with his how-big-is-your-tip-gonna-be routine, the same spiel that almost got him married up in Salem.

Fran was twenty-two.

A Stephen King fan.

A vegetarian except for beef jerky.

Also, most intriguing, the girl was first runner-up Miss Park Rapids, but should've won, which led Randy to say, "Yes, ma'am, I know the feeling," which led the girl to say, "My shift ends at noon."

"Is that right?" said Randy. "And what do folks do for kicks here in Park Rapids? Ice fish, maybe?"

"Some do. I'm the indoor type."

"Are you now?"

The girl eyed him. "You're broke, aren't you?"

"Not for long," he said, and gave her full-crooked. "What say you and me stick up a gas station?"

"Yeah?"

"Yeah."

"Noon it is," Fran said.

Randy winked at her, scrunched up the bill, put it in his pocket, and loped out the door, thinking he probably looked pretty dangerous from behind.

In Fulda, California, locked securely in his chilly bank vault, Douglas Cutterby sat cleaning and oiling an over-under, double-barreled ATI Crusader shotgun, working slowly, chatting with Lois in his head, reminiscing about the fun and profits they had shared over the years. Community National, he reminded her, had been the equivalent of a playground for adults, a rumpus room stocked with slot machines that never stopped spitting out shiny silver dollars. Why go and ruin it? Thing is, he whispered to her in his head, we both know what you had in mind. Under barrel for Toby, over barrel for me. I'm right, aren't

I? Yes, I am. And you should've known better. Sitting there on that park bench, the hundred K in your lap, you should've taken into account that I can have a stern side, that I'm a bank president, that I don't let my sympathies get in the way of farm foreclosures, that business is business, that it was your own carelessness that left this lovely, well-oiled shooting iron in easy reach.

A pity, my love.

So much for wedding vows.

So much for romance.

Douglas sighed, rose to his feet, and placed the disassembled Crusader in two oversize safe-deposit boxes.

But listen, he told her. Don't let a little buckshot sabotage the happy memories.

In the same instant, on the far side of the North American continent, a murmuration of several thousand starlings performed their ancient ballet two hundred feet above the White House, darkening an otherwise brilliant autumn afternoon. Synchronized to the millimeter, the starlings moved as a single elegant organism, upward and downward, north and south, while on the earth below a former big-city mayor strolled through the Rose Garden arm in arm with POTUS. "I *can't* lose, of course," POTUS was saying, "because I am who I am, but if I *did* lose— don't laugh, I hate it when people laugh at me—if I *did* lose, I wouldn't have to leave this place, would I?" He swept his gaze across the White House lawn. "All that baloney about how it belongs to the People, but get serious. It's *mine*, isn't it?"

"You bet it is," said the former big-city mayor. He stopped and gestured at the sky above them. "Holy shit, you see that, sir?"

"See what?" said POTUS.

"Those birds up there. Six or eight of them, I swear they just collided."

"Yeah?"

"Well, I think so, but maybe . . . There go three more!"

POTUS shrugged.

"Tough luck," he said. "They're black birds, aren't they?"

Randy had been waiting for Fran long enough. Noon was four hours ago, his feet were killing him, and the heating pads had become a problem.

He reached under his shirts, tried to loosen them, but it was like tugging on something stuck to a sidewalk. He tried his fingernails, tried sucking in his stomach, but finally he said, "Christ in a barrel," and looked around for somewhere private to peel off the pads. Four doors down was a shoe store, Larry's Shoes and Slippers.

A minute later Randy was auditioning a pair of loafers—reddish brown, like Angie's hair, and actual leather. "I'll try 'em on," he told the guy helping him. "But first things first. Where's your restroom?"

Randy followed directions to the tiniest bathroom he'd ever seen, barely enough room to pull off his shirts and go to work on the heating pads. Big trouble, he realized. The packing tape had fused to his chest right where his ticker was ticking. He got out his jackknife, tried sliding the blade under a pad, but nothing doing, the tape held like rubber cement.

There was a light rapping on the door. "Okay in there?" the shoe guy said.

"Pretty fair," said Randy. "Any chance you got a shoehorn?"

Randy turned on the hot water faucet, splashed himself, and

managed to hook a thumbnail under one of the pads. Damn if he wasn't gonna have a talk with somebody over at the Walgreens. He tried again with the jackknife, still no luck, then looked in the mirror. The pads gave him a nice V shape like you see in comic books and prison weight rooms. For now, he decided, he could live with this. He tucked in the shirts, flushed the toilet, and stepped out to find the shoe guy waiting with a shoehorn and a frown.

"Everything work out okay?"

"Not bad," said Randy. "Let's try on them loafers."

Randy took a seat, kicked off his cowboy boots, slipped on the loafers, and took a stroll down a carpeted testing aisle. At the end of the aisle was a shoe mirror.

"Those tassels," he said skeptically. "A little fruity, you think?"

"Tassel makes the shoe. Tassel's the crown jewel." The salesman took out a pocket calculator and tapped some buttons. "I can get you twenty percent off."

"Off what?" said Randy. "Bottom line. How much?"

"Comes to eighty-eight and change."

Randy shook his head and said, "Pretty steep for cowhide. By the way, are you Larry?"

"Am I Larry?"

"That's what 'are you Larry?' means."

"Well, no," the man said. "I'm Mel."

"So where's Larry? Riding his toboggan?"

"Larry's my kid brother. We take turns here. I don't see why—"

"Just making sure it's mano a mano, you and me," said Randy. He paused and smiled. "You do trade-ins, right?"

"Well, not—"

"Those boots of mine, they seen some action over the years. You ever do rodeo? Say it's a rainy day, four inches of slop on the ground, Brahmas pissing and pooping like there's no tomorrow, but them boots, I'll tell you straight up, your feet barely even get soggy. Five-hundred-dollar boots. Got 'em for two hundred off a clown buddy—he's dead now—been dead six, seven years—unfunniest clown in history, but he knew a good boot and that's the Lord's truth."

"We don't do trade-ins," said Mel.

"Yeah, well, think it over. Let's go see what's in your cash register."

There was a little over three hundred and forty in the register, small bills, not great but better than broke.

Shoe stores were brand-new stickup territory for Randy. He selected the forty-inch high-top shoelaces, yellow ones, fixing up Mel nice and comfortable in the bathroom, down by the sink drainage pipe. Mel didn't say a word, not with the buffing cloth in his mouth.

"What we're gonna do now," said Randy, "we're gonna wrap up our business here. Give me a head bob if that's okay with you."

Mel bobbed his head.

"Excellent. Now, those five-hundred-dollar rodeo boots are all yours; these eighty-eight-and-change loafers are mine. So far so good? That tallies up to you owing me four hundred and twelve bucks, cash on the barrelhead. But you already paid me three-forty out of the register. End of the day, I'm still short seventy-two and change. Question is, what are we gonna do about it? If you got ideas, speak up."

Randy gave him a few seconds.

"Well, guess what," he said. "I got my own idea. There's this pair of ladies' heels I spotted, sixty-seven bucks without the discount, so what I'll do is, I'll box up the heels in a size six and a half—that's my girlfriend's size—and we'll call it square. If that's not fairer than fair, I don't know what is. Deal?"

It took time but Mel's head bobbed.

"Smart businessman," Randy said.

He shut the bathroom door, rounded up the ladies' heels, hung a Closed sign in the store's window, and was outside waiting for Fran way before he started laughing.

39

WANDA JANE EPSTEIN STOOD AT GRAVESIDE WHIS-
pering to her best friend Hedda Todhauser: "That asshole blew
away his wife, robbed his own bank, and not a speck of evidence
against him—no weapon, no witnesses, not a flake of dan-
druff. Cross my heart, though, Dougie's our man. He's a can of
poisoned Crisco."

Hedda made a huffing noise. "I kind of go for the silver hair,
though. If he'd work on the potbelly—"

"Hedda, he's a serial killer."

"The rich, widower kind," said Hedda. "Besides, he only
killed Lois, right? That's not serial."

"Serial starts *somewhere*."

"Not so loud."

Wanda Jane took Hedda's arm, pulled her away a few steps,
and surveyed the hundred or so mourners equally split between Republicans and Mexicans. It was a double interment,
two open graves, two closed coffins. On Lois Cutterby's side of
the aisle were Fulda's movers and shakers. A sorrowful Douglas
Cutterby stood flanked by Mayor Chub O'Neill and Chamber
of Commerce President Earl Fenstermacher, the two of them
attending Douglas like a pair of gargoyles in front of a library.
The Cutterby contingent was respectably somber, respectably
furred, respectably black-suited, and respectably bored silly.

The mood near Toby's hole was celebrative, more like Cinco de Mayo than Black Friday.

"Kind of awesome," Hedda whispered. "Yin and yangy. The American experiment."

"The Haves and the Pedros," Wanda Jane said dryly.

"What?" said Hedda.

"Nothing. Look at Dougie—he's flirting with me."

Hedda shook her head. "He's blinking, honey."

"Bullshit. Nobody blinks with one eye."

Later, after Lois and Toby were safely in the ground, Wanda Jane and Hedda cleared their heads at the only decent restaurant in twenty miles, a Holiday Inn near the Oregon border. Wanda Jane ordered two whiskies and a platter of ribs; Hedda ordered two whiskies and the shrimp scampi, and for a couple of hours they talked strategy.

As things stood, Wanda Jane explained, it was a half-solved crime. The bank's camera clips plainly showed Toby walking into the lobby with a hoe in his hands, the spitting image of Matt Dillon, the one on *Gunsmoke* reruns. At first, it looked like a standard holdup—Lois with her hands behind her head, Lois leading the way into the vault, Toby following on her heels. When the vault camera picked them up, Toby's mask had disappeared. Why? Made no sense. The clips were grainy, jerky, and at times worthless, but the general sequence of events seemed clear: Lois holding what appeared to be a trick-or-treat bag, Toby stuffing it with cash. At one point Toby took a step toward Lois and seemed to give her a quick peck on the cheek. Or maybe not—maybe it was the camera angle. Either way, after three or four seconds, as Toby stepped away from her, the barrels of a shotgun appeared at the corner of the frame—Lois leveling it waist-high—then came an eerie, soundless flash of light, a quick glare, like Baghdad under nighttime air assault.

"Up to that instant," Wanda Jane told Hedda, "you'd think you were watching *Bonnie and Clyde*. The only surprise, really, was why they let the camera record any of it. It's not as if they didn't *know* there were cameras."

"Unless," said Hedda.

"Unless what?"

"Well, unless they thought the clips would end up in a dumpster. Or erased."

Wanda Jane smiled. "Doug Cutterby."

"So put him in jail," Hedda said, "with somebody like me."

Wanda Jane polished off the first of her whiskies. "Thing is, there's still the proof problem. Right now, everything points somewhere else. Randy's prints on the hoe, all over the Matt Dillon stuff."

"Randy Zapf?" Hedda said. "No way, hon. Randy'd snag his balls in the vault door."

"My thought, too," said Wanda Jane.

"So where does that leave you? Up a creek, I guess."

"Not quite. Cutterby *knew* those prints would be there. The guy was bragging, showing off how smart he is."

For a time, both of them sat thinking. They had been friends since tenth grade, led the cheers for the Fulda Trojans, skipped their senior prom to pull an all-nighter with a bag of mushrooms. And then for twelve years they'd gone their separate ways. Hedda moved to Sacramento, married a man, divorced him, and eventually returned to Fulda, where she now ran a one-woman enterprise as owner, trainer, bookkeeper, instructor, and janitor of the Todhauser CrossFit Spa. At six four and a hundred and ninety-some pounds, Hedda had matured into a woman of consequence, formidable but lonely.

Now, she sighed and said, "Okay, maybe I can help you out. Pin Dougie under a barbell, beat a confession out of him."

"Not sure it'll hold up in court."

"Who's talking court? Then deep-six him. After he fathers my children."

"Naturally. How's the shrimp?"

"Tastes like whiskey so far." Hedda wiggled an empty glass. "So what's the plan? I can tell you want to nail the guy. Obsessed, I'd say."

"I am," said Wanda Jane, surprised by Hedda's sharp tone. "Guy's wife is slop on a park bench, meanwhile he's licking his chops at me, talking structure. Anyway, I'm a cop."

"You're a dispatcher."

"A dispatcher cop. For the time being, at least, I'm the law, me and Elmo, and Elmo couldn't investigate his own toilet paper." Wanda Jane shook her head hard. "Look, I can't ignore the obvious. Lois walks out of the bank with a hundred thousand— that's for sure, it's in the clips—and last we see her, she's headed down toward the park, same place she used to meet Toby for on-the-house slobber sessions. Next morning she's hamburger. No money. It's gone."

"You have a theory?"

"Sure I do. All three of them were in on it—Lois, Toby, and Doug. Everybody screws everybody else."

Hedda sat thinking for a moment, then grinned, then leaned back and laughed.

"Love it!" she said. "Commerce American-style!"

"Makes sense, doesn't it? Lois zaps Toby. Doug zaps Lois.

And I'd bet a zillion bucks Toby planned on using his hoe on lovely Lois. I mean, that peck on the cheek? Kiss of death. And those camera clips—all three of them assumed they'd be erased, but then Doug realizes only Lois and Toby would be incriminated, so the clips became this huge, huge plus for him. Dougie's home free. He has the cash, he has Randy for a fall guy, he collects insurance, he's an instant bachelor, and he knocks off a nice piece of cuckold payback. Clean sweep."

"Sweet," Hedda said.

"Except it's a theory."

"And?"

"We need proof."

"We?"

"You."

"Wait a minute," Hedda said. She leaned back in her chair, squinted at her shrimp for a second. "You're the cops, I do CrossFit."

Wanda Jane nodded. "Exactly right, I'm a cop. I'd get nowhere. And I'd have the whole entrapment problem. On the other hand, an ordinary law-abiding citizen—somebody six foot four, let's say—all you'd be doing is kissing and telling. In court, I mean."

"So what you want, you want me to screw a confession out of him?"

"I wouldn't put it that way."

"How would you put it?"

"Well," Wanda Jane said. "I'd call it batting practice."

In the morning, Mayor Chub O'Neill stopped by the station to let Wanda Jane know he'd be interviewing candidates to replace Toby Van Der Kellen. Wanda Jane listened and nodded.

New blood was fine with her; she had no interest in hassling Mexicans.

For way too long, Chub sat reviewing developments with the investigation, which boiled down to the feds pulling out the stops in tracking down Randy Zapf, who apparently was on the run with a Cutlass full of Community National's money.

"What we'd appreciate," Chub said as he stood up to leave, "we'd appreciate—Fulda would appreciate—I'd personally appreciate cutting Doug Cutterby some slack right now. I'm told you and your pal Hedda paid him a visit last night."

"An unofficial visit," said Wanda Jane. "Passing along condolences."

"Well, fine and dandy, but Doug got the feeling—" Chub shook his head and chuckled. "Condolences, I'll tell him that. He seemed to think . . . He's pretty much in shock for the moment, losing Lois and all. They were a team, after all."

"They sure were. The Addams family."

The mayor blinked at her and said, "Condolences. Doug'll be relieved to hear that. I'm relieved. Fulda's relieved."

"Listen," Wanda Jane said. "All we did was bring him a pie."

'Well, not *just* a pie."

"You mean the mushrooms in the pie?"

"Guess I did mean that. Doug called me this morning pretty upset, thinks maybe your friend Hedda might've spent the night."

"Grief counseling," Wanda Jane said.

"I'll bet it was. But since you're with the PD here, it doesn't look—"

"Hey, Chub, I didn't even go inside. Hedda did. She's an adult, he's an adult. Where's the problem?"

The man waited a second, then shrugged.

"No problem. Except Fulda's a small town, onions and sugar beets. Not a whole lot of opportunity for career growth. I hire, I fire. Got it?"

"Is that an or-else?"

"Not exactly," he said.

"What exactly?"

Chub's smile was still there, but it was a mayor's smile. "Let's call it a reality check. Lay off Cutterby." Chub's smile broadened. "Gotta run, but have yourself a boring day."

Wanda Jane watched the man turn and march out the door with an I've-got-ribbons-to-cut air of royalty.

She sat at her dispatch console for a good ten minutes, not really thinking, just feeling the heat in her head, then she flicked on her cell phone and called Elmo and told him to pin on his deputy badge and meet her at the station.

"Right now?" Elmo whined. "I'm swamped here, I got a pool hall to run."

"This will be more fun," said Wanda Jane.

Douglas Cutterby had calmed down. Over a ham and cheese omelet, which carried the tart aftertaste of fungus, Douglas told himself no harm, no foul, although it was true he'd been alarmed to awaken that morning to a bed littered with pizza crumbs. The two women showing up at his front door last night had set off warning bells. Smelled wrong: the Epstein girl in her PD uniform, the tall, muscular one in gym shorts and an extra sporty sports bra. He barely knew either of them except in his fantasies.

Now, cleaning up the breakfast dishes, Douglas found himself chatting in his head with Lois, filling her in on last night's developments. True enough, he told her, things had been uncomfortable at first, but after Epstein drove away, and after that first slice of late-evening pizza, he'd warmed up to what's-her-name, the Amazon with a no-nonsense attitude toward grief management. You'd have been proud of me, Douglas told the absent Lois. This girl says, "You can cry on my shoulder or you can pull down my shorts," and I say, "Whoa, Nellie," and she says, "Have another slice while you think it over," and I say, "What's your name again?" and the Amazon says, "Todhauser," and I say, "That's German, isn't it?" and she says, "*Du bist ein tease.*"

I don't want to rub it in, he told Lois, but now that you're dead, this old goat plans to learn a foreign language.

He showered, put on a suit and tie, then decided to skip work that day. What he'd do, he'd peel a few hundred hundreds off the stash in his safe-deposit box, drive down to the CrossFit spa, suck in his stomach, and see if Miss Todhauser was interested in spending Christmas camping out in the wilds of the Tahoe Ritz-Carlton.

Sound good, Lois?

Elmo Hive had been born into a Boston fortune, spent his younger years padding the fortune, summered on the Vineyard, wintered in Zermatt, married and divorced a cousin of Whitey Bulger, supped with the Shrivers, and all the while yearned to be a nomad nobody nowhere. He succeeded at age fifty-four. There had been no dramatic life event, just a low-key "enough is enough." He swapped his State Street law offices for a failing pool hall in Fulda, California, where the Brahmin Elmore became the clownish Elmo. He lost the Kennedy accent. He ignored Christmas cards from his Yale Law buddies, drove a 2014 Chevy Silverado, learned to install water heaters and tap a beer keg, worked part-time for the FPD, and lived a solitary, contented life in a four-room apartment above Elmo's Pool & Suds. For entertainment, he liked shopping for clothes at the Salvation Army down in Redding, where, for a song, he picked up brown pants, brown shirts, and brown work boots—hayseed camouflage. Over time, the disguise had become the real thing. Granted, he had two hundred million squirreled away, but for the most part, Elmo thought hick thoughts, talked hick talk, dreamed hick dreams, and at the moment stared at Wanda Jane Epstein with a hick's slack-jawed confusion. "You want me to bodyguard Hedda?" he asked. "She don't need bodyguards, she needs female saltpeter."

"I didn't say *bodyguard*, Elmo."

"You said don't let Douglas hurt her."

"I didn't say that either. I said keep an eye on her. Stay close, I said."

"That ain't bodyguarding?"

Wanda Jane tried to simplify. "Listen, Elmo, you're a cop, right?"

"Sorta," he said. "Sometimes I ride around in Toby's squad car. When he's sick or lazy or something."

"Toby's dead, Elmo."

"Right."

"So you and me, we're the cops. Cops protect people. Doug's dangerous. Follow me so far?"

"Sure do," Elmo said slowly.

"You sound doubtful."

Elmo frowned. "The thing is, Hedda seems . . . You know, she wrestles fat Japs and stuff. What am I gonna do? I'm fifty-eight, couldn't take down a guppy."

"Nobody's asking you to wrestle anybody," said Wanda Jane. "Just stick tight. Go where Hedda goes, especially when she's with Cutterby. If there's trouble, show him your service weapon."

"Not sure it works. Where you gonna be?"

"Here and there. Doug's taking her down to Tahoe over Christmas, probably through New Year's, maybe even longer—mourning period, I guess. Once they're out of town, I'll toss the guy's house again, top to bottom this time. But I'll need you to . . . What are you chewing?"

"Skoal. Like some?"

"Next life maybe. Anyhow, I'll need you to tail them down to Tahoe, keep an eye on Hedda. Don't make any Christmas plans."

Elmo removed his Seahawks cap and inspected it for several seconds. Slowly, he said, "You sure about this? Tailing people, tossing houses? No warrant?"

"Not right now."

"Awful tricky," he said. "Illegal, too. Fourth Amendment. I assume Hedda'll be wired, right?"

"I wouldn't say *wired*. Her cell phone has a recording app."

"Same difference. Illegal in California. All parties need to consent."

Wanda Jane looked at him. "Elmo, what the fuck? All of a sudden you're Barry Scheck?"

"Tossing in my two cents," he said mildly. "If you want to record pillow talk, I recommend you move the action to

Nevada. Only need one party's consent there. Entrapment laws are weaker."

"Who the hell *are* you?" asked Wanda Jane.

"Me? I'm Elmo."

"Elmo what?"

"Esquire," he said.

40

ON THE TOP FLOOR OF YOU!, IN THE WALNUT-
paneled, soundproof boardroom of Pacific Ships and Shipping, nourished by canapés and hydrated with Perrier, seated
in matching swivel chairs that had cost the company $13,000
apiece, the principals had assembled to settle the fate of Boyd
Halverson Birdsong.

The meeting was in its second hour.

Evelyn presided, Junius seethed, Dooney scoffed and said,
"What's to decide? We turn him in. Buy tickets and popcorn
for the trial. Bank robbery, home invasion, grand larceny."

"Attempted wife theft," said Junius.

"My Bugatti, that's worse."

"Alienation of affection."

"And my bowling alley, for crying out loud. Ask me, we
crush him like a bug."

"Like a worm," said Junius.

Evelyn had tired of the petty bickering.

"Great," she said. "So here's what we've decided. Junius,
you're calling off your pervert hoodlum—two mashed toes,
that's plenty. You're writing Community National a check for
eighty-one thousand. Tack on a couple thousand for interest,
okay? If you have to, you're buying the whole bank. Dooney,
you're—"

"Call me Dad."

"Dooney, you're bailing out JCPenney. It's a private company now, so make an offer, the whole shebang, whatever it takes. Just make sure Boyd gets his job back. And the place in Bemidji? That goes to me, free and clear. And fast."

Evelyn looked at Junius, then at Dooney.

"Fair summary?" she said.

Henry Speck did not care for Enni's tone of voice, or for the pistol she was waving around, or for the big bushy-bearded guy with a chipmunk's name who sat grinning at him from a rocker on the porch of Henry's rented cabin on Lake Larceny. It was an unseasonably warm November morning, easily in the mid-forties, and the freak Halloween snowstorm was a thing of the past. Another freak had replaced it. Enni had become Peggy, and Peggy was snarling.

"You want me to *walk*?" Henry said.

"Fifteen miles to airport, good for you, good for me!" yelled either Enni or Peggy or both. "You a dangerous son-of-a-bitch child molester Speck creep! Walk!"

"Child molester?" Henry said. "You signed my consent form."

"Ha!" she yelled, definitely the Peggy from Eau Claire. "I'm seventeen! Maybe twenty! Barely!"

"Which one?"

"Which what?"

"Whoever's talking right now. Peggy or Enni?"

"Both of us! Twins!"

"Well, there you go," Henry said. "Add the ages together, it comes to thirty-seven. You're over the hill."

"Go!" she yelled. "Scary slime son of a bitch! Walk!"

"*I'm* scary?"

She tapped the tip of his nose with Boyd's Temptation. "First pay the fee," she said, going singsong, probably Enni now. "Then you go walk-walk-walk!"

"Fee? What the fuck?" said Henry.

He looked at the bearded guy for help—Alvin somebody—but Alvin was enjoying this.

"You're charging a fee?"

"Two hundred fifty an hour," the girl, or girls, said. "Cheap for the tasty cradle rob."

"Hey, I don't . . . What's the grand total?"

"Thirty thousand even," said the bearded guy. "But Enni gives discounts. Peggy doesn't."

"Which one am I talking to?"

Enni, or Peggy, rolled her eyes, and yelled, "I tell you already! Twins! Double trouble, you pay double!"

"Sixty grand? For what?"

"Listen, bubba"—definitely Peggy now—"I tap-danced."

Henry wasn't sure how to play this. The gun looked real.

"I loved you," he said. "Really."

"Okay, discount." Now it was Enni, almost for sure. "Six thousand. Fair and square."

"Credit card, you said?"

"Okey-dokey," the girls said.

The bearded guy—Alvin—grinned, and said, "Minnesota, man. If it ain't the flies, it's the Finns."

Hours later, near nightfall, as Henry plodded into the outskirts of Bemidji, he had come to terms with his interlude in lake country. A con was a con. Naturally, Junius would moan and groan when he saw the bill, but toes had been squashed, the job had been neatly handled, and it wasn't his fault that the local help was expensive.

On the connecting flight to Minneapolis, Henry removed his shoes and massaged his feet, happy to be heading back to L.A.

He leaned across the aisle and said to the young lady in 4-B, "You ever try hot sauce?"

The young lady said, "Old hat. Where's the party?"

Randy had been waiting outside Larry's Shoes and Slippers since noon. Now it was coming up on dinnertime, still no Fran, and he was starting to think he'd gotten the day wrong. Noon tomorrow maybe. Or maybe noon the day after tomorrow.

He checked both his wristwatches, which were ticking fine, and decided to give it another half hour, fifty minutes tops, just in case she was deciding whether to go with pantyhose or no pantyhose for the gas-station stickup. No way of telling, he thought.

Exasperated, Randy changed posture, folding his arms like the Duke in *Tall in the Saddle*. Pain in the ass, for sure, but at least he was looking sharp in these excellent new loafers. Mel had been right about the tassels. Crown jewels, no doubt about it, which got Randy to reviewing the whole shoe-store gig, smiling at some of his moves, how he'd taken his time robbing the place, and how good old Mel wasn't crazy about trade-ins or about getting shoelaced to the plumbing.

Randy kept a list in his head of his top twenty extralegal gigs, and this one was way up there, maybe number three on the hit parade. Hoeing Cyrus, that was thirteen. Carl was eighteen. The grape farmer, hard to rate, somewhere in the top ten. Probably number one, he reckoned, had to be that time up in Eugene, Oregon, just a regular electrician's job, wiring the renovation to this filthy-rich guy's house—new bathroom, two new bedrooms, big-ass study—putting in the overheads and outdoor floods and switches and outlets and cable and intercom and security, a pretty fair job, two full weeks at forty bucks an hour, not great but not bad considering at the time Randy didn't know diddly about intercoms or cable or security. Finally, the job's almost done. The rich guy's going away for the weekend, probably to Honolulu or someplace, who cares, so he gives Randy a key to his house, tells him to finish up while he's gone. Very trusting guy, Randy decides. Anyhow, Saturday morning, Randy shows up for work, uses the key to open up the house, wires away for a few hours, installs a four-hundred-dollar doorbell, installs a half-dozen Swarovski light fixtures, rambles around, checks out the Sub-Zero, has a beer, has another beer, catches the Dodgers-Pirates on that sixty-four-inch Sony plasma in the study, messes around with the intercom, and the whole time there's that hot key in his pocket. After a while it starts to feel like this is his own personal house, like he owns the place; that's exactly how it feels when he's got the key right there in his slim-cut Levis. So he forgets the intercom. Goes to work on the security system, which gets him to thinking there must be some serious stuff worth stealing here, not just the Sony. All Saturday night he thinks that. Thinks, Why not? Sleeps in the rich guy's bed, which is too soft, ends up on the rich guy's couch. Sunday morning comes, Randy's up early tossing the place for who knows what, maybe cash, maybe pearls from Honolulu. He finds sixty bucks in a suede loafer. He finds a Batman ring looks like it came with Cracker Jacks. Then he spends the afternoon ripping the place apart. He muscles the Sony out to his Cutlass. He steals the DVD player and the spanking-new Technics speakers he'd just hooked up. He steals an Eagles CD with "Hotel California" on it. He tries on the rich guy's suits, mostly Armani, tight in the crotch but

close enough. He grills up a nice fat porterhouse. He fills a re-
cycling bin with some pretty fair Wedgwood, helps himself to
the wine collection, swipes a coffee maker, thinks about renting
a truck for the rugs and mahogany pieces but can't figure how
he'd unload the stuff. At this point, he reasons, most other
thieves would probably call it a day. Not him. He's got pride.
Monday morning he's still on-site, still messing with the intercom, a NuTone, and around three in the afternoon he's finally
got the sucker up and running when the rich guy walks in
fresh from Honolulu. The guy looks around, asks where's his
TV, Randy tells him it's out in the Cutlass where it belongs,
with the Batman ring. Randy dings him with a hammer. The
guy goes down, tries to get up, so Randy dings him again, in
the throat, claw end of the hammer. All the security in the
world, he thinks, but it doesn't come to squat when you hand
somebody your keys.

"Ding," Randy said, a good professional word.

Yes, sir, he decided, Mr. Honolulu definitely topped the hit
parade. First one is always sweetest.

He chuckled and checked his wristwatches again.

Almost eight thirty, dark as hell, not a soul on the street,
and the heating pads were getting a lot more than just uncomfortable. Like wearing a wetsuit four sizes too small, he
thought. Or a boa constrictor.

He waited a few more minutes, thinking Fran might be running late, then shook his head and decided he had better things
to do. First, get rid of the pads. Second, see about tuning up his
Cutlass. Third, check on old Mel. Not in that order, though.

He looked up and down the street one last time, made sure
the coast was clear, then strolled into the darkened shoe store.

In the bathroom he turned on his cell flashlight. Mel seemed to be doing just fine down there under the sink.

Randy knelt beside him.

"Hey, bro," he said genially. "Just wanted to say you were dead-on right about them tassels. Spiffy as all get-out, and that's coming from a satisfied customer. Everything good on your end?"

Mel said nothing, didn't nod or shake his head.

"Cat got your tongue?" said Randy. He gave Mel's cheek a pinch. Then he remembered the buffing cloth, pulled it from the guy's mouth, and said, "Sorry, partner. For a second there I thought you might be mad at me. You mad at me?"

"No," Mel said.

"No," said Randy. "That's a solid answer. No means no, right? End of story. Want me to tighten up them shoelaces?"

"No," Mel grunted. "But go strangle yourself."

"Tried that one time, no fun," Randy said. "So, Mel, a couple things I forgot to mention. My boots, I'll need them back. Turns out loafers won't cut it on a bronc. Second thing—this one's a question. Any chance you belong to Triple A?"

"I almost suffocated," Mel said.

"Yeah, yeah. What about Triple A?"

"Never heard of it."

Randy sighed. "Listen, Mel, here's a couple words of advice. Show some respect for your customers. Yes or no? You belong to Triple A?"

Mel rolled his shoulders and went sullen-silent, so Randy dug out the guy's wallet and flipped it open and found what he needed. He studied the plastic card under his flashlight, making sure it hadn't expired.

"That last name of yours, Mel? How exactly do you pronounce it?"

"Smith," Mel said.

"Great. Reason I ask, there's some people say Smythe, like with a *y*, like they're big shots from Pittsburgh. You know where Smith comes from? It comes from rodeos, and that's a pure fact. Blacksmith, right? Way back in . . . whenever horses got invented, that's where it comes from. You know that?"

"I do," said Mel. "Take the boots. Can we forget the buffing rag?"

"Tough one there, Mel."

"I won't yell or anything."

"For sure?"

"Absolutely."

"Boy, I don't know," said Randy. "Not great stickup policy." He made a soft little commiserating sound. "Tell you what. Let me think it over while I ring up Triple A. Be right back. Don't go nowhere."

Randy tested the laces, moved to the checkout counter, collected his old riding boots, picked up three more pairs of shoes for Christmas presents, then punched in the Triple A service number. As he waited for a live human to come on the line, he went to the store's front window and peered across the street at the closed-down café, thinking Fran might finally be getting her act together.

Nothing but snow and icy sidewalks.

Norwegians, he told himself, were off his partner in crime list. No exceptions, not even for runner-up Miss Anything.

Five minutes later, after some back and forth, he'd set up a Triple A rendezvous in the Walgreens parking lot, explaining that he needed a battery charge, maybe a tow. He clarified for the operator that his name was pronounced with a *y* sound.

Back in the men's room, Randy put his mind to brass tacks.

He stuffed the buffing cloth down Mel's throat—deep this time—took a pee, washed his hands, said his goodbyes, and made tracks for the Walgreens lot. On the way, loaded down with boots and shoe boxes, he felt a quick, cold stab of pain in his chest, then some shortness of breath. Too much excitement, probably. Or those heating pads still taped to his ribs. He figured the Triple A guy would have a tool to take care of it.

41

TWO AND A HALF WEEKS BEFORE CHRISTMAS, HEDDA
called from a truck stop halfway to Tahoe.

"This is going faster than we thought," she said, sounding
breathless. "Doug wants a head start on the holidays. Six thirty
this morning, I'm doing burpees, next second I'm bobbing for
apples in his Caddy. He thinks we're getting married."

"Tahoe?"

"The Ritz. I impressed him."

"The Ritz, that's California. Make him change it." Wanda
Jane closed her eyes, tried to draw a map in her head. "Tell
him you can't be yourself in a Ritz, too ritzy, you need a Best
Western. The Nevada side. Nevada—it's important."

"Well, honey, the Ritz sounds—"

"Just do it. Nevada. Any luck so far?"

Hedda laughed. "So-so, I guess. If you want to nail him on
bank fraud, yeah, a ton of luck. Dougie can't stop yapping about
all the ways he screws people like you and me. Wait'll you hear
this greedy hog."

"The recorder works okay?"

"Not great, good enough. No murder stuff yet, but give it
time. I mean, listen, Doug's seventy if he's a day, and he's treat-
ing this like his now-or-never moment."

"You're a trooper."

"That I am. Did I mention we're getting married?"

"Don't kid around," Wanda Jane said crossly. "He's a hyena, Hedda. You know what to do if things go wacky?"

"Mace and run."

"Or just run. I'll light a fire under Elmo; he'll be there in five hours, max. Soon as you know, text me the hotel—name and address. And be careful."

"Don't sweat it, hon. I'm a giant."

At the wheel of his leased Escalade—and the Caddy was definitely his, leased or otherwise, because God knows he was shelling out big bucks each month, or at least Community National's big bucks—Douglas Cutterby found himself talking to Lois and Hedda Todhauser almost simultaneously.

To Lois, in his head, Douglas was saying: Look at me, love-bug! Free as a bird!

To Hedda, aloud, he was explaining how bank depositors almost never check their monthly statements, certainly not closely enough to notice double debits. So let's say, for instance, customer Joe Blow writes a check for $52.50, and there it is on his statement, $52.50 on the nose, then a month later, on Blow's next statement, there it is again, $52.50, but lazy, dumbass Joe Blow forgets that the same check already got debited so, lo and behold, Community National just raked in a tidy $52.50. Then let's say—just for the fun of it—let's say your bank does that twice a year to three thousand different customers, and let's say only twelve customers actually catch the double debit; well, in that case, all you do is say, Sorry, our mistake, and you credit back the $52.50, but you're still looking at almost—hold on, let me think—you're looking at a net profit of almost two hundred grand at the end of the year. Do that for thirty years, you've got your own island in the Caymans, just like Lois and me—whoops, just like me.

To Lois, in his head, he was saying: Okay, I *realize* you came up with that scam, but what Miss Todhauser doesn't know won't hurt her. Just look at those stars in her eyes. Reminds me of you way back when, back before Hubcap Toby, back before I had to correct the situation . . . Surprise, wasn't it? Trick or treat, I say, and you say, Doug, and I say, Go down on this, and you look at the twelve-gauge and almost say something else but not quite.

Douglas turned onto 89 South toward Tahoe, slowed down a little, and said to Hedda Todhauser, aloud: "Speaking of lazy customers, how many do you think actually compute interest due each month? Take a guess."

Hedda lifted her head and said, "Don't know."

"Correct," said Douglas. "You don't know, I don't know. Real close to zero, though. Maybe some tightwad in Omaha knows. Everybody else, they figure the *bank* knows what it's doing, but here's the sweet truth. At Community National we do personalized banking, meaning we decide how dumb somebody is and pay interest accordingly. In other words, our friend Joe Blow gets sixty cents a month on his checking account instead of the buck twenty he should be getting. You think Joe notices? You think Joe cares? You think *anybody* does? Sixty cents here, eighty cents there. Chisel away for thirty years, I'll tell you what, you can lease a couple dozen Escalades and have a pocketful left over for the roulette tables. You a roulette gal?"

"Not roulette," Hedda said. She sat up and unwrapped a stick of Doublemint. "Poker, maybe—I'm a sure-thing gal. But, boy, are *you* smart."

"No dummy, I'll admit. The joys of banking. You know those 1099-INT statements at the end of the year? You think anybody bothers to—?"

"Later. Where are we staying?"

"The Ritz, doll. Best for the best."

"No can do," said Hedda.

Douglas glanced at her. "No can do the Ritz?"

"Performance anxiety."

"Well," Douglas said jovially. "We don't want that, do we?"

After they'd cruised around the lake's southern shore and turned northeast into Nevada, Hedda selected a cinder-block motel outside Stateline, where they parked alongside a fleet of Yamahas and Harleys.

Their room—the honeymooners' suite—had the smell of a YMCA shower stall. The room featured miniature cakes of Ivory soap, Stud and Studess bathrobes, and a Joy-Ride bed that at the push of a button emitted the voice of Kenny Rogers covering "Endless Love."

"Comfy, isn't it?" said Hedda.

They dined right down the road at a not-bad steak house. Over appetizers, Hedda took out her cell phone, pretended to check messages, opened the record app, and placed the phone screen down on the table in front of her.

"Let's talk turkey," she said. "Tell me about Lois."

Douglas made a dismissive motion with his shoulders. "The past is past. How's the calamari?"

"Excellent. But losing Lois, you must . . . Her funeral was like, you know, not all that long ago."

"So it was," he said. "Which puts it in the rearview mirror. And, of course, Lois would've wanted this for me"—he swept an arm in a broad gesture that encompassed Hedda, the restaurant, the adjoining motel, and all of Tahoe—"she would've given my wallet a squeeze and cheered me on."

"Did you kill her?"

"Did I kill who?"

"Lois. Did you kill her?"

Douglas laughed.

After a thoughtful sip of wine, he said, "I'm impressed. Cards on the table—that's your style, yes?"

"More or less."

"Hmm," Douglas murmured. "You want to know what I'm thinking right now?"

"Sure. What?"

"I'm thinking: Why is a great-looking, thirty-something CrossFit gal eating calamari with an old buzzard like me? That's what I'm thinking. In fact, that's what I've been thinking since you showed up with a pizza and those tattoos on your ass. I've been thinking, Gee whiz, isn't this unusual? Unusual along the lines of impossible. Can't happen."

"Is that what unusual means?" said Hedda.

"In my experience, yes. My experience, I'll add, is considerable."

Hedda returned his toying, smarter-than-you smile.

"Your wife," she said cheerfully, "was a cold, calculating, manipulative, greedy bitch. So am I. You're single. You're rich. I'm single. I'm poor. What's wrong with being first in line?" She took a chance and moved her hand to his lap. "Cards on the table. Did you kill her?"

"Wow," he said.

"Wow means yes?"

"Wow means you remind me of Lois."

"Except I'm a foot taller, twenty years younger. And my hand's in your lap."

"Except all that."

"Douglas."

"What?"

"Did you kill Lois?"

"What if I did?"

"Then tonight we take the Joy-Ride for a spin."

"And if I didn't?"

"Then I overestimated you."

42

ON THE SHORES OF LAKE LARCENY, BOYD HALVERSON practiced walking on his heels. He paged through the *Iliad*, taking comfort in the foot problems of Achilles. He thought anti-suicide thoughts. He embarked on a rigorous antilying campaign, a struggle that was torpedoed when Angie turned toward him one evening, and asked, "How did you end up dropping your kid?"

In Los Angeles, Jim Dooney slipped a travel brochure under Calvin's dinner plate and said, "Someday soon, I want to show you Jakarta."

Across town, a half block off Rodeo Drive, Evelyn asked her yoga master if anyone had ever truly achieved stillness of mind. Evelyn listened carefully, and said, "Why not?"

In Park Rapids, Minnesota, Randy Zapf stood waiting for Triple A. He had been waiting half the night. Fran was still a no-show, his Cutlass was still a no-start, and the heating pads were now superglued and fast-frozen to his aching abs. Any day now, Randy was scolding the universe, you can start showing me some respect.

At the same instant, aboard a jiggling Joy-Ride in Lake Tahoe, Nevada, Douglas Cutterby joined Kenny Rogers in a tender duet of "Endless Love."

* * *

And out in the dark, somewhere in the expanse of North America, as Christmas approached, as speechwriters toiled and as pastors preached, mythomania claimed its thirty-millionth victim, maybe a crow, maybe a nurse in Kansas, maybe a doctoral candidate in Ohio. By that point, a Latino-hating Texan had fatally swallowed the replacement lie—twenty-two people lay splattered across the floors of a Walmart Supercenter in El Paso. Also, by that point, POTUS had enthusiastically welcomed skinheads, Nazis, xenophobes, and orthodox white supremacists into the cozy, all-American fellowship of "very fine people." Mythomania had become the nation's pornography of choice. From the eastern shore of Chesapeake Bay to San Diego's Naval Air Station, internet chat rooms blustered with vigilante outrage at the browning and Blacking and yellowing and Jewing and Musliming of the homeland. A car mechanic in Louisiana took a sledgehammer to fifteen Korean-made automobiles; a Miss America finalist showcased her sequined KKK robe in the evening gown competition; a barbecue joint in East Texas was firebombed for serving sushi; a TV evangelist in Virginia announced that America's problems "began and ended" with the failure to assassinate Susan B. Anthony. In San Jose, a captive parrot began lying. In Washington, D.C., the Senate's Clean Up America caucus voted to dismantle the Statue of Liberty, crate it up, and ship it back to the Frogs. "Another plot," said a spokesman for the Senate Majority Leader, "to dilute us with the tired and the poor and the wretched refuse." Ellis Island was declared America's Chernobyl.

Meanwhile, in small-town Fulda, California, Mayor Chub O'Neill had proclaimed December 25 "Truth Teller Day." Plans were underway for a nondenominational Truth-Telling pageant,

an extravaganza peopled with shepherds and wise men recit-
ing from a script authored by Earl Fenstermacher.

"The writing," Chub told his brother Dink, "is godawful, but
I love baby Jesus belting out 'Yankee Doodle Dandy.'"

"You don't think he's too Jewish?" said Dink.

"Maybe a little," said Chub.

43

IT WAS A FOUR-HOUR WAIT, BUT AROUND MID-night, after Randy had called Triple A threatening to cancel his membership, a black undersize tow truck pulled up behind his Cutlass in the Walgreens lot. A guy in a parka and pajama bottoms stepped out. The man was about Randy's age, early thirties, midthirties. He slipped into the Cutlass's driver seat, tried cranking the engine, gave up, and went to fetch his portable battery charger.

"Just curious," Randy said once the Cutlass was running. "You think I can get these wheels up to Bemidji tonight? First-class car but there's a speed problem. Can't quite hit thirty."

The man kind of shrugged, kind of didn't. "Fifty-fifty, I'd say. Another hour, it'll be snowing again. You a gambler?"

"Born that way," said Randy. "So when can you get her up and running?"

"Awful hard to say," The man's gaze skidded across the Cutlass. "Ten days, twelve days."

"Yeah?"

"Before Christmas for sure."

Randy blew out an exasperated breath. "Well, okay, before Christmas, but I'm holding you to it. One other question. You know anything about heating pads?"

* * *

An hour northward, on Lake Larceny, Angie had encouraged Boyd to revive his antilying campaign and was now presenting him with the opportunity to cleanse himself. "Lying is like farting," she said earnestly. "Everybody does it, nobody confesses. Confession, that's all that separates the damned from the saved, and you need to start coming clean or you'll be ducking pitchforks. Cleansing means you find yourself a smart, merciful confessor and put in some serious hours. I'd volunteer, except I'm not all that merciful."

"Sure, why not, I'll give it a shot," said Boyd. "You know any confessors?"

"Not offhand. Try God."

Outside, a light, steady snow was falling. They sat in Dooney's great room, a fire burning, Boyd's feet propped up on a half-packed suitcase. Weather and inertia and sore toes had delayed their departure for California.

"If it helps any," said Angie after five minutes had passed, "I'll give you a personal example. This one time in church—my dad's church, small congregation, just seven of us—I sort of dozed off during the sermon, and my mom caught me, and before I knew it, I was on my knees up by the altar—the altar was my dad's old gun case turned on its side—and my sister, Ruth, she was making faces and rolling her eyes while I was busy confessing, which got my goat, so I recanted right then and there; I told the whole congregation it was a trance, a religious trance, and the archangel Claudia had entered my spirit and was editing my dad's sermon, getting rid of the mescaline, so naturally I had to face the music for the next year or two, I had to recant the recant; I had to confess to stuff I didn't even do, like masturbating and eating other people's potato patties.

I'd have been better off just confessing and getting it over with."
Angie looked at him sideways. "You see the point?"

"I do," Boyd said. "You're a liar."

Hedda called Wanda Jane from a ladies' room in Harrah's.
Douglas was at the roulette wheel, down six thousand, having
his troubles.

"This has to be quick," Hedda said. "Did you get the recording attachments I just sent?"

"I did. In the car it sounded like you were—"

"Nothing Doublemint can't cure. Anyway, so far Doug's
playing it cute, Mister Cryptic, thinks he's God's gift to murder. I have ideas, though."

"Is Elmo there?"

"At the bar. Looking bored."

"Okay, listen," Wanda Jane said. "Anything bad happens, just
pound on the wall. Elmo's set up in the room next door to you."

"What can Elmo do?"

"Yell. Wave his six-shooter. What ideas?"

"Sorry?"

"You said you have ideas."

"Oh, yeah. Doug plays roulette, sucker's game, losing his
shirt. I thought I'd scout out a poker table, win his money back.
Might seal the deal. Sex and money."

"Reverse order for Douglas," said Wanda Jane.

Hedda sighed. "Probably. But you know something? I'm
starting to admire the guy. Don't ask me why."

"Why?" said Wanda Jane.

"He's all salamander. He doesn't pretend to have morals."

"Hedda?"

"What?"

"You can do better, honey."

"In Fulda?"

Wanda Jane Epstein spent the next twenty-four hours tossing the Cutterby house and came up with nothing—no shotgun, no pile of cash. At five in the morning, half blind with fatigue, she returned to her tiny one-bedroom apartment, showered off the Cutterby grime, and put in a call to Hedda down in Tahoe.

Hedda's phone immediately kicked into message mode. Wanda Jane waited twenty minutes, tried again, still no answer. "Call me," she told the machine. "Doug's smarter than we thought. We need to rethink this."

She fried up two eggs, sat down to eat, then lost her appetite. Second guesses kept nibbling away at her. All she had, really, was the bone-deep certainty that Douglas had blown his wife into bank heaven. Yet even that, she realized, amounted to little more than intuition mixed with a big dose of revulsion. Titty talk, she kept telling herself, didn't equal wife killer. Only two objective facts pointed at Douglas, and Wanda Jane understood that both of these could easily be explained away. He'd known in advance that Randy Zapf's prints would be all over the hoe, all over Toby's ridiculous cowboy disguise. Sure enough, prints everywhere. But so what? An educated guess, Douglas would say, or something similar, and then he'd come up with a story about Randy hanging around the bank, whatever tall tale popped into his head. Also, Douglas had admitted to being aware that his wife and Toby were sharing fluids on a regular basis, which suggested motive, but motive didn't put a twelve-gauge in his hands. Open marriage, she could hear him saying, even bragging.

The truth, Wanda Jane admitted as she tossed out the eggs,

was that she'd allowed her own history to cloud her thinking. Since early middle school, when her breasts exploded and then re-exploded, she'd been enduring a kind of quadruple life, a mix of pride and anger and power and self-hatred. One day she'd flaunt them, the next day she'd flatten them with ACE bandages. "The Twins," Hedda used to call them, with more envy than humor, but soon enough Hedda experienced her own growth spurt, upward in her case, hitting six four by her junior year in high school. Size, for both of them, had become identity. Hedda became Stilts; Wanda Jane became Twins. Neither of them was happy. Miserable, in fact. More than miserable. Granted, she and Hedda were enormous in very different ways, but enormity itself was the problem, and it was enormity that kept them away from dances, kept them out of parked cars containing boys, and kept them together through twenty years of friendship. They had cut classes together; they had pierced noses and tattooed butts together; they had eventually lost their virginity—not together, exactly—to the same obliging basketball coach. Together, at least in spirit, they had suffered through Hedda's brief marriage to a man three inches shorter and seventy IQ points dumber than she, and together they had discussed, often and in detail, their almost perverse impulses tending toward self-destruction.

Now, after trying Hedda's cell again, Wanda Jane was struck by something that had been bubbling inside her, something ill-formed and without words. As she reached for her car keys, the words appeared. *Betrayal*, that was one word. Endangering a friend, using a friend, preying on a friend. On the short six-block drive over to the Fulda PD station, she tried reaching Elmo, but this time not even a machine answered, just a buzzing sound followed by a click and a dial tone.

Swiftly, angry at herself, Wanda Jane unlocked the station, found Toby's retired service pistol in a file cabinet, grabbed a box of bullets, and left a voice message on Chub O'Neill's cell, letting him know he might want to speed up the interviewing process if he wanted a police force. "Right now you don't have one," she said, then she trotted back to her Camry and headed for Tahoe.

Three and a half hours later, when she stopped for gas, Elmo finally picked up.

"Hey, calm down, sweetheart," he told her, his voice distant and goofy sounding. "Cell service here, it's on and off. Clean air seems to interfere with—"

"I'm nobody's sweetheart, sweetheart. What about Hedda?"

"Hedda's Hedda, happy as a clam." Elmo's voice fell into a chastened, deflated monotone. He waited a moment. "Last I saw, she was cleaning up at a poker table, an all-nighter, guys walking up in their visors and sunglasses, walking away broke. Cutterby looks like he's wired up to a female ATM, the kind that keeps spilling chips in his lap."

"Last you saw?" said Wanda Jane. "When was that?"

Elmo hesitated. "Yeah, well, that's a problem. She played until—I don't know—about four in the morning, won about eight grand. Twenty, thirty minutes later, I tucked them into bed and got some shut-eye. Woke up an hour ago. They'd checked out."

Wanda Jane stood quietly for a second, pumping another five dollars of gas into her Camry's tank.

"You there?" Elmo said.

"His Caddy's gone?"

"It is. I had a peek in their room. Cleaned out. Air conditioner still running, loud enough to wake the dead, so I'm guessing they switched hotels, couldn't tolerate the roaches no more."

"You're a lawyer. Stop talking like Cousin Clem."

"Habit," Elmo said.

"Bad habit. This is no joke."

"Yes, that much I understand," said Elmo, now Elmore. "But I believe you're pretending to be a real cop, so let's both of us keep things in perspective."

"Okay, sorry."

Elmore waited a moment and said, "Soon as I can, I'll start giving parking lots the once-over, see if I can spot the Caddy. Like I say, Cutterby seemed like a pickle in a hot dog bun. Hedda's okay."

"Let's hope," said Wanda Jane.

"Get here when you can."

"Another hour, hour and a half. Meet you where?"

"Harrah's," he said. "Easy to find."

As she pulled back onto 395 South, Wanda Jane made herself push away bad thoughts. Hedda was thirty-four, weighed in at one ninety–something, and could manhandle the front end of a Volkswagen. Smart, too. And plenty cynical enough to watch out for snakes like Doug Cutterby.

Ten miles up the road, Wanda Jane told herself to get real.

Smart and cynical wouldn't do it.

Volkswagens wouldn't do it either. You couldn't outmuscle a shotgun. She was in a dither by the time she'd parked beside Elmo's pickup in the Harrah's lot.

"One favor," she said as he walked up to her. "I don't need Rube Elmo right now. I need Esquire Elmo."

"That would be Elmore," he said gently.

"Yeah, that one. I've sold out my best friend. Sent her where I wouldn't go."

He nodded. "The thought occurred to me. Let's go inside, figure out how to fix this."

In a bar just off the casino's main lobby, they sat over cups of coffee. Calmly, in very few words, Elmo explained that he'd already checked out the lodges and hotels around Stateline, no sign of Cutterby's Cadillac. He proposed that they separate and work their way up opposite sides of the lake, meeting somewhere around Incline Village. "Make it the Starlight Empress. We'll hook up there if we don't find anything—just stay cool, okay? It'll take time, probably the rest of the day, but we'll track 'em down."

Wanda Jane shook her head.

"I've got mulch for brains," she said. "What's wrong with me?"

"Nothing's wrong. Sense of justice."

"I took advantage of her."

"Maybe, maybe not," Elmo said. "Fact is, you didn't want to mud-wrestle with Cutterby. Hedda doesn't mind one little bit." He smiled, reached out, and gave her hand a bashful squeeze. "Basically, you had the right idea. Doug's a horn tooter. He just might start blabbing secrets under the covers."

"So you think he did it?"

"Did Lois? Bet your ass I think so." Elmo looked down at her hand, studying it briefly, then looked up again. "Let's not jump to worst-case conclusions. Doug was a man on a mission last night, visions of poker chips and German poontang. "We've got time, I think."

Wanda Jane stood up and said, "Mulch. Let's go."

Elmo took the California side of the lake; Wanda Jane took

Nevada. Every half hour they kept in touch about their progress, which was slow going on both sides of the lake. Wanda Jane had been here only once before, as a twelve-year-old, and she was surprised at how infested the place was with fast food joints and casinos and motels ranging from pricey to barely habitable. Even now, on a Friday in late December, the Christmas ski traffic made it a slow crawl up U.S. 50 to where it curved northeast above Glenbrook. Along the way, she pulled into a half-dozen parking lots, even a couple of small ones, but there was nothing resembling Cutterby's gas-guzzler.

Well after dark, a light snow falling, she pulled up next to Elmo at the Starlight Empress in Incline Village. Neither of them had good news. They stood beside Elmo's pickup for a few minutes, surveying a lot jammed with everything but a limo-size Cadillac.

"You're the lawyer," Wanda Jane finally said. "Any advice?"

"I advise we get out of the cold," said Elmo. "Donner weather out here."

"And after that?"

Elmo thought for a moment. "Good question. The ex-lawyer says we call off the vigilante stuff. Get some help. Pool-hall Elmo says we order up some hot chicken soup, hot anything, and try again in the morning. She'll probably call before then. Almost for sure."

"You think?"

"Yes, I do."

"I don't," Wanda Jane said. "You go inside. I'm taking a stroll."

Four hundred feet away, Douglas Cutterby conversed with Lois while consuming a somewhat overdone room-service T-bone.

Hedda's phone lay on the table before him, its recording app open and running. Hedda herself had gone downstairs to check the hotel's lost and found.

What this earthy young lady doesn't know, Douglas was now remarking to Lois, may end up hurting her, don't you agree?

Lois had no opinion one way or the other, which caused Douglas to smile and say, mutely, with his mouth full: Your newfound ambivalence is music to my ears, sweetie pie. Not that I don't miss you terribly. Not that I don't have a regret or two. Remember that look on your face? Well, of course you don't—how could you? "Don't you dare!" you were about to say, and then boom! Ambivalent in less than a heartbeat! No more opinions! Now, I'll confess you earned your load of buckshot, but nonetheless I do wish you were here right now—the abased you, the disfigured but vastly improved you—yes, and I do wish you could behold your Dougie's appeal to the softer sex, although soft is hardly the word for the acrobatic Ms. Todhauser. Her palate, perhaps. Otherwise—and I need not paint pictures—otherwise dear Hedda can be described as six and a third feet of animated concrete. Face it, hon, you were going mushy here and there. Martinis jiggling at the waistline. The shotgun trimmed you down a bit. In any event, mushiness aside, crankiness aside, and, of course, cuckoldry aside, you share a great deal with my earthquake-proof new consort. Hedda turns out to be a whiz with numbers—poker, in her case—and with some training, she'll make a first-class vice president of Community National. Or so I had thought. Until this. Just listen.

Douglas turned up the phone's volume and played a short segment featuring his own jovial baritone detailing a dozen counts of bank fraud.

Now that, he told Lois, was recorded in the midst of . . .

well, forgive me, in the midst of what we'll call *fireworks*. Seriously, I'm wounded. I liked her. And, unfortunately, there's more. Listen.

He played a longer clip, enjoying the baked potato more than the steak.

I owe you an apology, he told Lois. But how was I to know she was recording it all? Am I a mind reader? All the same, I do apologize. I mean, it was an intimate thing between you and me, husband and wife, that look on your face when you almost said, "Don't you dare," and when I said, "Suck on this, darling," because we both knew you were planning exactly the same for me—don't deny it! We had a great run, baby. And I'm sorry I kissed and told. Not quite kissed, I suppose, but dissolved our relationship. And told. I'm sure you know what I mean. Question now is, how do we handle Ms. Todhauser? Ideas?

Lois always had ideas, or used to, and it was hard for Douglas to accept silence. He turned off the recording app, returned the phone to his pocket, finished the baked potato, and put his mind to solutions. No reason to rush. Close call but no damage.

Ten minutes later, when Hedda walked in, Douglas said, "Find your phone?"

"No," said Hedda. "I need your keys. I'll check the car."

"Good idea," said Douglas. He tossed her his keys. "Then maybe some poker when you're back? The night's young."

Wanda Jane made her way through the Starlight's parking lot, double-checking for Cadillacs, then she circled the entire hotel. It was nearly ten in the evening, icy cold, and she'd wrapped herself in a ratty old blanket stashed in her trunk. After twenty minutes, she ended where she'd started, in the blinking glare of Christmas lights near the casino's front doors.

What made her stop and look out toward the frontage road she wasn't sure—probably nothing, just a place to look—but across the road was a fair-size restaurant with a fair-size parking lot, and even from a distance, Cutterby's big black Caddy stood out among its dwarf cousins. Wanda Jane crossed the road, cupped her hands against a passenger-side window, and was turning away when Hedda trotted up, and said, "Peeping Tom?"

They hugged—Wanda Jane on her tiptoes.

"I've got fifteen minutes, that's it," said Hedda. She unlocked the car, looked inside for a few seconds, and slammed it shut. "Let's grab a quick coffee."

The restaurant was jammed, nowhere to sit, and they ordered takeout and stood with their coffee in a little alcove near the cash register. The fifteen minutes went by quickly. Hedda explained that the hotel's lot had been full, that the car had been valeted across the street, that her cell phone was missing, that she'd gotten Douglas to admit almost everything—not quite admit, maybe, and not quite everything—the word was *gloat*—and that Wanda Jane should stop worrying, all was well, she was having fun; Douglas was talking about buying them a chalet up here in the Sierras, and for a murderer, for a banker to boot, the guy had a certain swashbuckling joie de vivre, a gentlemanly flair, a red-blooded appetite for martinis and car sex and money.

"Missing phone?" said Wanda Jane.

"Yeah, that part's a bummer. I thought it might be in the car."

"So the confession—?"

"Down the drain, but no worries. Tickle his pickle and the guy coos like a geriatric newborn. All I need is another phone."

"Take mine." Wanda Jane dug out her phone and handed it to Hedda. "You have Elmo's number, right?"

"Sure do. Look, I have to get back; he'll start wondering."

Wanda Jane finished her coffee in two gulps. Even indoors she was freezing.

"Okay," she said. "But stay in touch this time. I was worried sick."

"You're a nervous Nellie. Doug doesn't have a clue."

Hedda took Wanda Jane's arm as they crossed back to the Starlight Empress. At the front doors they hugged again.

"You know what?" Hedda said.

"What?"

"Don't laugh, but I wouldn't mind a chalet up here."

Douglas and Hedda were just entering the casino's poker room when his phone played "Sentimental Journey."

"Lois's theme song," Douglas said. "I better take this."

He moved away, turned his back to her, and spent the next several minutes mostly listening.

At one point he said, "My bank's not for sale."

Not much later he said, "*How* much?"

Then, almost immediately, he said, "May I call you Junius?"

44

JUNIUS KIRAKOSSIAN WAS SWIVELING IN HIS swivel chair on the top floor of YOU!, gazing out toward Catalina, a little sad, a little angry, and a whole bunch depressed. A man should not have to buy a bank, he scolded himself, in order to keep a wife a wife. Or to keep a wife's ex out of San Quentin. Or to get a good night's sleep.

What, he wondered, would a candy man do with a two-bit bank? Especially a crooked bank. Especially a crooked bank in the middle of nowhere. He cared about banks even less than he cared about ships and shipping, which was scarily close to zero.

What he cared about was Evelyn.

She hadn't exactly phrased it as an ultimatum—more like do it without the either-or. Since returning from Minnesota, his wife had been sweet enough, even loving enough—more than ever, in fact—but now there was a big helping of the father churning away inside the daughter. It's a bank, she'd said flatly, and it's what I want. Then came the smile. Then the Dooney stare.

Junius swiveled, slapped the button on his intercom, and asked his secretary to bring in the airline tickets for his flight up to Tahoe.

"Three other things," Junius told the intercom. "Cut a check for eighty-one thousand, make it out to a guy named Douglas

Cutterby—that's C-U-T-T-E-R-B-Y. Then get my father-in-law on the line. And tell Henry to come in."

"Henry's delayed," said his secretary.

"Delayed?"

"Caught a bug from somebody he met on a plane. If you want, I can reach him at the Minneapolis Radisson."

"What's he doing in a Radisson? What's wrong with La Quinta?"

"I guess he's recuperating, sir."

"Yeah?"

"Massage therapy. I hear it works."

Junius swiveled back toward Catalina. "Forget Henry, just get me Dooney. What time's my flight?"

"Noon. You've got three hours but, you know . . . it's Christmas Eve. Airport congestion."

"All right then, call my wife, tell her I'll be back in a week or so, this'll take some time. Maybe two weeks, no telling. Ask if she wants me to pick up a couple more banks on the way home. Maybe a gallon of blood."

"Sir?"

"Nothing. Forget that, too."

"Tell me about it," Dooney was saying, his voice scratchy and hollowed out over a speakerphone. "You think a bank is trouble, try making an offer on JCPenney. I barely know where to start."

"Progress?" said Junius.

"Here and there. Sort of. Right now, Calvin's on the other line with Plano. Hold on a sec." After a minute or two, Dooney said, "Okay, I'm back. Where's Plano?"

"Louisiana?" Junius said.

"Got me. All I know is I'll be there tonight."

"Jim, I've been thinking," said Junius, hesitating for a second. "This bank up in Fulda, I've looked at the financials. The whole operation is worth maybe ten cents if you can get it on sale. It's basically a bank without money. Drained dry."

"Right, I noticed that," said Dooney.

"So what if we deep-six the acquisition? Just hand over eighty-one grand and call it a day? That gets Halverson off the hook—like a loan repayment, you know? Everybody's happy."

"Not Evelyn. Buy the bank, Junius."

"But Jim, it's a shell game. They loan themselves money—fake names, naturally—then they charge the bank eight percent for the pleasure of loaning it to themselves. Tip of the iceberg. They must be running a dozen other scams, probably more. The toaster giveaway, you see that? Free toaster, just deposit your life savings at zero percent."

Dooney laughed. "Pretty clever, that one. My kind of business."

"Peddling nerve gas?"

There was some quiet before Dooney said, "Is that a criticism, Junius?"

"No, I was—"

"Because I'll tell you something. If some poor slob in Togo wants to settle a grudge, needs to defend his wife's honor, who am I to stand in the way? I ship the stuff, I don't . . . I don't *prescribe* it. Anyway, I'm an old man. I want to make things right with my daughter. Buy the bank."

"I don't see—"

"You arguing with me?"

"I wouldn't say argue, Jim. I'd say . . ."

Dooney made a show of clearing his throat. "A few things

you should remember, Junius. First off, PS&S can afford a crummy little bank, that's obvious. Am I right?"

"You are. Always."

"Good point. Second thing, Evelyn wants a clean slate for what's-his-name—Birdsong, whatever—so buying the bank covers that. You own it, you control it. Clean slate. And bear in mind, there's also that whole deal we had when I set you up as CEO. You occupy the swivel chair, I call the shots. I say buy a bank, you buy a bank. I say make my daughter happy, you make her happy. And then finally—let me finish here—finally, I'm tired of getting chased all over creation by a deranged liar with a bad temper. The tension, it's corrupting my relationship with Cal. Buy the bank. Clear?"

"Pretty clear," Junius said.

"And Junius?"

"Yeah, I'm here."

"That baseball team. Unload it. You're a laughingstock."

Along the shores of Lake Larceny, the days of December turned abnormally mild and sunny. Angie and Boyd were alone now. They had the lake to themselves. There were no boats, no fishermen or vacationers, no people at all, no motion except for what the wind would do to water and trees, and for the first time since late August, when Boyd had crossed the street to rob Community National, he was without ambition of any sort.

It was not lethargy. It was the absence of desire. He wanted nothing and December complied.

Even Boyd's dreams, which for years had boiled with wanting, were now as placid as this uninhabited Indian summer. He did not want love or joy or revenge or salvation or Evelyn. He did not want to live. He did not want to die. He looked out at the lake sometimes, enthralled at how equally unwanting it was, and how the deep, restless water cared nothing for its own beauty or buoyancy or eventual fate. On those occasions Boyd was struck by an amazed, almost disbelieving recollection of how he had once so ferociously cared. Ludicrous, he'd think. Yet it was true that until recently he had wanted very much, even desperately, to blow a lifetime of lies out of his head; he had wanted Jim Dooney to witness it; he had wanted to soak Dooney in complicity and brain splatter.

All that had once made sense. Now it embarrassed him.

Were all suicides, he wondered, founded in such flimsy fantasy? At best, Dooney would have sighed with displeasure, changed clothes, and called in a cleaning service to mop up his front doorstep.

In those deceitful days before full-scale winter, under a false sun, Boyd spent aimless, undemanding hours out on the dock, neither content nor discontent, submerging his toes in the frigid waters, obedient to Angie's orders.

The treatment seemed to help. The pain was receding and with each day he was able to gimp another ten or fifteen steps.

Not that he had a destination in mind. Destinations required a future, just as wanting required a future, and the very notion of a future—any future—struck him as bizarre. If there was a consequence to near suicide, Boyd had begun to realize, it was this hollowness inside him, an absence of even the most modest aspiration. The next meal, the next day, the next anything—there was no nextness. How could there be? No future, no next.

And so the days meandered into other days. December coasted toward Christmas. Twice now, Angie had postponed

their return to California. She made up flimsy excuses; she decorated the great room with pine boughs; she went oddly quiet,
more like a taxidermist's idea of Angie than Angie herself; she
seemed afraid. They slept separately, Boyd in the camper, Angie
before the fireplace in Dooney's great room, but at one point
he awoke to find her beside him in the Pleasure-Way, her face
inches away, inspecting him as if he were something new and
strange and a bit frightening. She said nothing. After a time,
she turned onto her back and lay watching the dark.

In the morning, neither of them spoke about it. Instead,
Angie said, "I need to get something back from you, Boyd. Anything. I'm afraid you'll lose me."

Boyd nodded.

He thought about it all day.

That evening, without meaning to be cruel, he said, "I'm
sorry. I'm a loser. Everybody knows that. Even I do."

She looked at him. An hour passed.

"Losing me," she said in a tired voice, "would be a tragedy."

Snow was falling. A wind was howling.

The lights went out.

Over the following days and nights, absolute winter came to
visit and this time it stayed. By December 16, five and a half
feet of snow had accumulated; pipes broke; there were cracklings in the trees outside. The camper was no longer habitable,
and Boyd looked on as Angie wrestled one of the two barber's
chairs down to the great room and set up a makeshift bed for
him in front of the fireplace. Though the mansion was a year-
round structure—the only such place on Lake Larceny—it was
heated by a trio of oil-burning furnaces that refused to burn,
or burned only at will, clanging in complaint. An electric oven

kept the kitchen warm, but the top two floors, with their eleven bedrooms, hair salon, and billiard parlor, might as well have been wide-open to the outdoors. Even the great room's huge fireplace threw out only a few sparse feet of livable warmth.

By day, they wore sweaters and overcoats, ate canned chili, took turns in the barber's chair, and waited for whatever was coming.

Late at night, especially in the vulture hours before dawn, Boyd revisited his own history of misdeeds. His toes were an excellent reminder. To his surprise, there was sometimes a small sizzle of pleasure inside the pain, the pleasure of a debt repaid, certainly not forgiven but perhaps accounted for. He should not have called his mother a fat ass. He should not have declined his father's invitation to throw around a football. He should not have claimed polo as a hobby. He should not have trumped up a Purple Heart, a brain tumor, and a résumé riddled with fantasy. He should not have replaced a Birdsong with a Halverson. If he were a courageous man, Boyd told himself—the vultures now hissing in the dark—and if he could somehow make himself believe in a future, he would one day look up the lovely Peggy and the lovelier Enni—both of them, why not?—and plead for a recrushing of his toes.

Maybe look up Dooney, too. Have a laugh. Pull out the Temptation and see what happened.

Once, in the midst of Boyd's 4:00 a.m. history lessons, he became aware of Angie talking in her sleep. She had usurped the barber's chair, consigning him to the floor beside her, and in the near dark of a dying fire, she jerked and moaned and half sat up and released little exclamatory bursts of animal utterance that were not gibberish exactly, not without meaning, more like a language entirely her own. It went on for two or three minutes, then she lay back in the barber's chair, put a hand to her mouth, and fell silent.

At another point, a day or two later, Alvin appeared at the door with four bags of groceries. He had little to say—almost nothing. He stomped snow from his boots, nodded at Boyd, nodded at Angie, and carried the bags into the kitchen and placed them on the counter.

"Well then," he murmured, then looked at Angie for a second and walked back toward the front door.

Boyd stopped him.

"I need to ask something," he said quietly. "You ever handle confessions?"

"Randy's here," Angie said on a sunny morning three days before Christmas. "Not here here. But in Bemidji. Bombing me with texts. He'll find this place eventually."

"Okay," said Boyd.

"Okay?"

"Sure. I've got more toes to crunch."

And then a day or two later, Boyd hobbled down to the lake, where he swept away some snow, took off his boots and socks, sat down gingerly on the dock, and pressed his bruised feet against a patch of shiny black ice. The morning was weirdly bright—bright without heat—and all around him the world sparkled. Boyd closed his eyes briefly, wishing he'd brought sunglasses, and when he looked up, he noticed a figure in a hooded red parka plodding toward him across the frozen lake. Man or woman, Boyd could not tell. The figure was dark and smudgy against the winter glare, a quarter mile away, moving as if in slow motion on what was probably a pair of snowshoes. After five or ten minutes, near the center of the lake, the figure stopped, pulled a long slender tool from under the parka, bent forward, paused a moment, then plunged the tool into the snow and ice beneath him. He—or possibly she—did this repetitively. There was a cracking sound. Then several cracking sounds. Boyd reached for his socks and boots, put them on, and pushed unsteadily to his feet. When he looked back at the lake, the red parka and the tool and the figure in snowshoes had vanished into a sparkling piece of nothing.

Was this real?

Boyd doubted it.

Here is what happens, he thought, when everything means nothing.

Randy Zapf showed up on Christmas Day. He had been delayed by car trouble, blizzard trouble, money trouble, and big, big trouble nailing down Angie's whereabouts.

"I'm Randy," he said when Boyd opened the door. "And I bet we're gonna have fun together."

45

"GO FOR A WALK, COME BACK IN A COUPLE OF hours," Angie said. "I need to talk to him privately."

"Hours?" said Boyd. "It's twelve degrees out there."

"Hot coffee," she said. "Bring a thermos."

Boyd left through the kitchen door, avoiding trouble, limping over to the Pleasure-Way to escape the cold. He got the heater going, put on three JCPenney sweaters, sat down, and did nothing for a while, then picked up his unfinished Churchill biography. He hadn't glanced at the book since . . . when? August? In Mexico? A yellowing corner of page 382 had been turned. Another nine hundred pages lay densely in wait.

Settling in, still goose-bumpy and shivering, Boyd waded into the Boer War, almost immediately wondering what a Boer was, thinking he should look it up, but then deciding he didn't give a damn. About that or anything else. He was tempted to skip ahead to the final few pages, where all biographies more or less ended in the same place.

After more than an hour, when he hit page 433, the camper's heater began to lose its own war, surrendering to Minnesota.

Boyd put on two more sweaters, both top-grade acrylic, added an old corduroy jacket and three pairs of woolen socks, and then, with nothing better to do, he set off across a frozen Lake Larceny to investigate what he'd come to consider the apparition of a red parka and a figure on snowshoes. The going was slow and difficult: deep, crusty snow, slick ice beneath it. A wolfish wind chewed on his ears and nose, sometimes biting through corduroy and five layers of Penney's acrylic. His toes alternated between numbness and electrocution. Maybe this, he mused, was nature's payback for a life of perfidy and pseudologia fantastica.

He counted his steps. He thought about Enni with her monkey wrench, his mother gulping milkshakes in front of *High Society*, Evelyn saying, "Polo, you're kidding?"

Several dozen blackbirds lay frozen solid in the snow.

Near the center of the lake, he found what he was hoping not to find. A small ragged circle of snow had been scooped away to expose the ice. Nearby, half drifted over, lay a cheap shovel, an iron-black ice auger, and something that looked like a chisel mounted on a metal broomstick. At the center of the circle was a hole. Or what had been a hole. It was now an ice scab, its sheen of a brighter and clearer quality than the ice around it.

Boyd turned away. He did not want to look. Don't, he thought, but then he did. A Pompeian red parka pressed up against the ice scab.

Boyd recalled a piggyback ride. "Hey, Dad," Alvin used to say.

In Jim Dooney's kitchen, a pair of stools had been drawn up in front of an open electric oven. Angie sat on one of the stools; the other was vacant.

"Where's James Dean?" Boyd had just asked.

"Where's who?"

"Your buddy. The cowboy."

"Randy's not a buddy. Not a cowboy either. Who's James Dean?"

"A nobody, because he's dead," said Boyd, "but my mom used to send him love letters."

Angie shrugged.

She looked the worse for wear, exhausted and jittery. On the floor in front of her were six pairs of shoes. In her lap was a rubber thong.

Boyd pulled off his boots and jacket, gimped his way to the vacant stool, and sat down with the thought that he may never stand again. The oven's heat seemed unearthly.

For a time, they did nothing but sit on their stools, avoiding each other's eyes. Boyd thought about the red parka, thought about saying something, not sure how or what, but then Angie let out an audible breath and muttered, "You've made a mess of things, haven't you?"

"That I have," said Boyd.

"I'm going back to California. Very soon. You can ride along or not, it's up to you. I'm done."

"California? You and James Dean?"

"His name's Randy and he needs me." Her voice was low, chilly, and distant sounding. She looked down at her lap and said, "I told him he could use the camper. Temporarily. Till I figure things out."

"He'll need to fix the heater."

"Fine. Randy's a fixer."

"Okay, good, but there's one other thing." Boyd hesitated. "It might make things worse."

"Just say it."

"Maybe . . . I don't know. Maybe you're not in shape for this."

"Say it or I'll scream. Say it this second. I'm in a screaming mood."

"What's up with the thong?"

"That's it?"

"Yes, it is. A thong?"

"It was a present!" she said fiercely. "From Randy. He was thinking of me, *caring* about me. And it's my color—yellow's my almost color. A billion bucks says you didn't even *know* that!"

"How's the fit?"

"What?"

"Snug enough?"

"Boyd," she said slowly, "are you *trying* to make me insane?"

"No," he said. "I'm trying not to tell you that your other boyfriend is out there under four inches of ice. You can scream now."

Angie stood looking down at the iced-over hole. Boyd stood beside her. "I'm not sure it's Alvin," she said.

"The parka," said Boyd. "It's Alvin."

"An accident, you think?"

"No."

"Oh, well."

"That's all you can say?"

"For now, I guess."

Snow and two crows tumbled from the sky. Angie removed her mittens and pressed the palms of her hands against the transparent scab of ice. A cold and windy half hour passed. "Sometimes," she murmured, "I want to give God a piece of my mind. He can be such a jerk."

"He heard my confession," said Boyd.

"God always hears."

"Alvin, I'm talking about. We *both* confessed. An all-nighter."

Angie looked down at the ice scab, turned away, and said, "Lot of good it did."

That night she had a great deal to say. She'd been talking in her sleep again. Boyd reached out, gave her shoulder a shake, and said, "Wake up, it's a dream."

"I *am* awake," she said irritably. "This is private. It's between God and Alvin and me."

The temperature on Lake Larceny hit minus twelve degrees the next morning and did not move a degree higher over the following seventeen days. A fifty-ton tree snapped in half at its trunk. The power failed. Cell service was intermittent. A raven fell stone-dead on the mansion's back porch.

With still another cold front sliding in from North Dakota, and with the Pleasure-Way's heater frozen solid, Angie helped Randy Zapf prepare a bed of quilts and cushions in front of the great room's fireplace. There would be rules, she explained. No threats. No dirty looks. No uncivilized language. Randy would never speak to Boyd; Boyd would never speak to Randy, and if either of them wished to communicate with the other, it would be done through Angie, who would translate and pass along the gist.

Randy swatted the air and said, "Suits me," then flashed a friendly grin at Boyd and said, "Ask the old guy if he ever floated upside down inside a keg of grape juice."

Angie said, "Boyd, did you ever—?"

"I heard him," said Boyd. "Ask if he's James Dean."

Angie said, "Randy, are you James Dean?"

Randy said, "Ask who the fuck James Dean is."

"Fuck is not civilized," said Angie, "but I'll ask. Boyd, tell Randy who James Dean is."

Boyd, who lay under a half-dozen blankets in the barber's chair, his feet elevated, his head tilted back as if to receive a shave, said, "Inform this ignorant lumphead that James Dean is—was—the third most famous human being in America back in 1956. Matthew McConaughey almost, but no bongos."

Randy said, "Big deal, tell him I don't—"

Angie said, "I haven't translated yet. Boyd thinks you look like Matthew McConaughey. Say thank you."

"Yeah, thanks," Randy said. "Now ask what a bongo is."

"It's a drum, for Pete's sake," said Angie. "Why bother?"

"Ask anyway," said Randy. "That's the rule."

"Boyd, what's a bongo?" Angie asked.

Boyd said, "A bongo . . . You could say it's skin stretched over air, like this imbecile's head."

Angie sighed. She was toasting marshmallows on a long, wavy-bladed *takoba* sword Randy had supplied from the trunk of his Cutlass. "Boyd says a bongo is skin stretched over air, like your head."

"Is that what he says? Ask him if that's what he says."

"Is that what you said?" said Angie.

"Word for word," said Boyd.

"That's what he said," Angie said.

"All right, do me a favor and ask Lover Boy if he ever rode a bronc. Two to one, he don't know what a bronc *is*."

Angie sighed, and said, "Boyd, Randy wants to know—"

"A bronc," said Boyd, "is an abused horse. Ask Dumbo if he ever played polo."

"Both of you, last warning, act your age," Angie said crossly. "Randy, have you ever played polo?"

"Yeah, sure."

"You've played polo?"

"Almost positive," said Randy. "Isn't that like when you ride big dogs and hit stuff with a hoe? I've played that game a time or two."

"He says he's played polo," Angie told Boyd. "Let's stop."

"In a minute," said Boyd. "Ask where he picked up the loafers. Ask if he teaches ballet down at the Y."

"I better not," Angie said.

"Did he say ballet?" said Randy. "Ask."

"This isn't civilized. We're stopping."

Angie stood up, ate two marshmallows off the sword, snuffed out a pair of candles, then slipped into one of Jim Dooney's sleeping bags. "My head hurts; that's it for tonight. Tomorrow, we start packing for California. Day after tomorrow, we hit the road, snow or no snow."

"Can I bring up one last thing?" Randy asked.

"If it's civilized," said Angie.

Randy was still grinning his friendly grin at Boyd. "I'm just wondering. Can you ask this ancient scumbag if he knows what first dibs means?"

"Forget the rules," said Angie. "You ask."

It took half the night for Boyd to settle down. He lay tossing and turning in his barber's chair. Angie, too: she lay near the fire, wrapped in her sleeping bag, talking nonsense in her sleep. At one point she turned toward Boyd, and whispered, in English, "Stop eavesdropping. I'm in church."

Randy lay a few feet away, cradling his sword. "Didn't you hear?" he said. "She's in church, Lover Boy."

"Am I missing something?" said Boyd.

"You sure are," whispered Angie.

They spent the days after Christmas preparing for departure. Randy and Angie shoveled out the long gravel driveway, their work twice undone by heavy snowfalls. In mid-January, Randy hooked up a fresh battery and took the Ferrari for a test run into Bemidji and back. "Needs giddyap," he said afterward. "But I guess it's okay if you never mounted a Cutlass."

Boyd filled a suitcase and a plastic garbage bag with his few belongings. Angie packed their cash—she wouldn't say how much. The Pleasure-Way was a lost cause.

"We'll take two cars," Angie said. "Randy's junker, my sex mobile. You'll ride with me, Boyd. Say goodbye to the camper."

"Bye," Boyd said.

"You're excited. Life's an adventure, isn't it?"

They pulled out at first light the next morning.

Randy led the way in his Cutlass, Angie following at the wheel of the midnight-blue Ferrari 812 Superfast, Boyd sitting stiff-legged and morbidly disposed beside her. The roads were slick. Heaps of dead birds lay in the ditches. Angie drove cautiously, with both hands, her seat levered fully forward, her lips compressed, a sofa cushion boosting her line of vision above the Ferrari's steering wheel. After a time, halfway to Park Rapids, Boyd had the sudden and ferocious need for a cigarette. He tapped his pockets, an old habit, then opened the glove compartment and found his Temptation wrapped in a suicide note. "Tell Angie," Alvin had written, "that I'll be pissed off if you can't steal stuff in heaven."

Boyd slipped the note in his pocket where cigarettes should have been.

The going was slow.

They would not reach California until early June.

46

ON THE LIMO RIDE FROM DFW UP TO PLANO, JIM
Dooney was telling Calvin that JCPenney might make a decent
acquisition. "People gotta eat, people gotta poop, people gotta
wear clothes. Tell me if I'm wrong, Cal. I'm not wrong. Imagine
if all our ships sink, all the ragheads stop buying nerve gas,
we've still got underwear to sell. We've got shoes, too. Suit
jackets. Socks, belts, plus-size pantyhose, high-end makeup,
low-end purses, and some pretty fair-quality luggage to pack up
all the dry goods. Plus, we land the whole shebang in a fire sale."

"How much?" asked Calvin.

"For the chain? Peanuts. A few billion."

"How few?"

"Seven, nine, who knows? We negotiate, that's why we're in
a limo, isn't it?"

Calvin took Dooney's hand.

"You're a good father," he said.

"Am I?"

"Nine billion to buy a guy's job back?"

"Yeah, I guess. If it pleases Evelyn, it pleases me." Dooney
returned the pressure of Calvin's hand. "Of course, there's self-
interest involved."

"Of course," said Calvin. "You're a businessman."

Dooney shrugged and peered out at Texas rolling by, mostly
strip malls and fake cowboys driving Land Rovers. "Like I told

Junius, now I'm telling you, I'm too old to keep looking over my shoulder. Let bygones be bygones."

"Good point. You could use a shave, though."

"You think?"

"And a trim around the ears. You don't want to look like a bum."

"I look like that?"

"Not to me, Jimmy. To me you look hot."

They rode in silence for a time before Dooney said, "Acquisitions like this one, Cal, I *feel* hot. I feel like I could snap up the Grand Canyon, buy the Washington Monument. You know the feeling? Buy Chicago, buy Yellowstone, put in hostile takeover bids on . . . on everything! The Declaration of Independence? Buy it. The Constitution? Buy it. All the schools, all the libraries—swallow up the whole sorry bunch, no more Darwin and dirty words. Buy it all! That's my dream, Cal, that's my fantasy, that's what'll make this country great again."

"Come on," said Calvin. "Think big."

In Tahoe, Wanda Jane sat with Elmo in the Starlight Empress's coffee shop, both of them fiddling with their empty cups as they waited for Hedda to call. She was overdue. "Every hour on the hour, that's what I told her," Wanda Jane was saying. "Hedda promised."

"The world gets in the way," said Elmo.

"That's what scares me."

Wanda Jane scanned the banks of slots and gaming tables over Elmo's shoulder. It was nearly ten in the evening. The place was filling up with the post-Christmas crowd, and something about the leftover holiday decorations and the hum of money changing hands told Wanda Jane they were in over their heads.

Fortune favors the brave, she thought, except when it favors the house.

"Stay here," she said after a moment. "I'd better try—"

Elmo's phone buzzed.

He answered, listened, and grinned at Wanda Jane.

"For you," he said.

Hedda's voice was rushed. She was calling from a business suite upstairs, had only a minute to talk. "Listen, I'm really, really sorry to be late," she said, "but there's this guy here, this skinny old dude, he wants to buy our bank, cash deal. Doug and I are putting the squeeze on, but the guy's a penny-pincher, keeps trying to whittle us down. Pretty exciting. Big fat bucks. And this business suite, you should see the spread I'm looking at right now, a whole side bar laid out with smoked salmon, these little lobster sandwiches. Champagne. Heroin. You name it."

"Heroin?"

"I'm kidding."

"You were supposed to call, Hedda. Every hour."

"How could I? Selling a bank, hon. It takes time. Probably another two or three weeks, I bet."

"You said *our* bank."

"I said *our*?"

Wanda Jane's eyes slid toward Elmo. She gave him a little wag of the head. "Slow down," she said.

"I *can't* slow down. Doug said make it quick. We're at crunch time, brass tacks, whatever you call it."

"Hedda?"

"Yeah?"

"What's with the 'we'?"

"We," Hedda said. "Doug and me. Out of the blue, this pip-squeak from L.A. rolls in, wants to snap up Community National. Dither, dither. We've got an agreement in principle, I'm pretty sure, but I can tell the pip-squeak isn't too happy with our financials—you know—our actual assets."

Wanda Jane closed her eyes for a moment, tried to think, and said, "I'm confused. Last I knew, you were taping him. Now you're his business partner?"

"Not just business," Hedda said.

"You're joking?"

"Sort of. I'm on the fence. Doug's talking the Caymans. Honeymoons."

"He's a murderer."

"I know. Fly in the ointment."

There was some silence.

Wanda Jane said, "Get out of there. Right now. Hedda."

"Jeez, I don't know. If you can't get love, you get laid. Can't get laid, get rich. It's my shot."

"Shot like Lois."

"Not necessarily," Hedda said, and laughed. "Look, I got to run, honey. I'll call when I can."

When Wanda Jane handed Elmo his phone, he said, "Complicated lady."

Evelyn, too, was on the phone, speaking through a distant, tinny-sounding wireless connection to Angie Bing, who sat double-parked in front of a shoe store in Park Rapids, Minnesota. "Randy and Boyd are inside," Angie said, "returning a bunch of shoes that don't even come close to fitting me. It's taking forever—Randy lost the sales slip. Anyway, we're finally on the way home, back to sunny skies."

"Good for you," said Evelyn. "But don't rush it. Shoes are important."

"What's *more* important?" said Angie.

"Nothing," said Evelyn.

"Ankle bracelets," Angie said. "Maybe engagement rings."

"Only maybe," said Evelyn. "Shoes first. How's the weather?"

Angie reached for the Ferrari's heater knob, couldn't find it. "Better. Ten below. You ever drive a Ferrari?"

"A couple," said Evelyn. "When I was young."

"I swear, you need pilot training. Where's the heat knob?"

"I don't believe there is one. Touch screen, I think."

"What touch screen?"

"Maybe I'm confusing it with my Bugatti," said Evelyn. "The one you sold."

"Oh, yeah. Actually, Alvin sold it. Alvin's dead now."

"Alvin's dead?"

"At least his parka is dead. Boyd says it's my fault, says I made him lust after me. Which is completely nuts. Alvin was a lost soul."

Evelyn made a sympathetic sound and said, "That's where shoes come in. How's Boyd?"

"Walking again. Kind of. He's a tough nut to crack."

"You'll crack him."

"Yeah?"

"Girl to girl, Angie. You know I'll always love him, right?"

"Of course I know."

"I know you know. Obviously, I don't tell Junius, and mostly I don't even tell myself, I swallow it, but just because something's impossible doesn't mean . . . Well, you already *know*. So what I'm trying to say—I'm not even sure what I'm trying to say—but I think I've smoothed things out for him. Not smooth, I take that back, but maybe smoother."

"I'd better hang up now," said Angie. "Here comes Boyd."

"Tell him I pushed the reset button."

"Button?"

"Reset. He'll understand. Let's you and me go shopping someday."

In Plano, after three weeks of stalled negotiations, Dooney made his third from final offer. A squad of JCPenney attorneys stared at him.

"All right, we'll sweeten it," Dooney said. "Four billion."

Three of the attorneys walked out. Those that remained coughed and examined air.

Dooney pushed back his chair.

"Tell you what, I'll consult with my barber. Maybe I can plunk down another billion."

In the top-floor business suite of the Tahoe Starlight Empress, Douglas smiled his savvy smile, moved Hedda's hand to his lap, shook his head with the knowing look of a scammer appraising a raw beginner, and told Junius, in so many words, to stop chiseling and get real.

"We've been at this forever," said Junius. "I missed Christmas; I missed New Year's. What are we waiting for, Groundhog Day? We had an agreement, I thought."

"In principle," said Douglas. "There's still the fine print. That extra two million to ice the cake."

"There *wasn't* any extra two million. You mentioned it three seconds ago."

Douglas arched an eyebrow.

"Now, now," he said, also archly. "Exaggeration gets us nowhere. The thing about agreements in principle is that agreements in principle aren't agreements. Not till the ink dries. So then, do we tack on the two million or do we eat more lobster sandwiches?"

"I'll have one," said Hedda.

In Larry's Shoes and Slippers, Randy Zapf had tired of explaining and re-explaining the obvious fact that a customer can misplace a sales receipt. He told Boyd to step outside and inform Angie that it might be a few more minutes.

O. J. had it right, Randy was thinking. The shoe didn't fit, case closed. He watched through the storefront window until Boyd was safely in the Ferrari, then he turned to Larry and said, "One last time, them shoes fit like canoes. Fork over my refund."

Larry said, "No receipt, no refund. It's in black-and-white."

"Black-and-white where?" said Randy.

"On the receipt."

"Yeah, well. You see the problem?"

Larry, who seemed distinctly nervous, even fearful, swept his eyes across Randy as if checking out a police lineup. "How many times do I have to explain this? I didn't sell you those shoes. Mel did—so you claim." He hesitated. "You sure you didn't hear about our stickup?"

"Not a chickadee's chirp," said Randy. "So, these shoes, they're in boxes that say Larry's Shoes and Slippers. Plain as day. Now I'm sorry about your brother, I liked Mel, but if he wants to suck on buffing rags, that's his business. Tell him to get well."

"How can I tell him?" Larry said.

"When he wakes up. Tell him then."

"Mel's not waking up."

Randy made a show of sighing. Why, he wondered, was everybody out to screw everybody else?

"All right, listen," he said. "Let's say I'm a shoe salesman. Let's say I come in here with these shoes that don't fit, and I say, 'Hey, you want to buy some shoes?' and you're supposed to say, 'Let me take a look,' and so you take a look and make a lowball offer, and I say, 'No way, Jose, but I'll haggle,' then we haggle for a while, and finally you hand me a hundred or so and we shake hands and shoot the shit, we talk about how freakin' cold it is, then I stroll out of here with my hundred and we don't even call it a refund, we call it the American way."

"I'll give you ten bucks," Larry said, "if you go away."

"Now we're getting somewhere," said Randy. "Make it twenty."

"Make it five."

"Ten it is. I keep the shoes."

"Almost forgot," Angie said to Boyd six hours down the road. "Evelyn called. I'm supposed to tell you she hit a reset button, whatever that means. She says you'd understand."

"I do," said Boyd. "But I don't believe it."

"She sounded sure."

"Evelyn would. She's dreaming. There aren't any resets."

They were nearing the North Dakota border, Randy leading the way, and the pace was slow. A hundred yards ahead, the Cutlass was coughing smoke from its customized twin tailpipes.

"May I ask something?" said Angie.

"What if I say no?"

"No is negative, Boyd. In fact, that's my question—why

do you have to be so negative—so *black*—about everything? What's wrong with Gee, I'm in a Superfast, I'm on the open road, my feet feel better, I think I'll have lamb chops for dinner, Evelyn hit a reset button? What's wrong with that?"

"Watch it. Randy's pulling over."

After the tow, in a Popeyes next door to Jack & Jackie's Last Chance Auto Repair just off U.S. Route 10 West, Randy was saying, "My Cutlass, it's like them horses I ride, it don't know what half speed means, it's either full-out gallop or it's napping. Follow me? You gotta find some zip in that jalopy you're driving. My wheels, they just can't go that slow. A bronc needs to *buck*, understand?"

"I thought it was your muffler," Angie said. "I thought the whole exhaust system fell off."

"Yeah, but that's because there weren't nothing to *muffle*. Measly sixty mph, a Cutlass muffler says screw this and blows itself up. It's like car suicide."

Across the road was a Sleep Sound motel, where they spent the night, and the next night, and then seventeen more nights. Cutlass parts, it turned out, were hard to find. They watched TV, fattened up at Popeyes, and not much else. Randy sulked. Angie told him to behave. There was nothing unusual, she said, about two fiancés.

On the ninth day of February, Angie paid the fourteen-hundred-dollar repair bill and they resumed rolling down U.S. 10 West, crossing into North Dakota with an optimistic eye on California.

"There, you see?" Angie told Boyd. "Another reset. Who's dreaming?"

* * *

Wanda Jane was speaking with Chub O'Neill, who gave her a flat no, he wasn't covering Tahoe expenses. It had been three weeks, going on four, and Chub wanted to know if she was trying to bankrupt the town of Fulda.

Wanda Jane disconnected and handed Elmo his cell phone.

"No dice. Chub says, quote, 'Are you crazy?'"

"That's it?" said Elmo.

"Not quite. He says—I'm quoting again—he says, 'Who the blankety-blank do you think you are, the FBI?' Then he tells me to stop harassing a quote 'pillar of the Fulda community.' Says he won't cover the mustard on a hot dog—Chub's words, not mine."

"Cheapskate," Elmo said.

"We could sleep in your pickup, I guess. Save a few bucks."

"We could. Or we could get married."

"Get what?"

"You and me. Just an idea."

"You're proposing?"

"I'm suggesting options."

"Elmo," Wanda Jane said, "you smell like a pool hall. I barely know you."

Elmo wrinkled his forehead, thought for a moment, and nodded. "True, I guess. But most likely we'd get to know each other."

"You're being funny? Cornpone humor?"

"Right," said Elmo.

"So what do we do?"

Elmo looked at his watch and said, "It's after midnight. I'll spring for two rooms. We'll take turns manning my phone. Forget I brought up the nuptials stuff."

Wanda Jane said, "Not so fast."

Twice now, Junius had flown back and forth from L.A. to Tahoe, and on a subzero night in mid-February, he pulled out a check for eighty-one-thousand dollars and slid it across the table toward Douglas.

"I'm done dicking around," he said. "Your bank got robbed. You didn't report it. You *couldn't* report it. We both know why."

"Ah," said Douglas.

"That check there, it's repayment in full. You don't want to cash it, I'm on Delta back to L.A. For good."

"Ah," Douglas said again, this time with a smile.

Junius said, "What am I, a throat doctor?"

He reached out to retrieve the check, which Douglas swiftly covered with the palm of his hand.

"Keep talking," he said.

It was three in the morning. The champagne was low, Hedda was half dozing in her chair, and the Starlight's business suite had the smell of unrefrigerated lobster.

Junius unsnapped his briefcase, extracted three documents, and pushed two of them toward Douglas.

"That first one, it's a loan agreement. Postdated. It says you loaned me eighty-one grand back in August. Sign it. This next one's a receipt. Loan repaid. Sign it. That'll straighten out your books."

"I thought we were talking about buying my bank?"

"We were," said Junius. "Until you started nickel-and-diming me."

"And what's that last document?"

"This fat one?" said Junius, and he held up three inches of financial data. "This one you don't need to sign. It's the one that goes to the FDIC if you don't hurry the fuck up and sign the first two. The one that puts you in jail."

"That one?"

"That's the one," Junius said.

"You still want to buy my bank?"

"Depends."

"On what?"

"On my mood, I guess. I don't *want* to buy it, obviously—I've made lollipops that are worth more—but my wife, she wants a bank pretty bad. So here we are. You signing or do I catch a flight?"

"Interest," Douglas said.

"What interest?"

"On the eighty-one. I loaned it to you way back in August, correct? Almost half a year. Five-point-six percent. Plus the two million extra we already talked about."

Junius stood up and said, "Nice to meet you."

Douglas said, "Sit down. Where's your sense of humor?"

Halfway across North Dakota, Randy Zapf glanced at the Ferrari in his rearview mirror and thought a trillion things all at once. He could hardly breathe, hardly keep his eyes on the road, except in North Dakota there wasn't anything else to look at unless you liked looking at snow and fences and telephone poles and dinky farmhouses every thousand miles or so.

Polo, he thought. What happened to first dibs?

He thought about the rubber thong Angie didn't seem to appreciate. He thought about the bank he didn't get to rob. He thought about Cyrus and Carl. He thought about friendly old

Mel. He thought about the *takoba* in his trunk and how he'd weld it to his Cutlass like a hood ornament after he used it for its natural God-given purpose. That got him to thinking about God, which led him to wondering why God invented North Dakota when he could've invented more Californias, or another Oregon, or even a Wyoming without all the wasted space.

Sorry, God, he thought, but who the hell plays polo?

Randy took a look in the rearview mirror again, eyed the clunker of a Ferrari trailing him by a couple hundred yards, Angie at the wheel, the polo-playing-bank-robbing has-been sitting there beside her like Señor King of the Roost. First dibs meant hands off. First dibs meant go find your own dwarf.

He thought for a while about what you could do with a twelve-volt battery and some copper wire.

He thought about selling North Dakota to the Canadians.

And then he thought: Why does that cop have his flashers on?

47

HENRY SPECK'S SYMPTOMS WERE MILD: A LOW-grade fever, a headache, a cough, and a run-down feeling he attributed to excessive exercise. It had been a vigorous twenty-three days in the Minneapolis Radisson Blu. Why they called it Blu, he had no idea. Nor did he know much about the young lady he'd encountered aboard the flight from Bemidji, only that she understood how to use room service, taught physics at a college over in St. Paul, and talked too much about angles of inclination. Hot sauce, though, had been a bust. "I thought it was a metaphor," she'd said, and when he asked what metaphors were, she'd said, with humorless affect, "Screwed your brains out, have we?"

Not much later she'd left.

Which was a good thing, probably. Chills, too. Sore throat. Henry jotted down the professor's vitals in his log, giving her a seven-plus out of a rarely achieved ten, estimating the rest, including her name, which he logged under Anonymous. Then he slept for two full days, awakening to find himself feeling much, much worse. What he should do, he thought, was relog the young lady under Deadly.

He took a long, unhelpful shower, stood sweating and shivering at a window, stared out in disbelief at two-below Minneapolis, and then, with a sigh, put in an overdue call to

Junius, whose smartass secretary answered. "He's in Tahoe," she said. "But he left instructions. You have a pencil?"

"I'm sick," said Henry, "so let's be gentle."

"Number one, get your egotistical, playboy ass out of the Radisson. Three hundred eighty a night, twenty-three nights, you know what that comes to?"

"Chicken feed. Sick pay."

"Comes to almost nine grand. Number two, Junius doesn't pay for sick, so book a flight to L.A. Number three, coach. Number four, clean out your desk. Number five, stay away from the boss's wife."

"What about you?" Henry said. "Are you on the stay-away list?"

"We tried that."

"Did we? I don't see your name in the log."

"You don't *know* my name."

"Maybe it's filed under Homely," said Henry. "One sec, let me look."

The North Dakota Highway Patrol officer, who was fed up, handed Randy a ticket for a broken taillight, inoperable windshield wipers, obstructed license plate, failure to wear a seat belt, unlatched trunk, expired driver's license, and reckless endangerment. "And if I hear 'flatfoot' one more time," the officer said, "we'll talk to a judge."

"Reckless how?" said Randy. "I was doing fifty."

"You were driving with your thumbs."

"And that's illegal?"

"That's dirt stupid."

"Stupid's illegal?"

"In your case," the officer said, "stupid gets the death penalty. You're in North Dakota."

Randy chanced a quick peek into his rearview mirror. Angie had pulled up behind the cop car. It was time, he decided, to cool it.

"All right, chief, you win," he said. "Deal is, I thought you looked—don't get mad at me—I thought you might be part redskin. Flatfoot tribe."

"You thought that, did you?"

"Sure as heck did."

"It's Blackfoot."

"What is?"

"My tribe. Blackfoot."

"So I nailed it, right? I guess that makes you a Flatfoot Blackfoot, or maybe the other way around. Same thing, I reckon."

"Get out."

"Sure thing. But after we're done here, you want to race?"

Angie smoothed things over, citing IQ issues, flirting a little, and after a time, the cop tipped his hat, gave her the ticket, glared at Randy, and drove away. "You didn't have to say IQ issues," Randy muttered. "I got feelings, don't I?"

"Do you?" said Angie.

"Well, sure I do."

"What, for example?"

"You know, I get hungry and stuff. And I would've creamed him in a good fair race."

Angie took the lead in the Ferrari; Randy sulked but followed a half mile behind in his Cutlass; Boyd sat watching telephone poles as they turned off I-94 and headed straight south into South Dakota. "That was a good example," Angie was saying, "of what a Christian has to put up with. Randy won't stop being Randy. And he won't let me un-Randy him. Same deal with you. You don't let me un-Boyd you. Are you listening? Right now, this instant, the way you're staring out the window like I'm not even talking, that's the Boyd I keep trying to un-Boyd. What if I never volunteered anything? What if I never started a single conversation? Never *ever*? What if I never opened up, never bared my deepest soul? Then what? If you were a good, moral person, Boyd—if you believed in something except evolution—you'd be a fisher of women, you'd be saying, 'Angie, tell me about yourself, your saddest secrets, don't be afraid,' and I'd probably say, 'I'm embarrassed,' but then you'd keep after me until I told you about summer camp when I was ten, swimming and bonfires, all that, and how I had this special scholarship for indigent kids—SIK, that's what they called it—I was a SIKie. My family, we lived in a double-wide, Boyd. We couldn't afford underpants, much less summer camp. So I'm a SIKie, I'm wearing other kids' socks and panties—you think that's not embarrassing? You think I didn't steal apples and pork chops and smuggle them into my room at night and stuff my guts with real food? This wasn't *Dirty Dancing*. This was *Dirty Angie*. Did I let poverty ruin my life? I did. For a while, I did. For quite a while. But you know what? Tenth grade, I had this terrible dream; it changed my whole attitude. I hope you're listening, this is good, you'll identify. In the dream I've just showed up in heaven, I'm at this big medieval gate, and I'm waiting for somebody to open it up, like Saint Peter or his helpers, and I wait there forever—literally, I mean—I wait and wait, and it starts getting dark, I'm cold, I'm freezing, but there isn't any gatekeeper, and I look through these iron bars and there's heaven, but all the streets are empty, not a single soul—literally—all the palaces are deserted, all the harps are locked up, it's a ghost town. Somehow I squeeze through the gate and start walking around, trying to find somebody to ask what's going on, and I peek into heaven's game room, and all the pinball machines are blinking, the buzzers are buzzing, but . . . no souls, no saints, no Jesus, no virgins, none of the bigwigs. Both casinos are empty. The throne room looks like somebody's retirement party just ended, a total mess, champagne glasses everywhere, and I'm still walking around, but now I'm getting scared . . . The parking lot, Boyd, it's jammed with a kabillion cars, but they're all rusted and broken down, and when I get to the nursery, which I guess is where all the stillborn babies go, the place is dead silent, just a billion empty cribs and nothing else. And none of the stoplights are working, and the TV screens are full of static, and the doorbells are disconnected, and when I pick up a telephone, all I get is one of those recordings telling me to try again later. See what I'm saying? Nobody home."

Ahead was a sign for Deadwood.

"Turn off here," said Boyd. "I want to see Deadwood."

"You get the point?" Angie said later, high in the Black Hills. "On Dooney's doorstep that night, that was your black time. Blackest time, I guess. Almost exactly like my dream—black-black-black—I'm in heaven but there isn't a single light on. And I'm all alone, that's the scariest part, not even some lowlife angel's assistant who got admitted by the skin of her teeth. All alone *forever.*"

"I get it. No need to explain."

"But for you, Boyd, there's a bright side."

"What's that?"

"Salvation, obviously."

"Angie—"

"I know you think I'm too Pentecostal, but you need black to get bright, that's all I'm saying. And now you're on the downslope, you haven't touched booze in a month, you haven't shot any buses, you haven't put a bullet in your head. Your soul is quiet. You sleep a lot. You watch telephone poles. You took your punishment and didn't complain. You were nice to Evelyn. You kissed her."

"She kissed me," Boyd said.

"Same thing."

The road to Deadwood climbed into the clouds then descended into a deep bowl filled with thicker clouds.

"That dream of yours," said Boyd. "You made it up, right?"

"So what?" said Angie.

The Black Hills were not black, exactly. Dark-green black, sometimes reddish black, and ghosted with clouds, like *Brigadoon*, which had been Boyd's mother's favorite movie back when his mother weighed three hundred and five pounds, back when his father invited Boyd to step outside and toss around a football, and back when Boyd was ashamed of his own shame.

People began dying three days after they checked into Hickok's Resort and Poker Parlor. No one was yet dying in Deadwood, but they were dying in Seattle and Manhattan and elsewhere, and people kept on dying for months and months. Masks were hard to find. Angie tore a Mexican shirt into three pieces, folded and safety-pinned the pieces, and said, "Better than holding our breath, I hope," even if holding their breath was exactly what they did, or seemed to be doing, over the coming brutal months in Deadwood. In part, Boyd suspected, Angie was delaying again—she seemed quietly scared of something. She would start to speak, then stop. She looked at him as if he were in shadow, dimly visible, growing dimmer, not quite real.

They occupied three separate rooms. They lived off what Angie called, without a whisper of irony, their remodeling fees, the sum of which had been collected after the disposal of a bowling alley, a Bugatti, and a good deal more. Most evenings they dined together downstairs in the Chuckwagon Room, adjourning afterward to Angie's suite for the nightly deathwatch on CNN. The threesome dynamic was uncomfortable. Angie sometimes cuddled up on Randy's lap like a little girl, casting a solemn, you-better-make-your-move-soon look at Boyd. Other times she practiced social distancing with both of them. On his part, Randy rarely spoke to Boyd, instead speaking about him in the third person with a calculating curl to his lips, as if casing a 7-Eleven. "This wee-wee," he'd say, "would look good in Saran Wrap."

"Tied up with tassels," Boyd would say, though his heart wasn't in it.

As they watched the fatalities pile up, Randy provided political commentary, a presidential mix of ignorance and blustering authority. "If you believe in this cooked-up virus hoax," he volunteered one evening, "you probably believe that Jackie Robinson was actually a Negro, or that somebody walked on the moon, or—I don't know—that this pinhead here actually robbed a bank."

"Oh, he did," Angie said quickly. "I helped. With the getaway mostly."

"Sure, sure," said Randy.

"What does sure, sure mean? Either Boyd robbed a bank or he didn't. And he did."

The sound on the TV had been turned low, and for a few seconds Randy studied Wolf Blitzer.

"I'll put it this way," Randy finally said, then said nothing.

"That settles it," said Boyd.

"Damn straight," said Randy.

Occasionally—tentatively, on Angie's part—they talked about pressing on toward California, but the contagions conspired against them. Boyd's toes went red and lumpy. An embittered, ham-handed Deadwood physician applied metal splints, prescribed an antibiotic, and told him the alternatives were bed rest or a permanent wheelchair, either was fine with him. Time trickled by. The world had locked down. In the hills above town, buzzards circled the carcasses of close relatives while Boyd and Angie circled each other. Something was happening between them; their options had narrowed; there was the feel of desolation and a kind of terminal foreknowledge. Partly it was immobility. Partly it was boredom. For all its historic fame, Deadwood, South Dakota, was a very small town—even Fulda seemed supersize by comparison—and the available entertainment options, if casinos were not one's cup of tea, had the variety of a mud puddle. Boyd spent two weeks in bed, feet elevated. Later he hobbled around on his heels. Near the end of the month, as mythomania and SARS did their dirty work, they ventured out to the graves of Wild Bill and Calamity Jane; they toured an old frontier house; they inspected fourteen buffalo statues; they browsed in Wild West knickknack shops, where Randy purchased a colorful postcard that featured the exterior of their hotel. That evening he addressed the card to a cop named Bork, care of the L.A.P.D. "I like to keep in touch," he told Angie, "with my friends."

The minutes ticked away, casualties mounted, and all across America mythomania presented its daily butcher's bill. Mothers shamelessly lied to their daughters. Fathers lied to their sons *and* daughters. Lawyers lied to clients, airlines lied to stranded travelers, and the liar in chief gamely lied about everything. Boyd felt responsible. In a way, he *was* responsible. Remarkable, he thought, how he had become his country, or how his country had become he. It was not so far-fetched, he speculated, to believe he was the originator of it all, the ur-liar of liars, the wellspring, the Pharaoh of Fantasy, a Johnny Appleseed seeding falsehood from sea to boiling sea.

By early April, casinos *had* become their cup of tea, a fantasy of last resort. Angie's remodeling stash bankrolled them. Randy indulged in the free drinks and blackjack kept Boyd off his feet. Officially, casinos had been shut down statewide, but for hotel guests—and for all-American profit—the Hickok's manager turned a blind eye. "Wild Bill," the manager said with a furtive flick of her eyebrows, "didn't give a hoot or a holler about runny noses. Shut up and deal, that was Bill's motto, and that's ours. Free country, isn't it? At least it used to be. Back before we had an African running things."

Whiling away the killer days of April, they tempted fate in the Hickok's dimly lighted, almost completely deserted gaming room, hitting fifteens and sixteens with the gambler's listless dream of actually pocketing a dollar or two. They lost. They increased their bets. They lost. Randy, who had trouble with addition, was the first to sour on blackjack. "This game," he growled over a free watered-down bourbon on ice, "should be against the law. What say we steal back the money they stealt from us?"

"Stealt?" said Boyd.

"Okay. Stealed."

"Stole."

"You know what?" Randy said. "I have a better idea. Let's stick you on my sword and have a wussie roast."

"Boys," Angie snapped. "Shut up and play cards."

And then on April 18 the sun finally showed up for its annual visit to the Black Hills. The clouds lifted, the temperature rose into the fifties, and Angie asked Boyd if he would join her on a stroll into the hills. Boyd declined, summoning the excuses of old age and tingly toes. He suggested they have a drink on the hotel's glassed-in veranda.

"Old age, that's a new one," Angie said after they'd ordered. "You used to say you *aren't* old."

"That was when I had a mission," he said, smiling at her. "Now I'm . . . missionless. *Old*, you could say. It's a slippery world, isn't it? For example, when you think of Winston Churchill, you don't picture youth, you picture a fat old man. But, of course, there once was a time when Winnie was *not* fat. And *not* old. And not pompous. And not dead. Once he was a war hero. Once he was a little boy."

Angie shook her head and said, "Who cares? How old are *you*? Tell the truth."

"Forty-seven," Boyd said.

"You told me fifty-three. And forty-nine."

"I jump around, don't I?"

"Boyd, does the truth matter to you? Even a little?"

"Don't be ridiculous. Why should truth matter?"

"Because the truth is true."

"Well, maybe," Boyd said. "But give it time. Fat, skinny, old, young, mission, missionless. Give it lots and lots of time, give it infinity, then everything's true. Or nothing's true. A good argument against suicide."

Angie shrugged. "And what about that whiskey you just ordered? I thought you vowed—"

"Gerbils are consistent, Angie. I'm a lesser creature."

Boyd's whiskey and Angie's Pepsi were delivered, and for some time they sat looking out at the most beautiful hills, the most beautiful mountains, on earth, but also the most forbidding and most mysterious and most quieting.

When she spoke again, Angie's voice had the quiver of fear he'd been noticing over recent weeks. "Do you want to talk about California? What'll happen then? When we get back?"

"If you do."

"Evelyn loves you."

"I'm sure. And I love her."

"But it's impossible, she says."

"And she's right. Love is true. Impossible is true. That's the truth."

"So."

"I don't think there is a so, Angie."

"No so?"

"Doubtful."

"We could live together."

"I don't think so."

"You just said 'so.' So there is a so."

"I said, 'Don't think.' So there's probably not a so."

"Boyd, is your new mission to make me hang myself?"

"My mission," he said, gently, even feeling gentle as he lifted his glass, "is to have one more of these."

Later, as they walked across the veranda into the hotel's lobby, Boyd put a hand against the small of her back, a reflex from the past. He swiftly withdrew it.

"That's more like it," she said.

A second afterward, she said, "Is that Randy?"

Then she said, "Are those handcuffs?"

48

IN TAHOE, TOO, AND IN LOS ANGELES, AND IN
Plano, Texas, other life stories veered off track, or took an intermission, or fell into stop-time, or drifted into the gloam of
a viral Brigadoon.

On a cold night in Tahoe—four in the morning, therefore
no longer night by the tick of the clock—Wanda Jane Epstein
stood hesitating in the second-floor hallway of the Starlight
Empress, at the door to room 242, Elmore Hive's room, thinking: Why are you doing this?

She raised a hand to knock, then pulled it back.

A floor above, Junius Kirakossian was trying for the seventh
time to reach Evelyn, who was not answering and who had
not answered for a day and a half. "I'm stuck here," he told her
machine. "This epi-damn-demic, it's like when the Twin Tow-
ers came down, cancelled flights and deserted hotels, nothing's
moving, including this Cutterby jerk. Every time we have a deal,
he asks for something new. Wants to stay on as bank president
even if I own the damned bank . . . Where are you?"

A few doors away, in room 305, Hedda was telling Douglas
to stick to his guns, no reason to rush, it was a seller's market,
and besides, nobody was going anywhere, not in Tahoe, not in
the whole country, and—also besides—agreements in principle didn't mean much if you didn't have principles. "You don't

have principles, do you?" she said, and Douglas stepped into the shower and said, "Does a shotgun?"

"Not that you'd notice," Hedda said. "So you killed Lois?"

"Scrub my back," said Douglas.

Seven hundred miles to the south, in Bel Air, Henry Speck said to Evelyn, "Am I your first CFO?"

And in Plano, Texas, Jim Dooney said to Calvin, "I'm not buying a goddamn department store, not at this price. That smartass lawyer, he called me . . . What was the word?"

"Unsavory," said Calvin.

"Oh, yeah."

"And a fossil. And a crook."

"Right, so forget the acquisition. I'll get leverage some other way. Maybe donate to their favorite charity—the Retarded Lawyers of America. Money talks, I promise you. Halverson will get his crummy job back."

"Okay, okay," said Cavin. "Let's touch up those sideburns."

Randy flashed a grin as Angie and Boyd moved toward him from across the lobby. Surrounding Randy were four gentlemen in cheap gray suits and white masks. A fifth gentleman, also in a white mask but wearing a blue windbreaker stenciled with the letters FBI, secured the handcuffs and bent forward to give Randy a brisk, no-nonsense pat down. "Spread 'em," the man said, and kicked Randy's loafers apart.

"Easy-pleasy," Randy said. "I surrender."

Nearby, at the hotel's registration desk, a group of elderly slot players, all from Spearfish, South Dakota, looked on with interest.

"They got me!" Randy yelled as Angie approached. His voice

was merry, even delighted. He nudged the windbreaker guy. "Jaywalking, am I right? Throw the book at me!"

One of the elderly slot players pumped her fist.

"Loitering!" Randy crowed. "I confess!"

"Yeah, loitering," said the tallest and grimmest of the gray-suited officers. He pulled off Randy's belt. "Plus armed robbery, seven counts. Plus murder, three counts, and we barely started counting." The man turned to Boyd and Angie. "You know this asshole?"

"Not me," Boyd said. "I'm a nobody."

"I know him slightly," Angie said. "He's my fiancé. One of them."

Randy laughed and gave a jiggle to the handcuffs, making music. "You know what?" he said. "Looks like we got some mistaken identity here. I'm Matthew McConaughey."

"Who?" said the oldest of the gray suits.

"You're asking who's Matthew McConaughey?"

"Yeah."

"Well, how should I know? Ask the bank robber over there—he's the McConaughey expert."

Eyes went to Boyd. Boyd's eyes went to Angie.

Angie said, "Excuse us, we're late for blackjack."

The third of the gray suits, a burly man with FBI eyeballs, opened his jacket to display a belt badge and a holstered Glock. "We know who the bank robber is, and the bank robber's wearing bank-robber cuffs. Your prints, buddy, are all over the hoe."

"You got my hoe? When do I get it back?"

"You have the right—"

"Yeah, yeah, let's go clear this up." Randy executed a little bow for his audience of slot players, winked at Angie, and gave Boyd a malevolent glare. "Back in a jiff."

When he was out the door and gone, Boyd said, "Murder?"

Angie said, "Randy can be impetuous."

Wanda Jane knocked, Elmo let her in, and she said, "From now on I call you Elmore. If I forget—if I make a mistake—stop me. It'll take getting used to."

"Okay," Elmo said.

"You know what made me think twice about this?"

"Sure."

"What?"

"Well, for starters," said Elmo, "I never look at your chest."

"Good guess."

"Not a guess. A strategy."

"It worked," she said.

Silver-haired, bluff-faced Douglas Cutterby smiled at Junius and said, "Do I stay on as president or don't I?"

"You don't," Junius said. "You sell me a bank and go away."

"That's final?"

"Pretty final."

"Final, I believe, doesn't have a pretty," said Douglas. "What say we add another half million to the purchase price? To finance my retirement?"

"What say I walk out of here?"

Hedda, who sat thoughtfully at Douglas's side, said, "Here's another idea. Split the difference, appoint me president. I'm local, people know me—a nice smooth transition. Obviously, I'd be only a figurehead." She looked at Douglas, then at Junius. "Just an idea. No more squabbling. Everybody's happy. We all go home."

"Interesting," Douglas said.

"Experience?" said Junius.

"I own a gym. I turn a profit."

Junius rose to his feet. "Stay tuned. I need to make a call."

Henry Speck had caught a half-empty flight out of Minneapolis, arrived at LAX sicker than ever, and now wondered how he'd found the stamina to take advantage of this golden opportunity.

"Leave your mask on," Evelyn said. "Pull it up high. I don't want to look at your face."

A half hour later, Henry asked, "Yes or no? Am I your first CFO?"

"You're my first goon," Evelyn said.

"*Goon* is strong," Henry said, feeling feverish but complacent.

"Gorilla?"

"How about we go with mechanic? I like mechanic."

"Meaning you fix things?"

"Fixed you, didn't I?"

Evelyn had known this was coming, known she had wanted it to come, and now it had come and gone—something mindless. Her mind exhausted her.

"*Mechanic* does the trick," Henry said. He felt his knees weaken and wondered if he was about to pass out. "You have an aspirin? I don't feel so hot."

Evelyn looked at him and said, "Now you tell me."

Henry said, "Is that your phone ringing?"

On a scale of one to ten, Randy decided, Deadwood was one of the cooler places to get arrested, possibly a nine, definitely an eight, up there with Chicago and Tombstone and Dodge City, not quite Wichita, better than Detroit, and to top it off, the forty-minute van ride down to Rapid City had a first-class feel to it, good scenery, plenty of headroom, the whole FBI posse keeping an eye on him like he was Sam Bass or Doc Holliday.

The Pennington County Jail turned out even better. Who'd expect it? The meat loaf wasn't bad at all. Three squares a day. Hot showers, plenty of soap. Nobody arguing if you pointed out that Jackie Robinson wasn't a Negro and JFK probably was. Best thing of all, Randy was top dog here. Murder one, three counts. No competition. And if that didn't impress anybody, Randy told himself, well, so what? He had plenty more excellent counts up his sleeve.

All told, not so bad. Carl and Cyrus, bless their sloppy-dead souls, would get a kick out of this. So would Mel. So would a certain dinged-up rich guy in Eugene, Oregon, and a certain grape farmer, and one or two others Randy could name if he had to or wanted to.

What ticked him off, really, wasn't jail. It was Angie.

Once a week, during his twenty-minute personal call, she kept wasting time on small talk, mostly about her scumbag bank robber and how he was finding God, or at least opening doors for her.

"I gotta ask this," he'd finally said. "Are you sleeping with him?"

"You think God sleeps with people?"

"I'm talking about—"

"Boyd doesn't either. I've tried, believe me."

"You tried?"

"Randy, wake up! Trying doesn't mean I'd *do* it; it means he'd have to marry me, just like you."

"Well, shit on a shingle, if that's—"

"If you want to talk dirty," Angie had said, "call the devil."

She'd hung up with eleven minutes still left on his call.

"Have you ever noticed," Douglas said to Hedda, in bed, in the wee-hour dark of their Starlight Empress room, "how hard it is to open things these days? You buy a can of peanuts, a bottle of ketchup, there's always that plastic sealer you need to peel off except you can't get a grip on it, so finally you have to stick it with a knife or rip it with your teeth. Pickle jars. Vacuum-sealed bags of coffee. D batteries—try opening a pack of those babies, you'll end up in a hospital. Pints of potato salad. Toys. Lawn fertilizer. A box of shotgun shells."

"It might be a safety issue," Hedda said. "Consumer protection, all that."

"Sure it's a safety issue. That's not my point. Business, my sweet. If you're serious about running Community National, then lesson number one is you need to make things hard to open. Follow me?"

"I don't."

Douglas chuckled. "Ask yourself this. What's the purpose of a business? Making money, correct? For a banker, therefore, the idea is to keep money *in* your bank, not let it drain *out*. Let's say somebody wants to withdraw ten thousand bucks and wire it to Aunt Betsy. A good banker makes it hard. Insists on a driver's license, asks for a password, tells them the password's wrong even if it's right. Like with a ketchup bottle. You put those plastic sealing do-jobbies over people's life savings. Somebody wants to cash in a CD? Sorry, that'll be seven business days, twelve business days, whatever you can get away with. Sorry, ma'am, that's an early withdrawal, we'll be keeping ninety days' interest. Sorry, we don't have your signature card on file. Oh, and before you withdraw your funds, we'll need you to answer these two or three account verification questions. What's your spouse's grandfather's mother's middle name? What was your great-great-uncle's favorite hobby? And so on. Easy in, hard out."

"Are you saying I get to be bank president?"

"Not quite yet." Douglas gripped a breast and gathered his thoughts. "Lesson number two. Ever notice how every time you call an airline—I mean *every* time, *every* airline, no exceptions—you get this recorded message saying something like, 'Our call volume is unusually high, please wait.' But the message *never* says, 'As usual, our call volume is ridiculously high, please wait.' The message *never* says, 'As always, we're totally backed up, and it looks like we always will be, so please shut up and wait.' The message *never* says, 'We're too cheap to hire enough people to answer the telephone, so fuck you, please wait.' Am I right?"

"Drives me nuts," said Hedda.

"Drives the whole universe nuts. But, boy, great business practice! Answering phones costs money. I mean, you need to hire people and then you need to pay them. You need to buy computers and desks and headsets for all those extra employees manning the extra phones. Pension plans, sick pay, taxes, supervisors. On and on. Bam, there goes your profit. So at Community National we're just like the airlines—make 'em wait. Only one teller on duty. *No* tellers on duty from eleven a.m. to one thirty p.m. And we *never* answer our phones—ironclad policy. What we *do* offer, we offer a special phone-answering deal, small fee of ninety-nine ninety-nine a year, you get to listen to our recorded message about how unusually busy we are, sorry, please try again later. It's like with computer printers. Those little extras—ink, for example. You buy that nice expensive printer except it doesn't print diddly without ink, and those itty-bitty ink cartridges, that's where the money is, month after month, year after year, everybody's shelling out for half an ounce of platinum-priced ink just so their printers actually *print*. Same with Community National. We've got our own extras. You want to write a check? Buy our forty-nine-dollar check booklets, they'll last you six weeks, then buy another one. You want a bank statement? That'll be fifteen bucks. You want a money order? That'll be two and a half percent. You want a stop payment? That'll be twenty-five bucks. You want a safe-deposit box? That'll be whatever the market bears . . . Anyway, tip of the iceberg. And I haven't mentioned the loan end of the business. That's where the juice is."

Hedda pulled up a sheet to protect herself. It was well after midnight. A pandemic was raging, and the hotel was eerily silent.

"I get the picture," Hedda said. "Screw the customer, right?"

"Well, we don't advertise it that way, but you're on the right track." Douglas pulled down the sheet and regripped. "In any case, lesson number three—and this is a basic principle. Low interest rates on deposits, high interest rates on loans. The heart and soul of any bank."

"That hurts," said Hedda.

"Of course it hurts. That's business for you."

"No, the squeezing. It hurts."

"Oh, right. Apologies. I get carried away. But we're talking money here. The high-low principle: If a customer borrows money, gouge him. If a customer deposits money, gouge him. Or her. The basic idea is old hat, but at Community National we call it Cutterby's Law—last in, first out."

"Sounds sexy," Hedda said. "Did you kill Lois?"

Douglas hesitated and looked at her with mild rebuke. "You want to be a bank president or don't you?"

"I do. Did you kill her?"

"Lois?"

"You bet. Lois."

"Well," Douglas said, "that's a trifle off topic, isn't it? I was schooling you. Paving the way."

"And I appreciate it, Doug, but did you kill her?"

Again he hesitated, then he shrugged and beamed a banker's smile at her. "Hypothetically, perhaps—pure maybe—one might surmise that I terminated an unhappy partnership. Details forthcoming. In the Caymans. With spousal testimonial privilege. Fair enough?"

"Douglas, I can't—"

"Drop it. Let's wrap up our tutorial. First in, last out. Historically—twenty-six years in a row—Community National has been the very *first* bank in the country to raise loan rates and reduce deposit rates. And the very *last* bank to *reduce* loan rates and *raise* deposit rates. You see the beauty of that? Nobody, and I mean nobody, gouges the way we do."

"So you killed her, right?"

Douglas laughed, shook his head diagonally, and appraised Hedda in amused silence for a time. "You're a stubborn woman. One in a million. Banker to the core."

No, Hedda almost said, I'm a Todhauser. Look it up, pal.

Instead, she wiggled in close to him.

"Give me a kiss," she said. "Plenty of tongue."

49

JUST BEFORE DAYBREAK, WANDA JANE AND ELMO
went looking for breakfast, passing through the Starlight Empress's nearly deserted casino and then turning toward a coffee shop that looked to be open for business. They sat on stools at a high counter, ate microwaved egg sandwiches, and watched a trio of bewhiskered Hell's Angels finishing off a long night at the roulette wheel. A lone custodian vacuumed a roped-off portion of the casino floor. Upbeat music rolled out of the ceiling. It was a forlorn Covid morning.

"Don't look," Elmo said, "but there they are."

"Who?"

"Behind you."

Wanda Jane turned and looked.

Arm in arm, unmasked, plainly in a lively mood, Douglas and Hedda were striding out of a poker room on the far side of the casino, Hedda with a handful of purple chips, Douglas with the florid, smirking expression of a man privileged to be in the company of Lady Luck.

"You know," Elmo said thoughtfully, "I always considered Doug a big man. Hedda's got five inches on him."

"In flats," Wanda Jane said.

"Flat what?"

"Shoes. Flats are flat shoes."

"I'll be."

"You didn't know that?"

"Guess not. So, if your shoes have pointy toes, do you call them pointys?"

"Elmore, lose the bumpkin bullshit. We're beyond that."

"Habit," he said.

They watched Hedda cash in her chips, hand the bills to Douglas, then laugh and take his arm again.

"Cute couple," Elmo said.

"I wonder if it's real."

"Me, too."

At the entrance to the lobby, Douglas stopped to speak with a short, elderly, almost emaciated man in a business suit that nearly matched the one Douglas was wearing, except pricier and better tailored. After a moment, the three of them stepped into an elevator.

Elmo took Wanda Jane's hand. "You okay?"

"Not really."

"Your friend, she seems maybe a little too . . ."

"Content?"

"A tad more than content."

"The thought occurred to me. She has her contradictions."

"That she does. How's the egg sandwich?"

"Awful. How's yours?"

"Awful." Elmo released her hand, leaned back, and looked at her. "I need to mention something. That audio clip Hedda sent last night. We've got enough to haul him in on bank fraud. End it right now. Put him away for ten, fifteen years."

"He murdered his wife."

"Evidence, though. That 'terminating the partnership' stuff, it could mean anything."

"That's the lawyer talking?"

"Yes, it is."

"What do you suggest?"

"You're the boss. You won't like what I suggest."

"Say it anyway."

Elmo seemed to listen to his thoughts for a few seconds. He stirred his coffee, took a sip, carefully put down the cup and said, "I've brought it up before, but we're over our heads. I suggest we grab Hedda, hog-tie her, stuff her in your car, and go home. This won't end happily."

"One more day?"

"I don't suggest it, no."

"Thanks. Right you are. One more day."

On the walk back to Elmo's room, Wanda Jane said, "By the way, that getting-married idea of yours, it was pretty sudden, wouldn't you say?"

Elmo shrugged. "For you, I guess it was. For me, I've been dreaming for years."

"You're on."

"I figured," he said.

April passed. May arrived.

Angie drove Randy's Cutlass up a mountain road, put it in neutral, gave it a shove, and watched it drop three hundred feet. She hiked the four miles back to Hickok's Resort and Poker Parlor, where she cried for a while and then told Boyd there was no point in waiting around, the adventure was over, they would be hitting the road that afternoon. "No more casinos," she said. "Unless we need to stop in Reno. Or Vegas. Let's map out a route. What'll it be—north or south?"

"I'm along for the ride," said Boyd. "Your choice."

"I *know* it's my choice. Reno is shorter. Vegas has more wedding chapels."

They rolled out of Deadwood on May 17, taking the southern route through Wyoming, then picking up I-80 into Salt Lake City, all in a single long day. In the morning they headed south toward Vegas on I-15. Angie had been talking for a day and a half, even in her sleep, and as they passed through Provo, she stopped to draw a breath, glanced over at Boyd, and said, "So what's your opinion?"

"About?"

"Everything I've been saying. You want me to start over?"

"Boil it down for me."

Angie clicked her teeth in displeasure. She was at the Ferrari's wheel, boosted by her sofa cushion, driving the way Randy had taught her to drive.

"For starters, what about Evelyn's email last night? Like a miracle, wasn't it? Your old job waiting for you back in Fulda, no questions asked. And no problem with the bank you robbed—she basically owns it now, or her husband does, or her husband's company or something. You aren't gonna scream thank you to your Heavenly Father?"

"My Heavenly Father turned off his hearing aids," Boyd said gently, "and I can't say I blame him."

For four hours she said little more. The car's radio gasped with invective and grandiosity. An elderly Korean woman in Palo Alto had been shot dead for being Korean. An Alaska school board had banned *Macbeth* for excessive feminism. Proof of lunacy was now required on American passport applications.

And then, seventy miles outside Vegas, thumb driving, Angie made a huffing sound and said, "What about us, Boyd?

I tell you my whole life story, all the good parts, and you sit there like a rock. Nine months now. Zero. Nothing even half-way personal and I barely know the man I'll be saying 'I do' to in a day or so. How do you think that feels?" She gave a sharp, violent shake to her head. "Evelyn warned me. I'm supposed to get you to talk—talk about *true* stuff, *real* stuff . . . otherwise it's hopeless. Otherwise I should let you out right here in the middle of the desert."

"Pull over," Boyd said.

"You plan to walk?"

"Pull over."

Evelyn was relieved, even happy, to have Junius back in bed beside her, his socks on, his bones sharp as tent pegs, his meatless arms around her as he described the woes of Tahoe: a mostly empty hotel, half the employees out sick, the other half social distancing so you couldn't order a martini, couldn't get it if you did order it, and how he'd survived on smoked salmon and week-old lobster sandwiches while trying to buy a bank from the slickest, oiliest, greediest, smiliest, silver-hairedest son of a bitch who ever conned a con. "It'll take a cool million," he said, "just to unscramble the books, then another million to cover the bad loans—mostly to the guy's own dead wife—then another million in reserve against lawsuits, then another million in psychiatrist fees to help me recover." He cuddled in close. "But you've got your bank, don't you?"

"Yes. And thank you."

"What's new on your end?"

"Not a thing," Evelyn said. "Is Henry off the ventilator?"

"Yeah, he's off, all right."

"What does that mean?"

"I guess one thing it means," said Junius, "it means he doesn't have to worry about *me* killing him."

Angie pulled over, put on her hazard lights, and walked with Boyd out into the desert, where, after two or three minutes, he stopped and looked back at the Ferrari and said, "There are two Santa Monicas. One is a fairy tale . . ."

In the small, cramped headquarters of the Fulda, California, police department, Wanda Jane Epstein, Elmo Hive, and Chub O'Neill had agreed—reluctantly, in Wanda Jane's case—to devote scant resources to the enforcement of local ordinances. Bank robbery and homicide were off the table.

"Facts are facts," Chub was saying, affably enough. "And the fact is we have two squad cars—one's in the shop—and we have two police officers, one's a dispatcher, the other's barely part-time. Homicide? No way. Besides, it's wrapped up, the feds have their man."

Wanda took a last shot and said, "Hedda's recordings, though . . ."

"County prosecutor won't go near it," Chub said. "Bank fraud is federal. Murder is state *and* federal. Nothing municipal. And the recordings . . . at best inconclusive. And at worst, they're inadmissible without Hedda testifying, which we already know won't happen."

"Just because she married the son of a bitch," Wanda Jane said, "that doesn't mean we should let Cutterby—"

"It does," Elmo said softly. "It means no prosecution. Darling."

Decisively, Chub clapped his hands and stood up.

"Settled," he said. "And, listen, that traffic jam down at the clinic. You'd almost think this pandemic is real. Get on it, okay? Double-parking, that's real."

When he was gone, Elmo said, "I'm sorry."

"Me, too," said Wanda Jane. "But what a mistake."

"Trust Hedda. She says he'll pay, he'll pay."

In the desert outside Las Vegas, a vast and very cold desert, as cars whooshed by on the road to riches, Angie said, "So you were embarrassed?"

"Ashamed," Boyd said.

A fairy tale, he made himself say, of spangled gowns and faces from the tabloids . . . heiresses on skateboards and yoga masters and street magicians and impresarios of salvation, of fixed noses and big money . . . Rosemary Clooney in her bathrobe and curlers handing him a five-dollar tip on Christmas Eve.

His mother, Boyd also made himself say, weighed two hundred and seventy pounds when he was in fourth grade. Three hundred and twenty by eighth grade. Three hundred and ninety by his sophomore year in high school. "My dad tried," Boyd said. "Coaxing her, bribing her. Nothing worked. Me, I mostly checked out. Made up stories. Pretended. I didn't bring friends home. Who would? It was this little stucco bungalow—you were there, you know—and my mom seemed to fill the whole house. I mean, the place *smelled* fat. This oily, sugary, blubbery smell, it soaked into the walls, into her hair and housecoat. She couldn't get in or out of the bathtub; she couldn't turn around in the shower. My dad gave her once-a-week sponge baths on the sofa, which is where my mom lived, on the living-room sofa, eating butter, eating Heath bars, getting fatter, watching movie marathons, William Powell and Hedy Lamarr and Peter

Lorre, all day, all night, getting fatter and fatter. Her ears got fat. She didn't fit on the toilet anymore. Couldn't bend down, couldn't get up, couldn't wipe. In the bathroom we had this orange piddle pad, the kind for dogs, so she'd just stand there and go, then later my dad would clean it up . . . I hated going home after school. I'd stand on the doorstep and take a breath and hold it and make a run for my room. I don't know. Not just shame. Contempt, I guess. She hit four hundred and twenty pounds by the day I graduated from high school—obviously she didn't make it to the ceremony—she barely fit in our beat-up old Eldorado—hooked on milkshakes and Myrna Loy movies—*The Best Years of Our Lives, The Thin Man Goes Home*—hooked on Tyrone Power, hooked on romance, hooked on getting fatter, I guess. She swallowed the lies. She swallowed the fantasy. I swallowed it, too."

Angie looked at him.

After a few seconds, she said, "I've wondered about that. You always seemed . . . you seemed pretty retro. Like you grew up in the 1940s or something."

Boyd laughed. "Not just me. Everybody. It's what we yearn for—a fucking Hollywood fantasy." Boyd looked out at the desert, bewildered. "Anyway, who wants to be a Birdsong? Not I! Screech!"

If the plane crashed, Randy thought, he'd have a couple of pretty decent cushions, what with the two beefy Feebies flanking him, both of them braggarts, as if those FBI letters stenciled on their windbreakers were complimentary tickets to a Billy Ray concert. So far it had been a two-hour flight, not counting the layover in Denver. Touchdown in Sacramento was an hour away, maybe more, and Randy was getting antsy. The handcuffs weren't helping any, or the leg cuffs either, or how his underpants kept riding up way too high. First class, this was not, but even so, the last row of coach was fairly prime real estate, almost best in the house, and Randy had a decent view of the toilet door and something that looked like it might be a cloud.

Conversation wasn't in the cards. But what the heck. If these FBI wussies didn't want to learn a thing or two about staying on a bronc, no problem, it was their education down the drain.

Randy was happy to be headed home, extradited, which beat the heck out of Rapid City, and soon he got to thinking about Cyrus and Carl, how they'd had the lowdown on executions in California, where nobody was getting zapped anymore, and how if you wanted to get zapped you had to go all the way down to Quentin because they were too chicken at Pelican Bay, and even at Quentin you didn't get to take your electric ride, you didn't even get to practice holding your breath for the chamber, it was just a regular old doctor appointment without any sizzle or bad smell. Too bad about Cyrus. Carl he could do without.

This led to that, and he was thinking about good old Mel when the plane's tires hit tar in Sacramento.

About time, he scolded Delta.

Shuffling down the aisle, he was rooting for a free trip up to Pelican Bay—close to home, good climate. But the smart money, he figured, was on Quentin.

Henry Speck's last hours were among the most pleasant of a medium-long life, thirty-three years of carrying around the Speck albatross, not to mention the burden of being the prettiest guy on eHarmony. Being unconscious, being ventilated, what he got to do was lie back and let the memories splash through pneumonia dreams. The hum of the ventilator was lounge music, a piano bar, and even if Henry didn't know the ventilator was a ventilator, and even if he didn't know where he was or why he was there, he floated merrily on the tides of disease, wherever the infection took him, revisiting in Technicolor the entries in his logbook, each an out-of-focus extra in his life story, butterflies on an L.A. afternoon. Enni tap-danced. Peggy snarled. Evelyn chewed on his bicep. He was romping through paradise. He was Secretariat.

"So I dropped out of USC, changed my name, and just wandered. Changing your name does things. It's astonishing. You unplug yourself and plug in somebody new, like updating a computer. If you can change your name, what can't you change?"

Angie waited.

On the highway, a hundred yards away, limos and RVs and semis whizzed by, each with its miniature Doppler effect, scooping up desert air and blowing it backward. Angie had left the Ferrari running along the shoulder.

Boyd nearly stopped there—he didn't trust himself, a couple of lies fluttered nearby—but he said, truthfully: "So if you're not a Birdsong, and if you never really were, then you can make your dad's heart stop ticking even if the guy just picked up one day and left forever. You can shrink your mother down to a hundred pounds, get her off the sofa, give her a gentleman suitor who's the spitting image of Cesar Romero—who knows, maybe the suitor *is* Cesar Romero—then you enlist yourself in the Marine Corps, kick ass for a few months, come home with a Purple Heart you picked up in a pawn shop, and after that, who cares, why not type up a résumé that makes it look like you're actually worth a damn? Exeter, Princeton. You're not a Birdsong. You're a story."

"Go ahead, cry if you want," Angie said. "I don't mind."

Boyd laughed and said, "I'm not at the sad part."

Look at Ms. Todhauser, said Douglas Cutterby, almost aloud. Doesn't she remind you of you? Not the now Lois, not even the recent Lois, but the Lois who was Lois way back when, before Hubcap Toby, before you decided to entomb me exactly where you are, in that grave that's proving hard to crawl out of. No doubt about it. Hedda's got some Lois in her. You agree, don't you? Great with numbers. Great in the sack. Smart as a whip but not half as smart as she thinks. The way you looked up at the shotgun that day. That uh-oh look. Don't take it the wrong way, angel, but I think of it as the Judas look. I know what you're thinking. You're thinking: Who are you to criticize; who are you to turn down the silver? And I'll admit you have a point there, no argument, but let's agree that things boiled down to you or me. Turned out it was you. That uh-oh look. I'm sorry, I'm honestly sorry, but it still makes me smile. Right now I'm smiling. Uh-oh! In any event, the thing about Hedda, if you look close, the thing is she's five parts Lois and five parts something else: she's a mixed-up Lois, a Lois who doesn't know what Lois wants, a Lois who's let CrossFit go to her head, a Lois who thinks she can have her cake and eat it, too, a way less careful Lois, a Lois who looks—forgive me, lovebug—a Lois who looks stunning in her honeymoon bikini, a Lois chipped out of sculptor's marble, a freshly married Lois, a Lois who thinks she can run a bank without cutting corners, a Lois who thinks she can turn the tables on a professional table turner. Look at her! Imagine uh-oh popping into those Teutonic eyeballs of hers. Imagine uh-ohs putting a pucker on those succulent lips. She has a surprise coming, doesn't she?

I miss you, darling. Especially the early days, back when we were young together. Remember that? Running our own little bank, you and me. How fun it was! Our annual spring housecleaning—remember? Tidying up the safe-deposit boxes, a wristwatch here, a Krugerrand there, and nobody the wiser—Granny's necklace, Mommy's earrings!

You know what I wish, Lois? I wish you were here to watch me put the uh-oh in Hedda's eyes. Uh-oh, where's Granny's necklace! Uh-oh, is that rat poison I taste?

"Just wandered," Boyd said to the desert and to Angie. "Drove a cab in Helena, loaded cattle cars in Nebraska, worked on my résumé."

"I'll bet it was impressive," said Angie. "The résumé."

"Yes, it was. A new me. Somewhere in there I got married the first time—I was twenty, maybe twenty-one. My wife didn't like me much, I didn't like her, so we got along pretty well until she found out I hadn't written 'Stairway to Heaven.' That was the end of that."

In a way, Boyd told her, all the wandering was like a rest cure, a refreshing two-year nap from which he eventually awakened back in Santa Monica, a new man with a new name and a new history, a bit groggy, surprised to find himself on the metro desk of a newspaper for which he had once been a fast-pedaling delivery boy. Still a window-shopper, yes, but in journalism he'd discovered a calling. After all, he'd had practice ogling other people's lives. And so, over time, this led to that: Pasadena, Sacramento, Mexico City, Manila, a year in Hong Kong, then a trans-Pacific flight to Jakarta, Evelyn seated beside him—a Princeton story, a polo story, a Kandahar story—and with enough interest in her eyes to end up in wedding bells—not actual bells, perhaps, but certainly a fancy wedding on the top floor of PS&S's Pacific Basin headquarters—a fancy wedding attended by fancy people, among them diplomats and investment bankers and Suharto's third oil minister.

Then nearly two glorious years in Jakarta, which were now an impossible tall tale, and then a dossier dropping on the dining table.

"We had a little boy at that point," Boyd said. "We called him Teddy."

50

"I'M COLD," ANGIE SAID. "ANOTHER FORTY MINUTES, we could be in Vegas. Can you talk while I'm driving?"

"Of course," said Boyd.

"And it might be easier to cry in the car. Nobody'll hear except God and me."

"Neither of you needs to worry. I won't cry."

"Who's worried? You think God worries?"

"No," Boyd said. "I'm very sure he doesn't."

Doubly masked, once by an N95 and again by Turmeric & Cranberry Seed Energizing Radiance Masque, Evelyn lay comfortably in the darkened therapy room of The Inner You, an esthetician humming at her side, ocean waves rolling out of speakers deployed in the ceiling above. Evelyn's thoughts rolled with the ocean. Too bad about Henry was one thought, and the next was Yes, but he was a creep, and the next was I *needed* the creep—it *had* to be a creep—creepiness was the therapy, the flushing, nullifying mindlessness of creepiness—wasn't that the opposite of and therefore the antidote to excessive mindfulness?—yes, it was—even if chewing on a bicep had embarrassed her, cheapened her, even so, it was what she'd needed, just to be chewing on a bicep. Creepiness was her punishment.

If she could forgive Boyd, she could forgive herself.

Junius was another matter.

There was guilt, plenty of it, but it wasn't the betrayal kind. Junius had come as advertised; it was like acquiring a toaster that toasted. No romance, no bubbles in the blood, but lots of hands-off affection. Junius had twenty years on her, eighteen if you split hairs, and it wasn't as if romance had ever been the object or even a consideration. The object had been punishment. She had punished herself with the fantasy of forgetfulness. She had punished herself for good reason, because she had deserved punishment, because she had earned it, because she had allowed Boyd to pick up the horror and carry it away from her, because she had allowed herself to believe a lie, or pretend to believe, and because she had allowed Boyd to protect her from herself, to protect her with the fiction that the burden was his alone, the nightmare was his alone, a little boy on a sidewalk. She required punishment. She believed in punishment. She believed in receiving it and she believed in delivering it. God knows, she had punished Boyd—punished him for saving her with a valiant lie—bitter, merciless, willful, love-killing punishment, because, of course, he loved her, and because, of course, she loved him, and because killing love was the punishment of punishments even as she punished herself. Live a valiant lie, you deserve what you get.

When her masks came off, Evelyn took a YOU! elevator up six floors to Junius's suite of offices, where she would punish herself a little more.

"I need to tell you something," she said.

"You don't," said Junius. "I'm not blind. Just don't cough on me."

Roomy was not the word for a Ferrari 812 Superfast, the word was *expensive,* and Boyd found himself looking back with affection at the chugging old Pleasure-Way, slow but comfortable, a recreational vehicle headed for nowhere. The Ferrari smelled of a daydream. Superfast, for sure, but headed toward the same nowhere, getting there quicker.

Boyd had his seat levered back, shoes off, his toes a reminder of misdeeds. The high Nevada desert swept by with its somber warnings of Vegas just over the horizon.

Jakarta, he was telling Angie, seemed to be its own sprawling, noisy, diesel-smelling daydream, almost a memory of someone else's life, the way a kid's sandbox is remembered forty years into adulthood. Granted, Jakarta had been real. But then again, how *could* it have been? "How *could've* I been so young," he said. "So stupid, so in love, so hepped up on erasing a paperboy named Birdsong? Did I think I'd get away with it? Hard to say, but—"

"Boyd, stop!" Angie said. "I *know* all this. You're leaving something out—something important."

"I'm getting there."

"You're trying *not* to get there."

"I've told you. We had a little boy. We called him Teddy."

"Right," said Angie. "And that's where you keep stalling."

It was a little after eight in the morning. Calvin had delivered breakfast in bed while Jim Dooney was on the phone with Junius Kirakossian, distracted by a dozen photographs spread out on his soiled satin bedclothes. He was snagged somewhere between wrath and mirth. "All right, I get it, you had to make a few concessions," Dooney was saying. "A million here, a million there, what's the difference? PS&S ends up with the bank, right? So stop chiseling. Unload your baseball team and we're back to even, plus some. What's the stadium worth—hundred million? Real estate alone?"

Dooney half listened for a few seconds, eyeing one of the photographs.

"Junius," he said impatiently, "my waffles are getting cold. What's there to complain about? We give Todhauser six months in the saddle—trial period, that's all you contracted for—then we pull the plug: 'Sorry, ma'am, adios, back to CrossFit' . . . Yeah, you told me already, she doesn't know zip about banking, neither do I, neither do you, so we install our own finance guy . . . Yeah, finance gal . . . Point is, it was a deal breaker, so we live with it. I've got bigger problems. *You've* got bigger problems."

The bedroom door swung open. Calvin stepped in, frowned at Dooney, and sat on the edge of the bed with a look that said eat your breakfast.

"*My* problems?" Dooney yelled. "I'll *tell* you my problems. I'm *looking* at my problems, these train-wreck photographs your wife sent me . . . I *know* she's my daughter . . . My place out in Minnesota, it's like the termites went crazy, ate up all the rugs and furniture and cars, ate the floors, ate my bowling alley, ate Cal's barber's chairs and the beds and the tennis court and the boat and the dock and a brand-new snowmobile and the whole damned billiard room." Dooney snorted, caught a breath, and let out a stiff, humorless chuckle. "Junius, please shut up. I'm talking here."

Calvin picked up a fork and wagged it in warning.

"Look, the answer is a big fat no. You're not keeping the team . . . Go ahead, resign."

Dooney disconnected.

"He resigned?" Calvin said.

"Idle threat. Tell you what, let's put on our masks and head out to Disneyland. Ride the rides, enjoy old age."

"Disneyland's closed, Jim."

"Yeah? Let's buy it."

Wanda Jane had moved into her new husband's four-room apartment above Elmo's Pool & Suds, which, for the residence of a longtime bachelor, turned out to be tidy, tastefully furnished, and far more comfortable than she had reason to expect. She was also happier than she had reason to expect.

They had married in Reno, honeymooned in the apartment. Already they were talking about children.

In the evenings, when she wasn't on dispatch duty, Wanda Jane liked helping out at the bar, or sometimes just watching him play one-man eight ball, first the solids, then the stripes. He'd run the table in under three minutes, then he'd run it again, then again, almost without focus, conversing the whole while in two different voices, sliding from Elmo to Elmore and back again. After he'd given up on lawyering, he told her, he had thought long and hard about going pro—"Pool, I mean. I had the moves but no discipline, and of course, there's always some sharpshooter with both of those. Same with the law. I cared about justice, didn't give a tinker's damn about billing hours. Big mistake for an attorney, caring about justice. I've noticed that in cops, too. I notice it in you."

Life had taken a swift, sharp turn, and both of them woke up surprised and went to bed surprised. The private Elmore had a quietly solemn quality, a reserve, a decency that Wanda Jane had assumed had been obliterated in the year 2016. He avoided absolutes. He held her hand while they watched the country go to hell on cable news.

On an afternoon in late May, they met with Chub O'Neill in his town hall office on Cutterby Boulevard. Chub had selected his brother Dink as Fulda's new full-time patrol officer. "Dink has it all," Chub explained. "Knows choke holds, knows weapons, almost got his GED, and he's my brother. Aren't you, Dink?"

"Pretty sure," Dink said from an armchair.

"Not funny," said Chub.

"I didn't mean it to be funny. Mom said she wasn't—"

"So, yeah, Dink's our man. Show him the ropes, break him in. If you liked Toby, you're gonna love Dink."

"That tattoo," Wanda Jane said. "Is that . . . ?"

"No, no. It *looks* like a swastika, but it's . . . What is it again, Dink?"

"Devil's Crossroad," Dink said.

"There you are," said Chub.

Outside, hooking Wanda Jane's arm as they walked up Cutterby Boulevard, Elmo said, "You ever consider running for mayor?"

51

MYTHOMANIA WAS THE NEW RABIES. IT DISSOLVED brain cells, infected blackbirds, skunks, and congressmen from Ohio. A lobster fisherman named Jib Walker, working out of Rockport, Maine, tweeted out the news that a "liberal cabal" had been caught reprogramming Minuteman missiles to strike targets in Austin, Texas; Tallahassee, Florida; and Baton Rouge, Louisiana. The War Between the States, Jib proclaimed, would soon go nuclear. Confederate uniforms had been issued. The governor of Texas had ordered women to speed up the gestation process to provide "fresh new troops," while meanwhile, walls and other entrenchments went up around the states of Tennessee, Alabama, Idaho, Florida, and South Carolina. Kentucky was digging a moat. In Washington, D.C., the United States Supreme Court ruled 5–4 in favor of a petition to suspend habeas corpus in the case of a young woman accused of violating the Required Child Delivery clause of Missouri's amended state constitution. And in Baskin, Minnesota, just north of the Iowa state line, the town council imposed stringent new proof of citizenship requirements, including duplicate videos of conception.

The contagion swept up the Yukon River, down the Missouri, through the Everglades. It breached the Hoover Dam, curdled the waters of Lake Mead.

In Fulda, California, Dink O'Neill had deputized his motorcycle gang, the Holy Rollers, charging them with the enforcement of his brother's decree outlawing the display of masks within the city limits—a practice Chub denounced as un-American, unnecessary, unfriendly, unappetizing, and now unlawful. Privately, Dink urged Chub to take things a step further. "Why not a Final Solution?" Dink said. "See if masks work when the chips are down. Like at Treblinka."

52

BOYD AND ANGIE SPENT ONLY A FEW DAYS IN VE-
gas, inspecting wedding chapels and restocking Angie's ward-
robe. On an early Sunday morning, after a dispute over the
extravagance of a Tiffany's tiara, they gassed up the Ferrari and
took U.S. Route 95 northwest toward Fulda. "I don't know why
you're so cheap," Angie was grumbling. "If you're so hot to get
married, what's the problem with a trousseau, a few trinkets?
And that third chapel we checked out? The one with all the
plastic flowers? We should've got it over with right then and
there. The minister, he was already practicing."

"He was drunk."

"He was excited for us. He called us one-half of a cute
couple."

"He was a smartass."

"He was God's right arm."

"He squeezed your ass, Angie."

"He was *testing* me. Making sure I wouldn't . . . You know
the difference between you and me? I actually *believe* in something." Her eyes pivoted sharply in their sockets. "And you're
still stalling."

Eighty-eight miles up the road, as they approached the Funeral Mountains, Boyd took the Ferrari's wheel for the first
time since they'd rolled out of Deadwood. He was almost himself again. To the left was Death Valley, to the right were the

purply flats of the Amargosa Desert, and in Boyd's heart was the steady beat of a JCPenney man heading home to whittle away at his fourteen handicap. The car's radio was at half volume: somebody complaining about twenty dead schoolchildren in Sandy Hook who weren't actually dead.

When Boyd switched off the radio, Angie muttered, "What's the problem? Recognize one of your acolytes?"

Boyd shrugged and stayed silent. He had the sensation of time trickling through his bowels. Maybe it was despair, maybe it was the pitiless universe.

Later he said, "We all need our fantasies, Angie. Even you. Harps and halos. Life everlasting. UFOs and laced Kool-Aid and Prince Charming zooming us off to paradise. Everybody on earth—we trade in reality for whatever keeps us going."

"You're defending deceit?"

"No, I'm describing it."

Angie grunted and sat thinking. "Well," she said after a mile or two, "I've always wondered why lying wasn't covered by the Ten Commandments." She looked out at the Funeral Mountains, which seemed aglitter with sapphires and molten silver. "Okay, so what are you saying exactly? Lying is good for the soul?"

"I'm saying I don't know if I can stop. I don't know if I *want* to stop. I'm not a grubworm. What's life without delusion?"

"It's called the truth, Boyd. It won't kill you."

"Won't it?"

"No, it won't. You're stalling again. What happened to your little boy?"

Boyd drove another three hundred miles, then Angie took over, then after dark, as they crossed into California, Boyd said, "Subdural hematoma. I loved that kid."

Another mile went by.

"An accident—could've happened to anybody. I'd been fired, my marriage was over, we were taking a walk, Evelyn said something, I said something, the boy wiggled, I dropped him. We thought he was fine. He cried for a while, then went to sleep."

"And didn't wake up?"

"No, he didn't."

"Boyd?"

"What?"

"You're lying, aren't you?"

53

BOYD HAD BEEN DOZING IN THE FERRARI'S PASSEN-
ger seat, lulled by four hundred thousand dollars of sleek ma-
chinery and late-night talk radio and a pair of headlights slicing
through northwestern America. He awoke with a start, dreaming of Alvin: a red parka stiff beneath the ice.

Boyd sat up, patted his pockets, and looked over at Angie.

"Hey, you," he murmured. "Okay if I smoke?"

She didn't seem to hear. Her face looked malnourished in
the greenish lights of the dashboard.

"Of course it's not okay," she finally said. "You don't smoke.
You don't have cigarettes."

"Where are we?"

"Oregon. We passed through Fulda an hour ago. I didn't
stop."

Boyd knew better than to ask questions. He nodded and
said, "I wish I smoked."

"No, you don't."

"Yes, I do."

Ten or fifteen miles later, he said, "I was dreaming about
Alvin."

"Were you?"

"A good person, wasn't he? Alvin, I mean. Did I tell you
we took turns confessing to each other? Long, long session.

I unloaded, he unloaded. This was—what?—a couple of days before he froze himself."

Angie nodded at nothing. She looked exhausted.

"I liked the guy, sort of. Called me Dad. Took care of me. Took care of you, too. Gave me a piggyback ride. A thief, I guess, but he . . . he knew how to take a confession."

"Go back to sleep, Boyd. I'm concentrating." After a minute or two, she said, "Ask me why I didn't stop in Fulda."

"Why?"

"Because I'm scared."

"Me, too."

"We're not talking about you—ask me why I'm scared."

"I'll ask if you let me smoke."

"You *can't* smoke. What'll you smoke, your toes?"

"Why are you scared?"

"Because if I stopped in Fulda all this would be finished. My whole kidnapping story—Mexico, your mom's house, then Texas and Minnesota and Deadwood and Vegas, and all those places in-between, like when you tried to dump me in Kerrville that time, and like how we'd have coffee together every morning, and like right now, just driving in the night, I don't want it to stop because when it stops, everything else stops, and there go all the dreams, like just being happy someplace, except where I'm really happy is right here and right now. It's not fair. Stopping's immoral."

"I think we should both smoke," Boyd said.

Randy was displeased with the Sacramento lockup. None of the improvements he suggested ever happened, not even the easy ones, like putting a little salt on their popcorn. His mood was sour. Angie had gone radio silent, never picking up on his weekly phone calls, and who else was there to call? His PD, maybe, but his PD wasn't the D part of a PD, because the PD was public but he wasn't any defender, and because he told Randy the best he could hope for was seventy-five to life, no parole. Mel's prints were all over Randy's loafers. Randy's prints were all over the hoe. Some genius had hooked him up to a wet grape farmer and to a couple of messy-looking ex-cons along a highway and to a dinged-up rich guy in Eugene, Oregon. "If you want," the PD had said, "I'll go the insanity route, but insanity isn't the same as stupid."

The PD was below average. The spaghetti was way below average. Seventy-five to life didn't sound so terrible if you didn't have to spend it in Sacramento. Pelican Bay, that was a whole different can of soup.

He wondered if Angie was taking good care of his Cutlass.

He wondered if Pelican Bay allowed sex visits with girl-friends, or if you had to be married, or if you could at least get away with a little hanky-panky on the phone.

He wondered if he should fess up to the fact that he didn't do the Fulda bank job, just that he was planning on doing it, that he wanted to do it, and that he would've done it except for getting called out of town at the last minute. A tough decision, that one. Fessing up to being innocent sort of took him down a peg, put a blemish on his record.

There was stuff to think about. Welcome to the big leagues.

"You know what I mean about stopping?" Angie was saying. "You and me, we've been together longer than some married people, almost a whole year now. I'm scared about what'll hap-pen if we stop."

Boyd was at the wheel again. It was seven in the morning

and they were passing by Corvallis, Oregon, heading north toward Portland.

"What happens is," Angie went on, "I get this hollow, jittery feeling in my stomach. Like one time in middle school when I was pretty sure I got a C on a history test. I didn't want to go to class the next day, didn't want to face the music. So I *didn't* go. I didn't go for almost three weeks. Every day, I'd go to English and math and art, but then I'd skip history and hide out in a toilet stall—you know, with my legs folded up so nobody could spot me—but finally some tattle-tale assistant principal called my mom, and she raised Cain and waved her frying pan at me and . . . You can guess the rest, I suppose."

"You got a B, I'll bet," Boyd said.

"I got a D."

"Yikes."

"Yikes is right. It's how I feel about going back to Fulda, facing the music."

"You'll be fine, Angie. I'm the bank robber."

"I'm not talking about *that* music. I'm talking about *our* music."

"We have music?"

Angie slapped his arm. "Unplug your ears! We're in a Ferrari Superfast, aren't we? We're on the road. Anything's possible. But if we stop . . . I mean, if we stop, then everything stops. Don't you see that?"

"How did you end up with a D?"

"That was the teacher's fault. Don't get me started."

Ten miles past Corvallis, they had breakfast, ran the Ferrari through a car wash, gassed up, and continued north with Angie at the wheel. For more than an hour, Boyd kept his mouth shut, but then he said, "Why do you drive like that?"

"Like what?"

"You know. With your thumbs."

"Randy taught me. Are you criticizing?"

"Well, it makes me nervous. Maybe you should try—"

"Randy's an expert driver. Do you hear me criticizing Evelyn? Do you hear me saying that Evelyn should've stuck by you through thick and thin?"

"Forget it," Boyd said.

"I already have."

"May I ask one other thing?"

"If it's not jealousy asking. Just because Randy knows how to drive and you don't . . . What's the question?"

Boyd shook his head and said, "It slipped my mind."

They had cruised through Salem and Portland and Olympia before Boyd said, "Oh, yeah. Where are we going?"

"You know where. Don't play dumb."

"Is it Evelyn's idea?"

"Evelyn cares about you. She's trying to fix things. Besides, don't you want to know why that D was my teacher's fault?"

On the fourteenth floor of Seattle's Grand Majestic Hotel, Angie and Boyd slept for twenty hours after splurging on a pair of queen beds and a magnificent view of Elliott Bay. Both of them were suffering Ferrari lag. Even after awakening, they lazed around for a couple of hours. Angie counted up their money—still a little more than thirty-two thousand. Boyd considered his options. Grab a few thousand. Take the elevator down to the lobby, buy a pack of cigarettes, and start walking. His toes, he figured, would take him at least a mile or two.

"I know what you're thinking," Angie said, "but you're not getting out of this. It's for your own good." She was slipping bundles of cash into an Italian travel valise she'd picked up in Vegas. "Evelyn says I'm supposed to lay down the law. It'll take only an hour or two. It'll clear the decks."

"Not my style," said Boyd. "I'm an avoider."

"Oh, believe me, everybody knows that. Which is why Evelyn told me to lay down the law."

Angie locked the valise.

"Right now, I need to call Randy." She slipped the valise under her bed, then stood and gave him a petulant stare. "A private call, if you don't mind. Go take a nice cold shower and pretend you're not steaming with jealousy."

"I'm *not*."

"Right. Go get wet. Work on the erectile dysfunction."

The shower should've relaxed him. Instead, it gave him the jitters. After ten minutes, Boyd toweled off and stood staring at his feet. The problem, he realized, was reality.

I can't do this, he thought.

He put on a Grand Majestic robe and thought, My father is dead. My name is not Otis Birdsong.

"You think you've got troubles," Angie said when he opened the door. "Randy's in a whole lot bigger trouble. Murder trouble. He'll probably—"

"My father," Boyd said, "is dead."

"Did you hear what I just said?"

"My name is not Otis Birdsong."

"Randy's been killing people!"

"My mother worked at Warner Brothers, I went to Princeton, I'm a war hero."

"Killing people! That's illegal!"

"I'm not doing it, Angie. I can't do it."

Angie threw her cell phone at the wall. "Boyd, what's *wrong* with you? Don't you know what murder is? A grape farmer! A *lady* grape farmer!"

"Nobody can make me do it. Not you, not Evelyn."

"Are you insane?"

"No," he said. "I'm unrealistic. I won't do it. He's a monster. Reality's a monster."

54

HEDDA TODHAUSER HAD KEPT HER SURNAME, KEPT
her recordings of Douglas, and kept the shotgun and the hundred thousand dollars she'd discovered in the Community National vault. The shotgun had been disassembled and stored in two oversize safe-deposit boxes, each of which rented for three hundred bucks a year. The hundred grand had been stashed with the shotgun parts. Clever, she thought. Rob a bank, hide the take in the very same bank.

Clever, and audacious, too, but not as clever and not as audacious as transporting the evidence down to the Fulda PD and dumping it on Wanda Jane's dispatch console. "Don't worry, I wore gloves," Hedda told Wanda Jane. "One of the perks of being a temporary bank president, you get the keys to the vault. I hope you're proud of me."

"I sure am," said Wanda Jane, "except you didn't have to go and marry him."

"We do what it takes. I'm not a halfway girl."

Wanda Jane looked down at the shotgun.

"I guess this seals it."

"Not really," said Hedda. "All that does is put him in prison. Next, I put him in hell. I'm a Todhauser."

"You sure are."

"Mushrooms tonight? With a bank president?"

"And maybe a mayor," Wanda Jane said.

* * *

Tightening up his mask, Junius Kirakossian drew a stale breath and said to Evelyn, "You got what you wanted, now I get what I want. I'm keeping my baseball team. You can tell that to Daddy. Either that or he finds a new CEO."

"Why don't you tell him?"

"I did. He laughed."

"That's a start—it means he respects you. Dooney laughs when people stand up to him."

"I'm not Daddy's valet. I run a solid company. My ships don't sink. We're not gassing children."

"Junius?"

"What?"

"Nothing."

Junius looked out the limo's window and watched midnight Pasadena roll by. He hated the damn mask, hated smelling his dinner. Without turning from the window, he said, "You know what I've learned? I've learned not to believe my own bullshit. That's progress, isn't it?"

"For sure it is."

"Like with my team. Losers, every last one of them, but guess what? Who sympathizes with a winner? You cheer for a winner, you idolize a winner, but you don't *feel* for a winner. Winning's a pipe dream. Even the winners know they're losers. Mickey Mantle—loser. Neil Armstrong—loser. Heroic, though."

"You, too?"

"Yes, ma'am. I'm a goddamn loser hero."

"Junius?"

Junius looked out the window. He didn't want to hear what he was about to hear.

"I won't say I'm sorry. I *am* sorry, but it's meaningless. I'll say I love you. You're a good man."

"Yeah," he said. "Feeling any better?"

"A little."

"Well, keep the mask on, watch your distance. I hear it'll pass in a week or two."

It was a twenty-minute walk from their hotel to a squat, undistinguished, 1950s-era building three blocks from the waterfront. They stopped outside while Boyd smoked his third or fourth cigarette in forty years.

"Puff away, kill your sperm," Angie said. "But you're going in."

"One more," Boyd said.

A half hour later, in the lobby, he squeezed Angie's arm and said, "I can't."

A cheery woman behind the check-in desk directed them to a waiting area furnished with a dozen or so shabbily upholstered chairs. The lighting was dim and gloomy. The place seemed to be cutting corners on electricity.

"Stay here, stay calm," said Angie, "and don't embarrass me."

"This isn't my strong suit," said Boyd. "Let's go."

"He'll be down in five minutes."

Angie slipped on her mask, moved back to the desk, exchanged quiet words with the receptionist, then sat beside Boyd and took his hand. Already Boyd yearned for another cigarette.

"Stop fidgeting," Angie said. "Put your mask on. It'll be fun. It'll be joyous."

"I already told you, my father's dead."

An elevator opened and Otis Birdsong stepped into the lobby.

"Mask up," Angie muttered. "Right now. Give him a hug. Kiss him."

"How can I kiss him?"

"Your problem. Fake it."

There was no hugging, no kissing. They walked down to a park along Elliott Bay, Angie doing most of the talking, explaining how she'd had a reunion with her own father years and years ago, how they'd straightened out a few things about child abuse and staplers and what God had to say about polygamy and what actually happened at Ruby Ridge and whether Jim Jones was a real prophet and why God invented tuberculosis. Not many people in the U.S. still died of tuberculosis, she was saying brightly, but her father did—he was barely fifty when it happened—so she was glad they'd had a chance to mend fences, or at least talk about all the broken fences.

She walked between them, hooking their arms, and said to Boyd's father, "Of course, my dad wasn't vaccinated as a kid. His family didn't believe in it, so they all ended up with chicken pox and measles and polio and mumps and everything." She pointed to a park bench and took off her mask. "Birdsong, I love the sound of it. Let me guess—Wales?"

"Venice," said the old man. "The one in California."

"Is that right?"

"Sixties. Made it up myself. Seemed like a good new name."

"Not a *good* name," Angie said, "a *beautiful* name."

"Yeah, I thought so. Some didn't." Otis Birdsong did not look at Boyd, but he might as well have. "Peace on earth, the Lovin' Spoonful. Headbands, love beads, all that shit, so why not go for a name with some kick to it? Birdsong, it was a pussy magnet. Had to bat 'em away. Sure as hell beat Otis Jones." He pulled down his mask, coughed, and shook his head in disgust. "Cocksuckin' masks. I forgot what fresh air tastes like."

"I don't care for the word *pussy*," said Angie. "Or that other word."

"Tough luck," said the old man.

"You know, it's pretty amazing," said Angie, "but I thought you'd be . . . a really nice person. That's how Boyd made it sound."

"Who?"

"Boyd."

"Who the fuck's Boyd?"

Boyd made himself smile behind his mask. There was no room for him on the park bench. He stood off to the side, reminding himself not to utter a word.

"Right there, the deaf and dumb guy, that's Boyd," Angie said.

"Never heard of him."

"Your son."

"Fuck *son*. Blackie's my son."

"Blackie Birdsong?"

"Why not? Poetry, isn't it?"

Angie looked up at Boyd and said, "Blackie, is it?"

The old man laughed. Without looking at Boyd, he said, "Borrow me one of those cigarettes."

Boyd complied.

The old man pulled matches from his shirt pocket, lit up, chuckled, and said, "Blackie's a nickname, naturally. Wouldn't hang it on a birth certificate, that'd be cruel, but I'll tell you something, Blackie fit him to a T, always did. He popped out that way—Rhonda's womb, I'm talking about—popped out blacker than black—his mood, I'm saying, his whole shitty view of the world."

"Do you always swear like that?" Angie said.

"Don't like it? Hit the road, Rhonda."

"I'm not Rhonda, I'm Angie," said Angie.

"Spitting image except for a thousand pounds or so." Otis Birdsong peeked up at Boyd, almost slyly. "Remember fat old Rhonda?"

"I called her Mom," Boyd said, despite himself.

Angie rose to her feet.

"This isn't going well."

"Going great," said the old man. "How about we take a ferry ride? Me and Otis Junior, we'll hold hands and make up."

"Otis Junior?" said Angie.

"Just Junior," said Junior.

"Your name's not Boyd?"

"Hey, feed me another smoke," said Otis Senior. "This is fun. Ask him about Rosemary Clooney."

Boyd vetoed the ferry ride. They had a pizza lunch at a café off Elliott Avenue, during which Boyd said nothing, barely listening as the old man reminisced about what a lying, unappreciative, antisocial creep his son had been. "Birdsong wasn't good enough for him," said Otis Senior, speaking to Angie, not once glancing Boyd's way. "I wasn't good enough for him. Fat old Rhonda sure as shit wasn't good enough for him. Our house?—not good enough for him. Used cars? No way. Jesus H. Christ, I'm his father; I bring home the bacon, so what's wrong with used cars? I was goddamned good at it, really good. Used cars kept the milkshakes coming, paid for Blackie's first wasted year at USC. How you think it feels, your kid ditching his father's name? Vanishes off the face of the earth—not even a postcard, zilch, telling everybody on earth I'm six feet under. Same with his sister—ditched her, too, drowned her off Catalina like Natalie Wood. And Rhonda . . . well, I'm not shitting you, he treated her like she was some circus freak, the fat one, wouldn't look at her and wouldn't talk to her and wouldn't lift a finger to help her take a piss. What kind of kid is that?"

"Are you asking me?" said Angie.

"Fuck no I'm not asking you. I'm telling you."

"What does the *H* stand for?"

"Which *H*?"

"The one between Jesus and Christ."

Otis Senior shot her a wary grin. He was in his mideighties, maybe older, but there was nothing infirm about his mouth.

"You think I cuss too much?"

"Not exactly," said Angie. "But I think somebody needs to put you in a dishwasher." She smiled at this. "What do you think, Junior?"

Boyd thought, I told you so.

He shrugged and pressed his lips shut.

As they walked back to the retirement home, Angie made a point of keeping her hundred and three pounds between father and son. She chatted about clearing the air and how sharing viewpoints had helped heal things with her own dad.

In the lobby there was the sizzle of silence. The old man pushed the elevator's up button.

"Well," Angie said. "Now bygones are bygones."

"Are you kidding?" said Otis Senior. He almost looked at Boyd but didn't. "Only reason I'm here is to say what a pitiful excuse for a son I had."

"That's a start, isn't it?" Angie said.

"I told you so," said Boyd.

It rained hard that night, stopped for a while, then rained harder. At one point Angie and Boyd tried standing under a pair of umbrellas on their fourteenth-floor balcony, looking out toward where Puget Sound should have been. The mood, like the clouds, was oppressive. "We're close to the end now, aren't we?" Angie said. She took Boyd's arm. "I guess nobody can fix everything."

"One time, I'm pretty sure, my dad said he loved me. I loved him, too."

"I know that."

"We should get some sleep."

"Was he always so cruel?"

"No, he was a Birdsong. The world and I disappointed him."

In the morning they drove south out of Seattle. By nightfall, they were thirty miles outside Fulda, California.

"Remember the rooster?" Boyd said. "Down in Mexico?"

"No."

"There was a rooster, I promise you. Beady little eyes."

"Sorry. I do remember when you shot a guy's table."

"Me, too."

"I don't think I can marry you, Boyd."

"No?"

"I don't think so."

"Well, I'm not surprised. Who *would* marry me?"

"Somebody would. You're an interesting atheist. I think I might cry now."

A while later, with the lights of Fulda in view, Angie said, "We could just keep driving, I guess. Never stop."

"I guess," said Boyd.

"But probably not," Angie said.

55

RANDY CONFESSED AND PLED OUT, SAVED ON AT-torney fees, took the hundred years, and counted himself a winner. He'd put in his oar for Pelican Bay—paddled hard, in fact—but apparently you couldn't choose your poison or your prison. Corcoran it was. Big deal. Corcoran would do the trick just fine.

He was already knocking off his push-ups, getting ready for the majors. Corcoran was Manson country.

Waiting around for the formalities, he thought, was a pain in the ass, especially because Sacramento made you wear a mask day and night, which naturally nobody did except when the screws gave you the evil eye, but even so, what about a man's right to blow his nose or sniff a little smuggled glue? Cruel and unusual, obviously. Like making you wear your own mini gas chamber.

On the plus side, Randy had become a whopper in a small pond, far and away the most respected resident in the whole Sacramento lockup, and he got a kick out of how the small-timers kowtowed to him, the assault and battery guys, like that Communist fella next door who kept calling him comrade. Sooner or later, Randy thought, he'd have to set the Russian straight on that, start explaining how shoplifting didn't qualify for comrade, not even close. For now, he thought, let the poor guy dream his dreams.

Masks aside—which was hard to do—the only snag had been pleading out to the Fulda stickup. That part had gotten complicated. Most guys, they mess up their alibis, but Randy had pretty much messed up his confession, mainly because he was innocent. Turned out he'd gotten a few facts wrong, like the fact that he wasn't there, and the fact that they had him on tape sticking up a McDonald's six hundred miles away, and the fact that Toby and Lois actually pulled the job, and the fact that Lois offed Toby, and the fact that all that was on video, and the fact that Doug Cutterby had just been arrested for offing Lois with his twelve-gauge, not to mention for heisting the heist, and the fact that Cutterby's DNA was all over the shotgun and all over a hundred grand in spanking-new currency that didn't even belong to him, because Toby and Lois did the actual heavy lifting.

Facts, Randy thought, were a nuisance, and it had taken some smooth talking to squeeze himself into the picture, get his share of the credit. Thank God his own prints were on the hoe, which helped with the accessory charge, almost nailed down conspiracy to commit.

All the same, he decided, it was embarrassing to be mixed in with a crew of amateurs. At Corcoran he'd keep his mouth shut. Stick to grape farmers and ex-cons, maybe throw in a shoe salesman, let it go at that.

For now, he did his push-ups, ignored the Russian next door, and worked on his prison patter—the exact words he'd use when somebody at Corcoran asked what he was in for. At night, in his off hours, he planned new jobs for when his hundred years were up. What he'd do, he figured, was heist an aircraft carrier, something fresh like that, though he'd probably need backup. Maybe the Russian.

On Saturdays, Randy had his weekly twenty-minute phone call with Angie. She seemed a whole lot friendlier now. Respect, probably. You could hear it in her voice. Last he heard, she was back in Fulda, counting change at Community National, but she'd promised to pay him a visit before he got sent up to the big leagues in Corcoran. "A whole hundred years?" she'd said. It gave him goose bumps. Funny how numbers impress people. Anyway, the problem now was conjugal visits. How to get the job done with a mask over his nose. Maybe the Russian would know.

By July 26, Covid deaths in the U.S. had surpassed 100,000, putting a dent in Fulda's mayoral election turnout. Of 2,070 registered voters, only 510 ballots were cast, half of which, according to Chub O'Neill, were fraudulent. Wanda Jane Epstein led the field with 256, Chub received 253, and Douglas Cutterby scored a single absentee write-in ballot. By that point, Douglas had been indicted on seventy-eight counts of bank fraud, seven counts of obstruction of justice, and one count of first-degree murder. His ballot had been submitted from the pretrial holding lockup down in Atwater. Six days later, Douglas was dead of pneumonia.

"All I did," Hedda told Wanda Jane, "was kiss him a lot."

"You're a Todhauser."

"And I warned him. Told him to look it up."

"Are you okay?"

"Fever, bad cough," Hedda said. "But I'll make it. How's Elmo?"

"Much better. He'll make it, too." Wanda Jane paused. "Kissed him to death, did you? Douglas?"

"Is it a crime?"

"No idea," said Wanda Jane, "but it's justice."

The hospital discouraged visitors, but on two occasions Evelyn talked herself to Junius's bedside, where there was little she could do except hold his hand. They had slept in separate beds, kept their distance, worn their masks around the mansion. She had quarantined herself. She had held her breath when they passed each other in the hallways. Soon enough, though, Junius was a sick man, and he kept getting sicker, and as Evelyn sat watching him shrink before her eyes, almost dissolving into the hospital bed, she pictured Henry Speck's bugs munching away at her husband's lungs and heart and head.

After three weeks, he was able to sit up. After another three weeks, he was back home, more emaciated than ever but with light in his eyes.

"Don't worry about it," he said. "Henry was a pussycat. I'm not."

In the heat of early August, after his discharge, they sometimes paddled around in their big pool, often saying nothing, other times locking on to safe subjects and bantering breathlessly until one of them couldn't manage it any longer. Neither of them was able to find a way to talk about what they needed to talk about. Once, Evelyn started to say, "I'm poison; I dropped my own baby. Now you. There's something about me—" But Junius growled, and said, "There's something about *everybody*, for Chrissake. Don't flatter yourself." He looked at her without compassion. A moment later he said, "I thought Boyd dropped the kid?"

"No," she said.

"Why'd I think that?"

"Because that's what I told everybody. Because that's what Boyd told everybody. He lied for me and then he made himself believe the lie, just like all the other lies. Except he was lying for *me*. You understand? Two seconds—that's how it happened—on a sidewalk—we were already in bad shape, our marriage, and I was furious and hurt and . . . and I was yelling at him and I had Teddy in my arms and . . . not even two seconds, one second . . . there was this warm weight in my arms then there *wasn't* weight . . . That's how it still is, last night, right now, tomorrow, weight then no weight, this slipping-trapdoor feeling, but Boyd lied for me and I lied right along with him, because the lying helped a little, not much, but of course I needed the lie. It helped me get out of bed. Helped me get rid of the crib and the bassinet and the fucking teddy bears, not that it ever changed anything, not that it ever erased that sound—not loud, just this soft crunching sound. Anyway, I believed the lie. At least pretended to believe. I made up details in my head. The lie, I mean. Boyd still carries it around for me. He *knows* it's not true, but he keeps on believing, and I guess it helps both of us."

"Huh," grunted Junius. "That explains it."

Two afternoons later, Calvin and Jim Dooney stopped by, partly to congratulate Junius on being alive, partly to say they were off to Jakarta for six months, no business, all pleasure. "Just to visit the scenes of the crimes," Dooney said with a laugh. "Cal's never been out of the country—it'll be good to show him around. Where it all started."

"Wear your masks," said Junius. "And I'm not selling the team."

"Bravo!" said Calvin.

56

BY EARLY AUGUST, MYTHOMANIA HAD CLAIMED THE governor of Florida, the governor of Texas, and all but twelve starlings in the state of Idaho. Passport applications were way up. Baby formula was selling at a premium. The Statue of Liberty was back where it belonged, crated up in the dank cellar of the Louvre. And just over the horizon, in November, a national election promised fun for Truth Tellers everywhere.

As summer sped toward its January meltdown, Boyd Halverson trimmed his golf handicap by two hard-won strokes. He slept well at night. He ran a tight ship at JCPenney. He drank moderately—a whiskey at breakfast, a whiskey at lunch, a double at day's end. On Tuesdays, he deposited his weekly paycheck in a renamed Community National Bank, where he flirted with Angie Bing and nodded pleasantly at Hedda Todhauser. Most evenings, he ignored Winston Churchill and instead reached for the *Iliad,* with its entertaining array of simpering, snarling, flagrantly mendacious gods and goddesses.

He was not an atheist, Boyd informed Angie over a taco lunch one afternoon. He was a Greek. He was a pantheist. He believed in infinite Big Bangs, therefore infinite universes, therefore infinite deities with infinite agendas. "Every billion years or so," he said, "the gods' terms expire and they get together in the Cow Palace to nominate fresh new gods. Poseidon's term expired centuries ago. He's an insurance adjuster for

State Farm. Athena sells perfume in a Dillard's. Point is, you take your chances—which god do you end up with? Clown or monster? Luck of the draw."

"Clever," Angie grunted. "But pagan clever."

"Good story, though. Plenty of fireworks."

"Have you stopped lying yet?"

Boyd swallowed a clever falsehood. "Yes and no. I guess you could say it's a long-term project. I catch myself fibbing sometimes, take a breath, and start over."

"Good enough. Starting over's a start," said Angie.

In late August they celebrated the one-year anniversary of their drive out of Fulda with Community National's money. The plan had been to make a night of it, but Angie wasn't feeling well, so they picked up a bucket of KFC and settled into her new apartment for some quiet reminiscence. She hadn't yet purchased furniture, not a single chair, and they used a pile of blankets as a sofa and dining table. "I'm not much of a home-maker," Angie said, a little nervously, "so I guess you got lucky on that account." In one sense, the occasion was awkward, full of broken sentences, but in most ways they were comfortable together. It was hard to tell what had changed between them.

Around midnight, Angie lay with her head in Boyd's lap, her legs stretched out across the blankets.

"I'm not sure what to call you," she said. "Is it Boyd or Otis or Junior or Blackie?"

"Make it Blackie for now. Memories."

"Bad ones, though."

"Pretty bad," Junior said. "But I need the punishment."

"You've been talking to Evelyn."

"I have been. Not often. She offered me her place in Minnesota next month."

"Did she?"

"I'd have to replace a few things."

"Is it okay with my head in your lap?"

"It's good."

"Will you kiss me once?"

"Why not?" said Otis.

They kissed for what seemed a long time. Afterward, Angie said, "I hope you don't think I was leading you on the whole while. I wasn't."

"I know you weren't."

"There's only one of me. I'm a missionary."

"I know that, too."

"One more kiss? I won't ask after that."

A little later she sat up.

"He needed me more than you did. His soul needed me."

"Oh, yes? Does he have one?"

"We're working on it. I wish you could've—"

One of the broken sentences happened. They were accustomed to this and both of them waited.

"I mean, I wish we could've kissed like that a long time ago."

"I do, too, but—you know." Boyd smiled at her. "Hard to kiss a missionary. Anyway, Randy *always* needed you more."

She thought about it, then said, "Probably."

She stopped again.

"I can tell you're better now, Boyd. Luckiest man on earth. You're almost good to go."

"It was more than luck, Angie."

"Was it?"

"It was you," he said. "You know it was you."

"I hope so, but there was luck, too. What if Dooney had been home that night? What if he'd opened that door?"

"I've thought about it. All the time, really. But still mostly you."

"Are you going to church, Boyd?"

"Blackie."

"Are you going to church?"

"I am. I hate it. Excellent punishment."

"What about golf?"

"Every day."

"Kiwanis?"

"You bet—Service, Pride, Charity. Right now, we're tearing down that shaggy old maze where Lois was killed, putting up swing sets and monkey bars. The new mayor's idea."

"Boyd?"

"Junior, you mean."

"Are you angry with me?"

"Not at all."

"You're allowed to be angry if you want."

"I'm sad for you, Angie."

"Sad because I married him?"

"Yes."

"Well, you should be. Prison weddings, they're awful—prisons echo like crazy. I do, I do, I do, I do, I do. It keeps coming right back at you."

"Okay, I'm angry. But not at you."

"At God?"

"At your next hundred years."

"Yeah, well." Angie went silent for a moment. "Good chicken, right? Finger lickin'?"

It was two in the morning when Boyd and Blackie and Junior and Otis walked the three blocks to their own small apartment over the JCPenney store. Boyd fussed around for a bit. He opened the *Iliad* and settled in. After half a paragraph, he laughed, tossed it down, took out his wallet, extracted a crumpled Blue Fly calling card, and picked up his phone.

He was on the edge of disconnecting when she answered.

"Enni?" he said.

"Enni's sleeping. This is Peggy."

"Put Enni on. It's important."

"Who's calling?"

"Tell her it's the toe guy," said Boyd. "He'd like to escort the two of you to dinner next month. A double date."

"Is that right?"

"Yes, it is."

"Hang on," she said. "I'll see what I can do."

ABOUT

MARINER BOOKS

MARINER BOOKS traces its beginnings to 1832 when William Ticknor cofounded the Old Corner Bookstore in Boston, from which he would run the legendary firm Ticknor and Fields, publisher of Ralph Waldo Emerson, Harriet Beecher Stowe, Nathaniel Hawthorne, and Henry David Thoreau. Following Ticknor's death, Henry Oscar Houghton acquired Ticknor and Fields and, in 1880, formed Houghton Mifflin, which later merged with venerable Harcourt Publishing to form Houghton Mifflin Harcourt. HarperCollins purchased HMH's trade publishing business in 2021 and reestablished their storied lists and editorial team under the name Mariner Books.

Uniting the legacies of Houghton Mifflin, Harcourt Brace, and Ticknor and Fields, Mariner Books continues one of the great traditions in American bookselling. Our imprints have introduced an incomparable roster of enduring classics, including Hawthorne's *The Scarlet Letter,* Thoreau's *Walden,* Willa Cather's *O Pioneers!,* Virginia Woolf's *To the Lighthouse,* W.E.B. Du Bois's *Black Reconstruction,* J.R.R. Tolkien's *The Lord of the Rings,* Carson McCullers's *The Heart Is a Lonely Hunter,* Ann Petry's *The Narrows,* George Orwell's *Animal Farm* and *Nineteen Eighty-Four,* Rachel Carson's *Silent Spring,* Margaret Walker's *Jubilee,* Italo Calvino's *Invisible Cities,* Alice Walker's *The Color Purple,* Margaret Atwood's *The Handmaid's Tale,* Tim O'Brien's *The Things They Carried,* Philip Roth's *The Plot Against America,* Jhumpa Lahiri's *Interpreter of Maladies,* and many others. Today Mariner Books remains proudly committed to the craft of fine publishing established nearly two centuries ago at the Old Corner Bookstore.